The Troublemaker Next Door

MARIE HARTE

sourcebooks
casablanca

Published by Sourcebooks Casablanca, an imprint of Sourcebooks, Inc.
P.O. Box 4410, Naperville, Illinois 60567-4410
(630) 961-3900
Fax: (630) 961-2168
www.sourcebooks.com

Printed and bound in Canada.
WC 10 9 8 7 6 5 4 3 2 1

Praise for Marie Harte

"Hot sex, good characters... Harte has a gift for writing hot sex scenes that are emotional and specific to her characters."

—*RT Book Reviews*

"Hot and spicy... The author takes you through a range of emotions."

—*Night Owl Romance*, Reviewer Top Pick

"Off the charts scorching hot. Ms. Harte wows with sex scenes that will make your heart pump."

—*Long and Short Reviews*

"Ms. Harte is an awesome writer. Her comedic timing is perfect. She creates endearing characters."

—*Romance Reviews*

"Marie Harte...knows what readers are looking for and gives it to them by the page full."

—*Fresh Fiction*

"With...charismatic characters and sexual tension that is hot enough to scorch your fingers as you are turning the pages."

—*Romance Junkies*

"Skillfully created...with sassy wit and snappy dialogue."

—*RT Book Reviews*

To my friends Cat and Teri for sticking by me. I love you guys. Hell-clickers, unite!

And to D.T. and R.C. for having patience when Momma was late with dinner. I love you.

Chapter 1

"BUT UNCLE FLYNN, YOU PROMISED."

Flynn McCauley shook his head, his eyes glued to the television, where the Mariners played out the top of the ninth inning. "Just let me see the highlights from last night's game. I promise I'll turn it back in a minute."

"But, but…" Colin tapered off, and Flynn watched the next few minutes in disbelief. He hadn't thought the Mariners could pull off the win. Damn, he owed Brody twenty bucks.

The frightening sound of a child's tears tore Flynn from the game. He stared at his nephew in shock. "*Colin?*"

Five-and-a-half-year-old Colin McCauley didn't cry when he skinned his knees, when he'd suffered a black eye from a wild pitch, or when his father had mistakenly thrown away his favorite T-shirt just last week, thinking the holey thing a rag. The kid was tougher than a lot of grown men Flynn knew, a mirror image of Mike in too many ways.

"Colin, what's wrong, dude?" Panicked when Colin continued to cry, Flynn hurried to change the channel. Then he offered him some of the soda Colin had been asking for earlier but wasn't allowed to have. Anything to dry up Colin's tears. "It's okay, buddy. Don't cry." He crossed the couch to hug him, concerned there might be something really wrong.

After a few moments, Colin stopped his tears and squirmed to get free so he could see the television. His grief dried up as if it had never been, not even a hiccup to indicate emotional trauma.

A remarkable recovery. "Are you, or are you not, upset about something?"

Colin took a long drag of soda and laughed at the screen. "Not now." He beamed, looking exactly like Mike—smug and annoying.

"Scammed by a kid. This is embarrassing."

"Ubie told me it would work, but I didn't believe him."

"Uncle Brody, right. Now why am I not surprised?" He had his best friend and business partner to thank for Colin's ability to lie with a straight face. "When did he teach you that?"

"At dinner last Sunday. Oh, watch this, Uncle Flynn. See how the monster eats the school? Awesome." Colin dissolved into boyish laughter.

Flynn sighed and sank into the couch. Babysitting duty wasn't so bad, or at least it hadn't been when the kid attended preschool. But if Colin was mastering Brody's tricks now, imagine what he'd be like at eight, ten… hell, as a teenager. Flynn resolved to have a firm talk with good old Ubie. No point in encouraging Colin to scam people if Flynn wasn't allowed to be in on the joke.

Flynn sat next to Colin, enjoying the cartoon despite himself. He rubbed the kid's head. Colin McCauley, future heartbreaker. He had good looks, a great sense of humor, and a quick mind, one that would keep them all on their toes for years to come. Mike had done pretty damn good with the kid, but Flynn liked to think he'd had a hand in Colin's greatness. At least the part of him that kicked ass at sports.

Just as the back door opened and heavy footsteps signaled Mike's return—*thank God*—the phone rang. And rang and rang.

"Flynn, answer the frigging phone, would you?" Mike yelled from the other room.

"What, are his hands broken?" Flynn asked the boy as he reached for the phone. "Can't he tell I'm busy watching you?"

Colin ignored him in favor of a cartoon sponge. Like father like son.

Into the phone, Flynn barked, "Yeah?"

"Um, hello?" A woman's voice. She sounded soft, sexy. Interesting.

Flynn straightened on the couch. "McCauley residence. How can I help you?"

Colin turned to look at him with interest. Flynn never used the good voice on anyone but customers or women.

"Is this Mike?"

"No, but I can get him for you."

"That would be great."

"Hold on." Flynn sought his brother and found him struggling with a tool belt and muddied boots in the kitchen. "Yo, Mike. Phone call."

"Take a message, Einstein. I'm busy here." Mike struggled with dirt-caked knots on his work boots, the scowl on his face enough to black out the sun.

Flynn flipped him the finger while he spoke to the angel on the phone again. "Sorry, but he's busy right now. Can I take a message?"

Silence, and then a long, drawn-out sigh. "Can you

just tell him that we're having a problem with the sink? I hate to bother, but my roommate threatened to cut all my hair off if I don't get this fixed soon. The problem has been going on for a week."

"Ah, hold on." He covered the phone. To his brother, he asked, "Why is some hot-sounding chick asking you to fix her sink?"

Mike groaned. "Hell. That's probably one of the tenants next door."

"Mom and Dad have new renters already? Since when?"

"Been four months now. You aren't that observant, are you? Didn't get the family looks or brains, apparently." Mike's sneer set Flynn's teeth on edge. Arrogant bastard. His brother glanced at the phone and sighed. "Tell her I'll be right over."

Flynn passed the message, then hung up. "I don't remember Mom telling us about renting the house again. All I knew is they had some renovations done since the last bunch trashed the garage. I thought the cars I'd seen in the drive belonged to her fix-it crew."

"Well, in case it's escaped your notice, the garage has been fixed for a while now. She rented the place out to three women who moved in around the middle of February. I think you and Brody were doing that job in the San Juans then. They aren't bad neighbors. Keep to themselves, really quiet, and I think one of them has been working on the flower beds in the front, because they've really taken off this year."

Trust Mike not to come to the heart of the matter. "Any of them hot?"

"And this is why Mom didn't mention them."

Flynn frowned. "Don't be a dick. Just because you refuse to, and I quote, 'open your heart to love again' doesn't mean the rest of us aren't interested."

Mike finally stepped out of his god-awful boots. The things were like boats that had been dipped in muck and rolled over in stink. "First of all, don't quote Mom to me at five o'clock on a Friday after I've spent all…" he glanced around and seeing the kitchen clear, continued, "…*fucking* day working on Jane Risby's kitchen cabinets. The woman changes her mind about what she wants at the drop of a hat, and I'm tired. Second, just because I'm not willing to marry and procreate *again* doesn't mean I'm against getting laid. But you don't piss where you eat, and my neighbors are way too close to deal with in the event a date goes south."

"Hmm, good point. So answer the question already."

Mike rolled his eyes. "The truth? Every one of them is hot. Not cute, or attractive, but one you'd want to bring home and keep around until breakfast the next morning. And the morning after that. So don't even think about hitting on them. I meant it when I said I don't want the fallout of pissed-off neighbors. Find someone else to bone while I find a clean pair of shoes."

"Mike, don't be an ass if you can help it." He ignored the dark look his brother shot him. "Come on, let me take care of this for you. A clogged sink is right up my alley. Hello, plumber here? I swear I won't hit on any of them." Today.

Mike narrowed his eyes but was either too tired to argue or he believed Flynn's crap. "Okay. But as soon as you're done, you come right back here. Leave them alone. I mean it."

"Yeah, yeah. Why don't you go nag your kid? I think he's drinking in the living room."

Flynn left just as he heard his anal-retentive brother yelling at Colin to take his drink back into the kitchen where it belonged. Satisfied he'd at least had a bit of revenge on his nephew, he grabbed a toolbox from his truck and walked next door.

Mike hadn't been kidding about the flowers. Seattle's rich brown dirt made for some killer growth, especially during the summer. Roses, lavender, and poppies scattered the front flower beds like a carpet of color. The grass looked freshly mowed, and the walkway had been swept free of debris. A nice change from the last couple who'd spent more time smoking and letting their bratty kids dig up the yard than tending to anything. The aging Craftsman looked as good now as the pictures he'd seen of it newly built. The slate-blue wooden siding looked fresh against the white columns and rails on the covered porch. A rocking chair sat next to pots of cheery geraniums, and a few pairs of women's sneakers sat by the front door.

He rang the doorbell and waited, wondering what the women who wore the shoes looked like, out of curiosity, not desperation. He had a few female friends he could see when he felt the need for companionship. Nice women he could be casual with, and a few he now stayed away from because the last times he'd visited they'd hinted at wanting something more serious. Casual hookups in bars didn't appeal to him. The threat of disease or waking up next to a woman dimmer than a busted lightbulb made him shudder. If his mother would just stop bugging him about settling down, about how she'd had three children by his age and blah blah blah responsibilities…

"Hello?" Dark brown eyes peered at him through the crack in the door.

"Hi. You just called my brother, Mike. I'm Flynn, here to save your sink." He held up his toolbox.

"Oh. Hold on." She closed the door and he heard her undo the chain. The door opened. "Come on in."

He made sure to wipe his feet on the mat before entering and took in the cheery feel of the foyer. The hardwoods looked clean and polished, comfortable furniture in the open living area neat and decorated like something out of a magazine. Bold splashes of color mixed with eclectic pieces, not at all the traditional style of his mother's place or his stark bachelor pad. Yet the room also felt lived in. Books and magazines scattered the coffee table, and plants thrived in the ledge of the bay window. A cool breeze blew through the window screens in the living room. The light scent of flowers and something delicious mingled, making him hungry and more than a little intrigued about the occupants of the house.

The woman in front of him lived up to Mike's description, and then some. To Flynn's discomfort, she reminded him of Lea, Mike's deceased wife. Short, curvy, and pretty with that same touch of innocence that had always made Flynn want to protect. She had dark hair and deep brown eyes, high cheekbones and full lips. From behind, she and Lea might as well have been twins.

"Name's Flynn McCauley," he said once they reached the kitchen. He put down his tools and held out a hand.

She took it with a smile and a firm grip, surprising

him. Not as shy as the softness of her voice would have him believe. "Abby Dunn. Nice to meet you. We've seen Mike a few times, but with us being so busy, we haven't been too neighborly, I'm afraid."

He glanced around. "We?"

"Oh, my roommates Maddie and Vanessa. They should be home soon."

He nodded. She tucked a long strand of dark hair behind her ear, and he noticed the differences between her and Lea. Her eyes had a bit more slant, looking more exotic and less girl-next-door. Her hair was straighter as well, not as wavy as Lea's had been.

Realizing he'd been staring, he apologized. "Sorry. You look a lot like someone I used to know."

She nodded, no longer smiling. "Your brother's wife. Your mother mentioned the resemblance. When Mike first saw me, he looked like he'd seen a ghost. I might have kept my distance because of that too."

"Please don't. It's been years. And Mike would have said something if it bothered him." At least, he thought he would have. "I'm just glad to see my parents renting to people who take care of the place."

She scrunched her nose. "Yeah. When we moved in, there was a faint reek of smoke. Your mother didn't seem happy about that." Abby grinned. "Gave us half off our first month's rent too. I like her. Don't tell her, but she's a soft touch."

Flynn chuckled. "You got that right." He looked at the counter to see a stack of detergents and items normally kept under a sink. On the floor, a few soaked towels absorbed water. "Oh boy. The sink problem."

She nodded. "But I think the water leak is my fault. I

knew not to use the sink, but the dishwasher was full, and I forgot. Normally it just clogs up, but today water dripped from underneath." She opened the cabinet under the sink and showed him. "Do you think you can fix this?"

"Better than Mike could. I'm the plumber."

"Good. You're exactly who we need."

"Just let me get under there and I'll have it fixed for you in no time. If you have something else to do, go ahead. Or you can wait and watch if you want."

She bit her lower lip. Lea never used to do that. "If you wouldn't mind, I was right in the middle of something. I'll be down the hall if you need anything."

"Okay." He got to work, grateful the clog would be easy enough to handle. The broken valve, not so much unless he had a spare part in his box. Which he did. Humming under his breath, he lost himself in his work. Once finished, he heard a raised female voice screaming in anger. Odd, because he hadn't heard anyone enter the house.

He slid out from under the sink, curious when he heard Abby try to placate the woman. But she wouldn't stop yelling. Hoping he wouldn't have to break up a catfight, though secretly enthusiastic about the idea, he moved to investigate.

—∿∿—

"Oh my God, Abby! Right there, in the office I visit ten times a day. He had the nerve to drag my hand over his crotch!" Maddie paced back and forth, still in shock about this disastrous turn of events. "I was supposed to be offered a huge job, a step toward a junior partnership, not an opportunity to fuck the boss!"

Abby's eyes were as round as quarters. "I thought you said Fred was gay."

"I thought he was. He's neat, he has a tendency to lisp, and he calls everyone, men and women, *sthweetheart*. It's all a front so no one feels threatened by him."

"Until he puts your hand over his penis during a business lunch." Abby nodded.

"No, after the lunch. The gourmet meal was to soften me up, play his cards. Dangle the carrot before me and tease me about giving Diane the promotion." Maddie threw her purse against the wall and shrieked. "The man has money coming out his perfectly groomed ass. He can have anyone he wants. Why would he do this to *me*?"

"Maybe because he can," Abby said softly.

Ignoring her, Maddie ranted. "I can't believe this. I had my whole future mapped out. More responsibilities, a major account of my own, then a junior partnership before I'd branch out and start my own design boutique. And now…"

"Now what, exactly? You didn't say what happened after he put your hand over his…you know."

"I squeezed. Hard."

"Ew."

"Tell me about it, it was instinctive. I wanted him to let me go, and he did," she said with some small satisfaction. "Then I dumped his coffee in his lap, told him to kiss my ass, and stalked out of there. I immediately turned in my resignation and told them to expect a call from an attorney."

"You're going to hire a lawyer?"

"No." She felt miserable. "My savings aren't for an

attorney, they're for my future. Realistically, by the time I go through with a lawsuit, I'll be broke. The case will have turned into a he said–she said match, and with his money, he'll buy the jury."

"There won't be a jury, just a hearing—"

"Exactly. Not even a jury." She wanted to cry. So angry. Men. "He dicks me over, Ben dicks me over. What the hell is going on with my life?"

Abby stood up and crossed the room to her. "I'm so sorry. So did he say anything after you stormed out?"

"I have no idea. I didn't wait around for the fallout. That ass!"

"Don't worry, you'll get through this." Abby patted her shoulder. "So on top of everything with your boss, what happened with Ben?"

Maddie kicked off her heels, imagining kicking them at Ben's head. "We broke up. He was getting too clingy, so I told him to man up or man out—as in, get out."

"Are you serious? What did he do when you issued that ultimatum?"

"He got out, or rather, he told *me* to get out. Told me it wasn't manning up to want his girlfriend to spend time with him. Oh, like my career doesn't matter because I'm an interior designer? Like being a doctor is so much more important." She saw Abby's wince and snapped, "He's a foot doctor, not a neurosurgeon. Give me a break."

Abby squeezed her shoulder. "I'm sorry, sweetie. I know you liked Ben."

"It's all right. He was wearing on me. They all do." She walked away from Abby and paced back and forth across the room. "Men. Nothing but a bunch of self-absorbed assholes who can't think beyond their dicks."

"Ah, Maddie, you might want to—"

"And really, Fred Hampton? Designer to the stars? Please. Forcing my hand over his lap was a stupid thing to do. His package did not impress. At. All."

Abby flushed.

"Come on. You write a lot worse than that."

"Uh, yeah, but you see, there's someone—"

"All my hard work, for what?" Maddie was on a tear. "I spent ten fucking years working to get to that place. Sure I learned. I interned, paid my way through school, suffered through the chrome years and the faux fur trends, which just won't go away. But this *insult*! In this day and age, with so much bullshit about being PC and sexual harassment has no place in the workplace, and my boss just made me feel him up in his own office during business hours. The perv! I feel like a total—"

She looked up to see a huge, green-eyed hunk filling out a white T-shirt and jeans like he'd stepped out of a Man of the Month calendar. One of *them*. A man. The enemy.

Abby cleared her throat. "Maddie, this is Flynn McCauley, Mike's brother. He was just fixing our kitchen sink."

Mortified but not willing to let him see it, Maddie gave him a disdainful once-over, ignoring the surge of her libido. "How *nice* to meet you. And would you like me to feel you up as well?"

He raised a brow and gave her the same thorough examination, lingering not on her breasts or ass, the way most men did, but on her face. Sure, why should this one be typical when it took all kind of XY degrees of perversion to make the world go 'round?

Annoyed all over again, she tossed her head, grateful her hair stayed out of her eyes, though God knew she had the frizz from hell going on, and stomped out of the room with a low, "And fuck you too." She took the stairs two at a time and slammed the door of her bedroom behind her. After locking the door and turning on the radio to mask any other noise, she lay down on her bed and let the tears fall. Could her life get any worse?

"Oh man, I'm really sorry." Abby apologized for the fourth time in as many seconds.

"Hey, don't worry about it. Sounds like your friend had the mother of all bad days." Flynn still had a hard time catching his breath.

Had Mike said the women were hot? He was out of his celibate mind. Abby had cute down to a science, and that resemblance to Lea which kind of freaked him out. But Maddie? She of the long legs, killer rack, and sultry face? Sultry, a word he'd never used to describe a woman. But damn, it fit. She wasn't pretty or cute, but with full lips, that flush on her cheeks, and those direct, man-hating eyes so dark they looked like never-ending night, the woman had a knockout punch he still hadn't recovered from.

"Maddie can be a little dramatic, but she had cause." Abby picked up her friend's purse and shoes and put them on the desk next to her computer.

It suddenly struck Flynn that in all the time he'd been standing there listening to Maddie, he hadn't noticed that the women had turned his mother's idea of a sitting room into an office. French doors off the smaller room gave it a bigger feel, and the hardwoods had been covered with a Persian rug in dark red accents. Dark red, reminding him of Maddie's hair. Man, he had a thing for redheads. All that temper… he could only imagine what she'd be like in bed.

"Flynn?"

"Sorry. Hey, you want me to go down to her boss's office and pound some sense into him?"

She blinked. "Probably not a good idea unless you want a lawsuit. Fred Hampton has a lot of money."

He shrugged. "That's okay. I know a lot of people who'd back me up. Heck, my nephew would alibi me with no problem. I'll go kick this Fred guy's ass, and we'll all pretend I was here fixing your sink while Colin watched me the whole time. Kid has the face of angel but can lie like a champ." Was it bad he sounded like he was bragging? Though the thought of beating the shit out of Maddie's boss had real appeal. Who the hell treated a woman like that but real scum?

"Nice offer. I'll pass it on to Maddie when she's in a better mood. Now, about the sink, how much do I owe you for parts or labor or whatever?"

He shook his head. "Your landlord should have handled this when the problem first happened." He made a mental note to talk to his mom and dad after he chewed out Mike.

"It's not their fault. I kind of dragged my feet to get it fixed. Vanessa usually handles the house issues, but she's been busy at work lately."

"Please tell me she doesn't work with Maddie." He liked saying her name. Short for Madison? Madeleine? He'd have to find out.

Abby snorted. "No way. Vanessa is an accountant. Very cut and dry. The woman means business when it comes to numbers. You need a good person to do your taxes, you should call her."

"I would if I didn't make my little brother, I mean, if my little brother hadn't already *offered* to take care of them for me."

She laughed and walked with him to the kitchen to grab his tools. "I have two sisters. They can be a handful. At least mine live on the East Coast."

"Lucky you." Cameron was such a snot. Thought he knew everything when it came to financial planning. From what little Flynn knew, his brother did, but it didn't help Cam's already huge ego to point that out. "If you need anything else, let me know." He fished a business card out of his back pocket.

"You really are a plumber." Her surprise disgruntled him, and she must have seen it, because she blushed. "I know you said you were, but I thought that might have been a little brotherly competition. As in, you're better at plumbing than he is. And besides, you don't look anything like our old neighborhood plumber. He was an older man with a big belly and that problem men get with their pants when they bend over."

It took him a minute. "Ah. Crack, the nonaddictive kind. The pants too low for you?"

She shuddered. "Way too low." So much for thinking the woman was shy. "But yours seem okay. Forgive me for making generalizations."

She walked him to the front door.

"No problem. But if you want, I could wear my pants really low for you the next time your sink clogs."

She winked. "Sounds good to me."

She shut the door behind him, and he heard her faint chuckle. He decided he liked Abby Dunn. Her roommate, on the other hand… That redhead he had no intention of leaving alone. Now that he thought about it, his mother wasn't exactly being neighborly by not inviting her new tenants over for a summer barbecue. He'd have to rectify that, but not until he had a few words with Mike. What had he been thinking to leave a houseful of women like that all alone? God knew what Vanessa looked like. Flynn had a sudden image of the three roommates scrapping around in a ring throwing Jell-O at one another, Maddie leading the match, and hustled back to his brother to yell at him.

Chapter 2

"MADDIE, OPEN THE DOOR!" VANESSA'S STERN VOICE refused to lower in volume. Determined to be heard, she also refused to go away.

Weary, puffy-eyed, and miserable, Maddie dragged herself off the bed and unlocked her door. Then she stumbled back to bed and flopped down. Vanessa entered with Abby right behind her, both looking worried—Vanessa looked worried and annoyed, but then, Vanessa needed stress to make her life complete.

"Okay, I want the whole story from beginning to end." Her cousin liked order as much as she liked giving orders. Straight and to the point, Vanessa would have been a terror to grow up with. She had a year on Maddie and used to lord the fact over her during family visits until they'd decided to live together a little over a year ago. Now she no longer had to mention what she'd drilled into them from move-in day. Abby, the little traitor, gracefully gave in, ceding Vanessa's dominance over the household.

Maddie ran through her situation, hitting all the pertinent points. "He took me out to lunch at a posh spot, and he made a ton of comments about me going places. How I was such a talented designer, how he'd seen me working so hard and was impressed. Then we returned to the office to work. Not an hour later, he brought me in to make me an offer—so I thought. Instead, he showed me something else."

"His etchings," Abby muttered.

"Might as well have been. He dangled the contract for Mishton Plaza, that new condo near Pioneer Square. I would have had carte blanche over the lobby and a few of the predesigned spaces, with an option for more. It's a primo job. And if I didn't want Diane to get it, all I had to do was say yes to spreading my legs and keeping my mouth shut about it."

"You, keep quiet? He didn't know who he was messing with."

She ignored Vanessa. "To seal the deal, a handjob right there in his office, smack-dab during the work day."

"This makes no sense." Vanessa frowned.

"You think I just blew a chance at making a living doing what I love, on what, a lie?" Incensed, Maddie tried to rise but Abby sat on the bed and latched on to her like a dead weight.

"No, I believe you. I just have a hard time believing no one's ever said no to him before. I bet he's harassed a lot of other women."

Maddie didn't know. She only knew he'd done it to her. Made her feel like a victim, and she hated it. "At first I just listened to him in shock. I mean, this is Fred, my gay boss, hitting on me. He's at least twenty years older than I am. I didn't expect it. Not of him."

"I'm getting grossed out all over again." Abby had a squick factor Maddie had never understood. The woman wrote dirty books, for God's sake.

"I don't like any of this. I'm going to look into an attorney for you." Vanessa held up a hand. "Stop. It won't cost you a dime, and I just want to see how you can fight this, if you even can. Unless you had witnesses, I think you're right about it being a case of he said–she said."

"No witnesses." Bitterness filled her once more. "Fred's office is his sanctum."

She told them everything, leaving out her terror about how she'd make a living in this downtrodden economy. Maddie had been working since she'd been ten. She'd always known what she was doing, where she was going. But now? Would she end up serving lattes at Starbucks? Her tears returned.

"Honey, it'll be okay." Abby muscled Maddie into a hug.

"Not if she spends her days like this."

"Nice, Vanessa." Abby huffed.

"Look, we all know that jerk will probably get away with it. But at least go on record about what happened."

Sound advice. "I did," she said, muffled against Abby's ample chest.

"Good. It won't help your career to get labeled as a whistle-blower, and by now Fred's had time to paint you as the company whore, but at least you did the right thing."

Abby scowled. "God, Vanessa, now even I want to go hang myself, and I've never met the guy." She patted Maddie's back, her best friend through thick and thin.

Oddly enough, Vanessa's blunt words made her feel better. "Actually, it helps to hear the truth. Let's say I get my job back. Then I have to pretend nothing happened. And after the stink I made when I yelled at the other partners about what he did, I don't want to work for Fred Hampton again. *Ever*. Worst case, he'll tell everyone he fired me, even though I said I quit. And I don't have to see that place again."

Vanessa cocked her head, the way she did when she pondered a deep and interesting problem. Like how to make two kids count as more of a tax credit. "What do Kim and Robin have to say about this?"

Maddie blew out a deep breath. "I haven't told them yet."

Vanessa snorted. "Like they don't know. Maddie, they do most of your contract work; they have friends all over that office. Of course they've heard by now. Knowing you, the floors below you heard how upset you were—with good reason. You're not exactly quiet, even on your good days."

Maddie glared. "I only told Pat and Jean, the partners. They said they'd look into it, but I know they won't. They do everything Fred tells them to."

"And Olivia, the receptionist, probably heard you," Vanessa continued. "The office isn't that big."

"So?"

"So Olivia has a big mouth. And she's part of the gay club."

Maddie's head pounded. "It's not a *club*. She's gay. Robin and Kim are gay. Lesbian. Say it with me, Vanessa. *Gay* is not a bad word."

"I didn't say it was. My point is that the gay people I've met in my profession tend to stick together, because they have more than one thing in common. I guarantee you Olivia already told Kim and Robin what happened. Five bucks says they're either calling you or knocking at the front door before the night is through."

As if on cue, someone leaned on the doorbell.

—∿—

Four margaritas and two buttery nipples later, Maddie felt no pain. Surrounded by her friends, she laughed and drank as if she had no worries. As if she wouldn't soon start on the same path her mother had taken so many years ago.

"To you guys. You rock." She licked the salt on the wide glass and took a large swallow, followed by a larger burp.

"Nice, Maddie." Kim sighed, taking dainty sips of her drink. "She's a sloppy drunk, who knew?"

"I knew." Vanessa tapped glasses with Robin. "Ever since she turned twenty-one. Can't hold her liquor either. That's why she never goes out to bars. Two tequilas and she'd be some guy's mattress for sure." She paused. "Or some girl's mattress, I suppose."

Robin grinned. "Cheers to equal opportunity."

Kim frowned.

Maddie sighed. "Oh, Kimmie. Don't worry. Your girl has never looked twice at anyone I know."

"Really?"

Robin coughed before clearing her throat. "Come on, Kim. You know you're the woman for me. So I look. I'm human."

Kim took another sip. "So you are. But don't forget where you put your boots every night. Under *my* bed."

Robin and the others laughed, looking at her construction boots. But to Maddie, their love was the sweetest thing. Robin, with her short spiky brown hair, her pretty blue eyes framed by the thickest lashes. She tried to be so tough and butch. But when she looked at Kim, her partner, she of the designer dresses, killer heels, and manicures, she had that soft gleam in her eyes.

A tear trickled down Maddie's cheek. She sniffed and took another drink. "Maybe I should switch sides. I haven't found any luck with men."

"Hear, hear," Robin and Kim said as one.

"And I… Where's Abby?"

Vanessa shrugged. "You know how she gets. When the guys have their poker nights, she's in the hammock."

"What are you talking about?" Kim asked and ran a hand through her long blond hair. Classically beautiful, Kim was every inch the blue-eyed blond. Maddie wished she felt something more than admiration for the woman's looks. Something like the lust she'd felt, despite her earlier embarrassment, when the hunk had been gaping at her.

Talk about hot. Such a broad chest, corded arms, thick thighs. He had to be seriously hung, a guy that large with such big feet… And why the hell should she care about that? Had to be the drink. "Vanessa, have you seen our neighbors?"

"Mike and Colin? Yeah."

"No, I mean the brother. The green-eyed stud. Finn, Frank, Flynn, something like that."

"I don't think so." Vanessa frowned. She didn't look nearly as drunk as she should be.

"How many drinks have you had?" Maddie heard herself slur but didn't care. She was sliding into numbness feet first.

"Two, Sloppy Sally. Geesh, what a lush." Vanessa shook her head. "Hard to believe we're related."

Kim laughed. "Give her a break. She broke up with her boyfriend, held her boss's dick, and quit her job all on the same day. She's entitled."

Robin shuddered. "Fred's dick. I think I just threw up in my mouth."

Kim kissed her. "See, that's true love, that I kiss you even though you say something so disgusting. Now someone tell me where Abby is."

Maddie leaned forward. "You wanna know? She's outside in a hammock, listening to the guys playing poker."

Kim blinked. "Why?"

Maddie had no idea, but Vanessa answered. "It helps her get in touch with her male characters. She needs to make her men sound like men. The neighbors get together once a week and talk about guy stuff."

"Guy stuff?" Maddie frowned.

"Tits and ass, who's getting laid, you know, guy stuff." Robin downed her drink. "And on that note, Kim and I are taking your room, Maddie. We're too buzzed to drive, and all this talk of tits and ass is making me need some Kimmie time."

"Bleh. Get out of here with your love talk. Making me sick." Actually, she did feel a little nauseous.

"Need help?" Robin asked.

"I have her." Vanessa swore. "Hell no. Not in here. Come on, princess." Her cousin hauled her to her feet and helped her to the bathroom just in time. The buttery nipples weren't so buttery when the schnapps discharged from her body. And then the margaritas stood up with a shout, demanding to be noticed.

—᠁—

"I'm telling you, from behind, I thought I was seeing a ghost." Flynn polished off another Heineken, ignoring Cam's gripe about hurting the local microbreweries.

"Seriously. You're giving in to the corporate breweries. Support real beer makers. Try one of these."

Flynn snorted. "I'm not drinking anything that has a rose and a dog on it. It's beer, for Christ's sake."

"It's actually pretty good. Light but full-bodied." Brody, Colin's collaborator on the tears-for-suckers play, twirled his bottle while they waited for Mike to put Colin down for the night. "So back to this woman."

"Abby Dunn."

"Right, the neighbor." Brody looked interested. "What was she like?"

Cam answered. "She's kind of short but really pretty. Black hair, brown eyes, and has a very curvy build. She's very nice."

"How the hell would you know?" Flynn glared at his younger brother, dressed in pressed slacks and a designer shirt, unlike the rest of them.

The McCauleys came from a long line of middle-class working stiffs. Even Brody, though not related by blood, fit the mold. But Cam, with his fancy degrees, smooth hands, and stylish clothes... They still teased their mother about bringing home the wrong baby. If not for the fact that all of them looked so much alike, Cam might have believed them.

"Because, you cretin, Mom and Dad trust me with the truth." Cam sipped from his beer like a girl. "I met them a few months ago, when Mom rented the place. She wanted my opinion."

"And?" Brody asked.

"And what? They're all employed, attractive, nice to talk to."

Flynn and Brody exchanged a look, and Brody said, "I know, right? It's like he's not human."

Cam flushed. "Screw you. Okay, fine. You want

me to talk on your level? Yeah, all three of them are sexy. You wouldn't have to do any of 'em doggie style because they're not bad to look at. Better now?" He stopped when they looked over his shoulder at Mike, who stared at Cam in shock.

"Holy shit. Maybe he is a McCauley after all."

Flynn and the others laughed, ribbing him until Mike joined them at the table in the dining room. He had the windows open, letting the evening breeze settle over them. Between the neighbors' flowers and Mike's assortment of color outside, Flynn felt like they were playing in a greenhouse, their only concession to poker night chips and beer.

Tonight they'd agreed on spades instead of poker, since Mike had bills to pay. He wanted electricity next month, not to line Flynn's pockets, or so he said. Frankly, Flynn thought he was just tired of losing. God knew Mike had money stashed in so many places it made Cam crazy trying to organize it all. But hell, Mike's house, Mike's rules.

As they started the hand, Flynn brought out the big guns. "So why the hell didn't you warn me Abby looks like Lea?"

The table grew still.

Brody blinked. "She does?"

Everyone stared at Mike, who sighed. "Who cares? Lea is gone. Abby's her own person and a neighbor. I barely even know her. And no, I'm not carrying some secret torch for my dead wife's look-alike. Get over it already. I've dated other women."

"Not recently," Cam added.

Mike scowled. "Not since *before* they moved in. It

has nothing to do with them, okay? Now drop it before I put your hard head through my wall. We're here to take Flynn and Brody down, not to discuss my love life."

."That you don't have." Flynn grinned. "So you're okay. Good to know you're not about balling Abby. I liked her."

Brody choked on his beer. "'Not about balling Abby'? Jesus, Flynn. It becomes clearer to me every day why we get more customers when I man the phone."

Cam nodded. "I'd believe that." He glanced at Mike as he slapped down a five of hearts.

"Hey, no table talk." Brody glared.

"What? I said nothing. I played my card."

"You slapped it. So he knows to come back with hearts again and not cut you." Brody never let Cam cheat. On the other hand, Brody defined the term *card sharp*.

Predictably, after Flynn's turn, Mike played a king of hearts, won the hand, and led the next round with hearts again.

"What about Abby's roommates?" Cam asked the question without care, a little too much disinterest.

Flynn shared Brody's knowing look and glanced down at his cards again. "Hmm. I haven't met Vanessa yet, but Maddie's a real firecracker." His brother didn't react one way or another, and he wondered if he'd misjudged Cam's interest. "A redhead with a temper." Hell, now the others looked interested, not what he'd intended. "Apparently her boss made some move on her today, and she told him to shove it."

"Good for her." Cam nodded. "It still surprises me professionals pull this crap. Mom would have a field day if anyone ever tried that with her."

"Yeah, but she'd have to wait until Dad pounded him through the floor first." Mike grinned, and they all laughed.

"I want to know why no one mentioned the neighbors to me before now." Brody frowned as he took the next hand. He and Flynn played with a harmony that soon had his brothers more than annoyed. "I mean, I get not telling Flynn. He acts like he's perpetually in heat. But I'm trustworthy."

"Bullshit." Flynn dealt a new hand. "Trustworthy? Then how about you tell Mike what you taught his kid to do."

Mike didn't mess around when it came to Colin. Mother bears had nothing on the protective instincts of his big brother. Only older than Flynn by two years, Mike had nevertheless made it his mission in life to defend him, Brody, and Cam all the way through high school.

"Brody, I'm waiting." Mike didn't look happy.

Brody muttered to Flynn, "You're an asshole, you know that?" To Mike he said, "I might have shown him how to palm a card or two."

"Not that." Flynn started to enjoy himself. He and Brody took the next few tricks not even trying.

"Ah, okay. Well, let me see. We haven't started pimping yet, and I was saving the crack pipe for when he turned double digits, the big one oh."

Flynn snickered and Cam laughed.

Mike huffed out a breath and threw down his last card. "You two aren't even concentrating. Cam, wake the fuck up and win a hand."

"Me? Quit browbeating Brody and concentrate. You know he's fine with Colin. Hell, all of us have changed that kid more times than I want to think about. He definitely takes after you in too many ways."

"That's my boy." Pride glowed in Mike's blue eyes. He was a helluva father. Just like their own dad. It made Flynn wonder if he'd ever be as good, if he'd ever meet a woman he'd love enough to even think about having a kid with.

"So just what did he teach Colin?" Mike had to know.

"The little punk had the nerve to cry. Had me shitting myself thinking something was really wrong with him, until I realized he'd gotten me to change the channel to his favorite cartoon and hand him my Coke."

"Which he's not supposed to have in the living room." Great, now Mike was frowning at him.

Brody laughed. "Sucker. The crying thing was to get women. I told him to practice until he can do it on command. Watch." In seconds, Brody had streams of tears down his face. "Please, I'll do anything. Don't leave me."

"Not bad." Cam seemed impressed. "I thought you were just a no-talent card player, but you're a second-rate actor too. Oh, and a knuckle-dragging toilet trouble-shooter, I forgot."

"That's plumber, geekboy. You keep adding your silly little numbers while Flynn and I get rich off manly work. Please, you're barely a glorified secretary."

Cam's grin turned evil. "Oh, man, I am so telling Mom you said that."

Considering their mother had been a secretary for over twenty years, Cam had serious leverage on Brody, and Brody knew it.

"Hell. If I'm going down, I'm going down swinging." He leapt from his seat and tackled Cam to the ground.

"Swirly time, mathboy. Courtesy of your neighborhood toilet troubleshooter."

Flynn was laughing so hard his stomach hurt, while Mike argued with the guys not to bust any heads and keep the noise down. He had a hard enough time explaining to Colin why he shouldn't act like his uncles in public.

While Brody wrestled Cam on the floor, both of them whispering insults and swear words so as not to wake Colin, Flynn grabbed another couple of beers for himself and Mike.

"Thanks."

"Sure." He toyed with the label. "Seriously, why didn't Brody or I know about the neighbors? It's not like I'm a dog. I'm not going to hump them in public." At Mike's look, he flushed. "For God's sake, I was twenty years old and drunk. The girl wasn't even real. It was a mannequin and it was all Brody's idea."

Brody and Cam started laughing on the floor while they tried to outwrestle each other. Brody had height and brawn, but Cam had agility and appeared as if he'd been bulking up.

"Hey, some muscle on the youngest."

"Yeah. I hear he's hitting the gym more." Mike flexed. The guy was huge. Hauling lumber around and hammering crap all day did that for a guy. "But still smaller, little man," he said in his best Schwarzenegger impression.

"Fuck you." Cam put Brody into a headlock.

Flynn wanted an answer from Mike. "Hey, I went over there and fixed that sink without a problem. Didn't even make a stink when the redhead went postal and started throwing her shoes and purse around. Not even when she yanked off her shirt and told me if I wanted to see them, I could. Then she invited me to touch them, and I…" he trailed off when everyone stopped to stare at him.

"No kidding? Maybe I should have gone over there." Mike scratched his head.

"Of course I'm kidding. Idiots." Flynn dodged the napkin Mike threw at him. "But she did have a hard time with her boss. And she did throw her shoes. I'm thinking Mom should invite them to a family barbecue to be nice. A late welcome-to-the-neighborhood deal. Abby didn't make a fuss about the sink, and she even tried to pay me for helping."

"I'm sold. I'll mention it to Mom next time I talk to her."

Which would be tomorrow. The woman called Mike every damn day. Flynn loved his mother, but he was okay hearing from her every few days. Not like he needed her reminding him to find a woman and settle down more often than that. Besides, if Mike mentioned to their mother the idea of inviting the neighbors for a party, it wouldn't set off any alarm bells.

"Okay, you losers. Want another shot at the title?" he asked Mike and Cam. "Let's drop the pussy games and go straight-up Texas Hold'em."

Cam shoved Brody off him and stood, brushing the dust off his pants and shirt. "Fine, but Brody doesn't get to deal."

"Agreed," Mike and Flynn said at the same time.

Brody scowled. "And in exchange, swear you'll forget the secretary crack. I love Bitsy." What he called their mother. "Besides, she hears that shit, she'll skin me alive."

Punishment enough, Flynn thought.

"Fine." Mike gave Brody the dad stare. "But if Mom invites the neighbors to the house, you and Flynn—"

Flynn huffed. "Why am I lumped with him again?"

"Have to behave yourselves. I live right next to these women. I don't want to deal with shit because of you two."

Brody shrugged. "Whatever."

"Yeah, sure," Flynn muttered. "Now cut the cards, Nancy. And prepare to lose your ass off."

Chapter 3

MADDIE GROANED. HER HEAD FELT LIKE IT WOULD split in two, and she had a nasty taste in her mouth. Like butterscotch vomit. At the thought, she visited the bathroom again in a hurry.

An hour later, after a shower and brushing her teeth white enough to glow, she felt more like herself. Except for the headache she needed to remedy.

"Drink lots of water and have a little toast," Vanessa said when Maddie walked into the kitchen. As usual, her cousin looked perfect. Neat, without a hair out of place. With her blond hair pulled back in a ponytail and dressed in shorts and a T-shirt promoting *Go Organic*, she looked ready to run minus the shoes. Vanessa didn't want shoes in the house because it added to a dirty floor. On that rule, Maddie agreed.

Dressed in jeans and a tank top, she felt more human, if not any less stupid. God. She'd quit her job yesterday. The panic that had receded during her drunken binge returned in a rush, and she forced herself to concentrate on the here and now before she lost her mind.

She would not spend the rest of her life working three jobs to make ends meet. She did not have a child to support and a nonexistent husband. Money sat in a nice little nest egg in her bank account. She would not starve, nor work herself to an early grave. Breathe in, breathe out.

"Robin and Kim left, by the way," Abby said as she joined them, holding a cup. She poured herself more coffee. Her reading glasses sat perched on top of her head.

"Busy night writing?"

Abby smiled. "Oh yeah. Apparently the guys were much more into smack talking last night than talking trash about women. Though they normally aren't insulting, unless the woman they're talking about is really bitchy." She stared at Maddie. "Or mean. Or vindictive."

"Why are you looking at me?"

"You should apologize. Flynn was really nice when he came over to fix the plumbing. And you weren't. I understand why." Abby waved away her protest. "But the real you is a wonderful, giving woman who works hard to be independent. Not a shrew who hates men."

"Well…" Vanessa drawled.

"Don't even start."

She laughed. "I'm going out for a run. You should get something in that stomach unless you want to feel crappy all day. I'll be back soon." She practically danced out of the kitchen.

"Pretentious snot." Maddie glared at the back of her cousin's head.

Abby sputtered on her coffee, laughing. "You really aren't a morning person, are you? Though it's eleven, and in my book, anything after ten is late. So eleven's more like early afternoon."

Morning or afternoon, it was a beautiful day. After making herself toast and pouring a tall glass of water, she joined Abby outside on the back porch to enjoy the weather.

"Tomatoes are doing well." She nodded to the

garden. "Cucumbers too. You have the greenest thumb I've ever seen."

"I do." Abby thumped her chest with pride. "I grew the biggest pumpkin in 4H ten years ago, I'll have you know."

"Dork."

"Well, what are your accomplishments, Miss I Can't Hold My Liquor?"

"I lettered in track. I'm faster than Vanessa," she bragged. "And I was voted most likely to succeed." *Yeah, how's that working for you without a job?* She coughed to hide her embarrassment. And hurt. And anger. She was done crying. No more tears. Her eyes looked puffy enough.

"I think this is a sign." Abby nodded.

"That I should become a lesbian?"

Abby choked. "Would you stop saying that? I thought Robin was going to jump you last night when you mentioned switching teams."

"As if that's possible. Unfortunately, I wasn't born gay. Besides, if I even blinked at Robin wrong, Kim would kick her ass. Then Kim would kick mine. Don't let her heels fool you." Maddie sighed. "It's too bad I like men." And on that note... "I can't stop thinking about what Mike's brother must think of me after yesterday. I wonder if he heard me yelling?"

"I think China heard you yelling," Abby said drily. "Finish your food and go over and apologize. Trust me, he was very understanding about it all, and it's not like you didn't have the right to freak out a little."

"How was he understanding?" Had Flynn spent his time watching her throw a hissy, then flirted with Abby? Abby, for all her obvious beauty, was clueless when it came to men. The guy could easily have been naked and ready to mount her before Abby'd realize he wanted her.

"He offered to go beat Fred up. When I told him it wasn't worth jail time, he then offered to have his nephew alibi him while he pounded your boss. Cute, huh?" Abby snorted. "Funny guy."

Sexy guy. She couldn't stop seeing that brilliant green color of his eyes and not think of him. It would have been easier if he'd been dressed up or trying to impress. But the guy had been wearing jeans and a white T-shirt. Short black hair, a face that made her think of way too many square-jawed heroes from her old romance books. And he'd been nice enough not to call her out when she'd accused all men of being assholes.

Or when she'd told him to fuck off.

"So you think I should apologize?"

"Yep. And scope out and see if he has any other brothers. I always hear him and Cam. We met Cameron a few months ago, remember? He's the nice, quiet one. Just as handsome as the other two. But that last guy, Brody, I think. I haven't met him yet."

"How many are there?" She couldn't imagine what his mother had gone through raising four or more handsome McCauleys. She'd probably been afraid they'd end up getting some girl pregnant. Maddie knew more than most how easy that was to do. *And I need to dwell on that like I need another buttery nipple.* Feeling queasy, she changed the subject. "So Abby, why do you really hang out here listening to them? I still don't get it."

Abby looked to the privacy fence separating them from Mike's house. They had plenty of distance, but she lowered her voice anyway. "I don't have brothers. It's hard for me to write scenes between guys. I mean, I can write sex scenes easily. I know sex."

"So it says on the bathroom walls."

"Witch." Abby laughed. "The dynamics between women are easy. Men are different. Reading about a man calling a woman 'my darling rose petal' is so '80s. I'm trying to get a more real, contemporary tone to my work."

"So go to a bar. Get some guy friends. Get over this shy thing. You're so weird, Abby. You're a knockout and you think you're fat."

Abby glanced over her shoulder at her ass. "I do have to lose a few—"

"You're funny and smart, but you let a jerk like Kevin make you feel like a fool."

"Gee, Maddie. Thanks for ruining my day." Abby frowned.

"My point is, you're one up on me in so many ways, but you're not nearly as confident as you should be. Heck, I'm pretty happy about myself, and I don't even have a job." And just like that, her self-assuredness plummeted. *Don't panic. It's just a minor setback, not a life-altering moment. I don't think.*

Abby stood, grabbed her by the arm, and tugged her back through the house. She opened the front door and shoved Maddie outside. "Stop thinking about yesterday and go see if Flynn is over there. If not, at least thank Mike for us. It's the right thing to do."

Grumbling at bossy short people who drank too much caffeine and developed attitudes like Vanessa, Maddie slipped on her shoes then walked the short distance next door. Like their house, this one had Craftsman-style architecture. A large porch with a hanging swing she envied, and pots of flowers all over the place. She'd never seen Mike outside tending to them, but then again, she spent most of her days from sun up to sun down at work. And for the past few months, she'd spent what little off time she had with Ben. That hypocrite.

It was all fine and dandy for him to ask her to cancel her plans for one of his benefit dinners or a call he had to make to a hospital, or to rearrange her life to suit his profession. But God forbid she cancel a date because she needed to confer with a client. She wouldn't compare interior design to medicine, but her career meant something to her, even if she wasn't saving lives. *Or treating athlete's foot*, she thought nastily.

The door opened in front of her, and she blinked at a sleepy-eyed stranger wearing nothing more than tan shorts and a smile. "Well, hello there."

The clear charm earned a smile from her, even though she still hated men. She could hate an entire gender and appreciate a work of art, though, couldn't she? He probably wasn't a McCauley, unless this one was a honey-haired throwback. His hair stuck up in places, indicating a good case of bed head. Amber eyes full of laughter and speculation teased her to enjoy the moment. She didn't know why, but his good mood seemed infectious.

"I just wanted to thank Mike and Flynn for the plumbing work yesterday. I don't want to inter"—he dragged her into the house before she could finish—"rupt."

"Just wait here. I'll be right back." He tore off down a hallway past the living room that looked like a bomb had hit it. Pizza boxes, soda cans, beer bottles, and peanut shells littered every available table and parts of the floor. Underneath the mess, she sensed the potential for a really nice house. But stereotypical man furniture took up too much space.

A brown recliner, leather couch, and tan curtains accented with, gee, brown trim, cluttered the busy living room. Not to be outdone, the big-screen television sat on the far wall, detracting from the focal point of the room, which should have been a gorgeous stone fireplace.

Just then, a groan shook a blanket, a few cans, and a pizza box that fell off the lump on the sofa. She hadn't noticed the hand dangling from the couch until now. To her shock, a man unfolded from the furniture.

No, not a man, a disheveled Adonis who blinked at her in shock. He wore nothing but a pair of low-riding boxer briefs. Every ridge of muscle in his abdomen and chest flexed as he took in a breath. Then he raised his hands to wipe his eyes, and she tried not to gape when his arms bunched and his biceps begged her to touch.

"Maddie?"

Flynn McCauley looked even better half naked than he had wearing jeans and a T-shirt. She tried really hard to remember how much she hated men. Just when she thought she could say something without sounding too out of breath, Colin McCauley walked through the living room looking barely awake. He wore Spider-Man underpants and rubbed his eyes, reminding her so much of Flynn that she smiled.

"Hi, Colin."

He stopped under the archway to the kitchen, turned to stare at her, and screamed, "*Girrllllll!*" Shrieking, he raced back the way he'd come, running with one hand covering his tiny butt.

Deep voices sounded from the back rooms. What sounded like Mike and the guy from the front door.

"Sorry about that. He's in an anti-girl phase. We keep telling him it'll pass." Flynn hadn't blinked yet. "Guess I should go put something on."

Not on my account. "Oh, right. I'm really sorry to bother you. But it's noon, so I didn't think—"

"Noon?"

"Yeah." And she thought she'd slept in. "Rough night?"

He glanced around him and frowned. "I guess. Man, when Mike sees this, he's going to shit a brick." He looked back at her and flushed.

Good Lord, could the man be any more attractive?

"Be right back." He darted around the couch and disappeared.

Mike appeared at the mouth of the hallway followed by the other guy and Colin. "Sorry about the noise, we—"

He stopped dead at the sight of the living room. Before he could say a word, the guy behind him started talking.

"Don't blow a gasket. Flynn and I will clean it up. All of it."

"You'd better, Brody, or I'll," he paused, checked himself, and finished with a glance at Colin, "I'll put you in time-out in the corner." He added in a low voice, "In a body bag."

Mike, at least, wore jeans and a T-shirt with some cartoon characters on it, which were mirrored by his son behind him. They looked so cute, like a matched set. She couldn't help grinning.

"Not my fault. Today, Colin got to pick what I wear," he said, seeing her smile.

"It's fair, because you never let me wear what I want to camp." Colin's mouth set in a stubborn line.

Uh-oh. Family squabble. "I'd better go. Sorry for intruding. I just wanted to say—"

"You threw away my favorite shirt." Colin tilted his chin, the same way Mike had when he'd looked at Brody. In challenge.

"Don't go." Brody magically appeared and gently nudged her away from the front door. "Want something to drink? Eat? I promise, the kitchen is clean."

"Are you herding me?"

"It's working, isn't it?" He whispered, "Didn't want you to see the drama behind you. Colin's playing it up because we're here. I knew the little guy wasn't going to let that shirt go."

She walked with him out of the room into the kitchen and sat at the surprisingly clean table. This room she liked. Done in muted grays, blacks, and blues, the ceramic tiled floor and granite countertops definitely suited Mike. Now if she could get him to part with the rest of his furniture, or at least arrange it another way, it would look so much better.

She couldn't help designing, and then she remembered again that she had no job.

"Who are you?" she asked finally. "I don't think we've met."

"I'm sorry." He held out a large hand. "Brody Singer. The unofficially adopted member of the McCauley clan." Flynn walked into the room and Brody added, "And Flynn's boss."

Flynn shot him a dirty look. "Try partner. Brody and I are the masters behind McSons Plumbing."

She shook Brody's hand. "Madison Gardner. But call me Maddie." She turned to Flynn. "And about yesterday…" She shouldn't stay, not since she hated men. Hated what they looked like with those muscular chests. Hated the strong muscles of Brody's thighs in those khaki shorts. Hated the way Flynn's strong neck drew her attention to his broad shoulders. "I wanted to say thank you for fixing our sink. I didn't get a chance before." Her cheeks heated, but she couldn't help it.

Flynn sat down next to her and lifted her hand. He shocked her by kissing the back of it. "Sorry you had such a bad day. If you want, I can go kick your boss's ass. It's no problem at all."

He did seem pretty serious. So did Brody, nodding behind him.

"Ah, no. That's okay. I'll handle it."

Brody took a seat across from her. "You're not going to still work for the guy, are you?"

"I quit." She swallowed hard, still coming to grips with the decision.

"Good for you." Flynn nodded. "I tell you, Brody and I worked for this real ass—dirtbag when we first started out. We learned as much as we could, then moved on. Luckily, I'm smart enough, and he's pretty enough, that we hired on somewhere else before making a go of it ourselves. You ever think of that? Working for yourself?"

Only all the time. "Yeah."

"Great. It's hard, but if you're bossy, like Brody is—"

"You're kidding, right? *I'm* bossy?"

"Then it's the best way to go," Flynn finished. "I love being my own boss. Of course, it helps we have a kick-ass accountant to do our books. You have someone who could handle the financial aspect of things?"

"Um, yeah." Vanessa. But… working for herself now? She'd need to build clients, start padding her resume, find a place to set up shop, start advertising…

"What do you do again?" Flynn asked. "I forget, something you said about designing, right? My aunt sells houses. Just the other day she was complaining about how much staging impacts a sale. Of course, I had to ask her what staging was, but when she told me, I was floored people will pay more for a house decorated the right way. I mean, it's the same house either way, right?"

A lightbulb clicked, and she wondered if she ought to hold off on submitting her resume to other designers. With a lot of luck, and a little bit of help, she could start working for herself sooner than she'd intended. Not designing. That wouldn't do for the immediate future. But maybe staging…?

"Thank you." Hope sparking in her breast for the first time since the disaster had struck. Bursting with it, she leaned into Flynn, cupped his cheeks, and planted a kiss on his smooth, firm lips.

No one moved or said a thing when she stood, waved, and left, brimming with positivity once more.

~~~

Flynn couldn't stop staring after her.

"That was gross." Colin made retching sounds, standing with his father right behind him.

Brody grinned. "Hot dayum, son, you look like you just got walloped with a lead pipe."

"I feel like it." And said lead pipe was growing in his pants. Holy shit. No question, he had to have that woman. If one innocent kiss had been enough to get him this hard, he could only imagine what it would feel like to be in bed with her.

"Uh-uh. No. I know that look, and forget it." Mike scowled.

In front of him, Colin scowled as well.

"You two are like bookends. One big, one small." Brody mussed with Colin's hair, and Colin slapped at him, until the two of them were mock wrestling. Colin gurgled with laughter while Brody tickled him.

"Idiot." Mike shook his head at Brody. "I mean it, Flynn."

"You're not the boss of me." Flynn grinned.

Colin agreed. "Yeah, Dad. Only Grandpa and Gramma can tell Uncle Flynn what to do."

"Ya think?" Mike reached for his son and proceeded to show him who was in charge until he cried uncle. Literally.

"He mean me or you?" Brody asked, watching the pair with affection.

"Please. I'm the boy's favorite. You all know it." But his mind was on other things. "Okay, Mike. Quit playing around and call Mom. I want her to invite the neighbors over next week. Make it Saturday. Brody and I are clear that weekend."

"Are you serious?"

"Yeah, I am. And don't mess with me on this, or I'll go right back over there and give her a kiss I won't walk away from. You get me?"

Colin gagged again, but Brody gave him a thumbs-up.

After being forced to clean up the living room by a man who'd lived like a slob the better part of his growing years, Flynn went home to change into work clothes. He and Brody had a job at three that ended up lasting a few hours, then he returned to his apartment and did a little cleaning of his own. Located downtown near the market, his place afforded him the opportunity to park his truck and walk to any number of shops for what he needed.

Since he rarely spent time at home, more often at Mike's, his parents', or working, he didn't have much more to do than dust and pick up a few odds and ends. He did some laundry and settled down to watch a movie. Something with blood and guns. And sex, which of course made him think of Maddie. Damn. He'd been a long time between women if just the thought of a date with her could make his heart race and his body come alive.

Annoyed at his hard-on that refused to leave, he fast-forwarded past the sex parts and tried to focus on the mindless violence. Not long after, he drifted into sleep. Unfortunately, he dreamed of nothing but Maddie.

———

Standing in front of her door the next day with a bouquet of daisies and praying his brother wouldn't see him, Flynn waited with a sense of nervous anticipation he hadn't felt in a long, long time. Before he could knock, the door opened.

Abby and a tall, beautiful blond stood staring at him in surprise. They were dressed in workout gear, showing off a nice expanse of sculpted legs. A nice way to break in a Sunday after a boring hour of church service.

"Hey, Flynn." Abby smiled. "Nice to see you." She glanced at the flowers in his hand and her smile widened.

"Don't tell me. You're the handyman." The blond tilted her head, looking him up and down. Cool, assertive, and attractive. But she didn't do it for him. Nor did the short brunette by her side.

"Plumber, actually." He held out his hand, not surprised when she gripped it with a firm shake. "Flynn McCauley."

"Vanessa Campbell. Nice to meet you. We'd stay, but we're already behind schedule."

Abby made a face. "Yeah, late for a date with death."

Flynn smiled. Abby looked pathetic, Vanessa impatient. A lot like him and Cam when his brother started nagging him to exercise. Luckily, the autocrat had been too busy with work lately to obsess about training. "I feel for you, Abby."

"I'll probably drop dead of a heart attack. Flynn, if I'm not back in an hour, call 9-1-1." She groaned when Vanessa grabbed her by the hand and dragged her into the front yard.

"A little warm-up, then we'll stop and stretch." Vanessa rattled off a bunch of tidbits about lactic acid and muscle memory while Abby griped and complained.

"Good luck," he called after the pair, then turned to see Maddie walking down the stairs.

The woman wore nothing more than a pair of well-worn shorts and a T-shirt that molded to her curves not constrained by a bra. *Thank you, God.* She really did have a killer rack. He could just imagine holding those breasts in his hands, feeling their softness as he thumbed over her nipples. Her hair was mussed, and she barely caught a yawn. When she saw Flynn, she stopped in her tracks.

"Morning. Or should I say, afternoon?" When she continued to say nothing, he asked, "May I come in?"

"Sure." She turned around, raced back up the stairs, and yelled, "Be right back."

"O-kay." Flynn walked inside and shut the door behind him. He'd spent the first few years of his life in this house. Something about the open airiness of it had always screamed fairies and pixies to him. Not that he'd ever tell his brothers he imagined fairies had lived in the garden, but hell, he'd been all of four. Then Cam had started walking, and they'd moved a few blocks over into a bigger spread. But he'd never forgotten his fondness for this place.

He shook his head when he saw his impression from Friday remained the same. Everything seemed so tidy. How could people live like this? No clutter, no mess. It was like Mike's, but without the funk of dirty socks and little kid smell.

"I had to change." She sounded out of breath when she found him in the foyer again.

"Sorry to put you out." He smiled, wishing she hadn't changed a thing. But with or without a bra, Maddie looked incredible. She'd brushed her hair, and he wanted to touch it, to see if it felt as soft as it looked. Her shirt still clung to her curves, but left more to the imagination since she'd put on underclothes.

"What's up?" She shoved her hands in her back pockets.

He forced himself to keep his gaze level with her eyes. He offered her the flowers. "These are for you. Not only for that apology yesterday, but for freaking out my nephew. I don't think a girl has ever seen Colin in his Spidey shorts before."

She flushed and laughed. "He hit a really high pitch as he raced from the room. I hope he's not too embarrassed."

"Nope. We McCauleys can handle a lot. Look at me. I'm not too scarred after you caught me in my briefs."

The pink on her cheeks deepened. "They weren't exactly briefs."

Pleased she'd noticed, he continued, "And hey, I surprised you this morning. I guess we're even."

She clutched the flowers. "I guess we are."

Silence settled between them, one fraught with a tension Flynn could only describe as sexual. He would have been content to stare at her all day. She had a darker complexion than he would have expected on a redhead. Not pale, her olive skin turned a delightful pink when she was embarrassed. Her face could have graced any of the magazines stacked neatly on her coffee table, yet her nose had a smattering of freckles at the bridge that stopped her short of perfection.

And her eyes... He was drowning in them, caught in the amber color that looked gold one minute, deep brown the next. He wondered what she saw when she looked at him. Did she feel the attraction? Was his interest flattering, or was he one more creep like all the rest who no doubt fell at her feet when confronted with such beauty?

"I should put these in water," she said in a husky voice that made him want to take her in his arms and carry her upstairs.

"Yeah." He cleared his throat and followed her into the kitchen, unable to look away from her curves. Man, that ass just begged to be held. "Ah, so the reason I stopped by. My mom and dad are having a picnic next Saturday and wanted to invite you guys. Think you all could swing by around two?" He hadn't confirmed the date or time yet, but he knew his mother wouldn't say no, and whatever she wanted, Dad agreed to.

"Oh. A picnic?"

"A barbecue."

"I'd say I have to check my calendar, but not any-more. I'm free for the immediate future." She paused. "Man, that doesn't sound good, does it?"

"You being free?"

"Me whining about my job again. I'm done with that. I'd love to go to a barbecue. I haven't been to one in years. That's really nice of your parents."

"Good."

"I can't answer for Vanessa or Abby, but if they're not working, I know they'd love to be there."

"Great." Good, great. She reduced him to one-word answers. He couldn't think about more than her mouth, watching her form each word with those plump, red lips. She'd been so soft yesterday, and that brief kiss had given him some wet dreams last night. Hell, he hadn't come in his sheets since he'd been a teenager. But this morning he'd had to dump his sheets in the washer be-fore joining his family for church. Church—talk about a buzzkill. Yet here he stood, across from the object of his fantasies.

"You okay, Flynn?" She frowned. "You look a little funny."

"Mike told me to leave you alone," he blurted.

"Why?"

"Cautioned me not to screw over his neighbors, because he didn't want to deal with a bunch of annoyed women."

"What do you mean?" She took a step back and bumped against the counter.

He closed the distance between them and caged her between his arms. It gratified him to hear her breathing as raspy and uneven as his. "I know you hate men. That you had a crappy day on Friday. And that you have some things to iron out. I just wanted to thank you for yesterday. Nothing more than that. Okay?"

She licked her lips, and he forced himself to keep an inch or two between them. Fucking her on the counter would have to wait, because her roommates would be back soon.

"Thank me for apologizing? But you don't have to—"

"Yes, Maddie. I do." She didn't understand. He *did* have to, or he'd lose his ever-loving mind. His lips met hers, and he forgot his own name.

Chapter 4

MADDIE COULD BARELY BREATHE. THE FEEL OF Flynn's mouth on hers sucked away her breath, her reason, her ability to think. His lips felt a lot different than they had yesterday. Still firm beneath her, he now exuded some kind of attractant because she wanted nothing more than to wrap her legs around his waist and hold on for the ride. And that scent. He wore a subtle cologne, a hint of citrus and man that made her want to snuggle close and sniff him while she rubbed all over his kick-ass body.

His lips teased, gentle yet persistent. He didn't rush her, and to feel a man like Flynn exploring like he had all the time in the world turned her knees to jelly. She'd never before experienced a kiss that put her at the center of a man's world. His concentration focused on her, on tasting her. With a slow swipe of his tongue, he coaxed her to open her mouth. When she did, he slid his tongue inside, grazing her lips and teeth. Then he stirred her entire body into a rhythmic beat. His tongue entered and retreated, as if he was making love to her mouth.

She groaned, totally turned on, especially when he moaned and deepened the kiss.

Her nipples hurt, hard and sensitive. Her body throbbed, and she swore she'd need to change her panties after this.

Flynn let her go to get another breath of air. She drew

in a deep breath seconds before he descended again, this time less careful, hungrier. Still, the aggravating man didn't touch her with more than his mouth, and the frustration built. She wanted his hands on her, to cup her breasts, slide between her legs, and make her feel so good.

It had been more than two months since any intimacies with Ben, and even those had been scheduled around his work or hers. Nothing spontaneous, and nothing nearly as good as this kiss from a man she'd just met.

A large hand settled on her rib cage, and she trembled. She absolutely loved having her sides stroked. Trust Flynn to accidentally find a sweet spot.

He gripped her tighter then released her, rubbing his fingers against her ribs with shocking potency. Then he broke the kiss, breathing hard. "Maddie. Holy shit." He leaned his forehead against hers, and to her surprise, he shook like she did. "I didn't mean to… That was… I just wanted to say thanks."

He pulled back, took his hand away, and placed it on the counter again. Not touching, but so close, he overwhelmed her with his size and strength. The pulse beat at his throat, and he swallowed hard.

What could she say? "You're welcome," came out in a throaty whisper.

"God, you're beautiful." He stroked a finger down her cheek then shook his head and stepped back. "I need to go. Some things to do before tomorrow. So I can count on you to show on Saturday at two?"

She nodded, not sure she could speak again.

"Great." He winced. "I can't think beyond good and

great right now." He didn't make sense, but then, he didn't need to. Not when he could kiss like that.

Still bemused, she walked him to the door and waved when he left.

Not sure she liked what she'd just turned into, Maddie forced herself to put on her shoes and go out for a walk. She locked the door behind her, tapped the key in her pocket, and lost herself in a muddied knot of sensation, images of a half-naked Flynn, and the uneasy notion that she'd somehow traded one obsession for another. Her work for the knockout plumber.

She returned to the house a few hours later to find two very annoyed women waiting on the front step.

"About freakin' time." Vanessa ripped the key from Maddie's hand.

"Oh, uh, sorry."

Abby scowled. "Locking the door is good. Locking it when the key's not"—she lowered her voice—"in its hiding spot is annoying."

Maddie cringed. Her fault, totally, since she'd taken the spare key from the flower pot yesterday. She had no intention of explaining why she'd been so distracted this morning, so she fibbed just a bit. "I'm sorry, guys. My head's not right. I can't stop thinking about work."

Abby raised a brow. "Oh? I was thinking a handsome man with flowers turned your head."

Maddie concentrated on thinking about work and work only. *Fred, remember what he did to you.* "Yeah, about that. Flynn came by to invite us all to his mom and dad's next week. Barbecue on Saturday. He also gave me flowers. Said he felt bad about what happened to me on Friday."

Abby started to soften. Vanessa wasn't moved.

"Yeah, whatever." Her cousin huffed. "Next time, moon around town after the key's back in the pot."

"Oh, ease up, hard-ass." Abby took Maddie and ushered her inside. "So what did your wandering thoughts tell you to do?"

The three of them walked through the house and pushed through the back door. They sat on the porch, staring at the masses of flowers and vegetables. A few butterflies appeared, and the scent of honeysuckle relaxed Maddie enough to share what she'd tentatively planned.

"Something Flynn said yesterday had me thinking."

"I'll bet it did." Vanessa wiggled her eyebrows.

"Get your head out of the guy's pants." Maddie frowned, inwardly telling herself the same thing. "After the initial panic of losing my job, I thought about all the places I'd send my resume, hoping Fred wouldn't blacklist me before I could find something else. I've always planned to one day run my own firm, but not yet. I don't have enough in savings, the clients, or the plans vested to start my own firm."

"But…" Abby encouraged.

"But then Flynn mentioned staging." At Vanessa's blank look, she explained, "You know, when someone wants to sell a house but their furniture makes the place look too small or too ugly? Then stagers come in and move the furniture around. Sometimes, depending upon how involved they get, they can paint the place, rent and position new furniture, all to make it more appealing to home buyers."

"Oh right. I watch those shows on TV all the time." Abby nodded.

Vanessa frowned. "Don't Robin and Kim already do that?"

"Kind of." Maddie needed to call them, to see what her friends thought of the idea. "Our firm—I mean, Hampton's Designs—used to use them to rent furniture and stage it when we sold ideas to clients. Kim and Robin mostly purchase the furniture in their warehouse for rentals. But I'd be designing with it."

"That's actually not a bad idea. You can still do interior decorating, but with so many people trying to buy and sell nowadays, you hit a decent market. Now you just need to figure out how much it will cost to do business, and to see what your competitors are up to."

Trust Vanessa to have to throw in some suggestions. Give the woman an inch, she'd run over you by a mile. And with her big feet, she'd hurt you when she finished.

"Thanks." They sat together enjoying the sunlight.

Vanessa, not surprisingly, had to ruin it. "So the flowers…"

"Yeah, the flowers." Abby leaned closer. "How come Flynn didn't bring me any? I was the nice one. I didn't say anything about men being pricks and hating them all."

Vanessa laughed. "Nice. No wonder he seemed so scared at the door."

"He wasn't scared." Maddie glared. "It was very thoughtful of him to bring flowers. And the invitation wasn't just to me, it's to all of us." When Vanessa and Abby exchanged a glance, she snapped, "What?"

Abby answered, making no effort to hide her grin. "Your lips look a little bruised, Maddie. And Flynn didn't just bring you cheapo carnations. That's a date bouquet if I ever saw one."

"You write fiction. What do you know?"

Vanessa had to chime in, "She knows plenty. Remember, she listens to those bozos every Friday night, for their 'man talk.' Personally, I think she gets off on the voyeur aspect of spying."

Abby blushed. "I listen. I don't look."

Vanessa shrugged. "Whatever. So Abby, is Flynn dating anyone right now?"

"No, he's not dating anyone right now, you big-footed heifer. He broke up with his last bimbo over a month ago."

"Perfect." Vanessa clapped her hands and smiled at Maddie. "Now *you* can be his bimbo."

Maddie wanted to slap her cousin silly. Instead, she counted to ten before she answered. "You're hilarious. Ha ha. I'm not a bimbo, and I'm not into men right now. Or women," she added before Vanessa could add another obnoxious comment. "I don't want to date any-one." *Yeah, hormones, listen up. No more men. Kisses or no kisses, he's not my type. He's too good-looking. Too muscular. Too everything.* "Remember, I broke up with Ben too. I didn't just lose a job. Besides, I have too much at stake right now. It's going to take all my energy just to get this job thing going."

Vanessa nodded. "You do have a point, and it's nice to see you behaving rationally about it. Research, plan-ning, talent. You can definitely make a go of it if you do it right."

"Thanks, I think."

"No, that's a compliment." Abby nodded. "She said

the same thing to me when I decided to stop working for other people and work for myself. At first she called me nuts for quitting my day job to write. Because let's face it, how many wackos out there with a blog are writing right now? I'm a wacko, and I write. But I had a vision."

"And another job or two to back you up," Vanessa said drily. "You segued into your own business before you ever considered writing full time. Now you make ends meet, barely, mind you—"

"Thanks so much."

Vanessa continued. "But you're smart about it. You're dedicated to your work, and it shows. And now you're venturing into, well, I won't say virgin territory, but those smutty books are making you some serious cash."

Abby's lips flattened. Oh boy. Not this argument again. "They're not smutty books, Vanessa. They're erotic *romance*. Not dirty, not porn, not smut. It's about love experienced through sexual connection. Something you wouldn't know much about."

Maddie's thoughts immediately went to Flynn. "And on that note, I'm out of here. I have some stuff to do, calls to make." Neither roommate looked up as she left, engaged in a familiar argument that would build until Abby stormed away madder than a scalded cat.

Once upstairs in her room, Maddie sank back onto her bed and wondered if she was doing the right thing. Granted, she'd been through a lot the past few days, but going it on her own? That was a lot to take on. Could she do it? Did she really have the nerve to try?

Not short on gumption, which she'd inherited from her mother, Maddie had been working since she could

THE TROUBLEMAKER NEXT DOOR   57

remember. Just her and her mom, and they'd never had much money. Every paycheck stretched thin. They scrimped and saved no matter the occasion. Second-hand became second nature, and Maddie had learned to make a dollar stretch like nobody's business.

Even Vanessa didn't know how bad it had been. When Michelle Gardner took her daughter to see relatives for a week or two during the summer and on odd holidays, the visits remained short and sweet. For years Maddie had begged to stay longer, until during one visit she'd overheard her grandmother bashing her mother. Apparently the mistake of getting knocked up at sixteen with a boy from the wrong side of the tracks never went away, no matter how hard her mother worked to make things right by Grandma Gardner.

Maddie had never known her father, a man who supposedly had his own troubles. Her mother never spoke ill of him. Hell, she never spoke of him, period. The woman had too much on her plate to worry about a deadbeat ex-boyfriend.

Michelle worked extra hard to make up for her youthful indiscretion. Too full of pride, Maddie had once heard her aunt say of her mother. But Maddie didn't think her mother had enough pride. At forty-four, with no education but the GED she'd managed to earn after giving birth to her daughter, the woman still worked seven days a week. Chapped hands, premature gray hair, and back problems made her mother look a decade older than her age. Yet the woman acted so pleased to still be living on her own, with no help or handouts from anyone. It saddened Maddie to return home, seeing her mother so physically beat down.

The stubborn woman repeatedly refused Maddie's offer to move her out West. She wouldn't allow Maddie to give her money either. Her mother had friends and a routine she had no plans to give up, especially not for a daughter she'd raised to be independent.

Maddie thought again about calling her mother for support. Mom would understand, and she'd offer both sympathy and sound advice, but Maddie didn't want to let her down. Every accomplishment, every accolade she'd earned had made her mother so proud. She didn't want to add her mom's disappointment and worry on top of her own anxiety.

With a deep breath, she rose from the bed and sat at her vanity, now free of any and all makeup. She plunked down her laptop and started researching, starting her life over from scratch.

Three days later, Maddie sat outside the Starbucks on Queen Anne on a sunny afternoon, glorying in the day. Her meeting with Kim and Robin had been more than productive; it had been enlightening. Not only were her friends excited for her to start her business, they'd wondered what had taken her so long. With them behind her, she planned to make a real go of things. Her fears of being two doors from the poorhouse had faded, though not disappeared completely.

At the thought, she knew she needed to bite the bullet. She pulled out her cell phone and dialed her mother's number. Despite the time difference, she knew Michelle Gardner would be hard at work at the diner.

Her mother answered, breathless. "Maddie?"

"I knew I needed to get my caller ID changed,"

Maddie teased then took a sip of her latte. "How are you, Mom?"

"Great, now that my baby girl has finally called. Hold on a sec." She muffled the phone, and Maddie could hear her ask for a few minutes.

Maddie would have felt bad about interrupting, but since her mother never did anything *but* work, the woman could use a spare minute to take a break.

"So why haven't you called me in forever? I was getting worried, Madison."

Maddie had talked to the woman two weeks ago. Her mother had a definite knack for instilling remorse, deserved or not. "Sorry, but I've been busy with work and trying to keep Abby and Vanessa from killing each other. Abby's got deadlines, and you know that's always a rough time to get through."

Her mother laughed. "I love that girl. So creative. And how is your cousin, anyway? Still trying to boss everyone around?"

"When isn't she? She's Aunt Loretta's daughter, go figure."

"Poor kid."

Maddie snorted, thinking the same. She made small talk with her mother, wanting to but not quite having the courage to mention her new venture as an entrepreneur. She wanted to prove to herself she could succeed before telling her mother.

For a few minutes, they discussed the diner, her mother's new neighbor, and life on the East Coast versus Maddie's cooler summer out West. Finally a conversation that didn't veer into Maddie's personal life, of which her mother never seemed to approve.

"And what about your doctor? You haven't said anything about Ben."

Crap. Might as well get it over with. "Ah, we're no longer together."

"Good. I never liked him. Though I did get worried that he lasted longer than the others you've dated."

Maddie hadn't expected her mother to be pleased she'd once again broken up with someone. "What? Why?"

"He was too stifling."

She thought her mother had liked Ben. A doctor with a decent background, and he'd always paid when they'd gone out. Maddie had never talked bad about him. So what wasn't to like? "You never even met him."

"I didn't need to." Her mother sniffed. "Everything you described about him sounded just like all the others you've dated. Dull. Not a challenge, and not what you need, honey."

They'd had this conversation more times than Maddie liked to count. Maddie tried to change the subject. "You know, Mom, it's surprising how nice it is today. The sun is shining, the birds are chirping. And for once, Starbucks isn't overcrowded."

"I know I made mistakes with you." Her mother talked right over her. "I showed you how to be strong. You're one of the hardest workers I know. But sometimes, in a relationship especially, you have to give and take. I never had that with your father because we were so damn young. I spent my youth trying to prove myself to my parents, who only ever saw what they wanted to see. But honey, I see your successes. I know you're smart."

Would she still think that if she knew Maddie had quit her job?

"When it comes to business, you have a terrific head on your shoulders. But your heart? Not so much. Don't do what I did. Don't bury yourself in work and forget about living. If you don't trust, you won't get hurt. But you won't live either." She could almost see her mother making that stern face and shaking a bony finger at her. "I know what Ben and those others gave you. Sex may be necessary at times, but it won't fill your holidays and special moments with joy. It won't hold your hand and walk with you to the movies. And it won't make you less lonely either. You need to find a man who fulfills who you really are."

God, not this again. She wanted to crawl under a rock when her mother mentioned s-e-x. Though they always spoke openly with one another, Maddie at times wished they had more secrets. "Okay, Mom. I'm hearing you." *Way too clearly*.

As if her mother had conjured him with talk of sex and fulfillment, Maddie watched a way-too-familiar face round the corner onto Queen Anne. Dressed in jeans and a green T-shirt that clung to every ridge and divot of muscle, Flynn McCauley strutted down the sidewalk like he owned it. He nodded to several people along the way, the hottie obviously a mainstay in the Queen Anne district. Drawing closer, he approached the coffee shop as if pulled by invisible strings.

Despite trying not to look directly at him, she knew the second he saw her because his eyes widened and his lips curled.

Great. She hadn't been able to stop thinking about him since Sunday. This would only add to her sleepless nights. Before she could get up and sneak back inside, he waved at her. There went her chance to indulge in a good dose of self-preservation.

"Hello?" Her mother raised her voice. "Maddie? Are you still there?"

"Sorry." Time to check for signs of drool. Good Lord, Flynn was hot, and way too much to handle while speaking with her mother. With her luck, her mother would insist on a conversation about available men while Flynn hovered nearby. "I have to go, Mom. I love you. Talk to you next week, I promise."

Her mother sighed. "I know, I know. You don't want to hear it. I'm sorry, but someone needs to tell you how to—"

"Mom. I *really* have to go."

Her mother muttered under her breath and finished with, "Fine. I love you too. Bye."

Maddie disconnected just as Flynn sidled up to her table. She forced a natural smile and tried to ignore the racing of her pulse. "Well, hello, Flynn."

"Maddie Gardner. My day is looking even brighter. Mind if I sit?"

Resigned, she nodded. "Sure. Have a seat." Out of the corner of her eye she saw a woman at the table behind Flynn ogling him. To help him out and no doubt prevent him from a future case of something contagious, she raised a brow at the woman. "Can I help you with something?"

The woman blushed and turned around, no doubt embarrassed to be caught staring. Smug and not sure why, Maddie tried to view Flynn's surprise visit as nothing more than a chance meeting between acquaintances. No reason she should be feeling so nervous or excited. This was Flynn, her neighbor's brother. He'd fixed her sink, for heaven's sake.

She hadn't realized she'd been tapping her fingers on the table until Flynn glanced down at her hands.

"You okay?"

No. I'm not. I want to have smokin' hot sex with you then send you far, far away, wouldn't paint her in a favorable light, so she blamed her mother. "I just talked to my mom. I've been better."

He chuckled. "Hold that thought." He returned minutes later. But he'd been gone long enough to allow her to get her hormones under control.

Or so she'd thought. When he sat and focused all that male attention on her, her palms started to sweat.

He tipped his head back and took a deep draught from a bottle of something orange. She couldn't look away from the cords of his throat as he swallowed.

He finished half his drink and smacked his lips. "Man, I needed that. So tell me about your mom."

She concentrated on her cup and intentionally eased her clenched thighs. Then she took another sip of coffee before speaking. "How much time do you have?"

He grinned. "Come on. She can't be that bad. You're nice enough. Kind of."

She liked his teasing. "Funny guy. My mother calls me once a week. Sometimes, if I'm lucky, once every other week. She loves me and she means well, but she's always trying to tell me what to do."

"I know the feeling. Hell, my mother lives a few streets down from Mike's. I see her all the time because I practically live at his place."

"Really?"

"Yeah. Funny I hadn't seen you before last week. I mean, I'm there practically every Friday. We play cards, the four of us. Me and my brothers and Brody."

"Seems like a nice crowd." A sexy crowd. All of his brothers looked alike. Strong, handsome, and too tempting to a woman who wanted little to do with men. Even Brody had been more than attractive, and she wasn't into blonds.

"They are. Except for my nephew. He's a schemer. Too smart for his own good." Flynn smiled.

The clear affection for his family gave her another insight into his character, one she couldn't help liking. Maddie didn't come from a large family, by any means, but she'd do anything for her mother, Vanessa, or Abby. Blood or not, her extended family meant everything to her. Something she and Flynn seemed to have in common.

"Colin's cute. He looks just like your brother."

Flynn frowned and took another sip of his soda. "Mike's a friggin' taskmaster. After you left the other day, he made me clean the place from top to bottom. Like he had nothing to do with the beers and half a pizza that disappeared in his big mouth."

Flynn looked so put out. She had to laugh. "That's nothing. I think Vanessa does white-glove tests when we're not around."

He chuckled. "Your house looked barely lived in. Trust me. You want to see a mess, you should see Brody's work in progress, as he calls it. He's a pig."

"But not you?"

"Nah. I like to be organized. Can't function if I can't find my crap right away. Of course, I've been told that's because I'm always late for everything, so I need it where I can find it before I have to dart out the door." His phone buzzed right then. "Hear that? My alarm so I won't be late. I'm turning over a new leaf." He winked at her.

"Late for what?"

"I'm due to meet Brody for a consult on a new job."

"Oh. Do you guys have an office around here?"

"No. I left my truck at Mike's while we worked out of Brody's. I need to pick it up and drive to the customer."

"Well, good luck on your consult."

He stood to leave, and she already missed his company. Which was stupid. He was nothing more than the neighbor's brother. Besides, she'd see him soon enough at the coming barbecue.

"See you Saturday, right?"

"You're reading my mind." She nodded. "I'll be there. It's really nice of your parents to invite us."

"Well, you can thank them by showing up and being extra nice to their charming son."

She blinked at him, all innocence. "Which one?"

"That would be me. Feel free to ignore the other Neanderthals hanging around for a free meal."

Before she could comment, he leaned down and shocked her by planting a kiss on her cheek. The warmth in that simple touch locked her body up, frozen in suspense to see what more he might do.

Flynn didn't pull back right away. He stayed so close she could feel his breath against her mouth, could almost taste the sweet orange that lingered on his lips. "See you soon, Maddie."

Then he stood and left, carrying his bottle as he whistled his way across the street. He didn't look back once.

She didn't look away from him until he turned out of sight. Holy hell, but the temperature had escalated in the last few minutes. She downed the rest of her lukewarm latte and fanned herself.

She needed to find a way to deal with her odd reaction to the man before Saturday. She almost wished she hadn't agreed to go, but she refused to shy away from the party because he made her uncomfortable. It would have been almost easier if he'd done it on purpose, but he couldn't know how he affected her.

Maddie Gardner dealt with conflict; she didn't let it deal with her. She'd told Fred Hampton to shove it, had lived for over a year with a small-scale dictator who hated the word *dust*, and had neatly fielded another call from her mother. She could handle Flynn McCauley.

She hoped.

On her way back home, she ran into Jed, a friend of Vanessa's she'd once met at a party. He seemed nice, safe, and uninteresting. Just the way she liked them, according to her mother. They chatted for a few minutes then parted after she promised to pass on a message for him.

Yet during the pleasant walk home, thoughts of Flynn, not her cousin or work, constantly intruded. And it bothered her.

Maddie had future plans that didn't include a guy. Period.

She tapped the cell phone in her back pocket, not surprised she still hadn't heard from Ben. They'd dated for a few months, been friends for even longer. Then they'd ended, and not one message from him asking about her pending promotion. Sure, her job had ended badly, but Ben didn't know that. They couldn't at least be friends?

After all, he'd been the one to demand she leave, not the other way around.

Well…in theory.

She wondered why her few relationships had devolved from new and exciting to okay sex to the big breakup. A definite pattern, she thought with resignation. Like most relationships, once the newness wore off and her partners no longer felt like king of the mountain for having conquered her, they demanded too much.

Her roommates hadn't been fortunate with Cupid either. So why did Maddie continue to dwell on relationships lately? It seemed like every time she turned around she thought about that amazing kiss on Sunday that had gone on forever but still hadn't been long enough. She found herself staring at the bouquet he'd brought her, making stupid excuses to visit the kitchen just so she could see evidence Flynn had been there.

What was it about him that nagged at her? She'd asked herself that question over and over, and after today she thought she'd come up with the answer— they had sexual chemistry. A natural connection and no big deal.

But she couldn't remember any of her past lovers having such an effect on her. No matter how much she tried, she couldn't make herself forget how good Flynn's lips felt on hers.

Biology was such a bitch.

Once home, she stepped onto her porch when a familiar voice called out to her. She turned to see Mike and Colin approaching. Mike walked, Colin skipped, and she couldn't help smiling at the pair.

"Hi, guys."

"Hi, Maddie." Colin looked much more cheerful than

the last time she'd seen him. He also seemed to be missing a tooth.

"Colin, I think something's wrong with your mouth."

He smiled, displaying a gap in his upper teeth. "I lost a tooth! I got two whole dollars too." He dug into his pants and pulled out two crumpled dollar bills.

"Wow. I think the most the tooth fairy ever brought me was a new toothbrush."

"Sorry to hear that." Mike smiled.

He stood a few inches taller than Flynn. They looked a lot alike, but whereas Flynn made her pulse race, her appreciation for Mike ran more to aesthetics. A handsome man with raw appeal and muscles on top of muscles. He also had that soft side to him, apparent whenever he looked at his son. But there was that same bland safety she'd felt earlier with Vanessa's friend. She liked that.

"Would you guys like to come in? I'm in charge of dinner tonight."

"What are you eating?" Colin asked and took a step forward.

Mike grabbed him by the collar. "Colin." He shook his head. "We just ate hot dogs. Actually, I wanted to invite you and your roommates to a barbecue this weekend. My parents like to have them, and it's past time we welcomed you proper. McCauley shindigs aren't to be missed. Plus, we owe you a public apology. Your first dealing with Flynn without the rest of us to keep him in line. I'm sorry for that."

She laughed. "He's not that bad. Besides, I think I was the one who scared him. It wasn't a good day to be a man in my house."

Mike nodded. "I'll bet."

"Anyway, I already told Flynn we'd love to come. I talked to Abby and Vanessa, and they have nothing going on Saturday. What should we bring?"

Mike didn't answer.

"Mike?"

"Sorry. I was thinking. If you have a favorite dessert, bring that. Otherwise, just bring yourselves." He paused. "So when did Flynn ask you about this weekend?"

"Sunday, and I just saw him half an hour ago at Starbucks. Why?"

He shrugged. "No reason. I just thought I'd nag him about communicating with the rest of us. Boy has no head for sharing information. Never has." He sighed.

She tried not to laugh again. The notion of Flynn as a boy didn't fit. She could see his stomach and that chest in her mind's eye. The scent of oranges over his lips... It was as if her memory had stuck a picture of him on a Post-it note and tacked it to her brain. "If it's a problem, we can—"

"No, no. My mom is dying to talk to you all. Whenever she gets a chance to talk to women, she's excited. Too many men in the family."

Colin thumped his chest. "Yeah. I'm a man. My tooth is *totally* gone." He tried to stick his tongue through the opening.

"We won't keep you any longer. See you on Saturday. Two-ish." Mike handed her a note. "The directions are on there. The folks are just two streets over and down a quarter mile. Tan house, blue shutters. Lots of cars in the drive."

"Thanks, Mike. See you, Colin." She watched them turn and leave, then entered the house to cook...something.

Hmm, hot dogs. That and some macaroni and cheese—now that sounded good and easy.

An hour later, as Maddie cleared her dishes from the table, Vanessa bitched about the meal, despite the fact that she'd arrived home late and should have been grateful to eat anything prepared at all. "I hate hot dogs."

"I know. That's why I made them."

Abby crossed her eyes behind Vanessa's head.

"I saw that."

"You should have been a schoolteacher. The dreaded Miss Campbell. Oooh." Abby raised her hands in mock fright. "I have work to do. Maddie, if you or teacher-creature needs me, I'll be on the computer."

"It's not teacher-creature," Vanessa grumbled as she ate her hot dog. "I hate when she calls me names."

"And yet the shoe fits." Maddie grinned. "I saw Jed Rawlins today. He told me to remind you about coffee supplies. Something about creamer?"

Vanessa sighed and shrugged out of her suit jacket. She wore her hair in a bun, the escaping strands actually softening her face. But far be it from Maddie to tell her cousin she looked pretty. Pretty had no place in accounting.

"You know, if Jed put half the effort into work as he does into taking coffee breaks, we'd probably be the preeminent firm in Seattle."

Maddie found Vanessa as intriguing as she sometimes found her annoying. Unlike her, Vanessa didn't seem to have any confidence issues. A rock of solid self-love. Not selfish or arrogant, just a woman happy with herself and her place in life. An oddity among women everywhere, but there she was.

"Jed would do better to be more like me," Vanessa continued, talking with her mouth full. She downed her carb-loaded macaroni and cheese like a Hoover set to high. "I'm too busy doing my damn job to worry about sugar, creamer, or the who's-dating-who chatter by the watercooler."

Maddie blinked. "Do they really have watercoolers at your work? I thought that was just an expression. 'Watercooler talk.'"

"Yeah. We do. It's purified water. Not bad, but I bring my own."

The queen of self-sufficient would. Maddie sighed.

"What's wrong?"

"Have you ever had a problem in life you couldn't solve? Ever had a problem too big to handle on your own?"

Vanessa paused. "Nope."

"Bitch."

Vanessa smiled. "Jealousy will get you everywhere. There's nothing I like more than envy." She glanced down at the crumbs on her plate. "As far as hot dogs go, I guess these things aren't bad. Mac 'n' cheese isn't either."

"Want to lick the pan?"

"Sure."

Maddie grimaced as her cousin took every piece of macaroni from the pan and ate it. "You should be really, really fat. How is it I eat one hot dog and my butt explodes? We're related. I should have your metabolism."

"Must get it from your dad, whoever he is."

And that's one of the things Maddie truly appreciated about Vanessa. She didn't coddle or softly gloss over hurtful details. She went straight at life with a one-two punch. Because Maddie knew Vanessa loved her, she normally didn't take her comments as digs, but rather as unfortunate truths.

"But look at it like this. Aunt Michelle is a pretty redhead too, but she burns two seconds in the sun. You must get that Mediterranean skin from your dad. So big ass, but nice skin. It all evens out."

"I actually never thought of my ass as big, but thanks." Maddie shook her head, amused and not sure why. Her gaze caught the flowers that looked as fresh as they had when she'd put them in water.

"Hmm, more quiet thoughts about Flynn. I wonder how you'll react to your studly plumber this weekend." Vanessa carried her plate to the sink and washed the dishes. The woman would have a coronary if a dish remained dirty longer than five minutes.

"Oh shut up. He's not my studly plumber. I mean, he is studly, but he's not mine."

"She who doth protest too much, doth—"

Maddie scowled. "Doth this." She held up a finger and left the kitchen—and her cousin's laughter—behind. Instead of heading back upstairs, she sat down in the living room and opened her laptop, looking once again at the competition. Staging prices, services, realtors… She made more notes and forced herself to stop thinking about Flynn McCauley.

So of course later that night she dreamed about him wearing nothing but those damn boxer briefs and a smile.

Chapter 5

THANKFULLY, THE WEATHER HELD THROUGH TO THE weekend. Saturday afternoon, dressed in jeans and a T-shirt, Flynn tossed around the football with his brothers. He loved their get-togethers, when his parents grilled outside while he, his brothers, and Brody taunted and played ball with one another in the backyard. Suckers. As if any of them could out-throw him—the star quarterback.

He glanced at the back door again, wondering when the hell Maddie would show. It was five after two already. The ball knocked him in the head.

"Shit." When one of the older neighbors raised a brow at him, he lowered his voice. "I mean, heck. That hurt." He picked up the pigskin and moved to beam it back at Cam when his younger brother pointed at Brody. Flynn changed direction, aimed, and threw. Hard.

The ball hit Brody's chest with an audible *thump*.

Brody wheezed. "Bastard."

"Watch your mouth, Brody," Flynn warned, playing the good son. "We have guests present."

"Brody," Beth McCauley warned in a loud voice. His mother was standing next to his father, clear across the yard. He'd always said she had ears like a bat.

Brody scowled. Flynn and his brothers laughed.

His mother joined them, waving at Brody to pitch her the ball. "Over here, Brody."

Her kid in name if not blood. Brody winced. "You sure, Bitsy? I don't wanna hurt you."

Flynn jeered him. "Like you could. You throw like a girl." He shot his mother an innocent look. "No offense, Ma."

"None taken, you big oaf."

Cam snickered.

Brody threw the ball with a gentle push, and she caught it with no problem. She threw it to Flynn with some oomph, and he pretended to have a hard time catching it.

"Don't bobble it, son. Two hands, bring it in tight."

He frowned when the guys shook their heads at him. Could they not see he'd been teasing? "I know how to catch a ball, Ma. Gimme a break. High school, college. I started varsity for three years, woman."

"I'm sorry, *what* did you call me?"

Only their father could get away with calling her that. "Ah, nothing, Ma."

Colin raced out the back door and missed bumping into Flynn by inches. Behind him followed one of the neighborhood kids. "They're here!" He grabbed the ball from Flynn and took off.

Maddie, Vanessa, and Abby walked out the back door into the yard. Feeling like Pavlov's dog but unable to stop himself, Flynn took a few steps toward her before he realized what he'd done. He deliberately shoved his hands in his pockets and walked to his dad, hoping he hadn't looked like a lovesick fool. Not that he was lovesick. Far from it. But hell, a man would have to be a eunuch not to look at Maddie Gardner.

Then Maddie caught his gaze and blushed.

Fuck if he could forget yesterday's short peck on the cheek. A little kiss, and he'd thought of nothing more than her soft lips when he'd jacked off last night.

"Ladies, glad to see you could make it." His mother took the plate of brownies from Maddie and tugged her along. Her friends followed. "You remember James, my husband. Flynn, my son."

The charming one. He hoped Maddie remembered. He hadn't really been kidding. Flynn didn't want her talking to the other guys. Sometimes being close in age to his siblings wasn't such a hot deal.

To his pleasure, her smile seemed warmer when she lit on him.

His mother shoved the brownies at him, breaking their connection. "What?"

"Go put them on the table, but *don't* eat them." She motioned to one of the picnic tables that held a ton of food. To the girls, she said, "You know Mike and Cameron. Have you met Brody yet?"

Flynn hurried to the table and returned, wanting to hear everything they said.

Abby asked, "How many sons do you have?"

Brody caught the football Colin tossed him and joined them. His eyes widened when he saw Abby, but he didn't say anything more than, "Pleased to meet you."

"Thanks for inviting us over, Mrs. McCauley," Vanessa said. A sexy, sophisticated blond, yet she didn't hold a candle to the redhead who blushed when Flynn looked at her. God, he hoped his hard-on wasn't too obvious in his jeans. Time for a cold drink. Definitely something alcoholic.

Brody cleared his throat. "Nice to see you ladies

finally made it. We're starved, and the general"—he shot a thumb at their mother—"wouldn't let us have anything to eat until you made an appearance."

They smiled at the bastard before his mother whisked the women away and pointed out Colin, his friend, and a few of the neighbors who'd joined them.

After spending an hour doing his best to keep things casual by steering clear of Maddie and interacting with his brothers, Brody, and the neighbors, Flynn couldn't stand it any longer. He approached her by the sidelines of a makeshift badminton court.

He nodded behind him at the picnic table. "The brownies look good." Flynn didn't know why talking to Maddie felt so awkward. Maybe because he couldn't stop looking at her mouth, knowing how she tasted. Like a cold beer on a perfect game day. Refreshing, addicting, and so goddamn good he wanted to get drunk on her.

She stood with him while they watched the others play badminton. His mother and her games. He'd done his time with that tiny racket while Brody did his best to beat him down with that stupid shuttlecock.

Cock. Not a good word to think around Maddie, because at just the mention of it, the damn thing wanted to rise and stay up. Thoughts about his mother, father, and neighbors watching him with a woody cooled him off. At least for now.

"Mike said to bring our favorite dessert, so we did." She smiled at Abby's heroic attempt to return Vanessa's volley. Brody leaned in to help her, but Flynn missed the end result because a small, unearthly tornado shoved him into Maddie.

He wrapped his arms around her and stumbled but didn't fall.

"Rory Templeton, you get back here this minute," Rory's mother yelled at him as the kid dashed away from Colin's squirt gun.

Colin cried victory, then the little punk turned it on him.

"*Colin*."

"Ha! I'm winning." Colin laughed and raced away, but not before shooting Maddie too.

"Sorry. He's competitive, like Mike."

She squirmed in his arms, and he realized he was still holding her. Her breasts brushed against his chest, and they both froze. He slowly dropped his arms. She slowly backed away.

He couldn't help looking down, captivated by the hard points of her nipples showing through her pink shirt. If he looked hard enough, he could make out the subtle lace on the straps of her bra too.

Oh man, not a good idea to look there. He wanted to take her inside and finish what they'd started last week.

"Competitive like who? I noticed you four trying to out-throw each other earlier."

"Well, I didn't want to look bad in front of company."

She laughed, a genuine chuckle that sounded both feminine and rich. It made him warm inside. "It's really nice of your family to invite us over." She subtly crossed her arms over her chest.

Denied sight of her ample breasts, he sighed. "Yeah, we're all about nice. Hey, you want a beer?"

"No thanks. How about something nonalcoholic?"

He grabbed her a lemonade, and they sat at a small

table watching his family mingle. Property in Queen Anne cost a bundle, but they'd been living here long enough that the original house had included the half acre of land. The backyard had been party central for years. An area for badminton, football parties, and for the past twenty-five years, kid birthday parties as well.

"Thanks." She drank it down like a woman dying of thirst, and he wondered if he wasn't the only one feeling awkward. "I can't believe how warm it's been this week."

"I love it. Makes work a lot easier than doing it in the winter, let me tell you."

She tilted her head, and a mass of dark red hair pooled on her shoulder. He was dying to sink his hands in the thick stuff. "I bet it's really hard in the winter."

It's really hard now. "Uh, yeah. Pipes freezing up. You wouldn't believe how many people go on vacation and forget to make sure they keep the heat up. Busted pipes, water heater problems, you name it. Your sink was one of the easiest problems I've had in a while."

"Glad we could help." They shared a laugh that felt natural, and just as good as kissing her. Which freaked him out. Wanting sex with a woman was one thing. But liking her this much, spending time with her like this, it didn't feel like his other forays into dating.

"So how's the job thing going?" he asked to take his mind from this emotional crap. He noticed his mother watching him and glanced at her, only to see her hurriedly look away. When her continued interest still failed to scare him from Maddie's side, he knew he had a problem.

"I've been working hard all week." Seeing his

curiosity, she continued. "I've come up with some quotes that can compete with other stagers in the area. There are a lot of people out there doing the same thing, but I do have a Fred Hampton's Designs background. As much as the owner of the firm is a complete jerk, the reputation of first-class work is there. I'm hoping it'll help."

"You know, my aunt is a realtor. I could call her for you. You should talk to her, see if she knows anyone who needs a house fixed up. She always says summer's a busy time to sell."

Maddie's eyes brightened before she shook her head. "No. I couldn't ask you to do that."

He frowned. "Why not? In my business, it's all about word of mouth and networking. If you're as good as I think you are, you won't need that much help once your name is out there."

"Why would you think I'm any good?"

"Because your house looks like something out of a magazine."

"Well, I try. But like I told you before, blame the neatness on Vanessa. She's like Hitler with a mop."

They grinned together while they watched the neat-nik trounce Mike.

"She's also competitive like nobody's business." Maddie sighed. "But she's family. I love her." She glanced around the yard. "I like your family. I think it's great how close you guys are with your parents."

"Well, Mom won't let us get any farther away. It's like she has this huge arm that drags us back the minute we mention moving."

———

He's leaving? Maddie blinked. "You're planning on moving?" The thought upset her, and it had no reason to. She didn't have anything going on with Flynn, not at all.

"Nah. I just like to tease her. We're not momma's boys, but we love her. We have a tight family. It helped a lot when Lea passed. Mike's wife," he explained in a low voice. "When a tragedy like that hits, it hurts everyone. But we stepped in and took care of Colin and Mike, made sure they had time to grieve. And us too. We loved her; she was family. But you know, the cooking, cleaning, all that stuff. My mom and dad were really there for Mike and Colin, you know?"

His hand rested on the table, and she put hers over it. "That's nice."

He looked down at their hands, then back into her eyes.

Oh God, she could see the variations of green in his irises, and she couldn't look away.

"Maddie?" His low voice made her belly flutter.

"Yeah?"

"I was thinking—"

Two sets of large hands tore him away from her.

"Stop flirting with the pretty girl and get your ass in the game," Mike ordered from one side of him.

Brody winked at her from the other. "Sorry, Maddie. I know how this one can get to chatting, and he just monopolizes time."

"Like a parasite," Cam added from behind them.

They ignored Flynn's muttered cursing, which died the moment his mother approached.

"For God's sake, Flynn. Let the girl eat. She's too thin as it is."

Maddie's smile stretched her mouth. "Too thin? I really, really like you." She stood and walked with Beth toward the picnic table laden with food, where her cousin and Abby had just made themselves at home.

"Thanks for this, Beth. It looks delicious."

"Well, don't tell, but I already had a brownie. That's some dangerous chocolate there, Maddie."

Maddie grabbed a plate and filled it with food. Normally she'd avoid the greasy meats and starches, but she hadn't had so much fun in ages. Feeling like she belonged amidst the crowd, half of whom she still didn't know, she forced herself to sit at a long table with strangers.

The patriarch of the family joined her. "Mind if I sit?"

Before she could answer, he scooted her over and sat next to her. As big as Mike, and just as handsome. No wonder Beth McCauley wore such a wide smile. Talk about good genes. But though Flynn looked like his father, he had his mother's eyes.

"So how are you and the girls settling in?"

"Fine." They'd been in the house for over four months. The settling had passed. "Mike's been more than nice, when we see him, which isn't that often. He's the perfect neighbor."

James grunted. "Colin hasn't been bugging you overly, has he? The boy nags to see the house all the time. My boys grew up in there, you know."

"It's a lovely house. Really great architecture."

He smiled, and they spoke of the neighborhood, her job—briefly—and how much the East Coast differed from the West.

"I hear Flynn helped you with a problem the other day."

Her mind flashed to her kitchen, and Flynn's mouth. "Yep. Fixed our sink." *I wish he would have fixed a few other things.*

"He's a good boy. Can get a bit randy now and then, so if he gets fresh, smack him upside the head."

She'd been drinking when he said *randy*, a word she hadn't heard spoken since her grandmother had said it how many years ago? She choked, gasping as he tapped her back.

"You okay?" His face creased in a frown.

"Fine." She wheezed and drank some more, wishing now she'd taken Flynn up on his offer of a beer.

"He hasn't been a problem, has he? Don't feel like you have to tolerate all the McCauleys now that you're renting. I can have a talk—"

"No, no. Your sons have been more than helpful."

"Brody too. He's mine, as much as he thinks he's not," he muttered and glared at Brody talking with Beth and Abby. "Boy moved in when he was six and never left. Definitely family."

She wanted to say she knew the feeling, but she didn't. She and her mother had never been a boisterous household. And visits with Vanessa's calm, contained family didn't count either. "You have a terrific family. I grew up without brothers or sisters. I always wanted to do this, big family parties with the neighbors." She smiled at a few of them sitting close. Two couples with young children, a pair of grandparents, a single dad tickling his son.

"So where's your family?" he asked.

"My mom lives in Pennsylvania. Refuses to move, though I've tried to talk her into coming out here."

He nodded. "Well, she's probably set in her life. Got her own way of doing things. Much as I love my family, I realize my sons are independent thinkers. Have their own lives to lead, like you and your roommates do."

She agreed. "Yeah. I just wish Mom was closer. I miss her. I have Vanessa, my cousin. And Abby of course. She's my best friend. But they're not Mom." She leaned closer. "Between you and me, Vanessa's too bossy. As my mom would say, she's a bit too big for her britches."

James laughed, and his wife looked over at him. As did Flynn, who frowned and stood. He looked as if he meant to join them when Cam yanked him back down. Then Brody distracted him with something that made him laugh.

She'd never thought of humor as sexy, but hearing Flynn's laugh aroused her. Just what she didn't need sitting so close to Flynn's *father*. Talk about bad timing to like men again.

"You okay?" James looked from her to Flynn and narrowed his eyes.

"Fine. I'm going for dessert. Want anything?"

"I sneaked a brownie when no one was looking." He winked. "But I'll have another."

Laughing, she left to get him one. But she found nothing left, just a few crumbs, so she put a piece of Beth's apple pie on a plate for him.

"Mom's pie is pretty good." Flynn spoke from over her shoulder. "But if you bake pie as well as you made the brownies, I'll concede you the winner."

He took the plate from her and delivered it to his father. He darted away before his dad could smack him in the head, and she wondered what he'd said.

"Well, nice to see you come up for some air." Vanessa looked a little too smug.

Not in the mood for Vanessa's teasing, Maddie readied to rip into her cousin when a blast of water between the eyes shocked her into stuttering. "Wh-wh—"

Flynn hoisted her assailant in the air. "Aha! Gotcha, you little monster." He ripped Colin's squirt gun aside. "Well, Maddie? What should we do with him?" He handed her the gun and set a squirming Colin on his feet.

She eyed the gun, saw the dismay on Colin's face, and handed it to Vanessa. "I'll leave the weapon in my cousin's brutal hands."

"Hey." Vanessa frowned.

"Me, I'm more of a tickler myself." She watched Colin's eyes grow wide before she tickled him until he was writhing on the ground.

"Daddy! Help!" he said between laughter.

Mike tried to intervene. "My son, I must save you!"

But Flynn grabbed the gun from Vanessa and shot him in the face with a blast of water. Then Brody and Cam joined in with Super Soakers that appeared out of nowhere. Everyone started squirting everyone, and the party got down and dirty.

Maddie hadn't thought they'd stay so late. An hour, maybe two, to be friendly before they left for the day. Who'd have thought she'd enjoy herself so much?

Flynn's brothers turned out to be as fun-loving and teasing with her as they were with each other, except in a nicer, gentler way. Flynn had suffered a few tackles, not to mention headlocks and a body slam from Mike that put him on his butt. The neighbors seemed nice and interested when Flynn had mentioned her career as a professional stager and designer.

And then the guy she couldn't stop thinking about had told his mother about her new business. Beth had immediately called her sister, the bigwig realtor. Now Maddie had an appointment on Tuesday with Linda Donnigan that could be a big break in her new career. Maybe.

Abby and Vanessa stood with her as they said good night to the McCauleys.

"We had a blast, Beth." Abby had her hand on the front door. "Thanks so much for inviting us. What a terrific way to spend our Saturday. Normally by now we'd be on our hands and knees scrubbing something while Vanessa cracks her whip. Thank you again for saving us from a fate worse than death."

"A fate worse than death? I thought that was what you called running. Wimp," Vanessa scoffed.

Beth grinned. "Anytime. And Maddie, let me know how your appointment with my sister goes. You'll do fine with her. She's a lot like Vanessa, very businesslike and very successful."

Vanessa beamed. "Now let's go, my minions. Time to clean the house, from top to bottom. Muhuhahaha."

Maddie groaned. They started walking away when Flynn darted after them.

"Wait up." He handed Maddie the brownie pan. "Would you ladies like a ride?"

Would I ever. Flynn's brows rose, and she coughed with embarrassment when she realized he'd caught her staring at him like dessert. Good Lord, she'd been ogling his package. How embarrassing.

"That's great. A way to escape Vanessa. Sure." Abby

dragged her to Flynn's truck, a manly type vehicle with a Hemi, whatever that was. She shoved Maddie in the front seat while she hopped in the back. Then she leaned toward the window and yelled at Vanessa, "See you at home." To Maddie, Abby whispered, "You can thank me later."

Flynn arrived at their house in minutes. But before Maddie could get out of the truck, Abby stopped her. "Flynn, could you do us a big favor?"

"Sure."

"It's cleaning night, and I just remembered we don't have any more glass cleaner. Would you mind running Maddie to the store to buy some? I'll keep Vanessa at bay while you guys get it."

Possibly the lamest excuse she'd ever heard. But Flynn picked it up and ran with it before Maddie could decide how she felt about being dumped in his lap.

"Not a problem. I'll bring her right back." He took off the minute her roommate shut the truck door.

Aware of the quiet intimacy between them, she shifted in her seat. To her discomfort, her nipples chafed against her shirt, as if she wasn't wearing a bra.

Flynn maneuvered them through traffic away from the closest grocery and headed downtown. "As I see it, you have two options."

"Only two?"

He grinned, and that flash of amusement turned her inside out. She'd actually liked talking to him today. She'd connected to him, person to person, in a way she and Ben never had. That weird fluttering and nervousness returned. Half of her wanted to tell him to turn the car around and take her home. The other half wanted... She didn't want to think about what *it* wanted.

"I can get your cleaner for you, then take you back and give you to that whip-wielder Vanessa." He gave a pretend shudder, and she chuckled. "Or I can take you someplace where the music is great, the wine is even better, and we could watch a movie, or whatever."

The *whatever* grabbed hold of her and wouldn't let go. But the pragmatic part of her warned her to tread warily. This man made her feel different than the others had. He didn't feel safe, and he didn't fit in a contained mold, like Ben. Flynn set her on edge in a very sexual, very emotional way.

He screamed *trouble*.

So she surprised herself when she asked, "What kind of movie?"

Chapter 6

FLYNN MCCAULEY SAT ONE FOOT AWAY FROM HER ON a black leather sofa in his apartment, and she still didn't know what she thought she was doing. Two wineglasses perched on the coffee table while a movie droned on in front of them. She hadn't heard one word of dialogue since Mr. Sexy had put his arm over the back of the couch. He brushed her neck from time to time with long, calloused fingers.

She shivered again when his forefinger traced its way along her nape.

"Cold?" he asked, his voice husky.

Oh, he knew what he was doing. Yet she didn't care. A glance down at his lap showed he was just as excited to be next to her. Her entire body throbbed. *Everywhere*. She wanted to blame her sudden need for Flynn on her recent dating dry spell, but she had a bad feeling it was more than that.

"Come closer. I'll keep you warm."

Ridiculous considering how hot she felt, but hell, she'd use the excuse and hope she didn't come across as desperate. Then again, that pole in his pants told her she affected him in the same way. Randy indeed.

She let him draw her against his body and gasped. "You're like an inferno." A great big body of heat… that fired her own. Lust consumed her, the need to touch him, to feel his skin against hers. To taste him again and see if that kiss had been an anomaly or the prelude to the combustible chemistry she could feel blistering her libido.

He curled his hand over her shoulder and sniffed her hair. "You smell good."

"Like hot dogs and hamburgers?" she teased and put her hand on his knee. He tensed, and she liked the reaction.

"Better." He nuzzled her hair aside and whispered in her ear, "Like those chocolate brownies. I'm just dying to eat you up, Maddie."

The image that thought conjured made her more than wet. She arched her neck, too drugged by his touch to heed the signs of no return. He nipped her earlobe and trailed his mouth down her neck, sucking in places that torqued her body into a man-hungry machine.

"Fuck me, you taste so good." He stroked her hair, running his fingers through the long strands.

She let go of his knee and ran her hand up his thigh.

He turned her head to kiss her flush on the mouth, and she sighed her surrender, not wanting to stop this journey until they finished. Her body *begged* her to reach the end. And fast.

He moaned her name and licked his way past her lips. Still slow, not pushing her too hard. And his continued persistence totally turned her on. She put her hands around his neck and dragged him closer, trying to take charge of the kiss. But he refused to be rushed.

"Oh no. I've been waiting for this. We're going to take it nice and slow. If I don't come in my pants first."

She smiled, pleased not to be the only one needing more.

"Mmm, that's it. Sit back for me. Let's take off your clothes and make you more comfortable." The line should have fallen short, but he didn't seem aware of what he said as he stripped her down to her bra and underwear. "Christ, you're hot."

She blushed. She couldn't help it. She hadn't planned on any of this, but she could only be glad she'd chosen today of all days to go with pink lace. "Now you."

He removed his shirt, shoes, and socks, but left his jeans on. "Trust me, this will be better for both of us if I leave these on."

"You're not a minuteman then? Good."

He pulled her over to straddle his lap. "Minuteman?" His gaze settled on her breasts.

"You know, one of those guys who says he's a great lover but lasts a minute?"

He chuckled and ran his fingers over her breast. The heat shot from her nipple to her core and startled a gasp out of her. "And that's why I'm wearing the jeans. Seeing you like this... I'd be tempted to shove inside you and come hard." He kissed her, his fingers making magic over first one breast, then the other. "We need to take this slow."

"I'm, ah, I don't have any condoms."

He pulled back to watch her as he pinched her nipple through the sheer fabric. "I do."

She moaned and threaded her fingers in his hair, wanting his mouth on her in the worst way.

Willing to please, Flynn kissed the tops of her breasts, then sucked her nipples through the material of her bra.

She writhed over him, wanting to feel him deep inside her with a desperation very unlike herself. "*Flynn.*"

"Oh yeah. That's it, baby. You feel so good in my mouth." He stopped sucking her through the material and pulled the bra down, exposing her wet nipple. Then he took her flesh between his lips and applied his teeth.

She bucked, perilously close to coming in her underwear, and over his jeans. He'd called her *baby*, and it had sounded so natural, so *sexy*. Normally she hated endearments, but this turned her on in a big way. Embarrassed by how easy she must seem, she tried to pull back, but he wouldn't let her.

"Oh no. Come, Maddie. Let me feel you come in my hands." He pulled down the other side of her bra, exposing her breasts while plumping them together. He set his teeth on her other nipple, rolling the bud with a gentle bite. While he kissed and fondled her breasts with one hand, he dragged his other down her belly and beneath her underwear.

His fingers stroked lower, gliding over her swollen folds before delving into the heat of her. He groaned and sucked her nipple hard while he shoved a thick finger inside her. Her clit felt so hard, so sensitive against the pad of his thumb.

Flynn kissed her nipple and leaned back while he fingered her, watching her expression. She should have been embarrassed, but for some odd reason, she wasn't.

"God, I want to fill this pussy. You are so sweet." He sawed his finger in and out of her, but she wanted more. He seemed to read her mind, because he added a second finger, stretching her. "Tight, so fucking tight."

The hunger on his face undid her. He looked at her as if he wanted to devour her, as if nothing else existed right now but him and her. "Come all over me, baby.

Drench me, Maddie. We'll come hard, then we'll come again in my bed. Together."

He thumbed her clit and thrust his fingers back inside her, and she came on a cry, locked up tight around him. Her whole body pulsed, the pleasure so intense she felt dizzy. But as she rocked down to earth, she felt his tension and knew he had yet to find release.

"That was incredible." He kissed her, slowly removing his fingers. Without breaking eye contact, he sucked one finger clean and groaned. "I am two seconds from coming in my jeans. Scoot back a second."

She moved back and unbuttoned his pants, her hands shaking as she lowered his zipper inch by inch. He pushed his pants and underwear down his thighs, exposing the hot length of him.

She stared down at his cock and swallowed. "You're big." Holy shit, he was huge.

"And hard. And hurting." He wrapped her fingers around his cock and showed her how to stroke him. He released her hand but couldn't seem to take his eyes away from her holding him. Nor could she. "Oh man. I'm gonna come all over you. I can't stop it. Your hand looks so good there. So goddamn good." He groaned when she squeezed and moved faster. Ropy jets of come splashed over her hand and landed on his belly.

His face contorted in pleasured agony, and she couldn't look away. She slid her hand up and down once more, lingering under the head of his shaft, and a large spurt of semen shot out again. He jerked, his stomach clenching, and eased her hand away from him.

"*Maddie*." He lay back, breathing as if he'd just run a marathon. To her surprise, she sounded the same.

In a moment of clarity, she saw them as they were. Maddie, in a bra pulled down beneath her boobs, sat over his denim-covered knees in soaking-wet lace panties. Flynn's jeans and underwear gathered at his thighs. A mess covered his belly, his cock, and her hand.

He held a finger to her that held a bead of his semen. "Lick it," he said in a deep, gritty voice.

She didn't know him that well despite the fact that he'd just had his fingers inside her. Even though they'd kissed as if they planned on exchanging tonsils. Licking his come would be so very, very stupid.

But the demand in his voice, the sexual hunger rejuvenating in his eyes... She grabbed his hand and took his finger inside her mouth. Salty and male, the flavor of the man she planned to get to know much, much better.

He groaned and kissed her again, and she knew this was only the beginning.

***

Flynn couldn't believe he'd just come all over himself. Like a friggin' teenager, he'd shot his wad in seconds from her small hand. The sight of her dainty fingers wrapped around his cock had been permanently seared into his brain. Despite the fact he'd just come all over, he wanted her again. But this time he wanted to explode inside her.

"Let's clean up and do this again, in a bed this time." He hoped she wouldn't be the type for self-recrimination. She didn't seem like a woman with easy morals, nor did he get the impression she often went home with a guy and had sex. For one, she had the cutest blush on her cheeks and refused to look at him directly. And two, she'd been so damn tight inside. He'd bet it had been a while for her. Hell, she'd gone off as fast as he had. He took comfort in the fact and prayed she wouldn't think him a—what had she called it? A minuteman.

He swore under his breath as he stood with her and righted his pants. Then he used his shirt to wipe the mess from his belly.

"What's wrong?"

She'd slipped her breasts back in her bra, and damn if he didn't want to do her all over again. She could have starred in her very own adult movies. Large breasts, a tiny waist, long, thick red hair that framed a siren's face. And those lips. When she'd sucked that drop of come from his finger like a dream come true, fantasies of her mouth around his cock refused to go away.

"You have too many clothes on," he rasped and reached for her hand. He gave it a gentle squeeze and pulled her with him into the bedroom. "Let me clean up. And I swear, this time I'll be more than a 'minuteman.'"

She laughed, relieving him. "I think that was me. I lasted maybe thirty seconds. So embarrassing."

"Hey, I barely took a breath and came. The minute you wrapped your hand around me, I was toast."

"Well, I'm using the excuse that it's been a while."

"Me too." Good. She hadn't been with anyone. "So I take it you're not involved with anyone right now."

"No." She frowned. "You?"

"Nope." *And I'm not looking for a steady girlfriend* should have been the next words out of his mouth, but she beat him to the punch.

"Look, Flynn. This is weird. I don't do this, have sex with people I just met." She let out a long breath. "I'm attracted to you. And this might sound really stupid, but I like what we just did. I just don't have time in my life right now for anything more complicated."

He blinked. "So you just want the sex. No dating, no holding hands, no cuddling?"

Her lips curled. "Well now, we could cuddle after, maybe a little. But the whole boyfriend/girlfriend thing is impossible for me right now. What with my business getting started. If it gets started," she added in a softer voice.

Flynn wanted to get down on his knees and promise to continue doing whatever he'd done to receive this reward again in the future. A woman built like Maddie, who had a brain, could socialize, and didn't bed hop, didn't want more than sex from him. No pressure, no commitment, no games.

"Are you real?"

She laughed. "Are you? I don't think I've ever seen a man so well put together as you." Her gaze drifted down his belly and settled on his semi-hard cock pushing at his jeans.

"I wouldn't know how put together you are." He tugged her closer. "You're not naked yet."

"Neither are you."

He kissed her but stopped before he forgot himself. "Time to fix that. You need to stop worrying about this future success of yours and focus on something much better."

"Like what?"

"Like a nice, long ride on your favorite stud." He leered at her. "Neigh."

"I don't know how to ride," she teased.

"I'll show you. No worries, darlin'." His accent sounded terrible, but her smile told him it didn't matter. Once in his bedroom, he left her to finish cleaning himself in the bathroom. He returned wearing his boxer briefs and found her lying on his bed. Naked.

"Holy shit." He didn't know where to look first. At the pouting lips parted for his cock, or the swollen breasts and cherry red nipples begging for a taste. Or maybe the incredibly erotic sight of her legs parted, revealing a wet pussy and the trimmest strip of red hair over her mound. "If I had a camera, I'd—"

She leaned up on her elbows and scowled at him. "Get yourself slapped."

He pulled off his underwear and grabbed himself, hard. "You are so fucking sexy when you're mad. I swear, the other day when you were storming around your house, I wanted to throw you over my shoulder and haul that pretty ass upstairs."

She blinked. "You did?"

He couldn't wait. Doing what he'd been dying to, he joined her on the bed. Slowly crawling from the foot of it to just between her legs, he knelt before her. "Look how hard you make me." He rubbed his thumb over his tip, not surprised to find it slick. "Do me a favor, reach into the drawer beside you and grab a packet."

She bit her lower lip. "Wow. You're a lot to handle."

"And getting bigger looking at your tits. You are a wet dream, you know that?"

She snorted and dug in his bedside drawer for a condom. "Flatterer."

Flynn smiled. "You think I'm bad, you should hear some of my brothers' lines. No, let's not go there. No way I'm bringing them into this bed. This is just you and me."

She held out the packet.

God, he felt like the star in one of his X-rated fantasies. Why not indulge himself? Who knew if he'd ever be lucky enough to have her again? "Put it on me, baby. Roll it real slow over my cock."

Her cheeks flushed, and she sat up and rose on her knees to face him. Slowly ripping the packet, she took out the condom and put it over his tip. His entire body locked up.

"Yeah. Roll it down."

"You're so thick, Flynn. Sexy." She played with him, way too enthusiastically for his peace of mind. She cupped his balls, touching them with a hesitance that hinted at her unfamiliarity with a man's body. The way she took pains to be gentle with him, when he needed a harder touch, thrilled him. Oh yeah. *The naughty schoolgirl, and I'm her teacher*.

He watched her roll down the rubber until it rested above his balls. Constraining as hell, and he prayed he'd still be able to feel her heat when he pushed inside her.

"Now lie back." She did, and he crouched between her thighs. "Remember what I said about wanting to eat you?"

Her eyes turned molten. "I don't, I mean, I never..."

"Had a guy go down on you?" His cock bobbed, as if shocked as well.

"Ben wasn't into that. And for all I know I'm not, er, tasty."

"You haven't been with a lot of guys, have you?"

"I'm not a slut." Her brows drew close and her mouth firmed into a line.

"Never said you were. I like you. I want to make you feel good, not bad. I just want to know if I'm going to do something you don't like." Honestly, he didn't care if she didn't want this. Flynn knew how to use his mouth. He'd guaran-damn-tee she came all over him.

"Oh. Sorry." She reached up to touch his chest, and her hands trailed fire around his nipples. "If you have to know, one time, when I was still a virgin, I had a guy want to do that to me. But it wasn't that good. Frankly, it was embarrassing. He didn't know what he was doing, I didn't know how to tell him to fix it, and we never spoke after that."

"Well, Maddie, I think it's been a few years since high school."

"Thanks for saying I look old." Her humor touched him. He didn't usually talk this much when raring to fuck, but he'd never felt so at ease and horny at the same time with a woman. The whole thing made little sense, but his cock didn't seem to care.

"You're hot, and you know it. I just want you to lie back and enjoy. Trust me, you'll like the way I do it. And if you want me to adjust, just tell me. I'm real good with constructive criticism."

Her short laugh turned into a moan the minute his lips closed over her clit. So sweet. Her heady taste exploded on his tongue. Innocent and tempting, her essence made him hungry for more. He licked and stroked, paying strict attention to her reactions. She liked it when he ran his hands over her thighs, when he played with her pussy, penetrating with his finger in short, choppy thrusts. She especially liked it when he sucked hard, tickling her bud with his never-tiring tongue.

Her groans and pleas for more fell like music to his ears, notes of need, high and strong, and he wanted badly to give her what she desired.

"Flynn." She ran her hands over his hair and ground into his face.

He fucking loved it. Playing, teasing, he inched his pinkie near her asshole, wondering if she'd ever been fucked there. He wasn't into it himself. The preparation, the mess, the problem of making it right for his partner. But he'd done it to please others. There were other things they could do, however, that could excite without all the fuss.

"Flynn, I'm going to come." She released his hair to clutch the sheets beside the bed. "That's so good. Oh, Flynn."

He rimmed her ass with his pinkie and barely pushed it in when he nipped her clit and sucked hard, grinding his tongue over the bundle of nerves.

She screamed his name as she flew apart, and in seconds he covered her, nudged her thighs wider and shoved himself inside.

So tight, she clamped down on him like a vise as he rode through her orgasm. A fucking storm of pleasure he couldn't believe as he drove inside her.

"Maddie. Yes, baby. Hold me. Oh fuck." He couldn't stop himself from plunging deeper, harder, and then the tingle grew from his balls, up his spine, and obliterated all thought. He swore and shoved one last time, jetting hard inside the condom, the spasms almost painful as he emptied himself while inside her.

The condom muted the sensation, but he could feel enough to blow his entire mind. He wanted to do it all over again, but this time he wanted to shoot in her pussy, to pull out and watch his semen spill from her body. Totally insane, because Flynn didn't do bareback and never had. But Maddie...

"Baby, you okay?" he asked when he could stop shaking. He withdrew and pulled the condom off. Then he grabbed a tissue from a box on the table, wrapped up the rubber, and tossed it to the floor.

"Oh my God." Maddie continued to breathe hard, her gaze unblinking as she stared up at the ceiling. "What the hell did you do to me?"

"It was good though, right?" He started to worry maybe he'd misread the signs when she rolled over onto him and kissed him so hard he saw stars.

"Good? Try great. Incredible. Amazing. You earned yourself a big ego for what you just did. You are the man. Not any man. But *the* man. Flynn." She moaned his name, and he felt ten feet tall. "My body is still tingling. Holy shit."

The swear sounded right coming off her lips. No innocent girl, but a sensual woman who didn't hide how she felt. Again, he wondered just what he'd done to deserve her, then decided not to question a good thing. Except his thoughts immediately jumped to their next encounter. If they'd even have one. The thought of not being with her like this again depressed him, so he refused to consider this a one-night stand.

"Oh man. I'm supposed to be bringing home window cleaner." She pouted, and he laughingly rolled her onto her back.

He lay on his side next to her, propped up on his elbow,

and explored her breasts. "I didn't give these enough attention. Have I told you how incredible you are?"

Her cheeks turned that pretty pink again. "I believe you said I was hot."

"Yeah, but there's hot, and there's eternal hard-on hot. Your tits, ah, breasts, are the best I've ever seen in my life."

"I wonder if I can use you as a reference in my new career." She snickered. "Incredible tits, and she designs too."

"Hell, I'd hire you. I don't know many guys who wouldn't." He couldn't take his eyes from her body. "Do you work out or something? I swear I could bounce a quarter off your stomach."

"Are you trying for another round? I'm flabby." She pinched her stomach, but he saw nothing but the stretch of fit skin. "And my ass is starting to get bigger."

"Bigger is better. Trust me." He rubbed a hand over her hip. When he caressed her ribs, he saw her eyes light up. "Oh, you like this."

"I do. Stop that." She squirmed. "I don't think I can come again. Twice in one night is a record."

He shook his head. "You have been seriously underappreciated, Maddie. I tell you what. I'll show you what you've been missing if you promise we'll do this again after tonight." Before she could protest, he stopped her. "I know. No commitment. No boyfriend/girlfriend label. Look, I'm not in the market for a girlfriend either. Brody and I have been gearing up to maybe hire on some guys to work for us, we're getting that busy. I don't have time for a relationship, like you. And if Mike finds out we did this, he'll kick my ass."

"Scared of your brother?" She tangled her fingers with his, brushing their hands over her soft skin.

The sight of them joined made him feel funny, and he shrugged it off. "Hell yeah. Have you seen the size of his neck? The boy is like a farmer turned pro wrestler. He's friggin' huge."

"Well, I won't tell if you won't."

"Exactly. I'm not a kiss-and-tell kind of guy. You don't know me well enough to know that. Or that I don't cheat on girlfriends, not that you are, but I'm just saying. If we do this again, which I hope we will, it'll be just us, ah…"

"Fucking?"

"Man, I love that mouth." He leaned over to kiss her again. His cock twitched, and he wondered what the hell had been in that wine. He should have been more than tired by now. Instead, he wanted to bend her over and start again.

Maddie pushed him onto his back and rose over him, speculation on her face. "So you're saying you want to keep fucking but keep it quiet? A little something on the side, and we let no one know? My roommates aren't stupid. They're going to be a little suspicious I didn't come home right away."

"Good point." He had a hard time taking his eyes off her breasts. But when he saw her brow raised in question, he concentrated on what the hell she was saying. "I'll go with whatever you want. But whatever happens between us has to stay between us. I don't want you pissed at me and taking it out on Mike. Same goes for me yelling at Vanessa because you make me crazy."

"Actually, you can yell at Vanessa all you want." She

ran her fingertips over his chest. "I get your point. I'd like us to be friends at least. I mean, Ben and I were friends before we dated. We broke up and nothing. Not even a 'how are you.'"

"I don't want that for us. Not that there is an *us*, if you know what I mean," he amended, not sure why the thought of them together pleased him so much. "But you have to know, I want to do this again. And again. And maybe again after that."

She smiled. "Good to know. Me too. But I don't want to, um, it would probably be best if we kept this casual between us."

"Right."

"But you have a point. If we're kind of together, it would make me feel better, safer, if it was just you and me. No other women. Not that we're dating or anything."

Was she trying to convince him or herself? Interesting thought.

She continued, "A man is the last thing I need right now. No offense; I'm not talking about you."

"None taken." He shifted beneath her, letting her feel his cock against her thigh.

Her eyes widened. "Does that thing ever go down?"

"Not around you, apparently." He caressed her breasts. "So we should probably get you that window cleaner, hmm?"

"Well, yeah. But they don't need it right away, do they?"

He brought her lips down to meet his. The kiss this time felt sweet, easy. Familiar yet fraught with a tenderness he didn't understand. "They should wait."

"Vanessa is a tyrant." She kissed him back. For

all she talked about casual sex, nothing in her expression seemed light. Soft, sensual, affectionate. Maddie Gardner didn't make sense, and he wanted like hell to figure her out. So that they could have sex without complications, not for any other reason. He'd barely turned thirty-one. He wasn't ready for kids and the white picket fence yet.

"Your cousin reminds me of my brothers."

Her lips trailed over his mouth to his neck and ear. "Are they mean to you, cupcake? I bet I could handle them." She whispered the naughty things she'd do, shocking and arousing him that she could be so wicked.

His semi-hard cock grew to epic proportions. He let her play before reminding her just how much she'd been missing out on in life.

Chapter 7

IN THE END, THEY AGREED TO PRETEND TO SOME HOT and heavy petting for her roommates, but she'd divulge nothing more. Maddie didn't need scrutiny on her love life—*sex* life, she corrected. She had enough to worry about without anxiety over what her roommates might think.

She arrived home four hours later. As expected, the flicker of a television lit up the darkness of the living room. Abby and Vanessa were no doubt waiting up for her. The hour hadn't yet reached eleven, so she wasn't too late.

Armed with a bottle of Windex, she snuck into the clean and tidy house, so boneless she wanted to melt into a pile of satisfied goo. Flynn McCauley had touched her in places she hadn't known existed. And the things he'd done to her with that mouth defied belief.

She tiptoed past the living room, through the darkened hall, and put the cleaner on the kitchen counter. Moonlight through the window showed it to be spotless. Poor Abby, at home all alone with Vanessa, her rubber gloves, and Mr. Clean.

The lights snapped on and she shrieked and turned to face Vanessa and Abby.

"So, Skankerella sneaks home." Vanessa crossed her arms over her chest.

"Vanessa." Abby quirked a smile. "Although I like Skankerella. Mind if I use that in my next book?"

"Feel free."

Both friends scrutinized her from top to bottom. Maddie didn't mind. She looked the same as she had before she'd left, minus her panties. She'd refused to put the wet things back on, but Flynn promised to get them back to her. Discreetly.

"Man, they did it. I knew it." Abby held out her hand, and Vanessa started to reach for her pocket.

"Hey! I didn't do anything." She didn't want to fib to her best friends, but this thing between her and Flynn confused her. It meant something more than she'd expected, and she needed time, and privacy, to know what the hell had actually happened between them.

Vanessa huffed. "Four hours to get glass cleaner? Please credit us with some intelligence."

"Okay, so there might have been some kissing and touching involved. But we're taking it slow." The truth, if watered down some. "Neither of us wants a relationship, and Mike threatened to hang Flynn by his toes if he bothers any of us. I guess our neighbor is afraid if Flynn breaks my heart, I'll blame Mike and make his life miserable."

"A fair assessment. Makes you wonder how many other hearts Flynn's broken that Mike would warn him." Vanessa frowned. "Take it slow with the heart-throb. He's handsome, available, and not what you need right now."

"Thanks, *Mom*," she grumbled at her cousin.

"Well, one of us has to keep our legs closed and our minds sharp."

Abby sputtered with laughter. "That would be you, for sure."

"Don't even pretend it wouldn't be you." Vanessa snorted. "The woman who writes about it every day but never does anything with that imagination? The last time you got lucky you found a penny heads up on the sidewalk. And that was what? Last month?"

Abby sneered. "Yeah? Well if you didn't walk around with an icicle up your ass, you wouldn't be such a cold, frigid bitch."

Maddie stared from Abby to Vanessa in shock. "Guys?"

Abby's smile returned. "Did you like that?"

"Oh yeah. Frigid bitch worked. But you might want to hold onto the sarcasm longer. It takes practice, but it works for me."

"You two make my head hurt. I'm going to bed. I have a lot on my plate this week." Maddie shook her head and left them behind, her thoughts on other things. Namely, her new business.

And Flynn.

———

Abby waited until Maddie climbed the stairs. Once she heard the door shut, she held her palm out. "Twenty. I told you."

Vanessa frowned but put a crisp bill face-up on Abby's palm. "She said she didn't do anything."

"Please. I know Maddie better than she knows herself. She totally danced the mambo with snake man. Flynn was practically drooling when they left. Trust me, I know when a man's interested."

Vanessa chuckled.

"What?"

"Abby, you're blind when it comes to men. Oh sure,

when you're observing your roommates or planning out your next novel, you see all kinds of things. But you never see them coming your way, do you?"

Not liking the direction of this conversation, she asked Vanessa the question weighing heavily on her mind. "Do you think Maddie and Flynn will work?"

Vanessa pursed her lips in thought. "I don't know. From everything I saw today, he comes from a decent family with core values. He's handsome, intelligent, and financially responsible—I think. I'll know more after I've done some research on his personal finances."

"Are you serious?"

"Look. Flynn might not know it, but when he decided to take up with Maddie, he got himself two self-appointed guardians." Vanessa glared at her. "Or am I wrong, and you don't care if he uses my cousin—*our* roommate—and smashes her heart into tiny pieces?"

Abby scowled. "Of course I care." She thought about what Vanessa had said. "Do I even want to know how you'll get that information about Flynn's finances?"

"I'll work it out of Cameron."

"Their brother, Cameron?"

Vanessa nodded. "He's the saner one in the family. A financial whiz, or so I hear. I'll con him into giving up some deets about Flynn. Don't worry. You keep up the eavesdropping on poker nights. Maybe we'll find something we can use. And try to work info out of the kid. They normally break pretty easily."

"Vanessa!"

She laughed. "I'm kidding. Colin's a cute little boy. But seriously, he would be a great source of information. You should offer to babysit someday, then pepper the crap out of him. But you have to be subtle, or he'll go home telling dear old dad you're asking questions about Flynn."

"So why don't you do the babysitting thing?" Abby didn't want to remember the last time she'd been around children. Her sisters, flying mashed potatoes, nieces and nephews who refused to listen to reason, orange juice in her purse...

"I'm going to be working the brother for information. He's the baby of the family. It'll be easy."

Abby frowned. "He's older than you are, and I know because Beth ran through the family history with me. I think he's nearing thirty. He's no pushover, Vanessa. And he's not stupid."

Vanessa waved her away. "Yeah, yeah. Now I'm going to get some rest because I have to go in to work tomorrow. Without me, that project is dead in the water. God, the curse of the competent." She sighed and twisted her straight hair into a bun. "Don't forget. We need info. So get that kid over here and work him."

Abby watched her walk away and let out a deep breath. Vanessa had her heart in the right place, but manipulating a five-year-old for answers didn't seem kosher to Abby. Walking back down the hall, she turned off the television and entered the office. She sat in front of her computer, too tired to do any work, and turned to her bookshelves.

Ten titles, all written by Abigail D. Chatterly. *My hard work is paying off. Finally.* Yet the excitement she normally felt when looking at her accomplishments refused to come. The barbecue this afternoon had been fun, and a bit of a letdown. The McCauleys were wonderful

people. Everyone, from little Colin to his grandfather
James, had been more than sweet. If she could discount
the strange looks Brody had given her, she'd have said
the day had been a success.

It still weirded her out that she looked so much like
Mike's dead wife, Lea. But if it didn't bother him, she
didn't know why his friend would be so troubled. *Give
him a break, Abby. He's the only one who never saw you
before. Probably just a shock to his system.* But of all the
men who'd been at the party, he was the one she wanted
most to notice her. She'd heard him and his buddies on
and off for weeks, unable to place a face to his name.

But holy Hannah, Brody Singer had awakened the
woman inside her, and now that stupid woman refused
to go back to sleep.

Disgruntled, she tried to banish the tall, golden Brody
from her mind. Like Vanessa, she'd seen the chemistry
between Flynn and Maddie brewing all day. She'd also
seen Flynn's reaction to meeting Maddie last week,
when the poor man had stared so hard she feared his
eyes would pop out of their sockets.

And why shouldn't he? Unlike Abby, Maddie had
height, a figure most women envied—hell, *she* did—and
red hair, amber eyes, model good looks, and a pleasant
personality. Mostly. Then again, most men didn't care
about pleasant. They wanted hot, sexy, passionate—all
characteristics Maddie possessed.

The best thing that could have happened to her, besides losing that stifling job with snotty people, was
breaking up with Ben. "Boring Ben," as Abby had secretly nicknamed him. Maddie seemed to attach herself
to guys who didn't challenge her. Abby had a feeling

Maddie feared becoming her mother, loving the wrong man and facing the consequences.

Abby felt for her. She did. Her own family loved her. With the exception of one annoying older sister, they supported her and had helped her through school so she didn't have to take major loans. She'd never wanted for much. And when she'd met Kevin, she'd thought she'd found heaven on earth.

Not wanting to travel down that dark road again, she forced the memory aside and turned on the computer. Her heroes and heroines lived their own happily-ever-afters. If she had anything to do with it, Maddie would as well. Abby just needed time to figure out if Flynn would be a hero or a villain, a main love interest or a secondary character. Because unlike Maddie's other boyfriends, Flynn didn't seem the type to accept Maddie's distance. He had too much going for him to succumb to an emotionally withdrawn lover, not with a family like his.

The McCauleys were loud. Protective. Loyal. Loving. She'd seen it in his parents and brothers, in the way they all cared for Colin and treated their guests with respect and affection. Abby couldn't have written Maddie a better hero. Now to make sure Flynn wasn't a scoundrel in disguise.

Maddie continued to badger herself not to pick up the phone on Sunday. Hadn't she told Flynn they were casual? She'd see him when she saw him. Mike lived right next door. It was inevitable they'd bump into each other soon enough. And she'd had enough sex last night to last her several months.

It's the quality of the orgasms. Not the quantity, Maddie. Though three in one night had broken every record in the Madison Gardner Hall of Fame. She'd never taken the concept of multiple orgasms seriously. But after experiencing Flynn, she knew anything was possible. He'd turned her inside out with his hands, his tongue, his giant cock. She'd never been one concerned about size, but the way he'd used it and how he'd felt inside her... Flynn definitely knew how to please a woman.

And therein lay the problem. He must have had a lot of experience to know how to bring someone he barely knew to orgasm so quickly. Despite her long stretch of celibacy, Flynn had played her body like his own personal instrument. Just thinking about him revved her engines again. To her bemusement, she didn't like the thought of him with another woman. Jealousy, strong and sure, curled in her breast, and she wanted to slap herself for being so cliché.

Christ, I barely know him. It's not like I claimed him as mine or anything. And his past is just that, his past. So why had she felt such relief when he'd agreed to no other people in their personal lives while they dallied with each other?

She called herself an idiot and buckled down to iron out the details of her pitch to Linda Donnigan. Yesterday had been a blessing in disguise. Not only was Flynn's Aunt Linda a realtor, she was a businesswoman who didn't mince words and who had Robin's and Kim's respect. A brief message to her friends had convinced Maddie a meeting with Linda would not only benefit her but might benefit them as well.

With their excited support behind her, she needed to be totally sure of herself. Selling the product would be easy so long as she believed in it; she had to believe in herself.

She never would have guessed that might be a problem, but Fred Hampton's machinations nagged at her confidence. What if she hadn't been hired based on her ability, but because he'd planned to sleep with her one day? What if her designs and ideas had never been very good, but he'd helped her limp along because he had ulterior motives?

The negative thinking continued to abrade her nerves, until she wanted to throw the whole project out the window.

A knock at her bedroom door interrupted her pity party. "What?" she yelled.

Vanessa opened the door. "Here you go, Your Highness." She tossed Maddie her cell phone.

"Oh. Where was it?"

"On the counter, Captain Clueless. Wait, what's that, you ask? No, my day has *not* gone well. Jed Rawlins is a horse's ass *and* stupid. He wasted my morning with questions he should already have known the answers to. When I told him that, he had the audacity to ask about *you*. As if I'd set up my own flesh and blood with someone like him."

Vanessa tied her hair up in a ponytail, her agitation apparent in the brisk motion of her hands. "I'm going out for a run before the rain comes down. Don't thank me for the phone or anything." She slammed the door shut and stomped down the stairs.

Chuckling, Maddie looked at the phone and scrolled

through her unread messages. "And she calls *me* 'Your Highness.' Too funny." Maddie really felt for the people who had to work with her cousin. The woman had a high intelligence and a low threshold for foolish questions and stupid people. Hell, she barely tolerated Maddie, and they were cousins.

Robin had sent her a few notes. One message from a friend from Hampton's Designs expressed regret that she'd left without saying good-bye. Maddie made a note to call her back. She wasn't a bad person, probably one of the best young designers still there. Another text—a reminder from Vanessa to purchase paper towels, which she'd sent yesterday while at the barbecue.

Vanessa needed a serious set-down. Texting a grocery list while at a party signaled a woman on the edge of a meltdown. Muttering under her breath about her cousin, Maddie stopped at a text sent today from a number she didn't recognize.

> Just wanted you to know I'm **NOT** thinking about you. At all. Casually Yours, F.

The smile on her face grew. *Casually Yours*. As specified, they wouldn't cuddle or hug. Though, come to think of it, they'd done plenty of that last night. She'd insisted he didn't need to see her inside when he'd dropped her off after their rendezvous. She'd also nixed the idea of flowers or datelike behavior, in case he took it upon himself to display any. But a text between friends couldn't be construed as anything but platonic. Ordinary.

Noting the three-hour lapse between when he'd sent it

and now, she figured it safe to text back. It was probably
a good thing she'd misplaced her phone. Otherwise she
would have pounced on it the moment it rang and fought
with herself not to immediately text back. She typed into
her tiny keyboard, Not thinking about you either. But take
good care of that tongue. Casually back at you, M.

She returned to work, her woes forgotten as she threw
herself into the notion that Flynn's aunt wouldn't know
what hit her come Tuesday. Maddie's baby, Gardner's,
would do what the other companies couldn't. Not only
would she sweep the local real estate agents off their
feet, but her new venture would win back the confidence
Maddie had lost, and in the process, make her departure
from Hampton's Designs no more than a bad memory.

—⁓—

Flynn heard his phone chime and dove for it before Brody returned from the bathroom. They sat at
Brody's place drinking beer and watching a game. The
clouds overhead had looked ominous so they'd passed
on an outdoor ball game with friends. Though he dealt
with rain on a daily basis, living in Seattle, he hated
being wet.

At least Brody had a decent place—if one disregarded
the mess in most of the rooms save this one. He lived in
a house that had been converted into a duplex just three
blocks from Green Lake. Seth, the old man who owned
the building, lived right next door. He kept to himself.
On the odd days Flynn had seen him at the park sitting
on a bench, he'd had a story to tell.

Seth planned on living in his house until he died.
Brody did most of the upkeep and had a portion of his

rent deducted for it. But even if he hadn't earned a re-
duction, his friend still would have helped the old man.
Truth to tell, the crotchety bastard kind of reminded
Flynn of his own father. And since Brody idolized James
McCauley, it made sense he'd taken to Seth.

Flynn glanced at the bathroom, then at the phone,
back at the bathroom, then thought *screw it*. He looked
at the message then saved it. Tucking the phone back
into his pocket, he settled back on the couch to enjoy
the rest of the game.

Brody appeared and plunked down beside him, keeping the requisite three feet of man-space between them.
"What the hell are you smiling at, dumbass? We're
down by three and can't buy a hit." He swore when the
next pitch came in. "Strike? What are they swinging at?"

Flynn shrugged and took a swig of his beer.

"What happened?" Brody muted the television and
turned to face him. "Tell me."

"What? I'm watching the game. We're down, as
usual. But we'll come back."

"No. You're never this happy. You've been humming
all day. What's up with you?" Brody's eyes narrowed.
"You got laid, didn't you?"

Flynn choked on his beer. Was he that easy to read?
"Why does my good mood have to be tied to sex?
Couldn't I be happy because I'm watching the game
with my bud and drinking a beer?" He turned the label
and nodded. "One that isn't one of Cam's girlie drinks?"

"No, no. Don't screw with me. I know you." Brody
tilted his head. "You did the redhead. Hot damn."

It annoyed Flynn that Brody passed Maddie off as
just *the redhead*. The woman had a name. "First of all,

Maddie Gardner is not just 'the redhead.' Dickhead. Second, I didn't *do* anyone. I drove Maddie and Abby home last night. Watched a movie, went to bed." *So why am I so happy?* "If I'm in a good mood, it's because one of the cousins is thinking of interning with us."

Brody blinked. "No shit? Which one? Theo, Landon, or Gavin? No way it's Hope. And seriously, what's with your aunt naming them like that? It's like she *wanted* them to get pummeled growing up."

Flynn grinned. Aunt Linda's sons were good kids, but Brody had a point. They'd spent a lot of their not-so-distant past defending the Donnigan brothers, who didn't know when to keep their big mouths shut. "Theo. He just graduated and has been dragging his feet about college. The others are still overseas doing God knows what for Corps and country."

"Damn jarheads. Hope they're staying safe." Brody frowned.

"You know, I still say you should have joined the Corps." Like Flynn's father and cousins had.

Brody snorted. "I'm not into taking orders from anyone. And before you say it, yeah, I listen to your dad, but only because he has such a big mouth."

"True." Flynn chuckled. "Me, I knew what I wanted to do the minute my dad let me go with him during the summers on those construction sites. Remember? I'll never forget Roger Dellford preaching about plumbing being an art form while he smoked that huge cigar. Remember how he'd bring us a beer when Dad wasn't looking? Man, I loved that guy."

Brody clinked the neck of his beer against Flynn's. "Me too. And I'll add my thanks to Daring Dellford for his insight, his stogies, and his brew. We've cleared a shitload this year. If we could add on another team, we'd be golden."

"Maybe when Gavin comes home, I can convince him to work with Theo. Keep it all in the family."

Brody nodded. "Sounds good. Now back to our earlier discussion."

Like a dog with a goddamn bone. "Huh?"

"Dude, lie to your brothers, your mother, your nephew. But don't lie to me. I know you."

Shit. He didn't want to break Maddie's confidence, but this was Brody. He might be a pain in the ass at times, as well as a liar and a card cheat, but he was Flynn's best friend, blood brother, and pretend twin. Had been since kindergarten.

He sighed. "You can't tell anyone."

Brody's eyes gleamed. "I fucking knew it."

"Swear. I'm not kidding." He punched Brody in the arm.

"Ow. Okay, I swear. I won't say a thing to the family. You know I won't."

Gratified to see the truth, Flynn wondered how much to say. "I took the girls home last night."

"*You did both of them?*"

"Don't be an ass."

"Oh, right." Did Brody look relieved?

"And then I took Maddie out to get some stupid supplies to clean her house." At Brody's look of disbelief, he nodded. "Seriously. Vanessa's got this thing about cleanliness. She's a little scary."

"Sounds like it. So, Maddie?"

"We went back to my place. And we, ah, we kind of fooled around."

"Dude, you fucked her. I know that look."

"Shut up." He flushed. Damn it, he felt like a schoolgirl at her first sleepover, spilling secrets he shouldn't be sharing. "We're keeping it casual. She's not gonna say anything to her friends. And if Mike finds out, it'll just show him he was right not to tell *us*—yeah, you and me—about them moving in in the first place."

"Hmm. Good point. Okay. I'll try to keep all teasing to a minimum. Just between you and me."

"We're past the fourth grade, numbnuts. Grow up."

"Maddie of the long red hair and killer bod." Brody sighed. "I bet that was some piece of ass, huh?"

"Fuck off. She's not a piece of ass." Flynn restrained himself from punching Brody right in the face. "She's a nice person. We connected, but we're just friends. Don't push me on this."

Brody held up his hands in surrender.

Flynn didn't trust the sly look in his eyes. "I'm not kidding."

"Hey, point taken. Understood. You and your girlfriend—"

"She's *not* my girlfriend. She's too busy starting her new business for relationships. And we have this new team we're building. I don't have time either."

"Bullshit," Brody scoffed. "You're not looking because you keep coming up short. Not everyone is like your parents. Those two have some kind of lovefest going on I still don't get. But you might find a woman if you'd lower your standards. How many women in this day and age are actually stay-at-home moms who worship at their husband's feet?"

"Are we talking about Beth McCauley?" Flynn

drained the rest of his beer. "That woman raised us, yeah. But have you ever seen her worship Dad?"

Brody frowned. "Ah, no. But we both know that's what you're looking for, why your slutty girlfriends never measure up."

"First of all, they're not slutty."

"Half of them are fuck-buddies. Go ahead. Deny it."

He wanted to, but he couldn't. The odd thing was that he didn't consider Maddie one of them. "Let's discuss *you* and *your* hang-ups."

Brody turned and looked for the remote. "This isn't about me."

"Sure it is. If you were busy with your own slutty girlfriend, you'd stop hounding me."

Brody laughed. "Who says I'm not busy?"

"The fact that it's Sunday and you're sitting here with me. That the most you have to do on a Saturday is drool over Abby Dunn."

Brody's face darkened. "I did not."

Bingo. Now to exploit the weakness. He hated to go there, but Brody needed a wake-up call. "You think I didn't know about your thing for Lea?"

Brody blanched. "It wasn't like that."

Flynn softened his voice. "I know. We all loved her like a sister, but you saw something more. Christ, Brody, she looked exactly like the picture of that centerfold you used to keep under your bed. The one you found in seventh grade. Remember?"

Brody's cheeks had gone from white to dark red in an instant. "This is not what we were talking about."

"Sure it is. I'm friendly with Maddie, and you have a thing for her best friend, Abby. Don't ignore it."

"You want me to forget this conversation? Fine." He glanced around. "Where the fuck is the remote?"

"Brody, relax. Abby is really nice, but she's not Lea. Once you get past the appearance, you'll see there's someone else in there. Even Mike said so. He's not into her."

They sat a moment in silence.

"How can you tell?"

Flynn forced himself not to smile. "Trust me. Mike might miss Lea, but he knows the difference between his wife and a look-alike. If he'd had a thing for Abby, I would have been able to tell. And think about it. Mom would have been shoving her at him on Saturday."

Brody relaxed. "Good point. She pretty much left Abby alone. Then again, she sure was shoving Maddie at you." The smirk on his face returned.

"She did not."

"Sorry to say, she kept tabs on you the whole day. The only reason Mike and I dragged you away from your girlfriend? Bitsy ordered us to."

"Hell." If his mother sensed his interest in the woman, he'd be smart to duck her calls for a few days. His phone rang, and his heart raced on the off chance Maddie had phoned. It continued to ring.

"You going to answer your ass?" Brody asked with an evil smile. He found the remote but kept the mute on.

"Fuck." Flynn dragged his phone out, saw his mother's number, and put it back, disappointed but refusing to acknowledge why. "Look. You know I'm seeing Maddie on the sly, and I know you're a pussy too afraid to put a move on Abby."

"Dick."

"Back at you. So let's agree to disagree and watch the friggin' game."

Brody's smile soured. "Fine. But if you don't at least tell me if she's a natural redhead, I'll go to your mother with my suspicions."

Flynn allowed the slow, satisfied smile he'd been hiding to stretch his mouth wide.

"Hell. At least one of us had a good night." Brody held the sweating bottle to his forehead. "Lucky prick."

Lucky indeed.

Chapter 8

MADDIE STILL COULDN'T BELIEVE IT. SHE'D ACED HER interview with Flynn's aunt. The woman had a huge clientele and reputation as a top independent realtor in the Seattle market. And she'd been more than enthused about trying Maddie on for size as a staging consultant. After all Maddie's stressing, in one short meeting, Gardner's was born.

She knew she should have been patient, but she had to share her good news. She wouldn't let herself think of failure. Instead, she was determined she'd succeed. Calling her mother would seal the deal. No going back now.

While she relaxed in the living room, she dialed the number and waited.

"Maddie! Good to hear from you, honey. Hold on." Michelle jostled the phone. After a minute, she picked it up. "So how are you? You hung up pretty fast last week."

Fast? They'd talked for a solid half hour. "I'm sorry about that. You see—"

"But I suppose I should stop lecturing you about men. Not as if I'm an expert." Her mother's self-effacing humor helped take the bitterness out of her words. "You'll find someone if it's meant to be. But at least you're no longer with Ben."

Maddie silently counted to ten before she spoke. "You'll never guess what happened."

"Okay. I'm waiting."

She didn't know why she found it so hard to tell her mother, even after her pep talk. It was as if saying it made it more real. "I'm my own boss now. I left Hampton's Designs to start my own company. Gardner's. Great name, huh?" she joked.

Her mother didn't say anything.

"Mom?"

"You're happy? This is a good thing? I thought you'd planned on branching out a few years from now." In the background, the hustle and bustle of the diner could be heard.

"No, no. It's all good. Hey, why do I hear noise? Am I taking you from work? I thought you had Tuesdays off."

"I'm fine. You worry too much." Her mom laughed. "I took Sheila's shift tonight so she could take mine tomorrow." A pregnant pause sat between them. "I have a date."

"Huh?"

"I'm going on a date. Can you believe it at my age?"

"Mom, you're only forty-four. That's a far cry from ancient."

"Thanks." Michelle chuckled. "I've seen Hank every day for the past three years, but I never noticed him before. And then the other day, he asked me to dinner. Me. A tired old woman, dating."

"You're not old." She'd never heard her mom sound so excited. "Tell me about him."

Their conversation lasted an hour, and her mother disconnected after a lengthy discussion about her date and Maddie's career change. Maddie was excited about the future, but out loud, she reminded herself to be cautious. "Maybe. It's not a done deal, even though I hit it off with Linda." Then she circled back to the topic that floored her.

Her mother had a date. With a man. And she'd sounded thrilled. So why did her mother having a real social life, not just with friends or family, feel so odd?

"When you start talking to yourself, you need therapy." Vanessa's dry voice startled her.

"Damn it, don't *do* that."

"And don't curse in front of the kid."

She glanced behind Vanessa to see Colin McCauley grinning at her.

"Ooooh. You said a bad word."

"She sure did, kiddo. Now let's go see what Abby's up to." Vanessa shot her a smug look before toting the boy down the hallway.

More than curious, Maddie rose and joined them in the kitchen. Abby and Vanessa seemed engaged in a glaring contest while Colin munched on Maddie's precious bag of frosted animal cookies. Cookies that should have been hidden in her secret stash.

"What's going on?"

Vanessa shrugged. "I took an early day and ran into Cameron. He was supposed to watch over Colin after camp let out for the day, but he's behind on a project, so I offered to help."

Maddie couldn't help it. She laughed. "*You?*"

"I'm more than capable of watching a small child."

Abby smiled through her teeth. "Yes, *you* are. Need I remind you I'm writing right now?"

Vanessa blew out her breath. "Fine. Hey, Colin. Want to play some computer games?"

"Sure." He followed her down the hall toward the office—Abby's office—trailing crumbs.

"I thought you were working." Confused, Maddie felt like she'd started from the wrong end of a book.

"I *am*." Abby tore out of the room, yelling for Vanessa.

Maddie had a headache. Too nervous last night to sleep, she'd been up all hours reviewing her pitch and presentation materials. Today's meeting and the call to her mother had about exhausted her reserves. And though the impress-me pumps she'd bought for the meeting had worked like a lucky charm, they pinched her toes.

She grabbed her purse and trudged up the stairs when her phone buzzed. Expecting the inquisition from Robin or Kim, she answered. "Hello?"

"Son of a bitch!" The voice sounded suspiciously like Flynn. He swore again, even louder, and she pulled the phone from her ear, wincing. A crash, bang, and Brody yelling about Flynn's dubious parentage came through with a burst of static.

"Flynn?"

"Damn it." Silence, then the static disappeared. "Maddie? Hi. Sorry about that."

Giddy as a schoolgirl, Maddie practically skipped to her room and closed the door behind her. She sat on her bed, not bothering to hide her smile or her nervous jitters. Her knee bobbed like a jackhammer.

"Where are you?"

"I'm in hell, with Satan's personal plumber—Brody Singer." She heard Brody yell something before Flynn continued. "I just wanted to know how the meeting with Aunt Linda went. Wait a minute."

"Who, me?"

"Sorry. No. *Brody, wait a minute*. Now, Maddie, tell me about your day."

"Are you in a well?"

"Feels like it. So how'd it go?"

The excitement that had so exhausted her only moments before returned full force as she repeated her conversation with Linda.

"That's terrific. My aunt's a real shark when it comes to her business. If she liked you, you must be good."

"Yeah, well, next week will prove it. I have to stage a place. I'm checking it out tomorrow."

"Sounds like your new job is taking off."

"Maybe." She paused, her mind still stuck on her mother's alarming news. She needed neutral feedback. Flynn had a decent relationship with his own mother. He might serve as a sounding board. "Can I ask you something?"

"Flynn, come on!" She heard Brody yell in the background. "This is fucking *heavy*."

Flynn ignored him. "Sure, Maddie. Take your time."

She couldn't help laughing. "Poor Brody. I'll make this quick. I would have asked Abby, but she knows my mom, and I need someone impartial. My mom is going out on a date."

"A date?"

"Yeah. Some guy she says she's known for years. They're going out tomorrow night, and I feel weird about it. I want her to be happy, but I don't know." This was stupid. The man had a job to do. She should talk to Abby about her mom. "Heck, you're busy, I should just—"

"No, hold on. Let me think." She heard another crash. "Ignore that. You love your mom, right?"

"Yes."

"I take it your dad isn't in the picture if she's going on a date."

"He was never in the picture."

"Got it." No lengthy pauses, no judgmental silence. "How old is she?"

"Forty-four."

"Wow. That's young." To his credit, he didn't do the math. "Sure you should be concerned. She's young enough to give you another brother or sister."

"Oh wow. I hadn't even thought about that." She blanched, not able to envision her mother having sex. "The thought of my mom doing... That's gross."

"Trust me, it's even worse to hear them going at it. Don't ask." He muffled the phone. "*Brody, one more minute.* I'm back. Look, it's natural to care about your mom. But if you want her to be happy, and she seems happy, what's so weird about her dating?"

"Nothing, I guess. I just don't want her to get hurt." Hell, one careless mistake twenty-seven years ago had changed her mother's entire life.

"Does she get hurt a lot? Bad choices with guys?"

"No. This is the first time I know of that she's been out on a date." As she said it, she heard the words and felt like a complete moron. How could she think her mother hadn't had sex in nearly thirty years?

"So it's been how long since her last date?" More creaking, then what sounded like rushing water.

"Should you get that?"

"Nah, Brody's got it."

"My mom's never dated, that I know of. Since I was born, it's always been just me and her. But that can't be right. Can it?"

"If she's a nun, maybe. She probably didn't tell you about it. Then again, maybe she put all her energy into you. Who knows? But if it were me, I'd be cheering for my mom to have fun and mingle a little. It's not healthy for a person to be so alone. Take Brody. He's like a hermit, and I keep nudging him to get a life." The swearing behind him suddenly sounded muffled.

Flynn returned. "Oh man, I hope you didn't hear too much of that."

She cringed, not sure what Brody suggested could be physically possible. "Thanks for listening."

"No problem. You feel better?"

To her bemusement, she did. "Yeah."

"Well, congrats on dealing with Aunt Linda and living to tell the tale. Now I have to go fix what Brody broke. Talk to you later."

He hung up before she could thank him again. And then she called her mother. "Mom, it's me again."

"Are you okay? What's wrong?"

"Nothing. I know you're busy, but… This isn't your first date since I was conceived, is it?"

"Um, not exactly."

Relieved, she smiled. "Good. I'd hate to think of you being alone for that long."

"Not even I could handle that."

"Okay, well, I just want you to have a good time." She didn't want to say it but couldn't help it. "*And use protection*," came out as one word.

Her mother started laughing and didn't stop. "Oh,

God. Now I have the hiccups. Wish me luck tomorrow, sweetie." She disconnected, leaving Maddie satisfied and happier than she had a right to be.

Her mother had a life. Her future had started to unfold itself. And wonder of wonders, her friend, her casual, neighborly new friend, had called to see how her day had gone.

She lay back on her bed, closed her eyes, and felt the smile creep over her face.

Abby yanked Vanessa out of the study while Colin looked at her iPad. "What the heck are you doing?"

"I told you. We need to grill him. Use your wiles and find out what you can. I'm simply taking advantage of an opportunity here. Didn't you say the other day you're ahead of schedule?"

She frowned. "Yes, but—"

"You love Maddie like a sister, right?"

"I do, but—"

"Isn't it best if we find out if you-know-who is a loser before she falls for him? Because in case it's escaped your notice, they have a thing going."

"He hasn't called her since Sunday."

"Oh? Have you checked her phone recently?"

Abby conceded the point. "No. Okay. I'll put off my work, but you're cooking."

"Deal."

Vanessa caved way too easily. Abby groaned. She entered the office again and found Colin on the floor staring at a picture of her and her sisters. "Hi." He seemed shy now that Vanessa had gone. "You're in kindergarten, right? Or I guess, going into first grade after the summer."

He nodded.

"So, um, what do you do at summer camp? Math, reading?"

No response. He just blinked at her.

"Do you dance?"

"No."

"Do you sing?"

"Sometimes."

"What do you sing?"

He started with "Row, Row, Row Your Boat," and by the time Vanessa announced dinner, Abby and Colin were singing "The Farmer in the Dell" after two renditions of "Bingo Was His Name-O" and "Old MacDonald."

They finished their song and washed their hands in the bathroom, readying for dinner. Abby smiled down at the little hands next to her own.

"You look like my mommy."

Abby's smile disappeared. "I know."

"But you're not her, I know that."

He sounded mature for a five-year-old. "I'm not your mommy, no. But I'd like to be your friend."

"But not my new mommy?"

"Ah, no. I like your dad, but I think we'll just be friends. Is that okay?"

Colin looked her over, and the similarities to Mike were uncanny. Then he smiled, and his blue eyes brightened. "Okay. Can I tell you a secret?"

She leaned closer. "Sure."

He whispered, "I like Vanessa, but she's kind of scary."

"I know. She scares me sometimes too." She did her best not to laugh.

He grabbed her hand. "Do you think I could have a soda while I'm here?"

"Sure, Colin. We'll share one."

Seeming pleased with his new buddy, he smiled and pulled her down the hallway toward the kitchen. She saw no sign of Vanessa but two plates of food had been carefully laid out on the table.

Two sodas, crunchy spaghetti, and a limp salad later, Colin still hadn't told her anything useful about Flynn.

From what she'd learned, Flynn could burp louder than Brody but not louder than Colin's dad, who held the record for longest and loudest belch. Flynn was a middle child, which Mike referred to as the one needing the most attention. Flynn was also thirty-one, lived in a cool apartment by Pike's Place Market, and drove Colin to school sometimes in an awesome truck. A standard. As in, it had a gear shift. It amazed her what Colin retained. And then she struck gold.

He guzzled more soda. "And he likes kissing girls. Gross."

Hmm. "Really? I don't have any uncles, but my sister likes kissing boys. She has a husband and two kids. And my other sister has four kids." And was working on husband number three, but she didn't mention that.

"Uncle Flynn likes kissing a lot." He turned accusing eyes on her. "He kissed Maddie. Right on the lips."

"He did?"

"Well, she kissed him. And after she left, he just mooned after her. I heard Daddy tell Uncle Cam that. And then Uncle Cam said something about Uncle Flynn being gone."

"Gone?"

"Gone-er. And then Daddy made Uncle Flynn clean the living room before he could go, but Ubie played a trick on Daddy and got out of his chores."

Flynn a goner? What to make of that? "Right. So, um, are you going to be a plumber like your uncles?"

"Nope." He puffed up with pride. "I'm gonna be a carpenter like Daddy and Grampa. And I'll be rich like Uncle Cam, 'cause I'm smart, and Ubie says I can sucker anybody with my cute little face."

Ubie again. He sounded like a real prince. "Ubie?"

"Uncle Brody. U. B. Get it? Ubie."

Ah. Uncle Brody of the deep brown eyes, light hair, and gorgeous face. He looked like he could bench press her with one finger.

"Wait. Abby, Abby, watch this."

She stared in amazement as he crumbled into tears. "Colin?"

Then in an instant, he stopped. "Good, huh?"

"You little faker. What else has Ubie taught you?"

"Watch."

Half an hour later, after cheating at cards and rolling one of her quarters over his fingers that mysteriously disappeared into his pockets so she'd had to give him another one, he'd exhausted his impressive repertoire.

"Oh, nice. You have real talent, Colin." Great skills to know for a child headed to juvie. She wondered if Mike knew what his son had learned at Ubie's hands.

As if she'd conjured him, a knock sounded at the front door. After a harried apology for imposing, Mike whisked Colin away with a wave and a smile. Abby watched them go, wondering just what the hell they'd learned.

Brody was well on his way to making Colin a major troublemaker, and Flynn was a goner for Maddie. Maybe. But that still didn't answer all her questions about the sexy plumber. Still, she'd done her best to get answers.

Now Vanessa could take a turn investigating. Abby had work to do. And a dinner to make. That spaghetti could only be classified as edible by a little boy who thought soda and frosted animal crackers made a good combination.

Chapter 9

MADDIE'S CELL PHONE RINGING AT—SHE TURNED bleary eyes to her alarm clock—half past ten woke her out of a sound sleep. But she had no problem remembering her dream. Flynn had worn nothing but jeans unbuttoned enough to hint at the erection pressing against his fly. The wind had been blowing, his hair pushed back from his sun-kissed face. His eyes had glowed under the light of the showplace Maddie had designed. Encased in glass walls, the room felt like a giant fishbowl.

Which made it so strange that she and Flynn would start kissing and fondling each other while faceless strangers pressed against the glass outside to watch. Maddie still felt totally turned on at the notion. How weird.

She scrambled to grab her phone off the nightstand and hurried to answer. "Hello?"

Silence.

"Hello?"

"Damn. Did I wake you?" Flynn's voice.

The tingle between her legs returned with a vengeance. She cleared her throat. "Yeah, but don't worry. I've already had a few hours of sleep. An early night to celebrate my success with your aunt."

"You deserve it. She's a ballbuster, or so my uncle likes to say." He chuckled.

She laughed with him. After a minute, when the silence grew, she asked him, "Not that I mind, but what's up?"

"I said I'd talk to you later. It's later."

"Bored, Flynn?" Now totally awake, she sat up against her headboard and glanced down at her rumpled skirt. "Man, I shouldn't have fallen asleep in this getup."

A pregnant pause. In a sexy voice, he asked, "What are you wearing?"

Instead of laughing at the start of what promised to be a bad case of phone sex, she shivered. Her entire body clenched. She kept seeing him in that dream, feeling his mouth on hers while others watched. "Why? What are *you* wearing?" *Take that, Flynn*.

"Nothing. I'm lying in bed, stark naked, and thinking of you. So I thought, hell, why not call and see what Maddie's up to?"

Stark naked. Her mouth watered. "I'm still wearing the skirt and dress shirt I had on when I met with your aunt."

"Oh?" She heard rustling in the background. "You wearing heels too? Stockings?"

"With garters." She liked wearing them because they made her feel sexy. The one area Maddie had never had any qualms about—her sexuality. In touch with her femininity, the better she looked, the better she felt about herself. "The stockings go from the upper part of my thigh to my toes."

She'd never had phone sex before; she had a feeling tonight would be a first. Instead of feeling weird about it, she wanted to explore. Flynn made her feel fun, adventurous. She wanted to see where this might lead.

"Stockings, huh?" The raspy breath as he paused turned her on all over again. "Describe everything, from your head to your toes. Is that soft, silky hair of yours down? Are the ends curled around your nipples?"

She licked her lips and decided to just go for it. Maddie had never been a prude, though she'd never been one to be so out there when it came to sex. Then again, she'd never before been tempted to talk to a man the way she wanted to with Flynn.

"My hair is down, and it's starting to curl. The ends are touching my shoulders. There's one strand that's touching the top of my breast. My hair looks really dark against the white of my shirt."

"What color's your bra?"

"White, and it's lacy."

"Take off your shirt," he ordered. "Sit there in your bra and talk to me."

The naughtiness of the conversation was titillating. Flynn had a voice made for phone sex. "I'm unbuttoning, Flynn. One, then two, then three…" She took him with her through the steps. "Now I'm sliding the shirt over my shoulders and off my arms. The silk feels good."

"I bet your nipples are hard. They hard, baby?"

"Yes," she whispered as she dropped the shirt behind her.

"Pinch them. Imagine it's me there, taking those nipples between my fingers."

She pinched them and shifted. "My panties are damp."

"Shit." He moaned, and she wanted to know more.

"What are you doing, Flynn? Tell me."

"I'm holding my cock. I'm thick, baby. Really hard."

"And hot." She remembered holding him, touching him. "I remember how you came all over your belly.

That white hot mess, so tasty." Oh yeah, she was good at this.

"Damn, you're sexy." His breathing sounded harsh. "Slow down. Tell me again, those tits tight? Sensitive? Imagine my mouth over them, biting those nipples until you come."

She played with herself, imagining Flynn right there with her. But she needed two hands so she could touch herself all over while he talked. Placing the phone between her cheek and shoulder, she freed her other hand.

"I want to come with you inside me, Flynn. I'm empty."

"I know. I wish to hell I was there with you right now." He panted. "I'd fuck that wet, tasty pussy. And I'd lick you all over. I'd kiss those sweet lips."

"What else would you do? Would you put that hard cock between my lips and fuck my mouth?"

"Oh yeah. Take off the rest of your clothes, baby. Right now. But keep the garters on. The hose and the shoes too."

She stripped out of everything but the garters and hose. The shoes, unfortunately, she'd left downstairs. But he didn't have to know that.

"Okay." So needy she sounded, but then, she needed him. "Now what?"

"Now you lay there and take what I give you. You open that mouth, let me own it. In and out, my cock is filling you up. And that first time when I come, you swallow it right down. Thick and creamy for you, Maddie. Taste good?"

"Oh yeah, Flynn."

"Then I'll pull out and I'm still hard. For you. No lag

time in this dream." He chuckled, the sound dark and dangerous.

"But I didn't come yet."

"That's right," he whispered. "Because you've been a bad girl. Letting Brody see you naked."

"Wh-what?"

"I need to spank you. Maybe even fuck that fine ass." He paused. "What do you think, Maddie? Too much?" His question took her aback.

"God, not enough." Oh hell, she hadn't said that out loud, had she?

"Yeah, that's good," he crooned. "I'd paddle your ass red. Such a bad girl, teasing a man with what he can't have. I'll have to tie you up and make you pay. Hold you down so you can't move, then fuck you hard. Give you a rough ride, but I won't let you come yet. Not until you're begging me for it. Touch yourself, Maddie. Get your clit nice and wet."

"I don't need to touch myself for that."

"Good girl. To reward you, I'll lick that little bud clean. Suck the juice right out of you. Hell, maybe I'll turn around. Let you suck me at the same time. That would be so sweet."

She moaned, unable to help herself. "Yeah. Lick me." She increased the pressure on her clit, on fire and ready to burst.

"You hot, baby? Need to come?"

"I do," she confessed. "I need to come around you."

"I bet you have toys. A fat dildo hidden in one of your drawers. You have one of those?"

She blushed but answered honestly, "Yes."

"Get it. Put it inside you," he ordered in a gritty voice.

She didn't want to stop, but she wanted this. *Him*. Inside her. "Hold on." She put down the phone and dashed to her dresser, where she kept it behind her lingerie. She took out the dildo and hurried back to the bed and the phone. "Okay."

"Oh God. You have it right there?"

"Yes."

"Put it in your mouth. Suck it."

She did, moaning into the phone.

"Damn. I'm gonna come soon. You have me so hard. I can just imagine you lying there naked, that dildo between those lips." He groaned. "Take it out and rub your clit with it. Let my dick rub you, baby."

"It's dragging down my body. Between my breasts, down my belly. Oh yes, Flynn. That's it. Put your cock there, right there. Hmm." She rubbed herself and closed her eyes, imagining him there. His shaft on her flesh, between her legs, hard and ready to take her.

"That's it. Yeah, tease yourself. Get me all wet. Now slide it in, one inch at a time."

She pushed the head of the toy inside her and gasped as the thick dildo stretched her.

"All of it. How does it feel?"

"So good. Oh Flynn. You feel good. So deep inside me."

His breathing grew heavier, and she imagined him dragging his hand over himself. Jerking off while he talked to her.

She couldn't believe how much she missed him. "I wish you were here."

"Me too. I'd slide myself inside you, fucking you

until I came deep in you. No condom, nothing but me filling you with come," he growled.

"Oh, yes. More."

"Pump it. Fuck yourself with it. The way I'm jerking off with my hand, pretending it's your cunt. That hot, tight pussy sucking me hard. Taking me deep. So deep, Maddie."

She could hear him nearing his edge and was right there with him. The dildo felt good, but with her eyes shut and Flynn's voice so close, she could picture him with her on the bed. And his presence made all the difference.

The kink in her neck, the drift of cool air over her nearly naked body, the discomfort of the garters pressing against the undersides of her thighs. Nothing mattered but coming with Flynn. Feeling him deep inside her.

"I'm coming. Flynn, come with me."

She saw him in her mind's eye, that ecstatic expression of pleasure on his face, the way his green eyes deepened, so dark, mossy, and full of desire. She rubbed her clit and pumped the dildo in and out, needing him. Only Flynn.

"Come, Maddie. All over me. Yeah, hold me tight. Milk it. That's it." He continued to order as his husky voice grew thicker, raspier.

"I'm coming," she whispered and bit her lip as a blast of desire rocked her foundation. She clenched the toy hard, seizing around it as she imagined him coming inside her. No condom, no protection from her fierce lover straining as he shot inside her.

His hoarse shout on the other end satisfied her need that he know the same bliss, and she whispered to him, encouraging. "That's it. All inside me, Flynn. Come hard, baby."

"Oh fuck. Yeah, that's good. So much for you, Maddie. Just for you." He moaned her name.

"All for me," she agreed, holding the toy inside her.

They lay apart, together, spent. And for Maddie, oddly at peace. She didn't feel the least bit embarrassed, though she wished he'd been here. When she withdrew the dildo, she felt empty. Not just physically, but emotionally.

"I can't believe you did that," he said, his voice again even, and startled her.

"What?" Would Flynn regard her as a slut because she'd shared in something *he'd* started? To her surprise, she'd gotten off on phone sex. She'd never tried it, never would have even thought to try it. But with Flynn, it had felt right.

"You got me off faster than I would have thought. I was trying to last."

She sighed, relieved he wasn't blaming her for anything. "Well, you were just as sexy. All those throaty growls and moans. I bet you could make a fortune in the adult industry."

He barked a laugh. "Me in porn? Hell no. I don't have nearly the stamina those guys do. And I'm embarrassed I didn't last any longer on the damn phone. But hell, you're fucking hot. Looking at you is a wet dream, sure. But who knew you could make all those sexy little sounds? The little mewl when you come makes me lose it each time. I wish you could have seen how hard I was."

"Me too." She was tempted to send him a picture of

her naked, but she'd never considered herself stupid. She subscribed to the rule to never put in print—or via electronics—anything she didn't expect to be shared.

"I'd have given anything to see you playing with yourself. We'll have to do that again, with me inside you next time." Flynn's satisfaction spoke to the woman inside her.

She felt better than good that she'd made him lose himself so completely. "Next time? Who says there'll be a next time? Maybe I just had all I can take of you," she teased. "My time is valuable, you know."

He didn't say anything, and she wondered if she'd pushed too far. "Flynn?"

"Well, I don't want to overstep. I mean, I know this is casual between us."

She rolled her eyes. Casual phone sex. Right.

He chuckled.

"What's so funny?"

"So, um, you said your time is valuable. So do I pay by the minute or what?"

It took her a moment, but instead of being insulted, she laughed. "Asshole."

"Hey, that's just what Brody calls me."

She remembered what he'd said about spanking her, that Brody had seen her. "Flynn?"

"Yeah?" She heard him moving around and thought she ought to do the same, but she couldn't move. "What you said earlier about Brody… Where did that come from?"

"Why? You have a thing for Brody?"

"Not him. But it was weird. Tonight I had this dream about you, and we were kissing. Fooling around, but we were in this glass box and people were watching us."

"I like your imagination." She could hear the grin—and relief—apparent in his voice.

"It was really sexy. I never thought of myself as an exhibitionist or anything, but I liked it. Then you mentioned Brody watching us. Weird coincidence."

"Great minds think alike." He laughed. "So, you have a thing for voyeurism. Good to know."

Her cheeks heated. "I do not." Conscious to keep her voice down and hoping she hadn't made too much noise earlier, she warned him, "Flynn, forget I said anything, or else."

"Or else what?"

"Or else I'll charge you by the minute. And trust me. You can't afford me."

He chuckled again. "Don't I know it. Okay, okay. I was just teasing. Hey, I don't want to piss you off. Then you might never talk to me again. And I really, *really* like talking to you, Maddie."

Just like that, her heart raced again. But this time she felt something more, a softening toward him she couldn't explain. She chalked it up to good sex and told him good night. After she cleaned up and readied for bed, she settled down into a deep, dreamless sleep.

***

Friday night, Flynn couldn't concentrate. The gift he'd gotten Maddie burned a hole in his pocket. He shouldn't have picked it up for her, but he wanted her to have it. Through the grapevine he'd learned Maddie had named her new company Gardner's. Simple yet succinct. The company would succeed because the stubborn redhead wouldn't let it fail.

"Jesus, Flynn. Why don't you just *give* them your money? I taught you better than that," Brody bit out with disgust.

Flynn glanced down at his cards. Hell. He'd bet everything on a pair of fours. He'd thought he had three of a kind, but turned out he didn't.

Mike shuffled the cards and shook his head. "I know that look. Little brother has a woman on the brain."

Brody said nothing.

"Yep," Cam chimed in. "I'll bet she's pretty, has long, silky red hair, and a pair of—"

"Watch it, asshole."

Cam grinned. "Pair of roommates just as pretty."

Flynn felt like a grade-A fool. So much for keeping the teasing between them.

"Gee, Flynn," Cam asked with mock innocence. "What's it like to be so in looovvee?"

The others laughed and made kissing noises.

"You guys are so immature."

Mike laughed especially hard at that. He had to wipe his eyes. "Oh man, I needed that. Speaking of immature, answer your cell once in a while, dumbass. Mom has been calling nonstop trying to reach you, and I know this because she's bugging me about it. Why aren't you calling her back?"

"You know why." Flynn glared at the dickheads laughing at him. "She's throwing me at Maddie and waiting to hear wedding bells. Christ. Okay. The woman's a knockout, and I like her. Doesn't mean I'm tripping down an aisle or anything. Why don't one of you get a date and give Mom something to really talk about. Like an honest-to-God miracle." He laughed at that one, pleased when the three of them suddenly found him less than amusing.

"Let's see," he continued. "Cam hasn't been laid since the Steelers last won the Super Bowl. Um, 2009 ring a bell?"

Cam flipped him the finger.

"Brody is downright pathetic, which we all know."

"I don't kiss and tell." Brody stuck his nose in the air.

"That's because you're too busy teaching Colin your tricks. You know, Mike told me that the other day the kid was practicing next door. Bragged to Abby about how Ubie is teaching him all kinds of things."

Brody didn't look happy at the news. But he masked it well. To Cam and Mike, he probably seemed annoyed to be on Mike's radar. But Flynn knew he had a thing for Abby.

"And let's not get started on Mike," Flynn added in a louder voice to be heard. The others watched him with two parts glee, one very large part aggravation.

"Flynn, shut it," Mike growled.

"Mike, hometown hero and all-around good guy, is soon going to join the priesthood, to make dear ol' da so vera happy."

The others laughed. Mike swore. "Your fucking accent sounds more like you just walked off the short bus than Irish, dickhead. And in case you've forgotten where you come from, we're Scottish."

"Sure thing, Laird Michael. Of course you'd be more than familiar with our Scottish heritage. Sword, bare chest, kilts, and all."

Mike flushed. "Shut up, Flynn."

"What's wrong, my big strapping lad? Don't want the guys to know about—"

Mike tackled him to the floor and put him in a headlock in seconds. Flynn felt faint from lack of oxygen. In a low whisper, Mike threatened, "You breathe a word of that, I'll make you eat through a straw out your ass."

Unable to finish the taunt, Flynn tapped him and mangled an "okay."

Once released, he kept his mouth shut. If Mike didn't want the others to know he'd once modeled for a romance cover, who was he to say?

"I have *got* to figure out what you have on him." Brody shook his head. "Whatever it is, it's still strong."

Flynn coughed, trying to find his voice. "Fucking bruiser."

"That's right." The smugness had returned. Mike cracked his knuckles and looked at Cam and Brody. "Anyone else?"

Cam looked bored by it all. "If we're just going to watch some sap get pummeled, why not turn on the championship? Some mixed martial arts is better than Flynn strangling on the kitchen floor."

"Ass." Flynn glared.

Mike nodded. "Not sure who's fighting tonight, but I'm game. Brody, grab the food. Cam, the beer. And don't make a mess." The guys grabbed their assigned items and dashed into the living room, joined by the sound of the television.

Before Flynn could escape, Mike grabbed him by the collar and pulled him back, choking him again. "You okay?"

Annoyed, he pushed his brother away. "I'm not delicate, you big bull. I'm fine, I—"

His phone buzzed. Hell. His mother had taken to texting him now to get his attention.

"Might as well answer it. She won't stop until you do." Mike's resignation bespoke experience.

Biting the bullet, Flynn pulled out his phone and read his latest text. He barely contained his shout of triumph. *Finally*, she'd called him. "Hot damn. I'm going to the movies. Later, losers."

She waited for him down the street, and he had a brief fantasy of picking up a sexy hooker who would promise to do anything and everything he asked for a buck. He pulled up next to her and rolled down his window. Holy shit, she'd packed a bag. Would he be setting himself up by hoping she'd spend the night?

"Do me a favor," he said when she moved to open the door.

She stopped. "What?"

"Lean closer so I can see you."

She did, and to his delight, he could see cleavage and the delicate cups of a black lace bra.

"Now ask me what I want, and tell me how much it'll cost me."

"How much it—" She burst into laughter and entered the car. "Funny guy. First the phone sex, now this. You *should* be paying me, you know. I only look this good through perseverance and by avoiding pasta."

"From what I hear, you're not missing much, especially if Vanessa's cooking."

She cringed. "Yikes. I take it Colin filled you in on his dinner the other night?"

"Don't get me wrong, it was nice of Vanessa to feed the kid. But I thought spaghetti noodles were supposed to be soft."

She sighed. "They are. That's why I had a peanut butter and jelly sandwich that night for dinner." She glanced out the window as they drove. "I didn't thank you before, but what you said about my mom helped. So thanks." Turning to face him again, she smiled.

God, she looked so pretty sitting there so close to him. "I—"

"So I was thinking we could see a movie at your place." She sidled closer, as close as the seat belt would allow. "And we could see something I picked out."

"Sure." He swallowed, hoping against hope he hadn't misread the situation. What if by texting him about a movie, she actually meant they should watch a movie? "Ah, what's in the bag?"

"I thought I might spend the night. But if you have plans, I could…"

"*No*."

She glanced at him in surprise.

"I mean, no, no plans. I have plenty of space for you to stay." *And plenty of condoms if we need them.*

Chapter 10

Fifteen long minutes later, he pulled into his parking space and walked with her up the stairs toward his unit. They entered and, after a few minutes, sat together on the couch, ready for the picture to start. In his back pocket, he had two foil packets. He'd also put his phone far away from him on the kitchen counter, his ringer on silent.

"So what's the movie?"

She shushed him, and he crossed his eyes at her but fell silent. He made no overt moves, though his body couldn't help hardening each time she moved on the couch and brushed against him. She wore a thin button-down purple shirt and jean shorts, and her sandals sat a small distance away by the front door. Even her toenails had a sexy red polish, one that matched her trimmed red fingernails.

Shadows caught on her sculpted calves when she crossed her ankles in front of her. She leaned forward and he caught tantalizing glimpses of her back and midriff. He wanted so much to kiss her stomach and trail his tongue down her slender frame.

Fuck, he ached. He shifted in his seat, trying to relieve the pressure on his balls.

"…hope it's okay."

What had she just said? "Sure, whatever."

Then some chick's mournful crooning polluted his

speakers, and two women ran to each other on a beach, crying and laughing.

He swung incredulous eyes her way. "You brought a chick flick? To actually watch?"

She frowned. "I told you I wanted to see a movie. What did you think I meant?"

He didn't want to ruin any possible chances for sex later on. "Nothing."

A few seconds passed before he noticed the smile she tried to hide behind her hand.

"What?"

She cleared her throat. "Nothing. I just love this movie. It's so sad, but such a great film about the bonds of female friendship when the brunette dies and her best friend raises her daughter."

Probably too much to ask that the women took off their clothes and went down on each other before one of them died.

He leaned his head back on the couch, wondering if she'd notice if he fell asleep. After a while, he glanced over and froze.

Maddie's blouse lay unbuttoned, exposing a black bra that showed more than it covered. The transparent cups showed off her plump nipples. But what killed him were her fingers pinching one bud into standing tall. Her other hand... *fuck me sideways*... was moving beneath her shorts. She'd unbuttoned them, and he could see matching sheer material over her fingers plunging into her pussy.

"Mmm."

He could barely breathe.

She tilted her head back. "I'm so hot."

"Jesus." Flynn knelt between her legs and pulled down her shorts in one move. Then he eased her panties down and watched her finger-fuck herself. "Keep going, baby. Don't stop."

He ripped off his shirt and took off the rest of his clothes in seconds. Flynn pushed her shirt off her shoulders but didn't want to impede her hungry fingers. He noticed the front closure on her bra and unfastened it. He didn't ask but latched on to her breast like a starving man.

When the contact put his cock in touch with her thigh, he felt her hand move, and then slick fingers circled his shaft.

He groaned and moved to her other breast.

"Oh, Flynn. That's good, so good."

Her throaty encouragement made it difficult to stay the course. Especially when he knew her fingers had been deep in her sweet pussy. He wanted to slide inside her, to come hard in that hot core. He shivered with the need, pressing inexorably forward.

Forcing himself to release her breast, he tried to put some space between them. He sounded like gravel but couldn't help himself. "Put a condom on me or I'm coming inside you right the fuck now."

"Mmm." She reached up and kissed his neck, then nibbled her way to his ear. "Where is it? Get me the condom. Let me roll it over you. Every thick inch of you."

He pulled back to look at this hedonistic creature—someone straight out of his deepest fantasies. She seemed too good to be true, and though he knew he shouldn't trust his hormones, he could feel himself being led by his dick.

"What's wrong, Flynn? Don't you want to be inside me?"

"Yeah, I do. Stand up." He didn't give her a chance but yanked her to her feet in front of him and sucked her clit into his mouth. She keened and gripped his hair. He groaned. "Oh yeah. That's good."

He pulled her ass close, running his fingers over her seam and teasing with little prods to her anus. Her clit was hard and tight, a ripe fruit ready to burst all over his tongue. Flynn devoured her, kneading her ass as he licked and stroked. He shoved his tongue as far up her pussy as it would go, not getting deep enough inside.

"Flynn. Please," she begged, out of breath and trembling. "Make me come."

He doubled his efforts, gratified when she smoothed her hands over his hair and clutched his shoulders. She dug her nails into his skin, and the pain nearly got him off.

"Flynn. *Flynn*." She shattered, coming all over his lips and tongue as her pleasure took her over. In a daze, she moved where he positioned her, bent over the back of his couch while he hurried to shove a condom over himself.

"Now feel it while I fuck you." He rammed himself inside her, sliding right through the slick, tight passage. "Your pussy is so hot, baby. So fucking perfect."

He fucked her, deep strokes taking him balls deep before pulling all the way out. Each time he slammed inside her, his balls slapped her and she moaned his name. He couldn't be sure, but he swore she tightened around him again.

The cries coming from her throat were soft sobs of

pleasure. So incredibly sexy because she uttered them in breathless pleas. No fake orgasm, but the real deal from a woman he'd already satisfied. She made him feel so fucking good.

"Oh God. Oh God, I'm coming again. Yes, *yes*." She shook beneath him as he neared his own end.

The indescribable desire blossomed as he gripped her hips and surged into her time and time again. Claiming, taking, fucking until he couldn't stop the swell of ecstasy that shot out of him in jets of milky seed.

"Christ, Maddie. Oh yeah, take it. Take all of it."

His knees felt weak after he gave her one last push and collapsed on top of her.

Conscious of his weight, he pulled out and took her with him to the floor, lying on the carpet in front of the couch. He couldn't move, exhausted from another out-of-this-world session with Maddie.

"Oh, wow. You just keep getting better." She sounded drowsy.

"Same back at you. Holy shit, Maddie. I could feel you gripping me when you came, right through the condom. It was incredible. My heart won't stop racing."

He wondered if it was possible to fall in love after that kind of heart-hammering sex. He wanted to call it making love, but he'd been as fierce as Maddie seeking her pleasure. Then his.

She grinned and stroked his chest. "You should have seen the look on your face when you thought we were going to watch the movie. I wish I'd had that on tape."

He tickled her until she begged him to stop. "No, you have to say Uncle. Uncle Flynn."

"Uncle Flynn, now stop." She laughed. "Naughty

boy. You aren't my uncle. I thought guys always wanted you to call them 'daddy.'"

He smacked her ass. "Funny. But if we'd had a camera in here, I'd have centered it on you. Then I could watch all over again, the way you came all over my lips, the way you moaned when you came a second time. Beautiful, Maddie. So beautiful."

She blushed but didn't look away from him. Her eyes darkened and she kissed him. Unlike before, this touch felt soft, affectionate. Caring.

He should have run fast and far away. But something inside him softened. Good sex, the woman in his arms, he didn't much care. He only knew he didn't want this feeling to end.

Maddie yawned and woke in unfamiliar surroundings. It took her a minute to remember she'd stayed the night at Flynn's. He had her in his arms, her head on his chest, her body half across his, hugging him like a body pillow. She felt comfortable, cherished even.

At the thought, she tensed. She had a bad feeling she'd started to fall for him. As in, moving from *like* into something approaching that other L word. The one that didn't seem to work for the women in the Gardner family.

The light streaming through his window indicated early morning. She figured she might as well get up, though she felt no rush to leave the warmth and safety of his arms.

She pulled her head back and studied him as he slept. He seemed softer, more boyish at rest. His black hair curled around his neck, so soft and thick. She rubbed a few strands between her fingers, taken with their contrasts. Dark against light. His arm bunched and hugged her tighter. A glance at his chest and arms turned her on all over again.

Flynn was so strong. His body didn't have an ounce of fat, unlike hers. Whereas she had softer padding, his chest and legs felt like iron.

And speaking of iron… She turned, putting her back to his front, spooning. He groaned and angled his cock under her ass, prodding first her anus before he moved and fitted himself against her warm, moist opening. Though conscious they needed a condom, some crazy part of her wanted, just once, to feel him inside her.

Internal warnings of disease and the slim chance of pregnancy faded under her desire, and she pushed back, taking the head of his cock inside her.

"Maddie," he groaned and pressed his large hand against her belly, pushing deeper inside her. "Oh yeah. You're so hot." He continued to move until he seated the entirety of his length inside her. A familiar rhythm took over, and she had a hard time telling him to stop when he rubbed her clit with one hand and pushed on her belly with the other, thrusting in and out and rushing her impending orgasm.

"Condom," she whispered, despite wanting nothing more than for him to come inside her. So sexy, so natural to feel a part of each other.

"Yeah." He continued to pump, and then he ceased. "Wait," he croaked when she shifted. He held his breath and then slowly let it out. He withdrew from her body in a rush. "Don't move," he growled. He leaned back, fumbled in the drawer, and then she felt his hands under her, between her legs. "There we go. Again." This time he pulled her over his sheath-covered shaft and rocked in and out of her.

His fingers plucked her clit as he thrust, and she tightened around him until he couldn't mistake her impending orgasm for anything else. His thrusts grew faster, slapping against her with intensity.

"Yeah, with me. Now, baby." He grunted and ground his fingers against her. The dual sensation of being filled while he stimulated her clit sent her over the edge, and they came together in a loud, blissful moan.

Sometime later, he stirred and planted kisses along her shoulder and neck. "Helluva way to wake up." He sucked hard and nipped the base of her neck.

"Ouch."

"Just wanted to remind you I'm here."

She laughed and tightened her inner walls, and he groaned. "Hard to forget when you're inside me."

"Yeah, deep." He kissed her shoulder again. "I've never been inside a woman without protection before." His admission thrilled her. "It was a close thing, Maddie. I wanted to come inside you really, really bad." When she said nothing, he added in a softer voice, "You don't have to worry. I'm clean, and I pulled out before I was close enough to, ah, fill you."

She sighed. "It was my fault. I was awake. I should have said something. But I..." Should she admit she'd wanted it? Would that change their relationship from casual to something deeper? Could fucking each other's brains out be considered *casual*? Right now, she and Flynn connected. Physically, he remained a part of her.

But emotionally, she worried she might be growing to like him too much.

I can do this. I can keep a distance and still be friends.

He stroked her hair with a gentle touch. "What's wrong, Maddie? You can tell me. Was I too rough? Did I freak you out? I swear I meant to pull out sooner, you just felt so good."

"No. I don't blame you." *Let it go.* "It was perfect." *Tell him you're on the Pill. Let him know it's safe to go all the way without worries.* The imp on her shoulder continued to push. But she knew if they started having sex without protection, she would count on him being totally loyal to her, without question. It would feel like the start of a real relationship. And the thought of having to give Flynn the man-up or man-out speech and watching him kick her out made her want to cry.

"Maddie?" He stopped stroking her hair.

"I don't think I can move." She groaned and felt him relax. "You feel so good inside me. I got cocky."

"I think I got cocky."

She pulled away from him and turned over. She leaned up off his chest and looked down at him. So handsome. A thoroughly sated male looking up at her as if he intended on keeping her in his bed for the rest of the day. Man, she had it bad. And by it, she reminded herself, she meant *lust*.

"A comedian, eh?" The urge to lean down and press her lips to his grew. So she dragged herself off him. "Dibs on the shower. Sucker," she threw over her shoulder and laughed into the bathroom.

Flynn cooked them both breakfast after joining her in the shower. The man should have been named Mr.

Insatiable. He'd brought her to climax again while he'd jerked off, and watching him masturbate climbed the list of things to fantasize about when she next found herself flying solo.

As they ate—now clean and dressed—at his kitchen island, he asked, "So you sticking around, or do you want me to take you home?" He acted as if the decision didn't bother him either way.

"Well, I don't want to put a kink in any plans you might have."

He grinned at the word *kink*.

"Grow up."

"You know, that's just what I told Brody the other day."

"Speaking of Brody, I hope all that banging and those curses I heard on the phone didn't cost too much."

"Nah. We discovered a few more leaks than we'd thought we'd have to handle. Then Brody had a problem holding on to the hot water heater, which he wouldn't have if he'd waited—like I told him to—until after I called you." He grabbed their dishes and started cleaning up, to her amazement. "I would have called you sooner, but I didn't want to bug you. I'm not clingy, I swear. But I had to know how it went with Aunt Linda. She's a real pistol."

She didn't know how she felt about him trying to put her at ease. A part of her wanted to thank him for sticking to their agreement. No strings, a casual relationship. Sex on the side. But another part of her wanted to ask what the hell was wrong with him, that he'd let a woman like *her* run free without even trying to start a relationship.

The poor guy couldn't win either way, and the rational part of her brain forced her to accept and stick by the rules she'd first dictated. Besides, Flynn had agreed with her. He didn't want a girlfriend right now. Who was she to assume otherwise?

Trying to play it cool, Maddie shrugged. "I like your aunt. She's a savvy businesswoman. And she offered me some help. Told me her son would move any... What?"

He frowned. "She promised Theo to me first. My nephew is built like a linebacker, but he's young. He needs direction, so Aunt Linda asked me to try interning him as another plumber on the team. I figured to start him with us next week."

"Want to flip for him?"

He grinned. "I don't know. He'll take one look at you and leave me in the dust. You'll need to watch yourself. The little jerk thinks he's the reincarnation of Romeo."

"Little? I thought you said he was six-two. That's bigger than you, right?"

He took a hand out of the dishwater and pointed a soapy finger at her. "I'm six-two and a half, little lady. Theo's a teenager and not nearly as buff." He flexed, showing off muscles and shooting bubbles across the floor. "The kid will be lucky to one day have guns this big."

She batted her lashes. "Why Flynn, are you jealous of your *much* younger cousin?"

He snorted. "Keep it up, sexy. Hell yeah, I'm jealous. While I'm laying pipe next week, and I don't mean laying pipe the way I did this morning," he laughed at her blush, "I'll be arms deep in mucky water, and that kid will be tripping all over himself looking at your ass while he tries to follow orders."

She giggled and wanted to smack herself. Maddie didn't giggle. Ever. Clearing her throat, she conceded victory to Flynn. "Well, if you can't do without him, I'll find another strong, strapping man to watch my ass and move furniture."

Flynn narrowed his eyes. "Nah, take the kid. He won't give you any problems. If he even hints at being lippy, threaten him with me or my aunt. Or Mike. The cousins are all afraid of him."

"Of your teddy bear of a brother? Why?"

He grinned. "Never mind." He continued to wash the dishes while she wiped down the counters and the center island where they'd eaten. The domesticity of the arrangement oddly pleased her. Flynn didn't ask her to help; she wanted to. Not like at home where Vanessa, an autocrat even in the kitchen, would have ordered her to clean up.

"So you staying or what?"

She raised a brow. "You asking or what?"

"Oh, so it's in my court? Sure. I want you to stay. Take off all your clothes and sit up on the island. Then spread your legs and—"

"Flynn." She felt her cheeks heat.

"Or we could go walk around town. I could get you flowers to celebrate your victory over my aunt."

"It's not a victory. And I don't need flowers." Oh man, she was a sucker for flowers.

"Well, if I did get you some, not that I will, we'd be talking about a *friendly* bunch of flowers. Nothing serious." Did he continually mention their casual arrangement to remind not just her, but himself as well? She admitted she liked the idea he might have to keep reminding himself to keep it light. That meant he wanted their relationship to go deeper, even though they wouldn't. Unless, of course, she'd created all his feelings out of thin air, because she couldn't help her own deepening attraction. *I'm such a neurotic, needy woman. Ugh.*

She cleared her throat. "Right. Casual friends. Who have sex sometimes."

"Not just sex. Orgasmic, screaming, begging, wet, messy sex. Between friends."

She huffed with laughter, and Flynn winked. "Now how about you find me some quality chocolate, lady? After all, I need to keep up with my sweets. If you're not going to give me any of that sugar between your legs, I might as well have some that'll rot my teeth."

"Fine. Let's go." She tried to stop smiling and glare at him. "But no hand holding."

"Gotcha."

Chapter 11

SO FAR SO GOOD. MADDIE GLANCED AT FLYNN OUT OF the corner of her eye as they strolled through Pike's Place Market. He hadn't tried to do more than walk with her as they looked over the assorted crafts on the tables. At the far end of the market, tie-dye shirts, Seattle prints, and beaded jewelry occupied table after table with a few children's toys and crafts interspersed here and there.

Flynn paused, and she stopped with him.

"A googley-eyed frog?" The small fuzzy stuffed animal had eyeballs that jiggled when he shook it.

He turned to her and grinned. "Colin would like this." He withdrew a few bills from his wallet.

"Yeah right. Admit it; you're buying it so *you* can play with it."

He gave her a sly wink. "You think?" He picked up another one. "Green or blue?"

"Why not one of each? That way you'll have yours when Colin keeps his."

With a chuckle, he purchased both. The salesman handed him a bag and they continued walking through the crowd.

"See anything you like?" he asked when she skirted another table of silk tees.

"I'm a window shopper. I buy only after I've looked at everything."

He groaned. "I know your type only too well. When

I was little, my mom used to drag us around with her
when she went shopping. She'd spend all day looking
for clothes, then she'd go back and buy the first thing
she'd tried on. Used to drive me nuts. Hours of torturous
trolling for jeans and shirts—not a toy in sight—that
could have been prevented. I should be in therapy."

"That's called doing it right." She dodged a small
child barreling through the crowd, his mother hard on
his heels. "We didn't have much money growing up,
so it was easier to pretend I could afford something but
didn't want to buy it. I liked to think I was choosey,
when in reality I was just poor."

"Church mouse poor? Or middle-class, too-many-
kids poor?"

"Church mouse."

"Bummer." He reached for the rose a vendor held
out to him and handed the saleswoman a buck. Then he
turned and presented it to Maddie. "Here you go, mouse.
I *choose* to buy this for you."

"Thanks, Flynn." Oddly touched, she accepted the
smooth-stemmed rose and tried to distance herself. She
nodded at him, queen to peasant, and continued brows-
ing. "You may continue, sirrah."

"Come on, princess." They walked more before he
continued. "You said something before, how it was just
you and your mom. No brothers or sisters?"

He didn't sound as if he could imagine such an
existence. Then again, with his family, he probably
couldn't. "Nope. Just me and my mom. We'd visit
Vanessa and her family most summers. Her mom and
my mom are sisters. But we never stayed long. My
grandmother would spend our vacations harassing my

mother. We visited mostly so I could see what few relatives I had."

"Why'd your grandmother screw with your mom?"

"Well, my mom got pregnant at sixteen. My father didn't stick around, and she ended up having me with another year left of high school." Maddie sighed. Sad, familiar story. "She spent her growing-up years raising me, all by herself. She lived with my grandparents only long enough to get a GED, a job, and enough to afford a sitter."

"She sounds hard-core." Flynn rested his hand on her lower back and nudged her toward the outside of the aisle when a group of pushy tourists bustled by with cameras in hand. "Must be why you work so hard. Apple falling from the tree, and all that crap."

She laughed. "And all that crap. That about sums it up."

They stopped to watch the guys at the fish market hawking salmon and perch while they threw the fish around.

"This is such a fun place." Maddie didn't often come down here, not crazy at the idea of managing the market crowds. Many in the city viewed the marketplace as touristy, and she'd never been one to waste her time with sightseeing.

Flynn drew her closer to be heard over the burst of laughter and commotion around them. "I have a confession to make. Once, when I was six or seven, I came down here with my folks. When they weren't looking, I snuck over here and bought a tiny fish with my allowance. I hid the thing in Mike's room, and the stench got so bad my mom had to fumigate the house."

"Flynn." She couldn't help laughing. "Why would you do that?"

"He stole one of my baseball cards. Guys can get territorial about stuff like that."

She shook her head. "The highlight of my youth was spent working alongside my mom. We'd clean houses during the summers, when I wasn't in school. All money under the table, of course. The closest I got to your kind of trouble was when I stole the head off a Barbie from this girl I hated. She used to bully me at school. We had to clean her house, and I was so embarrassed that my mother had to pick up the little snot's socks. So when I saw Malibu Barbie, so helpless, so alone, just sitting there…"

"Nice." He nuzzled her cheek with his. He pulled away, but before he moved back, she swore he kissed the top of her head. "I knew we had more in common than you liking me. You have a mean streak, Maddie. I dig that."

He tugged her with him past the fish guys outside onto Pike Street.

"Wait a minute. What did you mean about us both liking you?"

He gripped his bag in one hand and grabbed her hand in the other.

"Hey, no hand holding."

"Come on, slowpoke. Consider my hand a leash. And about us both liking me, what's the problem here? I like me. Do you like me?"

"Not at the moment," she grumbled and fought a smile. For some reason, whenever he started to get on her nerves, he'd turn around and make her laugh. "But I think you have it backward. We both like *me*."

"Now that I can't argue." He cast a lingering glance

over her body. "In fact, I'd like to *like* you again right now. How about that alley? It's not too crowded…"

She socked him in the arm, taking care not to damage the sweet-smelling rose in her hand. "Is sex all you ever think about?"

"Pretty much."

"You're such a guy." But she couldn't complain. He really knew what to do between the sheets.

He stopped with her in front of a confectioner's shop and murmured in her ear, "If it were up to me, you'd be up against that brick wall around the corner." His voice lowered. "Your legs around my waist, my cock inside that hot pussy."

"Flynn." She blushed, turned on yet embarrassed someone might overhear him. Fortunately, people continued to breeze by. No one gave them a second glance.

"It's your fault. You bring out the bad boy in me. But that's actually a good thing, according to the magazines out there." He pulled her with him into the candy shop. "Eighty-five percent of women polled prefer the bad boy."

The pretty young woman behind the counter grinned.

To her, he asked, "Am I right?"

"Depends on where you got your stats."

"*Cosmo*."

The girl nodded. "They never lie."

"For God's sake." Maddie yanked her hand from the man and stalked to the decadent truffles on display behind glass. "Wait a minute. Why are you reading *Cosmo*?"

"I found it at Cam's place the last time I was over. The hotshot thinks by reading what the opposite sex reads, he'll have insights the rest of his 'idiot' brothers don't."

"Well, he got the idiot part right."

Flynn scowled at her and bumped her aside.

"Watch it."

"What are you looking at? Oh, truffles. Yum."

"You like chocolate?"

The girl behind the case beamed at them through the glass. "We offer the finest hand-crafted chocolates in Seattle."

Flynn smiled at the girl and asked, "Which are your favorites?"

He should have been asking Maddie. What the hell did he care what some young flirt with a bad sense of style—hello, too much eyeliner—thought?

"Hmm. I like the mocha dreams. But the vanilla bourbon swirls are popular too."

"Maddie? What about you?" *Finally*, he asked her.

"What about me?" She hadn't meant to snap, but she didn't like him chatting up the girl, who was definitely old enough to appreciate a man like Flynn.

He smothered the smile but not fast enough to hide it from her.

"Something funny?" she asked, ice in her voice.

"Nope. What kind do you want, baby? My treat."

Calling her *baby* like that. What an ass. Yet her ire faded as the girl seemed to understand they weren't just palling around. About time. "Strawberry, the vanilla bourbon, and a lime twist. That one, in the white chocolate. "

"Those are good too," Miss Perky offered.

Flynn nodded. "We'll take two of each." He made more small talk with the girl while Maddie looked around. When younger, she never would have imagined dragging her mother into a place like this. Four dollars a truffle? For one piece of candy? Yet here she was, twenty-seven years old and waiting for someone to buy her not just one piece but three.

She smiled, a sense of accomplishment just there within reach. Sure, Flynn was buying the candy, but if Maddie had wanted, *she* could have bought them. Window shopping with the added benefit of getting the prize.

Flynn had the girl add the box of chocolates to the bag holding the frogs he'd purchased. He said good-bye before latching on to Maddie's hand again.

"Bye," Maddie said over her shoulder before Flynn dragged her outside. She didn't protest his hold until they were out of sight of the store. Then she tried to pull free. "Didn't I say no hand holding?"

He immediately let go, which should have made her happy. Instead, she missed his warmth. "Sorry. I was just trying to make you feel better. You seemed a little jealous inside the store." The twinkle of mischief in his eyes annoyed her.

"Screw you, McCauley. I wasn't jealous."

He fell into step beside her as she walked down the street and turned onto First. "Of course not."

"I wasn't." She felt like a fool. She had been jealous, and after spouting all those rules about them keeping their distance from each other and remaining just friends. "It just seems to me that if we're together, even as *friends*, it probably looks like we're dating or something. And it's rude to come on to someone else's boyfriend, right there in front of a person."

She knew she wasn't making sense.

Flynn shifted his hold on his bag. "Sure, Maddie. You weren't jealous. Not at all. Not even a little bit."

"Oh, shut up. Come on, let's go to lunch." This time she dragged him down the street.

Twenty minutes later, they sat on the balcony of The Pink Door and watched the calm waters of Elliott Bay while a few boats drifted by. The day couldn't have been more perfect. Overhead, a scatter of cottony clouds stood out against the baby-blue sky. The sun shone in bands of orange, red, and pink behind a few puffs of white, lending the water a sparkle that rippled as watercraft slid through the calm waters. A light breeze wafted past them, bringing the scent of garlic and basil on the salt air.

She closed her eyes, awash in the moment, and started when warm lips covered hers.

The kiss lasted a second, and she opened her eyes to see Flynn staring at her in bemusement.

"What was that for?"

"Because I can," he said with familiar arrogance, but the smile curling his lips gentled his words. His eyes seemed darker, more mysterious as he watched her, and she surprised herself to realize she'd actually enjoyed her day with him.

"This still doesn't mean we're dating," she blurted, panicked and not sure why.

"Sure thing." He didn't react other than to drink the beer he'd ordered and stare at her.

"Something wrong?"

"I was wondering something."

Aha. The third degree. She'd been waiting for it. "Go ahead. Say whatever's on your tiny little mind."

He chuckled. "You're sexy when you're mean, did you know that?" He pulled a lock of her hair.

"Ow."

"I can be mean too. Now shut up and listen."

He obviously wasn't trying to charm her anymore. She relaxed, knowing they'd achieved balance. Just sex, a casual companionship, friends. *No more deeper feelings*—so she kept telling herself.

"Listening." She took a sip of her wine, letting it linger on her tongue while the breeze pushed the scent of stuffed mushrooms nearer. Which reminded her, they still hadn't delved into that box of chocolates yet…

"You and your mom are close, right?"

She answered warily. "Yeah."

"So why did you move so far away from home? To get away from the area you grew up in? From her? And before you tell me it's none of my business, I did confess that deep dark secret of the hidden fish to you. To this day my mother still thinks Brody did it."

She opened her mouth to answer, then closed it. "Brody? You knew him back when you were six?"

"We think of him as the blond McCauley. He grew up with us and shared a room with me until we hit high school. But that's another story. Stop stalling and answer the question."

Curious about him all over again, she decided to answer. She didn't exactly have secrets she needed to hide. "I love my mom to death. Hell, I've spent the last three years trying to get her to move in with me, back in Philly and now here. But she loves home and won't move. I wanted to get away from the area. Not that it's bad, it's just so…so…" She couldn't think of a word to describe it.

"So East Coast?"

"Yeah. Not that there's anything wrong with it, but if you've been there, you notice a different vibe in the air. At least it feels that way to me."

"You don't see me arguing. I love it here. I grew up in Seattle and intend on living the rest of my life here. Not that I'm against travel or vacationing around women in bikinis. Something about the beach really calls to me."

She grinned. "I'll bet."

He smiled with her. "But I like it here. I'm close to my family. Not that we have to always be together. I'm no momma's boy."

"You sure?"

He sighed. "Okay, so the woman is demanding. I try to be a good son, but I don't need her approval on every-thing I do. Hell, you wouldn't believe how she reacted to my last girlfriend just because she danced—which isn't important." He coughed. "I was just curious about your mom."

Danced? As in, a stripper? She didn't know, and didn't want to know. Especially when another niggle of jealousy flitted through her brain. "My mom, right. Well, in a nutshell, I love my mother, but I think she works too damn hard. She's proud, won't accept help from me at all, and generally thinks she knows how I should live my life better than I do."

"We talking about your mother or mine?" he asked wryly.

"Both, I guess. At least your dad seems nice. I was talking to him at the barbecue. You all look just like him," she teased. "I never knew my father. He got my mother pregnant then left. Haven't heard from him since."

Silence surrounded their table. But not to be put off, Flynn persisted. Like Vanessa, she thought with amusement, he didn't have a kill switch. "She never asked him for child support or anything?" He frowned. "I know he was just a kid, but hell, so was she."

"Nope. She never asked him for a dime. Michelle Gardner doesn't like to accept help from anyone. Very self-sufficient. And stubborn too." Her mother still refused to visit Maddie until she could afford it, unwilling to let Maddie pay for her plane ticket.

"Gee, Maddie. Stubborn and self-sufficient. Sound familiar?"

She would have told him something vulgar, involving his head and his ass, but the waiter arrived. He left them a large plate of appetizers they'd decided to share.

While she enjoyed the appetizer, it took her a moment to realize Flynn hadn't eaten. He was staring at her.

"Hmm?" she managed around a mouthful.

"I like watching you eat." The roughness of his voice reminded her of their night on the phone. Sexy, masculine, arousing. "Almost as good as watching you come."

She choked and needed her water to wash it down. "Damn it. Don't do that."

"Sorry." The chuckle following the apology laid waste to his sincerity. "It's your fault. You're too pretty and sexy with your mouth full. Makes me think of other things that should be between those lips."

Damn if she didn't feel a flutter low in her belly. "I don't know how you do it, but now I'll never look at mushrooms the same way again. And you've ruined me for my cell phone."

He seemed entirely too pleased with himself. "Good."

Then he changed the subject completely. To her surprise, they spent the next hour talking about her and her plans for Gardner's.

They left the restaurant after she paid the bill, at her insistence, and spent the rest of the day walking around town together. They went in and out of shops, where Flynn actually encouraged her to try on a few skirts and even shoes. She dithered over a few purses she'd been wanting for a while and settled her mind on a blue leather bag. When her business broke even, *because it would*, she told herself, she'd be back to buy that bag. Or one like it, if it took her another ten years to see ends meet.

"Maddie?"

They'd walked their way back up Third Avenue toward Queen Anne Avenue, each determined to outdo the other. A long trip home, but a pleasant one. Before she could overtake him up the final hill toward Queen Anne, he pulled her with him to a stone wall outside an apartment building, and they sat for a breather.

"Okay. I could use a rest. And a snack." She glanced at the bag, then back at Flynn.

He dug into it and took out the chocolates. But he refused to let her pick her own. "Let me." He pulled out a lime truffle and held it to her lips.

She took a bite, unable to look away from him as she chewed. The flavor burst on her tongue, sweet and tart, yet it was the intensity on Flynn's face that held her captive.

He ate the rest of the chocolate and blinked. "Damn, that's good."

She nodded, wishing she could put her confusing

emotions into words. Aroused, scared, baffled, she only knew she yearned for something more from Flynn, something she didn't need and shouldn't want.

Flynn wiped her lower lip and pulled his thumb into his mouth. "You missed a crumb." He licked his lips, and she wanted to kiss him, to see if he tasted like chocolate and lime. "Thanks for hanging with me today. I had fun."

"Me too."

"And I wanted to give you this. Don't make a big deal out of it," he warned and reached into his back pocket for something. He withdrew a slender gift wrapped in crinkled blue tissue paper. To her surprise, Flynn looked nervous.

More than curious, she opened the present and stared at a slender, silver card case. Engraved on the front was the word *Gardner's*.

"Consider it a business celebration. My mom got me one when we opened McSons, but I didn't have the heart to tell her no guy would be caught dead with something like that, especially not one in my line of work. But a snazzy designer like you? I think it fits." The smile in his eyes lingered.

Touched far more than she wanted to admit, Maddie kissed him and clutched the gift tight. "Thanks, Flynn. This means a lot."

He winked. "But don't think this means we're dating," he mimicked in a high-pitched voice, throwing her words back at her in a playful tone.

She couldn't help the heat from rushing to her cheeks, feeling flustered and out of sorts. They'd spent a perfectly normal day together, and it had been more than fun. Now this. So thoughtful, he made her want to cry.

Saturday evening approached, and she wanted to enjoy the rest of her weekend with him. *Clingy, Maddie. Back off. Like he said, we're not dating.* "Flynn, I—"

"Hold on." Before she could rise, he closed the tiny gap between them, exciting her and unnerving her at the same time.

"But I…"

"Hush." He kissed her. Unlike the others, this kiss didn't instill sexual urgency, but a soothing sense of belonging. Affectionate and tender, Flynn didn't even try to push his tongue into her mouth. He ended the kiss before it could truly begin and freaked her the hell out—because she'd *liked* the closeness.

Before she could complain that this felt all too much like a date, Flynn stood. He pulled her to her feet, had the nerve to slap her on the ass, and started back up the hill without her. "Come on, slacker."

She blinked, not sure what had just happened. But no way in hell would Flynn McCauley leave her in the dust. After tucking the precious gift into her pocket, she hustled to catch his long strides and yanked him back by tugging on the back pocket of his jeans.

Shining eyes full of laughter met her gaze. "You're so easy. Afraid I'm going to go all"—he used air quotes—"'relationship' on you?" He snorted. "You should be so lucky."

"Oh? I think it's *you* who should be so lucky." Irritated but relieved at the same time, she increased her pace. "And if you think I'm giving you a ride home after that sneaky kiss, think again."

They taunted each other back to her house and arrived laughing and out of breath.

"You're not as out of shape as you look." Flynn pretended to measure her ass.

"Jerk. I should say the same about you, but your fat ego would only get in the way." Yeah, in the way of his thick thighs, firm ass, and broad chest. And those arms. She bent over to catch her breath and look away from his sexy body.

The card case burned a hole in her pocket. She wanted to pull it out and stare at it, then see if she could capture Flynn's reflection if she stood closer, stupidly wanting to hold on to some part of him, if even for a few seconds.

"You're a good sport, Maddie." Flynn reached into his bag and handed her the box of chocolates. And the blue frog. "I'd have given you green, but you did mention you prefer blue."

She shook the frog and watched those stupid eyes bobble. "You're torturing me, aren't you?"

He grinned. "Yeah. Because now when you see him, you'll think of me. First the cell phone, the card case, the frog. Before you know it, I'll be everywhere. And you'll be begging for more Flynn. *More Flynn, oh yes, more…*"

She slapped a hand over his mouth when Mike walked outside his house and scowled at the sight of them together. "Keep it down, genius."

Flynn glanced at Mike and groaned. "Damn. Maybe Mr. Green can save me." He pulled out the green frog and made it dance.

She started laughing and couldn't stop. She laughed so hard she cried, and he just grinned at her. When she collected herself again, she knew what had been nagging at her. "Oh man, I just remembered I left my stuff at your place."

He shrugged. "I'll bring it by tomorrow. Don't worry, I'm not insisting you stay the night. I would, but then you might think I wanted a 'relationship.'" More air quotes. "I have to rest up for the family dinner tomorrow night, anyway. Just pray Mike doesn't out me about you, or my mother will grill *me* for dinner."

She batted her lashes. "Momma's boy."

"Witch." He had the nerve to pop her on the ass again while Mike watched them from next door. "Now go inside while I try to mollify Mike."

"Wow. Mollify. That's a big word, Flynn. I didn't know you had it in you."

"Now, now, Maddie. We both know I had it in *you*." He left with a knowing smirk.

She chuckled all the way into the house. Once inside, she pulled the card case out. She clutched it and the frog, no longer sure how to feel.

Chapter 12

THE FOLLOWING FRIDAY, MADDIE DUSTED OFF HER hands and took great pleasure in her finished work—the Horror on Howe Street, as she'd privately labeled her first big job. Linda had already taken a quick walk-through, and she'd been more than pleased.

Maddie glanced down at the check in her hands, still stunned that she was actually making a go of being her own boss. Her first job, and she'd *nailed* it.

Still high on her success, she treated herself to an iced tea at her favorite coffee shop and basked in the afternoon sun. She'd scored the last table with an umbrella, and thank God for that. Sweat made her shirt cling to her back. Moving furniture, designing, and stressing about the job had taken their toll. She felt greasy, sweaty, and knew her hair probably looked more limp than a dish rag. She could only hope she didn't run into anyone she recognized.

So of course she glanced up and saw the annoying man of her dreams. "Hell."

On the sidewalk coming toward her, Flynn argued with Brody. They both wore stained jeans and work shirts emblazoned with McSons Plumbing in bold blue letters.

On cue, Flynn zeroed in on her, and a huge smile lit his face. He left Brody behind and joined her without asking for an invitation.

"Hey, Maddie. How's it going?"

"I'm celebrating. Linda's house is ready for sale."

"Congrats." Flynn cupped her shoulder and squeezed. "Any problems?"

"Your cousin was a big help. I'm hoping to bribe Theo away from you. And Linda's planning on giving me a lot of work in the future."

Brody joined them. "Hey, Maddie. What's with the big grin?"

Flynn answered for her. "Maddie just nailed the deal with Linda."

"Good job." He grabbed Maddie's drink without asking and took a big swig out of it.

"Ahem. That was mine." She glared at him.

"What's his is mine." Brody winked. "So by extension…"

"Brody," Flynn warned.

"Kidding, kidding." Brody kicked Flynn. "Then go get me something to drink. It's your turn."

She watched Flynn leave, her gaze lingering a little too long on his ass, if the knowing look on Brody's face meant anything.

"So. I hear you spent some time this past weekend with my boy." He nodded to the shop behind them, where Flynn had disappeared. "Should I ask about your intentions?"

She flushed. "You know, you're much more irritating than you look."

He laughed. "I don't know if that's possible." His grin faded. "Flynn says you're mean, sexy, and for me to mind my own fucking business. And yeah, he said 'fucking.' So I'm telling you to go easy on him. He's fragile."

She snorted. "Fragile my ass. Your 'boy' is a lady killer. That grin, those pecs, gimme a break. If I were interested in a relationship—which I'm *not*—I'd be worried I'd get my poor little heart broken. But since he and I are keeping things casual, I'm not worried."

"Casual. Right. Is that woman-speak for fuck-buddies?"

She stared at him, agog. "Do you talk to every woman like this? Or should I consider myself lucky?"

He flushed. "Sorry. I just worry about Flynn. He's my best friend. And I think he really likes you."

She didn't know if she liked Flynn sharing so much with Brody.

As if he read her mind, Brody shook his head. "No. Dumbass won't talk about you. Even at dinner Sunday night, with Bitsy and Pop drilling him, he kept tight-lipped. Of course, I had Colin run interference. He bats those big baby-blue eyes and Bitsy melts."

She smiled. "He's a cute kid. And according to you and Flynn, he's devious."

Brody laughed. "You should see what he can do with a deck of cards. And he's not even six yet!"

Flynn returned with three bottles of water. He set two of them in front of Brody and claimed the last for himself, then sat next to her in a huff. "Tell me you are not hitting on Brody. I could see you two chatting it up like best pals from the inside of the store."

Brody cracked up laughing. "Oh man. All this jealousy. It's like *Days of Our Lives*, only real."

"Relax, Flynn." Maddie ran a hand through her hair, in desperate need of a shower. "I don't think anyone will ever love Brody as much as he loves himself."

Brody looked wounded and drank down one bottle of water before starting on another one. "Well at least I wasn't obviously staring at my girlfriend's rack. Really, dude. We're in public." He smirked.

Flynn cleared his throat and jerked his gaze from her chest.

Maddie's cheeks heated. "Thanks a lot, Flynn."

"Well, hell, Maddie, they're out there. It's like they're begging me to…" He grabbed the bottle in front of him. "Man, is it hot out here or what?"

Brody snickered. "Like they're begging you to what, Flynn?" Brody wiggled his eyebrows at her. "We just finished a monstrous job roughing in the lines. Then Flynn's laying down some pipe—"

Laying pipe brought back memories of Flynn's apartment, and she choked on her own drink when Flynn did the same.

"What's with you two?" Brody shook his head. "Anyway, so we're done for the day. Flynn keeps insisting he's too tired to hit the club the rest of us are thinking of going to. Maddie, how about it? You think you and your roomies might want to go?"

"Go where, and who all is going?"

"Me, Flynn. Cam's out of town and not Mike, because he's Daddy Dearest now and refuses to 'find solace in a woman's arms again.' Heard that in a chick flick once, but it fits the big guy."

The sunlight danced past the umbrella and struck Flynn's face, highlighting the chisel of his chin. The dark stubble on his cheeks gave him a rough, sexy look. And when the sun lit his eyes, they flashed like precious gems. She wanted to sigh into his mouth, to kiss him in front of Brody and all the other women eyeing him up like their next meal. From the look of him, Flynn wanted the same.

"Well, well, well." Brody's sly tone broke the moment. "Aren't we in a good mood? I tell you, Maddie, Flynn wasn't so happy earlier. When Patty Haynes shoved her hands down his pants, he nearly hit the ceiling."

"*What?*" She hadn't meant that to come out so strong. "I mean, what happened?"

Flynn glared at Brody. "Nothing. A grabby client didn't figure no meant no. When she *tried* to shove her hand down the back of my pants for a squeeze, she found out differently."

Brody started laughing.

"I don't know, Brody. I don't think that's funny." She remembered too clearly how humiliated she'd felt when Fred had done something similar to her.

"No, no. You have to understand the whole picture. Patty Haynes is tipping eighty. But she moves like lightning when she wants something. Personally, I think she keeps clogging things down her sink so Flynn will show up in his tight jeans and flex for her."

Maddie tried to keep a straight face. "Eighty, Flynn?"

"She's seventy-eight," he snapped. "And she looks a lot younger."

Brody continued to laugh. His eyes watered and he sounded out of breath. Then Maddie joined in. The sheer joy of the moment, the humor and the chagrined look on Flynn's face as he watched her, added up to gales of mirth she didn't try to temper.

Until an older woman at a table next to them politely asked them to tone it down.

———

Later that night, Maddie, Vanessa, and Abby followed Brody, Flynn, and four of their male friends into a popular downtown club.

Maddie considered the place more sophisticated than the typical college hangouts. This club seemed to cater to an older crowd. Patrons in their late twenties and up, by the look of things. The chrome and bright lights gave the whole place a spacey yet retro feel that blended seamlessly with the music. Rave and dance, her personal favorites. The bass thumped, and the atmosphere smelled of sweat, alcohol, and a wash of cologne and perfume covering blazing hormones.

Two bars sat on either end of the first floor. In between, a raised platform filled with tables and chairs surrounded an expansive wooden dance floor. A length of counter ran the perimeter of the platform, providing a haven for the predators watching scantily clad women and men gyrate to the music.

Most of the guys wore jeans or casual suits. Dressy but not flashy. The women looked like a mix of fashionistas, divas in costumes, and well-dressed hookers. Maddie hadn't seen so much blue eye shadow since the eighth grade.

She looked almost matronly compared to the women on the dance floor. She'd chosen a short black skirt and baby-blue top that hung off her shoulder, baring a blue bra strap that looked like part of the shirt, and a pair of strappy heels.

The club scene had never been her thing, but after the day she'd had, she'd wanted to reward herself with something new and fun. And something that involved Flynn.

Vanessa sighed. "I knew I was going to regret this."

"What?" Abby cupped her ear, managing to look both sexy and demure at the same time. Vanessa rolled her eyes and sat at the table Brody found for them away from the dance floor. The music didn't sound as loud back here, and Maddie sat with her, rubbing the back of her neck, aware of a tension headache developing. She removed the clip holding her hair off her neck and felt worlds better.

"Damn." Flynn stared at her, looking less than pleased, and walked away.

She noted Vanessa's attention focused on someone over her shoulder and turned to see Brody talking to Abby and some huge guy standing way too close.

"I thought she was right behind us." Maddie ran a hand through her hair, then set her clip on the table.

"And so it begins." Vanessa waved over a waitress and ordered two pitchers of beer for everyone.

"Should we help her?"

Flynn joined Brody, said something, and the big guy with them shrugged and left.

"Nah," Dave, Brody's friend, said next to her. "They have it under control. Trust me, Brody doesn't need Flynn's help. He's mean when he's riled."

Dave, Ted, Gary, and Rick seemed like nice guys. She'd met them earlier in the afternoon before she'd left the coffee shop. Flynn hadn't seemed to like all the compliments they'd given her, which boosted her ego, she had to admit.

"So Maddie." Dave scooted closer. "You and Flynn got something going on?"

"Why do you ask?"

Dave put his hand on the back of her chair, the way Flynn liked to. A classic guy move, apparently. An attractive man, his brown eyes met hers and traced her features, the gesture one of interest and speculation. "He was a little insistent about us keeping our distance."

She hoped her blush didn't show. "We're just friends. He's probably just being nice. I think he and his family have adopted us. We live next door to his brother Mike."

"Oh. Good to know." He grinned and opened his mouth to say something else. Then he disappeared.

Flynn had yanked his chair back and inserted his own. "Back off, Dave."

"I knew it." Dave slapped Flynn on the back and focused on the pitcher the waitress put in front of him.

"So how do you know these guys? You never said." Maddie accepted the glass of beer Vanessa handed her and watched Flynn. How did the man look so handsome but at the same time not look like he put effort into it?

"Dave and Ted know Brody from way back. Gary and Rick we met a few years ago on a job. They're electricians. When you work in trade, you kind of get to know the competition and the folks that have a knack for what they do. Gary and Rick are good. Ted and Dave, who the hell knows?"

He didn't seem too fond of Dave, who winked at her over Flynn's shoulder. Then Dave asked Abby to dance, and she happily said yes.

Brody plunked down next to Vanessa. "Good to see Dave's having fun."

"Hey, he's your friend." Flynn put his beer down. "What do you think of the place, Maddie?"

"It's loud."

He laughed.

"The color scheme is actually perfect for what they're trying to sell."

He leaned closer. "What's that?"

"Booze and sex. The contemporary colors, the flashy glitter of mirrors and lights. It's exciting, functional, and a little overwhelming, to tell the truth." On television, the club scene always seemed so electrifying and sexy. Maddie just wanted to dance to the music minus all the people. She felt on display. The term *meat market* definitely came to mind, though in this place one would think more along the lines of filets.

Even the sight of Flynn in form-fitting black slacks and a button-up gray shirt, the sleeves rolled back to show off his sexy forearms, wasn't enough to stave her annoyance with the crowd.

His lips brushed her ear when he leaned closer to speak again. She couldn't contain a shiver. "You think like a designer even when you're not designing. So what do you think of my apartment?"

She pulled back, nonplussed when his dark gaze focused on her mouth. When one of the songs seemed to grow louder, she said into his ear, "It suits you. It's contemporary, sexy, and basic."

"Base?"

When had he put his hand on her thigh? He handled her under the table, where no one could see, but she didn't want their relationship to be so obvious.

She stopped his hand with her own and put it back on his lap. Except he wouldn't let her go. He pulled her hand closer and brushed it against his erection.

"Mmm. Yeah. Base. Like my instincts right now."

She yanked her hand back and glared at him, not pleased he was getting so cozy with her while Vanessa and Brody sat across the table from them. None of this with Flynn tonight felt casual. She knew better than to let herself get too attached. Brody and Vanessa stood and asked if Maddie wanted to dance with them. She nodded. Time to get some air *away* from Flynn. She stepped onto the dance floor and lost herself in the music. She didn't look back for a long time.

An hour and a half later, she'd finally found her groove. Flynn kept his distance, and for the most part she forced herself to ignore him. She'd danced with Ted, Brody, and some other guys, surprised to find she was having fun.

Abby and even Vanessa seemed to be having a blast. They stayed with their group, pretty much, while she didn't discriminate between dance partners. All of it remained innocent. If a guy put his hand where she didn't want it, she simply stepped back to the safety provided by Brody and the others.

She would have been having a stellar time if she could stop fighting with herself. On the one hand, she didn't want Flynn crowding her, acting like her boyfriend in front of their friends. On the other, she didn't like him dancing with the cute blond… *three times in a row*.

Needing to get a handle on her conflicted desire and the grabby blond holding Flynn too close, Maddie excused herself from her current dance partner and headed for trouble.

———∿———

Flynn contained his boredom and kept his smile in place. Tricia had been hounding him to follow her into a back room, where some of the club-goers went to hook up. There were a few rooms scattered in the back, supposedly for supplies. But a twenty to the dude guarding the roped-off area and you could fuck like bunnies for as long as you needed—Tricia's words, not his.

He'd done his best to keep his patience, trying to politely but firmly refuse. He should have stayed closer to the group, but his "date" had made it pretty plain he wasn't welcome.

Touching Maddie with friends nearby had been a stupid thing to do, but Christ. She couldn't wear those clothes and *not* expect him to react. Her glare had only made matters worse. When angry, with all that dark red hair framing her face, she made him so fucking hard.

To top off his frustration, she'd been dancing with every asshole in the place. Everyone but him. Not that he'd asked. He wouldn't want to burden his *friend* with unwanted advances. But this distance stuff grated. Sitting with her earlier today had felt right. Normal. His best friend, his best girl… Maddie fit him. Sexually he'd never had better. Orgasms with her sent his mind spinning, and he couldn't keep himself from becoming aroused two seconds in her presence.

The sex part he could handle. But wanting to talk to her? Stopping himself twenty times a day from texting just to see how the new job was going? He felt like a goddamn pussy, wishing she'd call him just to hear her voice. When she'd seduced him last week, he'd felt like the king of the mountain. And when she'd blinked away thankful tears over that card case, he'd wanted to hold her. To offer comfort, not to cop a quick feel.

"Come on, sexy. Just once in the back. You're too pretty to be by yourself." Tricia, his new best friend, slurred her words. Was there anything more unattractive than a drunken woman who smelled like the last guy she'd fucked and wouldn't take no for an answer? She was too hungry for it.

But not as hungry as he was for a certain stubborn redhead.

At the thought, he frowned. What would really be so bad about them actually dating? Maddie could fit him into her schedule if she wanted. He'd devoted all last Saturday to her, when he should have been showing Theo the ropes.

"Tricia, I told you before. I'm here with someone."

A glance over her shoulder showed that same some-one zeroing in on him with a frown. Thank God.

"Flynn?" Maddie arched a brow at Tricia, who clung to him like a vine.

"Maddie, meet my very drunk friend Tricia. Tricia, honey, you have to let go." He sighed when the woman tripped and knocked into him, then giggled.

Maddie's eyes lost their touch of frost and crinkled.

"Glad you find this funny." He hissed out a breath. "I've been telling her I'm not available, but she won't let go."

"Tricia?" Maddie had to call her name twice more to get her attention. "See that guy over there?" She pointed toward Brody. "He was asking who the hot blond dancing with Flynn was." She leaned closer, right over Flynn, giving him a perfect look down her shirt. Oh man, she was wearing another one of those sheer bras.

"And Tricia, Brody's loaded. He's rich and wants *you*." Maddie eased Tricia away, and the blond stumbled toward the dance floor.

Flynn didn't wait. He yanked Maddie with him and moved past the bar and away from the masses, where Brody's buddy Carl guarded one of the roped-off areas Tricia had mentioned. Carl stepped aside, taking the bill Flynn discreetly handed him before moving back to guard the narrow hallway that led to a smaller corridor lined by three doors.

"Flynn?" Maddie's breathless voice made him groan. "What's wrong?"

"What's wrong?" he repeated, aroused, angry, and tired of feeling so out of sorts around her. Up one minute, down the next. He glanced at his cock—up *again*. He chose one of the doors and pulled her into a small closet that smelled like pine cleanser.

He tugged on the light cord and closed the door behind them at the same time, then locked them inside.

When Maddie just stared at him as if he were crazy, he lost it.

Chapter 13

"You want to know what's wrong?" Flynn scowled at her, frustrated, horny, and beyond confused. "I'll tell you. You've had me hard since I saw you wearing that tiny skirt. Your tits are playing hell on my control, and those heels make me think of nothing more than having them on either side of my head while I fuck you raw."

Her mouth opened.

"Yeah, that's what's wrong. And while I watched you flaunt that tight little ass at half the dickheads out there, I had some drunk chick hanging all over me."

He kissed her, shoving his tongue in her mouth with hunger, wanting to follow with his cock. Maddie pulled him closer, her breasts rubbing against his shirt. "I didn't like her near you. Not one bit." She nipped his lower lip then shoved her tongue inside his mouth.

Her aggression tipped him over the edge, and he forgot to be tender and careful. He wanted to possess her and make it hard for her to walk away. Flynn pushed her back against the wall, probably the only clean part of the room.

Her heels put them on a more even footing, and he kissed her without pause, barely stopping to catch a breath. The urgency consumed him. Fucking her in a public place, in a closet, with the fear of getting caught…

He reached low and slid his hands under her skirt. Up her thighs to her ass, bared by a thong.

"You've got to be kidding me." He cupped her ass and tugged on the thin string between her cheeks, increasing the friction between her legs.

"Flynn. You're making me so wet."

"Good. Because I'm close to coming already." He palmed her ass and lifted her off the ground, grinding himself against her.

"Please. Do it."

"Do what?" He sucked hard on her neck. "Tell me."

"Fuck me. Right now. Here."

Like she had to tell him twice.

He didn't bother taking off her underwear, just pulled the string to the side and shoved a finger inside her.

She arched back, and he wanted to rip her shirt off and suck on her tits until she came. But he had his hands full.

"Take the condom out of my pocket. Hurry up."

She tried but couldn't get to it through the tangle of limbs.

Swearing, he let her slide down the wall onto her wobbly heels. He unfastened his pants, took himself out and then ripped open the packet. He slid the condom on in record time, then decided to go for it.

"Take off the thong. I don't want you wearing panties tonight."

Her eyes grew round and her breathing quickened. "But I'll make a mess of my skirt."

"It's black. No one will know but you and me." He loved this, taking her out of her comfort zone and giving her something he'd bet no one else had. "Take it off." He didn't mean to sound so demanding, but he barely hung on. He could feel his pulse pounding in his cock, and the constricting latex didn't help.

She pulled the thong down and stepped out of it.

Totally bare, that thin strip of red hair over her pussy, her labia naked of anything but that sweet juice flowing like honey.

Flynn gripped her ass and lifted her. He pinned her against the wall and wrapped her legs around his waist. "Now hold on, baby. Here it comes." He positioned himself and thrust hard.

She gave a low cry as he worked her, fucking with brutal strokes as he raced her to climax. So turned on, she didn't take long. And her wet pussy sucked him deeper, her contractions all but milking his semen from him in rushes of pleasure.

He groaned while he came, amazed he'd had the audacity to actually have sex with Maddie in a club, with tons of people just a few feet away.

She kissed him, a slow, leisurely kiss that told him more than words how much she'd loved every naughty moment. The kisses started revving him again, and he had to pull back, not sure how much time Carl would give them before someone came knocking.

"Maddie, baby." He kissed her again, this time on the forehead. Totally not a sexual move, but it felt more intimate because it wasn't. She blinked, and he'd swear the look in her eyes could only be described as gooey. Womanly and soft, like the look Lea used to give his brother.

Too gratified to panic, he surged inside her one last time then pulled out.

"You made me all wet."

"Hey, it's not me. I'm all in here." He pulled the condom off and grimaced, looking for a place to trash it.

"The can is right there." She pointed to a trash can by the door behind him. He tossed it in then tucked himself back in his clothes and straightened up.

Maddie had cleaned up as well, using a tissue she'd found from a box on a nearby shelf. She threw the wadded piece into the trash. "Now what?" She looked a little nervous. Her thong sat on the ground in a sodden mess.

"Now you go around bare. Better not spread your legs while you're sitting down."

Her eyes looked overly bright, her cheeks pink, and her lips red and ripe. He finally did what he'd been wanting to all night. He crouched before her and lifted her skirt, captivated by her naked flesh.

He leaned close and kissed her, making sure to lick between her folds and rub his tongue against her clit. Then he stood and pulled her skirt back down. "Kiss me. Taste how sweet you are."

She pulled his neck down and kissed him, moaning into his mouth.

"Now we'll both know you're naked under that sexy skirt. I might take you off to the side and bend you over. When no one's looking, I'll lift the back of your skirt up, stand behind you, and take you there, where anyone can walk by and see. And you'll cream for it, won't you?" He blew into her ear, and she trembled.

"Y-you can't do that. What if someone sees you?"

"Sees *us*." He massaged her breasts and pinched her nipples with slight pressure. "So what? Half the people out there are stoned out of their minds."

"No, don't. I don't want—"

"You *do* want. But be a good girl and I won't fuck you on the dance floor." He gave her a wicked smile, really into this new game. He'd never had this much fun before. Man, he'd really been missing out on this hidden talent for kink. "I'll take you home in my truck and watch you suck me off while I'm driving. How about that?"

"What?" She might have sounded more annoyed if she hadn't been so breathless.

"While I finger you. You're so fucking pretty when you come." He kissed her again, a swift press of his lips. Then he smoothed down her hair and tucked her shirt and skirt back. He picked up her panties and shoved them into his pocket, determined to add them to the other pair he had at home. "Now let's go out and see if we can fool everyone into believing we didn't just fuck in the closet."

"Oh, God. We really did." Her eyes sparkled, and she laughed in spite of her horrified words.

They spent the next hour with the gang, but this time Flynn danced with Maddie, keeping the hounds at bay. Every time they touched or locked gazes, he seemed to fall a little more under her spell.

And he didn't care who watched them or who knew it.

Three weeks later, Maddie was grimacing at the mess of her accounts. She'd been dipping into her savings more and more. Between advertising, a website she'd insisted she pay full price for from Abby, and a new laptop, she continued to lose more than she made. That didn't even take into account the furniture rental expenses she hadn't counted on, but she'd needed to make the first few jobs for Linda perfect, to prove that the first house hadn't been a fluke.

Three days after the open house on the Howe project, the house sold for its asking price. The success had boosted her confidence, but these setbacks worried her.

Her phone buzzed, and she dropped everything to reach for it. Another note from Flynn. He'd been gone the past three weeks on a job for a friend in Anacortes. She hadn't expected to miss him so much, yet she looked forward to every one of his messages. She read this one and smiled to herself.

> I need to add to my collection. Wear a pair of
> red panties this Friday.

She texted back, What's in it for me?

The phone rang—an actual call. "Hello?"

"Maddie, honey, do we really need to talk about this?" Flynn's deep voice turned her into a pile of mush.

"Now, Flynn, it's only a few more days until we see each other. Keep it together." She paused, in a mood to tease. "I have to say, I'm looking forward to finally going down on you."

He groaned. "Why say things like that now? When you're too far away to make good on your promises?"

"Promises? I'm just making conversation." She heard his muttered curse and grinned.

"Plan to make that happen, you little witch. But you have to be wearing those heels and a red thong next time."

"In your dreams."

"Every night."

She laughed. "So how's the job going?"

"Well, it's Wednesday night and I'm hanging out by the sewer while Brody makes a few calls. How do you think it's going?"

"Ew. Sorry I asked."

He chuckled. "Actually, this is a great project. I was hesitant to take it, but I'm glad Brody talked me into it. The money is phenomenal, but even better, we've made some new contacts. This development they're building is classy. They want everything done right, and their philosophy is quality over cost. The best fittings, the best materials, and they want the best service to go with it."

She liked the pride she heard in his voice. He exuded confidence. Hearing him talk like that, who wouldn't want McSons working for them? "So you only have a few more days?"

"Another week and a half, actually, but Brody and I are taking the weekend off and coming home." He paused. "I thought I'd swing by Friday night and take you out for a bite. It's been a while since I had dinner with a pretty face. Brody wears on a guy, you know?"

"Not having any fun with the girls up north, hmm?" She kept it light, but deep down she didn't want him to find anyone else.

"Nope. Just me and my ugly partner. What about you? I heard from my aunt that my cousin thinks you're hot. You been sucking up to Theo lately? Seen Ted hanging around?"

"No Ted, and Flynn, get real. Theo's a kid. A nice, strong young man who's too useful to me to have sex with him. And just saying his name and the word *sex* together makes me cringe."

"Wait a minute. He's too useful to you to have sex with, but I'm not?"

"Yes. No. First of all, your cousin is too young for me. You and I have an arrangement. We're friends who have an intimate knowledge of one another and don't get bogged down in messy emotions."

He snorted. "That's a mouthful. And speaking of mouthful, I'm planning on driving around town with you on Friday before dinner. Plenty of time for you to take care of me since I'm so useless, don't you think?"

"You have a one-track mind." She tried but couldn't sound annoyed. "I like it."

"I'll pick you up at eight. Be ready." He disconnected the call in a hurry.

Maddie shook her head and returned to work. An hour later, she was ready to pull her hair out. It would have helped if she'd accepted Abby's offer of free tech support, but Maddie didn't want to take advantage. Like Vanessa, who'd offered her a discount rate on her accounting services that Maddie hadn't accepted, Abby would receive full payment for services rendered.

Gardners didn't take charity. Hell, she'd grown up watching her mother work herself to the bone to provide for the two of them. Michelle Gardner didn't take advice or money from relatives or friends. Maddie liked to think she'd evolved from her mother. She took as much advice as she could, though she only followed what made sense. When it came to money, however, all bets were off.

She'd always made her own way, and she refused to stop now. She just needed to settle down and figure this out. After several jobs for Linda, she had less than she started with financially, but a lead on several other projects. The problem with staging boiled down to logistics. She'd pieced together what she could, in addition to adding Flynn's cousin to her labor force before the teen started interning with McSons Plumbing.

Robin and Kim had loaned two of their employees and staging resources to get her business started. The help had been more than welcome, and Maddie treasured her friends for supporting her. Yet Gardner's was *her* business, and she'd better fix her own problems before they grew too big to handle.

She spent the rest of the night and the next day coming up with ideas while she sketched a few designs for the house she'd been hired to stage for a major showing next week.

"Hey, come see this." Abby's voice preceded her into Maddie's room. She looked around and frowned. "It's a mess in here. You need a real office."

"Ya think?"

"Don't be sarcastic, Ms. Crabby. Take a break and come see your new website."

Maddie followed Abby downstairs to the office. Since Abby had accepted the smallest bedroom without protest, Maddie and Vanessa had conceded her the sunroom. Abby kept it organized and ran her business with a skill Maddie envied.

"You know," Abby said, looking around, "I can make some room for you in the corner. Just move the desk from your room down here. We can find a filing cabinet or shelving to help you."

"Nice offer. I might take you up on that. It's just easier for me right now because I know where everything is upstairs. I'm kind of too busy to move everything around."

"Busy. That's such a great word. I love being busy. Means I can afford to eat." Abby grinned. "But think about it, Maddie. How awesome is it that you're already hard at work again in your own field? Do you have any idea how hard it is to do what you love and get paid for it? You took a crappy situation and turned it around all in the same minute. I mean, well, not really, but it's not like you've been out of work for a year. You're right back in the game! It's so exciting to think of being your own boss, isn't it?"

Exciting? More like nerve wracking. But at least Maddie had what promised to be a nice income, if she could figure out how to better manage her operating costs. "Yeah, yeah. Now show me this website."

Abby had taken her ideas and plied them into the perfect electronic venue. "I couldn't get you *Gardner's* as a domain name, because it's pretty popular, believe it or not. But I did get you MGardner's dot com. Close enough. You'll just have to add that to your business cards later. Now check it out."

She'd included everything Maddie had asked for and more. An appointments and scheduling page, contact listing, places for her to show off her portfolio, services and estimates, and an additional page for a link to Madison Gardner Designs, Maddie's future design boutique.

"Oh wow." She hugged her friend until Abby squeaked. "Thank you so much. This is terrific! When does it go live?"

"Soon as you give me some pictures for your

portfolio section. You need to ask Linda if you can use the photos from the Howe house too. Those would be great because they're recent. And a few testimonials from Linda, Robin, or Kim would work. I'd ask you to get something from Hampton's too, but screw them."

"Yeah, screw them."

Maddie all of a sudden felt the pressure to succeed. Stupid, since she'd already been working for a few weeks. But the website would be global, putting herself out there for real. An office space—not her bedroom—and business cards with her website address, a new graphic design just for her, for Gardner's…

She felt so official now. It wouldn't be a private failure if she didn't succeed. Everyone would know she couldn't handle being her own boss.

It hurt to breathe.

"Whoa. What's that panicked look?"

"Sorry," Maddie rasped. "Just feeling the reality settle in. I can do this. I'm fine."

"Exactly. Don't let fear drag you down."

Maddie huffed, her tension easing as she repeated her inner mantra. *I can do this. I am not afraid.* "Funny, but I remember you freaking out when you started. It's tough when the money's tight." *And you're missing Flynn.* Her conscious mind booted him right back out. *Ack. This is not about him. I can do this.*

"You've been working for over a month." Abby shrugged. "I'm not seeing the problem."

"I'm not making the money I need to be self-sufficient. I can't do it just on staging, not at this rate."

"Do you need a loan?"

Abby barely had two dimes to rub together. "No! I

don't want your money. I want *my* money." She took a deep breath and let it out slowly. "I just need to look at what I'm doing and fix problem areas." She swallowed hard and admitted, "It's tough, sometimes, when I'm talking to Flynn, and he's got another job. He's so successful. Confident and handsome and working all over the place. I'm trying not to compare myself to him."

"Don't. Give yourself a break. You're just starting out. At least you were smart enough to save for your future."

"Yeah." *And look where that's gotten me. I'm going broke.* She wasn't, but it felt like she was. Terrified of ever reaching the panic line she'd invisibly drawn over that account, Maddie jumped at every shadow lately. She didn't know why, but she felt like her mother. Alone, struggling to make ends meet, underqualified for the really good work, because she no longer had the backing of a high-name firm behind her. Yet she had so many more options than her mother had ever had.

"Why do I seem to have the worst timing?" Vanessa's drawl made the situation go from bad to worse. The queen of competent, she who ruled the land of never-makes-a-mistake. *Of course* she'd come home early from her spinning class in time to hear Maddie confessing a bit of self-doubt.

Annoyed and wishing she'd never moved in with her stupid—perfect—cousin, Maddie growled, "Go away, Vanessa."

"Free house. Besides, this is Abby's office, not yours." Vanessa wouldn't shut up. "What the hell crawled up your ass today?" She paused, and her eyes gleamed with mirth. "You're missing that man of yours,

aren't you? So much for hoping you'd be a new independent woman."

"Oh, fuck off, Vanessa," she snapped. "This isn't
about Flynn. I'm just having a bad day."

Abby looked startled, but Vanessa didn't flinch. She
walked right into the room and sat on the floor, stretching her toned legs. "So what started this tantrum, Abby?
She not getting enough action from Flynn?"

"Not now, Vanessa." Abby glanced worriedly between them.

Furious at the thought of Vanessa insulting Flynn,
who'd been nothing but nice, Maddie cut in. "Flynn has
nothing to do with this."

"Please. You've been pouting since he's been gone.
Your cell rings and you jump to answer it. You have it
bad for the playboy." Vanessa's disgust came through
crystal clear.

"Just because you're one cold bitch doesn't mean the
rest of us have to be."

Vanessa stopped stretching and looked Maddie right
in the eye with an icy blue stare. "I'm a rational adult
who doesn't give up just because things are hard. *Man
up*, Maddie." She sneered. "You have man problems.
You have money problems. You're not good enough and
never will be. Wah wah wah. Join the fucking club."

Maddie blinked. Vanessa sounded surprisingly bitter.
Unfortunately, she wasn't done. "It's called life. Deal
with it. All I know is my free time is too precious to
spend it listening to you whine about how scared you
are. Everyone's scared of failing. But sometimes you
have to put on your big-girl pants and step up to the
plate. You want your business to succeed, talk to the

right people and figure it out. But stop with all the drama. It's giving me a headache."

Vanessa rose from the floor, graceful as always, and stalked out of the room and upstairs. A door slammed and classic rock boomed above.

"Somebody other than you had a bad day." Abby pushed her hair back behind her ear. "Wonder what crawled into her Nikes and died."

Maddie didn't know what to think.

She wiped her cheeks dry, no longer weepy. "Thanks, Abby." She hugged her. "You're such a good listener. But I'm not talking to Vanessa until she apologizes. You can tell her that for me."

"Ah, sure. But I'm going to wait until tomorrow. Vanessa is on a tear, and I'm too small and cute to be crushed under one of her size elevens."

She and Abby shared a laugh, then Maddie walked upstairs and fell into bed. For once, she didn't dream about the future, Flynn, or her mother. And she didn't wake up until her alarm rang at seven the next morning.

Chapter 14

FRIDAY MORNING, MADDIE FELT A BUZZ OF ENERGY she hadn't felt in weeks. She exercised, ate a healthy breakfast involving more than a box of cereal and milk, and cleaned up after herself. Vanessa had already left for the day—good riddance—but Abby sat at her computer with a steaming cup of coffee by her side. She waved at Maddie and kept writing.

Maddie took her time in the shower, concentrating on all the positives in her life. Vanessa could be a real bitch, but she had a point. Dwelling on the negative didn't help anything.

That afternoon, after a business meeting with Kim that really helped her put her worries into perspective, she felt more like the old Maddie, the woman who knew her worth and made damn sure others knew it as well. Kim had started from the ground up. Maddie couldn't have asked for a better example of how to make a design business work. Readjusting her time and budget, she'd figured out how not to lose so much money on her jobs. She should have talked to Kim weeks ago, but she'd also needed to learn by experience. Now it was time to put her plan into practice. She'd be a success because she had to be.

Of all Kim's advice, one piece she'd said had stood out, because it sounded like something Maddie's mother had said. *"One thing to remember, Maddie. Don't lose yourself in work. Because one day you'll look up and see life has passed you by. It's Friday. Go get laid, have a terrific meal, then get back to the grindstone on Monday. Really. What do you have to lose?"*

Kim's words wouldn't leave her all day. She had a valid point. Hell, so did Vanessa. If Maddie didn't believe in herself, could she ask anyone else to?

That thought in mind, she readied for her night out with Flynn. After checking herself three times in the mirror, she grabbed her bag and went downstairs to wait.

In the living room, Abby sat on the couch watching television. She muted it when she saw Maddie. Abby stared at Maddie's blue heels, jeans, and leather jacket over a silk tank. Her sly expression promised trouble. "You look all spiffed up. Where are you going?"

"Out. With a guy, Miss Nosy."

Abby tapped her fingers on her knee, glancing from Maddie to the discreet overnight bag sitting on the floor next to her purse. "Hmm. Anyone I know?"

Maddie shrugged. Under her jacket, the deep V of her shirt shifted enough to advertise she wasn't wearing a bra. But Abby's attention seemed focused on Maddie's bag.

"Let me rephrase that. Where is Flynn taking you?"

Maddie sighed. "He's just a friend."

"Yeah, one you're boinking. Just tell me this. Is he hotter without his clothes on, or with?"

"Without."

"You lucky, lucky whore."

"Abby!"

Abby moaned and fell back on the couch. "Do you have any idea how long it's been since I've seen a penis? I mean, one not on the Internet?"

"And whose fault is that? I keep telling you it's past time you reentered the dating scene."

"Please. You're supposedly not even dating. A friend, my ass. You and Flynn are doing it. You like him, he likes you. You're dating."

Maddie inhaled and let her breath out slowly. She would not let Abby ruin her good mood. "No, we're not. Dating implies rules, compromises, and time spent reassuring fragile male egos. Flynn and I aren't like that. We actually have fun together."

"Outside of the bedroom?"

In the club, actually. She cleared her throat. "Yes. As a matter of fact, we had fun a few weeks ago walking around downtown. Not holding hands or making goo-goo eyes at each other." Technically they had held hands, but Flynn had called that a leash. So it didn't count. "Just talking and window shopping. Nothing major."

Abby sat up and stared at her. "Guys don't window shop. Especially not guys like Flynn McCauley. It was a date."

"It was not."

"So okay. What are your plans for tonight then? And that bag? That's overnight equipment, sister." Abby's tone had gone from hard to teasing.

As annoyed as Maddie wanted to stay, she knew Abby just wanted the best for her. "So what? I might spend the night. Like a sleepover." She batted her eyes. "His mom said it was okay."

Abby laughed. "I'll bet she did. So what's in the bag? Whips and chains? Lube? Some toys, maybe?"

"Abigail Dunn. Where do you get your ideas?"

"Not from my own love life, that's for sure." Abby scowled. "Now stop avoiding the question. What's in the bag?"

"A change of clothes and a six-pack of beer. Next?"

"Hmm. Okay. What are your plans for the night?"

Through the screen door, Maddie heard vehicles approach. Vanessa's car pulled into the driveway. Behind her, Flynn parked his truck and opened the door. Maddie didn't want to deal with Vanessa, so she picked up her bag and purse and turned to Abby. "Tonight I plan to give Flynn the best blow job of his life. We might see a movie, we might not. Then I'm going to spend the rest of the weekend whipping him into shape as my love slave. Any more questions?"

Silence reigned.

Abby crossed her arms over her chest and bowed her head. "You're my idol. I can only dream of one day aspiring to give great head like you." She lifted her chin and grinned. "We're *so* talking when you get back. I need material for my new book. Go get your groove on, and think of me while you're getting yours."

"Sorry, but I won't be thinking of you when that happens." Maddie gave her a smart salute, turned, and left the house. She met Flynn before he could walk up the steps to the porch.

His unhurried perusal slowed over her breasts and lingered on her heels. "In case I haven't said it already, I'm really looking forward to tonight."

"Me too." She didn't pause as she passed Vanessa. They exchanged a silent but graphic communication involving fingers until Vanessa slammed into the house.

"Whoa. What was that about?"

"Never mind. Let's not spoil the mood. Drive, Flynn. Somewhere out of the way, hmm?"

—⁓—

Three fucking weeks, an eternity spent without Maddie. Flynn had filled his days with work, his nights spent playing cards with Brody or watching TV. When he couldn't fall asleep without thinking about her, he'd remember their time spent in his apartment, or in the closet of that club. Images of Maddie's beautiful red hair, her breasts, and her long legs never failed to make him sweat. Then he'd remember how hot and tight she felt when he pushed inside her, how sweet she tasted when he went down on her. And he'd come in a heartbeat.

Now the woman he'd been thinking far too much about sat next to him wearing a tame enough pair of jeans, a jacket over a pretty top. But the heels… He'd fucked her in those the last time they'd been together. Did that mean what he thought it did? He'd only been half teasing about her giving him a blowjob when he'd called her earlier in the week. While a part of him—the part already hard and throbbing—wanted to feel her lips around him, his rational side didn't want to have sex with her this time.

He'd done nothing but think about her while working, and he'd come to the conclusion that by having sex whenever they'd met, he'd perpetuated her idea that he only wanted her for one thing. The woman didn't want a relationship, or so she'd said. But damn it all, Flynn had changed his mind. He did. With Maddie.

He'd been telling himself no sex tonight. He'd change things up, put her off her game and indulge in an honest-to-God date, with no strings attached. But those heels bothered him.

"It's warm in here." She fanned herself.

Before he could ask if she wanted him to roll down a window, she took off her jacket. The teal blue silk tank she wore molded to her curves. His mouth dried in seconds.

"No bra?" He tried to sound together, sophisticated. Like this happened to him all the time. But he'd never had a woman like Maddie, and the knowledge that at any moment she could twist in her seat and her tits might pop out made it almost impossible to concentrate. He gripped the wheel and focused on not crashing into the vehicles around him.

"I thought I'd go without tonight. Something new. You don't mind, do you?"

"Um, mind?" He hadn't made a sound that high-pitched since Brody had tagged him in the balls trying to steal home in last summer's big game. He coughed. "No. No, you're good."

Determined to see the night through, his way, he pulled away from the crowded streets and headed toward Golden Gate Park. Maybe they could walk a bit before the park closed and they went to dinner.

She crossed her legs. He widened his, hoping for some release from the hard-on from hell.

Out of the corner of his eye, he saw her finger trace down her breast, calling attention to her nipple. Christ, was she trying to kill him?

He cleared his throat. "I thought we'd go walk at a park for a little bit, then hit dinner. Okay?"

"Sure. Whatever you want."

"Jesus, help me now."

She laughed, the rich sound making everything inside him come to life.

"Just sit there and don't move or talk to me until I get us away from the traffic, okay?" It would be the longest twenty minutes of his life, but he'd suffered worse. Hadn't he?

"Sure." The silence between them only increased the tension.

"Okay, the quiet isn't helping."

"Helping what?"

"Helping me keep my mind off my dick," he snapped.

She laughed again.

"Tell me what the silent treatment between you and Vanessa was all about."

"You do want to kill the mood, don't you? My cousin. Hmm, where should I start? I was having a bad day, and she made it worse."

"How? What happened?"

She squirmed in her seat, and the material of her shirt slid over her breasts. "It's embarrassing."

"Yeah? Well, so is trying not to come in your jeans when sitting next to a beautiful woman. I'm dealing. Get over yourself and tell me what happened."

"So bossy."

He had every intention of bossing her around later. So much for trying to make their date platonic. "I am so weak," he muttered. At her look, he prodded, "Vanessa…?"

"I've been having a few problems getting used to my new job. How to spend my money, make better contacts. Just growing pains and nerves."

"We all have them. Hell, Brody and I still do. We go a few days without a client, he's climbing the walls."

"It's hard. Hell, you know all about it. I was just having a moment—"

"Like the one you had when I first met you?"

She blushed. "A little."

He laughed. "Wish I could have been there. You're fucking sexy as hell when you're ticked off."

"Shut up, Flynn." But he could tell his comment pleased her. "So Vanessa turned on her bitchy as hell mode. I didn't appreciate little Miss Perfect throwing in her two cents, and she didn't like me whining—again."

He shrugged. "Sounds to me like maybe she should be more understanding. You've been through the wringer the past few weeks. You're entitled to a bad day or two."

She didn't say anything, and he wondered if he should have just shut up and let her vent. He fiddled with the radio, suddenly feeling a little nervous.

"Oh, leave that song. I like it."

"Sure."

By the time they'd reached the park, it looked mostly deserted and the sun had gone down.

"Wait. Pull over there." She pointed to an empty spot under some trees away from the overhead light. When she reached for her jacket, he figured she wanted some privacy to put it on, not wanting the rest of the world to ogle those luscious breasts.

Her action relieved him. He didn't want her showing anyone else those perfect tits, but he didn't know how she might have reacted if he'd told her to cover them up. In no way could he imagine a scenario where that wouldn't blow up in his face.

He parked and moved to turn off the engine.

"No, keep it running."

She sat much closer, nearly in his lap.

"Maddie?"

She unbuckled his seat belt. Then her fingers ran over his thigh, creeping dangerously higher up his leg. She palmed his cock.

"Oh, fuck."

"Exactly. Now lean back and let me do what we both know you want." She licked her lips.

How the hell did a red-blooded man say no to that? To refuse a blow job from the hottest woman on the planet because he wanted her to feel appreciated for more than her mouth?

Hell no. Rejection at this point would only hurt them both. She'd feel insulted, and he'd expire from the worst case of blue balls ever on record.

The sound of his jeans being unsnapped sounded like a shotgun compared to the muted sound of the radio.

"Keep your eye out, Flynn. We wouldn't want to get caught."

"Right." His nervous cough turned into a moan when she unzipped him. He wanted to scoot the material down, but she stilled him.

"No. Let me."

The woman refused to make him more comfortable, which only turned him on even more. She pulled his cock through the slit in his underwear, exposing his long, thick shaft. Asshole that he was, his tip beaded with pre-come, unable to hold himself back. Even to himself, he looked huge. "Ah, Maddie, you sure about this?" Because no way in hell did he want to wear a condom for a blow job.

"Oh yeah. I've been thinking about this for weeks."

She slowly bent down. Her hair tickled his cock, then her breath washed over him.

"Maddie. Oh fuck. I'm not gonna last, baby. Not at all," he moaned as she fitted her lips to his cockhead.

The warmth of her wet mouth eased over him so slowly. The impulse to shove her head down and fuck her throat pulled at him. But he clenched his fists and kept his eyes on the rearview and side mirrors. The last thing he needed was to get busted for public indecency and stop this before it had even gotten started.

She moaned around him and pushed down. She had half of him inside her, but it wasn't enough.

She flattened her hand against his belly, while the other cupped his balls through his jeans.

Then she sucked, and he felt himself spurt a small amount into her mouth.

"*Fuck.*"

She made a noise that could have been a laugh then started to bob over him, that glorious wealth of red hair fanned around his crotch. A fantasy he couldn't help living out to the fullest.

Consigning himself to a quick orgasm, he threaded his hands through her hair and pushed her head over him with gentle insistence.

"Let me fuck that mouth, baby. So good."

He grunted, he groaned, and he nearly had a heart attack when she scraped her teeth under his crown, against the very sensitive part of his shaft.

"I'm gonna come in your mouth. You going to swallow me, baby? Take that come down your throat?"

She moaned and pressed her hand firmer against his balls.

He couldn't draw it out any longer. He had to come. He ached to fill her. "Now, Maddie. Oh God, I'm coming."

He moaned her name as he released, the tremors of pleasure more than he could bear as he jetted down her throat. The orgasm seemed to last forever. His thoughts fled, nothing but sheer sensation filling his body, from his balls to his brain.

Leaning his head back, he reveled in the climax and felt himself fall headlong into what felt suspiciously like love. He'd never been in love before, so he couldn't swear by it, but he'd never felt this emotion for any other woman he'd been dating—or not dating. Never.

Soft hands tucked him back inside his jeans and zipped him up. He didn't move, even when she kissed him, and he tasted himself on her lips. He never would have pegged that as sexy, but knowing she'd accepted him willingly turned him on in a big way. If only he had the energy to physically respond.

It took him minutes before his brain cells fired again.

"You okay, Flynn?"

He blinked his eyes open and turned to thank her, but his words stuck in his throat.

Her large eyes dominated her face. Tender and soft, yet brimming with feeling. Her shiny lips looked swollen. They'd been stretched around his cock and coated with his seed. So plump and pretty. But her eyes held him.

"Flynn?"

He pulled her forward and kissed her. Not content to let it stop at that and afraid to say anything for fear of blurting out the wrong thing or scaring her away, he tugged her onto his lap and just held her.

She sighed and laid her head against his chest.

Flynn hugged her, stroking her back and feeling so much affection for Maddie he didn't know what to do. They hadn't known each other all that long. But he felt like he knew the real her. The scrappy, hardworking, decisive woman who had courage, integrity, and loyalty down to a science.

He kept trying to tell himself that great sex didn't make a relationship, but it sure the hell made him want to try for one.

After some time, he nudged her back into her seat and buckled them in. He pulled out of the parking lot and drove to a seafood restaurant downtown. Determined to keep things light while he figured out a way to make Maddie see him as more than a sex partner, he teased her about Vanessa and Abby and told tales about his brothers.

By the time they'd been seated in the restaurant, their relationship felt the way it normally did. But deep inside, Flynn knew everything had changed.

Chapter 15

THROUGHOUT DINNER, MADDIE COULD FEEL SOMEthing between them growing stronger. Flynn laughed and joked, but he watched her with an intensity that drew her like a drug. God, she wanted to blow him again. She'd never been into oral sex all that much, but she'd felt so empowered taking him like that. He'd been putty in her hands, or rather, her mouth. Afterward, she'd expected a smart remark, a slap on the ass, or even a little hanky-panky from him.

She hadn't expected that hug, or the belonging she'd felt in his arms.

"I'd love to know what you're thinking right now," he said in a deep voice.

The waiter arrived and took away their plates.

Flynn ordered them coffee and asked, "Dessert, Maddie?"

She gave him an impish grin. "I already had mine. Just coffee's fine."

He blew out a breath and waited until the waiter left before he spoke. "Don't worry, baby. I'm not going to let you go without giving you a proper thanks."

"Gee, I can't wait."

His eyes flashed. "I'll bet. You liked making me lose my freakin' head."

"I must have. I keep letting you call me *baby*."

"You don't like it?"

Normally she didn't. But Flynn calling her that didn't demean her or make her feel like the proverbial little woman. She heard the affection in his voice, the intimacy, and it didn't bother her. Yet it should have. "I do like it, which makes me wonder what's happened to my backbone."

"Don't worry. You're still independent, feisty, and a little bit mean."

"Thanks." She grinned.

"A real working woman with attitude. In fact, just to make you feel better, I'll let you pay for my dinner and order me around all night. Heck, you can drive us home, too."

"Not that monster truck. And I don't want to pay for dinner. You asked me out, you get the tab."

"Fair enough." He stroked the condensation on his water glass. "What about ordering me around for the rest of the night? You plan on doing that?"

"I might."

"Hmm." He pursed his lips. "I might let you. First, answer a few questions for me."

"What do you want to know?"

He took a moment. "Earlier, you're okay with all that? What we did in my truck?"

"If I hadn't been, I wouldn't have done it." Great, now she felt defensive.

"I just… we pretty much have been, ah, careful, if you know what I mean. And in the car, it was just you and me."

She caught what he didn't say. No condom. "Flynn, I might be stupid, but I trust you."

The smile in his eyes lingered after his lips evened.

"I trust you, too, you know. I've been too tired the past few weeks to do more than work my ass off with Brody, but even if I hadn't been, I told you when we first agreed that I wouldn't be with anyone but you."

"While we're doing this casual, um, thing." Should she call their association a relationship?

His frown came and went in a split second. "I think we can call it a relationship."

Scary how he started to read her mind. "Oh?"

"I'm not seeing anyone else, and you aren't. You and Ben haven't been a thing in weeks, right?"

"Ben and I were over for a few months before we split. We hadn't been together sexually," she explained in a lower voice. "And we didn't seem to click the way we once had."

"I think you said something about him being too clingy when you were ranting to Abby." He grinned. "Remember? The first day I met you?"

Uncomfortable, she looked anywhere but at Flynn. She must have seemed like the biggest bitch. "Ben's a nice guy. I didn't have a lot of trouble with him, but I think he wanted more out of our relationship than I could give him."

"What? Kids? Marriage?"

"Hell no." Horrified at the thought, she shivered. "I can't imagine life as Mrs. Dr. Ben Foster."

"Mrs. Doctor?"

"Yeah. Ben was all about his career. He should have been proud of it. And he's really a nice guy, but everything had to be his way. His job came first. His socializing meant we couldn't do anything I wanted. I got tired of it. And he wouldn't give me any room to breathe."

Flynn looked her in the eye, his expression intent. "Do I make you feel like that?"

"No. Not at all," she hurried to relieve him. "You're so different from him. Easy to talk to. We get along. And the, well, what we do when we're together, it's very wow."

"Yeah." His gaze drifted to her mouth. "Wow is a good description." He grew pensive, and she wondered what she'd said or done to make him uneasy.

"Flynn?"

"I need to ask you something, but I don't want you freaking out."

Nervous, she nodded. "Just ask."

"Would it make you uncomfortable if I said I'd like to start going out sometimes? Not just for the wow, but to spend time together."

She frowned. "What do you mean?" She thought they'd already been doing that.

His cheeks turned pink and she stared in awe. Flynn, blushing?

The waiter returned with two mugs and a handful of creamers, then left them.

Flynn fiddled with the spoon in his coffee. "Well, I wouldn't mind hanging out with you for a movie or a game, cards, something like that. Sometimes it's late and you might not be in the mood, but we could visit. Or something." He mumbled the last, and she couldn't stop staring at Flynn McCauley sounding anything less than confident. "I mean, we are friends. Casual friends, but we're friends." He lifted his gaze to meet hers. "We trust each other."

"Yes, we do." She thought about it. "I guess it

wouldn't hurt if we went out sometimes. Just to have fun, I mean, without the…" A woman neared their table, and she paused until she passed by. "Sex."

"Now don't get me wrong. I don't want to stop that." The devilry in his smile relieved her. She didn't want to stop that either. She'd never connected so fully with a man before when it came to sex. "I just don't want you to think that's all I want from you. I think being normal, no-strings-attached friends would be great. Unless you think that's pushing it?"

Flynn seemed inordinately worried about burdening her with his friendship.

"Relax, Flynn. I know you're not angling for marriage or a commitment. Sure, we can be friends. We are friends." *Right. So why do I want to tell him that it's okay if we go out on dates? And that I don't want him to look for anyone else, because it'll ruin this good thing we have here?*

"I don't think I told you, but my favorite color is blue." He smiled at the hint of her shirt he could see past her jacket. "You into vanilla or chocolate? Cats or dogs?"

They traded more intimate details about their likes and dislikes. Her thoughts about sports, his about chick flicks. He also shocked her by bringing up her work again. Most men dismissed her job as unimportant and not worth a mention. Flynn knew more about design than she'd thought, mostly due to his aunt's and his mother's fascination with all things home and garden related.

"I'm just a blue collar guy. Plumber extraordinaire," he joked. "I majored in history, but mostly because I wanted to play ball in college."

"Which ball?"

"Football. Please." He snorted. "I also played a little baseball, but that was mostly so Brody wouldn't feel so lonely during the off season."

"How nice of you." She grinned.

"Yeah, I'm a nice guy like that. But I'm curious. You don't mind being out with me? I'm not a doctor."

She snorted. "And thank God for that. I don't want to spend time with someone who thinks he's Superman with a stethoscope."

"How about with a lead pipe?"

"We talking the game Clue, or your ability to leap tall buildings in a single bound with that tongue?"

"Well, there is that. But I'm not into leaping tall buildings, just a certain redhead who likes yellow and the number three."

"Don't forget milk chocolate and puppies."

"Right. I jotted that down when you weren't looking."

Somehow her sexy interlude with Flynn had turned into what felt like a real date. Maddie wanted to call him on it, to remind him they were friends with benefits, yet she didn't want to end their fun. Was it wrong for Flynn to want to spend time with her outside of a bed, closet, or car? The naughty part of her said yes, but the woman said no. Only a stupid person would reject an offer of genuine friendship from Flynn. He'd already conquered her in bed; he had no need to look for more with their relationship.

They returned to his apartment and watched a movie together. They'd agreed on *Alien*, because she liked the strong female lead and he liked the sci-fi aspect. Popcorn and sodas followed, and after, when she could no longer keep her eyes open, he carried her into his bed and slept with her.

She woke the next morning in his arms, but instead of the embarrassment or annoyance she might have felt had another man presumed to put her in his bed, she welcomed his attention.

It made her think back to why she'd argued against dating Flynn. Oh right, because she'd thought she hated men. That had lasted all of a week.

"I have no willpower," she mumbled as she made her way to his bathroom. She knew getting attached to Flynn wasn't smart. When they eventually split, she would hurt. Badly.

"Hey, you gonna be in there all day or what?" He banged on the door.

The morning attitude could go. She wouldn't miss that.

Finding an unattractive trait helped stave off the panic beginning to creep in.

The door flew open while she stared at herself in the mirror, toothbrush in hand. "Hey. A little privacy?"

"Get that ass in the shower. Now."

She tried to ignore the sight of his erection and all of his mouthwatering golden skin. "I'm brushing my teeth."

"In. The. Shower."

The crisp command made her wet.

She put her toothbrush down and glared at him, wishing she meant it. Then she turned on the shower and removed her clothes. She stepped in and sighed at how good she felt under the hot spray.

She heard him brushing his teeth, and then he stepped in behind her. "Not wearing a bra last night was naughty, Maddie."

She groaned when he locked his hands around her breasts and pulled her tight against him, her back to his front.

He cupped her breasts and toyed with her nipples. "Going down on me in a park? Touching yourself in the truck? Then falling asleep on me with those tits showing through that top?" He tsked. "Such a bad, bad girl. I think you need to be spanked."

"Really?"

"Oh yeah." He forced her to hurry the shower. He soaped all over, rinsed off, then waited while she did the same.

After he turned off the water, he dried them both off and shoved her out the bathroom door.

"Hey."

He lifted her in his arms, so easily, and his strength excited her.

"What are you doing?"

"I'm getting you back for yesterday."

She landed on the bed and let out a breath. Before she could move, he landed on top of her and pinned her down. He kissed her, and she melted beneath him. His mouth moved from her lips down her face to her neck.

He lingered on spots in between, but he continued down a path to her breasts.

"Pretty tits, Maddie. Look at your nipples, baby. You cold?"

"Jerk," she huffed, and he laughed.

He sucked one nipple into his mouth, and she arched into him. He cupped her breast and pulled at her nipple while he toyed with the other one. The time he spent playing with her increased her arousal, so that when he finally kissed his way down her belly, she was more than ready.

She spread her legs, aching for the feel of his mouth on her. He didn't disappoint. Flynn licked and sucked her to the edge of orgasm in moments. His thick fingers pressed for entrance to her sex, and as he sucked, he shoved one finger, and then two inside her, fucking her with his fingers as he ate her. The intensity of her orgasm scared her. But Flynn wouldn't let her hide. He bore down on her clit and added another finger, but this one he pressed against her anus.

Then he pushed and penetrated. She cried out and came all over his mouth, his name a mantra on her lips.

He rode her through it, kissing and caressing her sex with loving bites. When finished, she could barely think straight.

"Watch. See what you do to me." He straddled her waist and jerked off, his cock thick and wet as he stroked it. Long, slow drags that enthralled her. "I'm so hard around you, Maddie. You taste so good, and you're so fucking beautiful."

The rough words pulled at her ego, and more, at her heart.

Then Flynn moaned and tugged once more, coming in milky jets over her belly. "Oh, fuck. Yeah, Maddie. All over you." He rubbed it into her stomach, as if sealing some part of himself inside her very skin.

When finished, he panted and stared down at her, his gaze inscrutable.

"I think I need another shower."

He shook his head. "Not yet."

Too tired to go again, she tried to protest. But the

blasted man ignored her. The sly bastard pushed her past her denial into another rip-roaring climax. And then, before she could catch her breath, he took her in his arms and cuddled with her.

To her dismay, another brick in the wall around her heart crumbled and fell.

—◆◇◆—

Finally free of the Anacortes job, Flynn's routine returned to normal. Mostly. He was doing his best not to bug Maddie. He sent her a text when he wanted to call, and he limited his messages to three instead of the two dozen he wanted to send. The woman had burrowed under his skin, and he had a bad feeling nothing but more sex, dating, and hell, maybe even a long-term relationship would cure him.

Brody razzed him about her. Mike had nearly taken his head off with threats about not screwing with the general happiness of his neighbors. Cam had been spending a lot of time away on business, so Flynn didn't worry the narc would sell him out. Still, his brothers clearly saw how over-the-moon he was for the woman. How could she not see it?

He checked his watch for the fourth time as he finished up this solo job while Brody did paperwork back at his place. After cleaning up behind him and checking again with the homeowner, he left with a smile. Doing his best to keep to the speed limit when anticipation had his foot heavy on the gas pedal, Flynn finally made his way back to the parking garage.

After a quick trip to his place, he showered, gave the apartment a good once-over, and waited for Maddie.

A Wednesday night, middle-of-the-week get-together. Hopefully, the first of many. He wondered if the flowers on the counter were a bit much, but he'd seen her looking at them when they'd been to the market together. Maddie's weaknesses, that he could see, were flowers, chocolates, and his interest in her.

Before he could finish that train of thought, the doorbell buzzed.

He nearly tripped over himself to answer it and forced himself to be cool. No need to let the woman know she had him wrapped around her finger already. Power and control were important in dealing with this particular redhead. He knew it; she knew it. Now he just needed to balance his desire, his affection, and his need for her company without scaring her away. He hoped distance would be the answer.

He opened the door and smiled. "Welcome."

Maddie wore a pair of jeans and a short-sleeved brown sweater. Casual, comfortable clothes, but she managed to look like a model wearing them all the same. "Hi. Sorry I'm a little late."

She had shadows under her eyes. "You look tired."

"Thanks a lot."

He shut the door behind her. "Sorry. Truth hurts."

"Such a flatterer," she grumbled and toed off her sandals before making a beeline for his couch.

"What's up with the shoes?"

"Oh, Vanessa's a tyrant. She doesn't want us tracking mud in the house. It's become a habit." She sat on his couch and lifted her leg so he could see her foot over the back of the couch. Wiggling her toes, she said, "You have a problem with firehouse red?"

He'd never thought a woman's foot could be so sexy. Yet he had to ignore his hard-on when he answered. "No problem. Now if it was *doctor* red, I'd have issues."

She grinned before flopping down so he could no longer see anything of her but her foot hooked over the sofa. "What's on the agenda tonight?"

Besides ignoring the fact I want to fuck? He cleared his throat. "I don't know. Just thought we could hang out, TV or a movie."

She sighed. "Sounds perfect. I've been so busy lately I haven't been able to catch a breath." She told him all about her day, her new collaboration with her friends Kim and Robin, Theo and his continued support, and how Linda might be harder to work with than she'd first thought.

Flynn joined her on the couch, surprised to find himself actually invested in the conversation. Man, everything about her resonated on his level. Maddie didn't put him on a pedestal. She was better-looking than he was, in his opinion. She seemed to like him well enough, but she didn't do whatever he wanted. Even better, she didn't demand he wait on her. He'd had his share of women who wanted to be treated like queens all the time, and at his expense.

He sat close to Maddie but not close enough. He pulled her into his lap.

"Oh, that's nice."

He'd expected her to protest, so having her close and actually pleased about it made him smile. Then she snuggled deeper into his embrace, and his heart did that odd patter that concerned him.

"You're so warm. And so built." Maddie ran her

hands over his chest, stroking the muscle as if petting something soft. "How are you this handsome and not married already?"

He had to take a breath before answering, worried his answer would come out shaky. "Never met the right woman, I guess. You've met my parents. They've been married more than thirty years. I don't want anything less than what they have."

"You're so lucky. You have such a great family. Your dad seems nice." He heard the question there.

"He is. Don't get me wrong. He's not that nice. A hard-ass who used to make me pay for stamps when I was eight and would stand next to a light switch until I turned it off, just to teach me a lesson. But he was there for us. Sports, school, camping, you name it. Dad was into family. But you ask me, he got lucky when he met Mom."

"I like Beth."

"Everyone does." He nuzzled the top of her hair, wondering what kind of shampoo she used because she always felt so soft and smelled like wildflowers. "What about your mom?"

"I love her. I was happy growing up, but maybe a little lonely. And I always felt like we worked too hard for everything."

We, not *she*, he noticed. "Yeah?"

"I've been working since I was a kid. Cleaning houses with my mom, then odd jobs around the diner. I was a busboy, hostess, and waitress before I could drive a car. Then a bunch of other jobs to help pay the rent and maybe afford a pair of jeans my mom deemed too expensive." She shrugged. "I'm not complaining. I know

I'm a hard worker, and I'm really fortunate now that I'm doing what I love."

She was. "Probably doesn't mean much, but I'm proud of you. It couldn't have been easy to deal with your boss and leave your job. But it sounds like it's paying off."

Her hands stopped stroking, and he felt her breath hot against his chest, even through his shirt. She sighed, and he was reminded of the shadows under her eyes. The woman looked beautiful, but exhausted.

He knew just how to put her to sleep. "You mind if I catch the scores from the games real quick?"

"Go ahead."

He grabbed the remote from the table and turned to the sports channel. A few minutes later he noticed Maddie hadn't moved. He pulled back and saw her head tucked against his chest, her hair obscuring her face.

"What am I going to do with you?" He moved on the couch slowly, so as not to wake her, and settled back into a sprawl. Maddie covered him like a human blanket. Warm, curvy, and so damn pretty.

He stroked her hair as he watched a replay of the day's games and wondered why this bland, nothing date had been the highlight of his day. And why the idea of sex couldn't make it any better than it already was.

Chapter 16

Maddie woke when Flynn shook her.

"Time to go, honey. You have work tomorrow, right?"

She blinked and realized she'd fallen asleep. "What time is it?"

He groaned, and her mind immediately went to sex. That's when she felt him under her. "Two in the morning."

She'd come over to spend time with Flynn, talked his ear off, then fallen asleep on the man. How embarrassing.

In her haste to regain her dignity, she shoved her knee in a bad place.

He coughed and groaned. "Christ, hold on." He quickly disengaged, and the two of them sat on the couch not looking at each other.

Worry about bad breath, bed-head, and how rumpled her clothes must be redirected Maddie's thoughts from the fact she'd *fallen asleep on Flynn*.

He let out a loud yawn and she peeked at him. A hint of stubble covered his jaw, but other than that, he still looked sexy and a little bit dangerous. A man no woman in her right mind would ignore.

Not sure why she wanted to run and hide, Maddie resolved to walk out calm, in control, and at least presentable. "I'll be right back." She moved to his bathroom and made good use of her time. Now sporting brushed hair, an empty bladder, and minty fresh breath courtesy of his toothpaste and her finger, she returned to the living room and found him waiting for her by the door.

She didn't know whether to feel insulted or glad that he had no intention of having sex with her. Then again, they weren't dating or anything. She'd come over to spend time with him, friend to friend. No big deal. Yet she wanted him to make a move, to throw her against the wall and take her. Or maybe bend her over the couch, pull down her pants, and—

"Ready to go?"

"Yeah." How disappointing. Flynn hadn't made a move all night. At first she'd been hopeful when he'd tugged her into his lap. But he'd done nothing more than hold her.

She slipped on her shoes and followed him out the door and down into the attached garage, where she'd parked in his friend's empty spot. The air had grown chilly, and she shivered, wishing she'd brought her jacket. Then again, she'd only planned to stay an hour or two, not half the night.

At her car, they paused. She fished her keys out of her pocket and unlocked her door. Before she could get in, Flynn stopped her.

He turned her to face him, then caged her between himself and the open door. "Thanks for coming over, Maddie." His grin made her heart race. That affectionate expression on his face had never been there before that she'd noticed. "Believe it or not, I had a good time."

Before she could apologize for sleeping all over him, he stuffed her into her car and shut the door.

Not even a kiss good-bye.

She wanted to be angry about it, but this platonic barrier was for the best. She kept reminding herself of that fact all the way home.

And the next day. And the next.

She saw his truck parked at Mike's Friday night. Weekly poker night.

Flynn didn't come over to say hello. He didn't call or text her either. Just the way she'd wanted it. And his distance drove her *crazy*. On Monday, she tried to focus on work, on dealing with a demanding Linda. Linda pushed Maddie to work harder and smarter. To keep up with demand, Maddie hired more movers on a revolving schedule and now tackled two projects at once. Ideas for design came with greater frequency than they ever had when she'd been working for Fred. And she wondered if her newfound freedom stemmed from finally being allowed to set her own pace, her own way.

Which might have explained her fixation on Flynn. She'd found a man who didn't jump when she snapped her fingers. He hadn't taken advantage of her at his place. He bought her chocolates. A lovely card case. A frog. That stupid rose that she'd taken to a craft store to have pressed. Not for sentimental reasons, but to make a nice decoration she'd frame for her wall someday.

Oh bullshit. She liked the rose. She liked the damn frog. And she really, really liked Flynn.

Maddie huffed at her reflection as she stood over her dresser in her bedroom, wondering why Flynn's earlier text had her in a lather. The man wanted to play cards later in the week. *Cards*. A whole two and a half weeks of no sex, and Flynn wanted to play a dumb game.

Damn him.

The rules she'd made about them being casual could be fudged. Didn't he know that? Didn't he care?

Annoyed, she decided to call *him* for a change.

He answered on the third ring. "Yo?"

"Hey, Flynn. It's Maddie." No reason for her to sound so breathy, or nervous.

"Hi, Maddie. What are you up to?"

Monday night. They both had work the next day. But she couldn't think of anything but Flynn. "Not much. I was wondering if you wanted to play cards tonight instead of later in the week. That is, if you don't have to get to bed early or anything. I'm bored."

Stark raving loony.

"Well, I was going to turn in."

It wasn't even nine!

"But I wouldn't mind a game. Why don't I swing by and pick you up?"

"Sure. See you soon." She ended the call and hustled to get ready. In ten minutes, she wore her best sexy underwear, a short skirt, and casual T-shirt with flip-flops. Slutty but comfy. She hoped she confused the hell out of him.

Abby yawned and walked out of her office wearing holey pajamas, her glasses perched on the end of her nose. "This book is friggin' killing me."

Maddie laughed at her. "You spent all day in jammies? You look like a little kid minus the blankie."

Abby made a face. "So where are you going? I'd guess Flynn's, but you two have been pretty cool lately."

She wanted to pretend it didn't matter, but she couldn't fool Abby. "He's driving me *nuts*. One minute he's making me see stars, then he's all huggy-feely and friendly. I slept all over him last week. And I do mean slept. The man didn't even try to cop a feel."

Abby bit her lip, but Maddie could see the grin.

"What the hell are you laughing at?"

"Maddie, you told the man you didn't want a boyfriend. He's giving you what you want. I don't see the problem."

Furious because Abby was right, Maddie didn't know what to say. Then Flynn's headlights shone through the front window. "I'm fixing the problem right now. See you in a few hours."

Abby shook her head. "Dealing with you makes my head hurt. I need more coffee and characters who actually listen to me."

Maddie left Abby still muttering to herself. She jumped in Flynn's truck and smiled at him. She smelled a hint of cologne. He wore sexy jeans and a button-down shirt. Ha. She had him. Going to bed early, hmm? Then why did he suddenly look like a man out to impress his girlfriend? For once, the thought of being his girlfriend didn't bother her. That Flynn wanted to look attractive satisfied her wounded heart. *Pride*. Wounded *pride*, she corrected herself in a hurry.

His gaze lingered on her legs. "Nice skirt."

"Thanks."

He pulled out of her driveway and drove them to his apartment in record time, telling her about his newest job. "So the guy thinks he's Mr. Fix-It, and the wife is behind him shaking her head frantically, panicked the dude will actually try to take on the shower installation by himself. Brody talked him off the ledge while I started working." He laughed. "But we had to let the guy help fit some pipes together, so he can later claim he worked on his home project."

She loved his smile, the firm lips that curved when he grinned, the warmth in his gaze as he shared part of himself with her. Dopey reactions to a plumbing story, but she'd missed the guy.

"We're here." He parked and helped her out of the truck. "Nice flip-flops."

She wouldn't be caught dead in them in public, but she didn't want Flynn to think she'd dressed up just for him. "They're comfortable. So are the shirt and skirt. Feel." She put his hand over her belly and rubbed.

He didn't speak. His large palm curved around her abdomen and squeezed her side, and she thought she had him. Instead, he pulled away and cleared his throat. "Yeah, soft."

She followed him out of the garage and up the stairs to his apartment, dying to see if he had an erection. Her panties already felt damp, and she knew her nipples showed through her thin T-shirt and bra.

Once inside his apartment, he closed and locked the door behind them. "Drink?"

"A beer if you have one."

He looked surprised. "Yeah. Let me get it."

A glance at his front showed him aroused before he turned.

Bingo. More than pleased, she twirled a lock of hair around her finger, knowing she looked damn good. She joined him at his kitchen island. "Been busy?" *Is that why you haven't picked up your phone to actually talk to me?*

"Yeah." He took a bottle from his refrigerator, opened it, and put it in front of her. "Last one."

"We can share."

His gaze moved from her eyes to her mouth, then lower to her breasts, where it settled. Until she put the bottle to her lips. She opened her mouth and took a swallow, watching him watch her drink.

His lips parted, and he licked them.

"Thirsty?" She offered him the beer.

"Hell yeah." He downed half the bottle before putting it down. "You're doing this on purpose."

She played innocent and frowned. "Doing what?"

"Sucking that bottle like it's my dick. Wearing that short little skirt, teasing me with that ass. And those breasts. I can see your bra through the shirt, Maddie. Fuck. I'm hard and hurting. You going to make it better before we *play cards*?"

"Look. It's been two weeks. I have needs, you know." She walked around the counter and moved right into his personal space. She toyed with the button in the middle of his chest. "Would you rather I went somewhere else to satisfy them?"

His eyes narrowed. Before she could say another word, he turned her around and bent her over the counter of the island. His hands ran from her knees up her legs to her thighs. He paused and leaned over her to whisper in her ear, "You need a good fuck, don't you?"

She had a hard time catching her breath, lost in her desire to feel him again. "Yes."

"Shoot, Maddie. All you had to do was say so."

"Right. You barely called me for two weeks."

"So you called me."

She should have been more suspicious of the

satisfaction in his voice, but his hands continued their ascent. He lingered over her ass and explored her flesh.

"God. You're wearing lace. Not for long." He pushed up the skirt and pushed her panties down her legs. "Kick them off and spread your legs."

She moaned, so wet and needy she thought about begging him to hurry. But did he need her as much? Or had he satisfied his lusts with someone else? The thought pissed the hell out of her.

"You don't seem too eager to me," she said, sounding out of breath. "Maybe you're not ready to give me what I need, too busy giving it away to someone else."

He smacked her ass and rubbed the sting away. Then he did it again, and she let out a small cry. "Oh, that's nice. Don't worry, Maddie. I've been too busy with work to fuck my way through the city." He laughed, but the gritty chuckle sounded mean. "Not that I would, not with this waiting for me."

He flipped her over, so that she lay with her back against the island, facing him. "Take off your shirt. Let me see those tits."

When he talked like that, she saw his control erode, and it turned her on even more. She pulled her shirt over her head but paused when his lips tickled her navel.

"I said off. The bra too."

She tossed the shirt but had trouble unfastening her bra. Flynn didn't move to help.

She finally unfastened it, and he pounced.

Flynn yanked her bra away and latched on to her breast with a groan. He sucked and nipped, teasing with long draws of his lips.

On the verge of orgasm from his touch, she shifted under him, wanting more.

He let her go and stared down at her as he pinched both nipples. "Greedy girl. You hungry, Maddie? Want something more?"

So aroused, so incredibly moved by this man who looked at her with such intensity, she couldn't speak. She'd never been so turned on her in life.

"Get on your knees and suck my cock. Get me nice and wet." He stepped back and watched through hooded eyes as she sank to her knees on the cold, hard tile and unbuttoned the fly of his jeans. He pulled something out of his pocket and put it on the counter near him. A condom.

She smiled and watched as his long, hard shaft sprang free from his jeans. No underwear for Flynn tonight. Oh yeah, he'd been wanting her as well.

She settled her lips over him and gladly drew him deeper. His hands tangled in her hair, gripping not too hard, but with control. She moaned at the thought and sucked him, licking as she bobbed over him.

"Yeah. That's it. Get me so hard, so I can fill you, Maddie. Yeah, just you. Two fucking weeks of waiting. Little witch." His hoarse moans encouraged her to take him deeper into her throat. She scratched his thighs through his jeans and knew he felt it when he thrust faster.

Then he pulled out and let go of her hair. He yanked her to her feet and bent her over the island, belly down, while donning the condom. The cold granite under her breasts stimulated her anew, and she writhed, needing him inside her.

Flynn nudged her ankles, spreading her wider. He

bunched her skirt up around her waist. Then he was there, shoving hard up inside her. So thick and hot as he fucked her without mercy, not stopping for anything.

"Oh God. Yes. Flynn, *yes*." She didn't need anything but him, bumping that spot deep inside her that sent shock waves through her body. She'd never come without stimulation to her clit, but she was on fire. He thrust deeper and swore, and she came, an explosive melding of heart and body she couldn't describe.

His groans told her he'd reached his own orgasm, and knowing she'd brought him such pleasure only increased her own.

After a few moments, she started to feel the cold under her breasts, the stretch of her legs, and the rasp of his jeans against her ass.

"Hold on." Flynn withdrew and helped her stand. "You okay?" He turned her in his arms and kissed her. But the kiss deepened as they held each other. When he pulled away, his eyes shone with emotion. "Once isn't enough."

"No." And she feared it would never be enough. Not with Flynn.

He disposed of the condom and tugged her with him. "Come on. We're just getting started."

Two hours later, pleasantly sore and unable to think about Flynn without feeling him inside her, Maddie lay alone in her bed at home and stared at the ceiling. She should have been too tired to do more than sleep, but her brain wouldn't stop spinning.

Tonight, having sex with Flynn had satisfied every cell in her body. And it had turned her into a whimpering, begging woman unable to do more than cry his name. Sex had never been so good. And she'd never, ever, felt so tuned to a partner. She wanted Flynn. She liked Flynn. She thought about him all the time.

She had a very bad feeling she might be falling in love with him. A sure path that led to disaster. What to do about him remained the question. She fell asleep with worry on her mind and an ache in her heart.

The next two weeks passed in a blur. Maddie had two houses to work with. One she finished in no time. The furniture and color palette actually worked with the house, but the design and layout needed work. Easy. The other house needed a lot more labor, as well as time she didn't have.

She'd had to put off two arranged outings with Flynn, and she refused to allow herself to miss him.

Gratified by her choice to remain independent, she couldn't figure out why she felt so annoyed with everyone and everything.

When Kim and Robin threatened to kick her ass if she didn't go out and get hammered before coming back to their furniture shop, Maddie figured she'd better get a handle on herself. Robin really would kick her ass and not feel bad about it.

She moped around the house, unable to start anything with Vanessa, who was working late, or Abby, who'd gone grocery shopping. Maddie fell onto the plush chair and turned around, so that her bare feet touched the wall above the cushions and her head dragged on the floor, the rest of her body seated upside-down on the thick leather seat.

The blood rushed to her head, and she pondered

her current circumstances. Not being with Flynn was so damn difficult. He hadn't been a prick when she'd canceled on him, taking her refusals with good humor. He refused to yell or fight with her. Then again, maybe he didn't really miss her. Maybe he was glad to take a break from her. Had she become the clingy one in their pseudo-relationship?

The idea didn't sit well. After all her warnings and caution, to then be the one to turn around and be ultra-needy went against the grain. She had never, ever, been the one left behind. Hell, Maddie made it a point to stand strong. She did the walking away, not the other way around.

"Hello?"

The familiar voice instantly made her happy.

Which annoyed her.

"Don't you ever knock?"

An upside-down Flynn regarded her with bemusement. "Is this some kinky version of yoga? Because if so, sign me up."

She realized his focus had shifted to her midriff, currently bared by her gaping shirt. On a muttered curse, she sat up and tugged it down. "What are you doing here?" Inwardly she cringed. Great. Now she sounded like a shrew. And with her hair all over the place, she probably looked like a witch.

Flynn blinked at her. "Ah, wow. This is probably a bad idea. I'm sorry. I'll go."

"No, wait." She stumbled over her feet to stop him and a felt like a complete idiot. Go, stay. No wonder the guy wanted to rush from the house. She didn't even like herself. "I'm sorry. It's been a rough few days."

He gave her a sympathetic nod. "Sorry. I know you probably want to relax, and I'm bugging you. It's just..."

Flynn looked haggard, now that she took a good look at him. "What's wrong?" She grabbed his arm, relieved to feel his solid strength beneath her fingers.

"It's Colin."

"What? Is he okay?" The little guy had such a special place in the McCauleys' hearts.

"I'm watching him tonight while Mike is doing some work with my dad. Problem is, he's misplaced his favorite stuffed animal, and I don't know what to do to help him. I was stupid and offered to get help to find the thing, which helped calm him down a little. He's freaking out. Is Abby here? I'll even take Vanessa."

"Wow. You must be desperate."

"I am." They both heard Colin whine across the yard for Uncle Flynn. "I'll just tell him no one was home. Don't worry about it. I'm sure we'll find the thing."

"No, wait. I'll help." Glad for the excuse, she looked for her shoes.

"You don't have to." Now Flynn seemed uneasy. The poor guy. A bitchy girlfriend—*friend*, she reminded herself, who happens to be a girl—and a crying nephew. She found her shoes stuffed under the leather chair. "Let's go."

Twenty minutes later, they still hadn't found Colin's Ubie. Named after the man who'd given it to him, the bear supposedly had a cute smile and the same coloring as the leather sofa. Colin frantically darted all over the house trying to find it, with Flynn hard on his heels.

It would have been comical if the little guy didn't look so stressed out about it.

"When is Mike coming home?" she said under her breath.

"Another hour." Flynn sighed. "Go on home, Maddie. I'm sorry for bothering you."

She felt terrible. He looked so put out. When Flynn cared, he really cared. "You love Colin so much. You're such a great uncle." She surrendered to impulse and hugged him. Strong, capable Flynn, putty in the hands of a small boy hankering for his bear.

"I found it! I found it, Uncle Flynn!" Colin raced through the house carrying a rugged bear. His joy promptly faded when he looked at them hugging. Then he burst into tears.

Astounded, Maddie hurried to his side and crouched down. "Colin. Are you okay?"

He nodded and threw his arms around her neck, shocking her.

She hadn't held a small child in years, not since she'd accompanied Abby home one Christmas and picked up her niece. Colin was a lot bigger than a baby. He smelled like popcorn and chocolate. His arms were surprisingly strong for a child his size.

"He wants you to pick him up," Flynn whispered. He tugged Ubie from Colin's hands.

She struggled under his weight but stood with him, and he immediately locked his legs around her waist. She patted his back, whispering words of comfort until his sniffles quieted.

"Want to sit on the couch with him? He likes that. We can turn on his favorite movie," Flynn offered.

She nodded and sat down on the couch with the little boy in her arms. He pillowed his head on her chest, and the strangest tug of longing hit her. She looked down at his mussed black hair and stroked it, taken with the silky softness. His lashes looked long and thick against the pale lids of his eyes. So innocent, so precious.

Flynn sat next to her. "Want me to take him?"

She couldn't speak. Instead, she shook her head and tightened her arms around the boy. When Flynn put an arm around her shoulders, she didn't protest. And before she knew it, she laid her head against his chest, comforted by the surety of him. The love he had for his nephew brought tears to her eyes, piercing the part of her that secretly wished he had more to spare.

She watched the television with a quiet joy, absorbed in the boy, the man, and the animated movie with an odd mix of affection, desire, and security. She wondered if Mike knew what a treasure he had in his family, and especially in the brother who would do anything for his nephew.

Chapter 17

FLYNN SHOULD HAVE FELT WORSE ABOUT WHAT HE'D done, but he was a man at the end of his rope. For five bucks, a pack of Raisinets, and Jiffy Pop, Colin had done the McCauley name proud. He'd given Flynn just enough time to tear Maddie away from her bad mood and give him the attention he'd needed. The kid's tears had been an added, if not necessary, bonus. That hadn't been in the script, but trust Colin to show off. The boy had a lot more in common with Brody than Mike wanted to think.

Now the little dork lay nestled in Maddie's arms looking way too content with himself. Jealous, Flynn forced himself to behave. Christ, could the woman be any more perfect for him? He could tell she didn't have a lot of experience with kids. She'd held Colin with an endearing awkwardness. God knew the kid weighed a ton for someone so young. But she'd held on tight, not letting go, showing an instinctive need to protect that called to Flynn. He wanted to be more than her lover and friend. He wanted Maddie as his wife. *Good God, I mean it. I love her.*

If he couldn't convince Maddie to give him a real chance at togetherness, he didn't know what he'd do. He couldn't eat. He had trouble sleeping. His brothers kept making fun of him. His mother had watched him with that knowing eye the last two Sundays. Hell, even being the recipient of Maddie's wrath earlier hadn't dissuaded him from caring. She turned him on. Big time.

He grazed her neck and stroked her hair.

She still held Colin tight, but a glance at the little faker showed him ready to rouse. Kid had a hard time missing his video games, even for a con as well played as this.

"I'm going to put him to bed." Seven o'clock, but hopefully she wouldn't realize how early it was. "He'll be more comfortable in his room."

Her arms tightened around Colin. Oh hell. She didn't want to give him up. The woman who claimed to not want anything to do with a relationship held onto his nephew, looking like she'd cry if he pried the kid from her arms.

In a softer voice, he said, "It's okay, Maddie. I'll take care of him."

She looked at Colin again before meeting Flynn's gaze. "Oh. Right. Sure." She pulled the little guy away from her chest and held him to Flynn.

He lifted Colin up and squeezed him to make sure the kid remained quiet. Once down the hall and in Colin's room, he closed the door behind them. "Colin, here's an extra five. You earned it."

He noted the empty box of candy but saw Colin had half a bowl of uneaten popcorn. "Look, you have maybe another forty-five minutes before your dad gets back. If he knows I gave you this crap, I'm toast."

Colin nodded. He knew the score. "So did it work? My crying was pretty good, right? And freaking out about Ubie?"

"Outstanding." Flynn ruffled his hair. "Remember, this stays between you and me. Just play your game, quietly, and give me some time with Maddie. Then I'll send her home and you and I'll wait for your dad. None the wiser," he warned.

Colin nodded, too happy to play his video games and eat in his room to object. "Cross my heart and hope to die."

"Stick a needle in my eye," they said together with a grin.

Flynn turned to the door. His hand on the knob, he paused when Colin called his name. "Yeah?"

"I like Maddie. She's soft. Not like Gramma. Different."

The kid had no idea. "Yeah." He cleared his throat. "So you think I should try to keep her?"

Colin nodded.

"Then you can't tell, okay?"

Colin crossed his heart again.

Flynn put a finger to his lips, waited until Colin nodded, then walked out of the room and closed the door behind him. He rejoined Maddie, who stared unseeingly at the television.

"You okay?"

She gasped. "Oh wow. I didn't see you there. Is the little guy all right?"

"As rain." He sat down next to her. "I can't thank you enough, Maddie. He seemed to calm down with you here."

She gave him a shy grin, and his heart tumbled and broke at her feet.

I am so fucked. "So, um, I know you've been busy and all, but would you like to play cards tonight?"

"What kind of cards?"

"Ever played cribbage? It's fun and perfect for two people. It's mostly a numbers game. Runs and pairs, numbers that add to fifteen." *Or my personal version of sixty-nine, if I get really lucky.*

"Sure." Her enthusiasm pleased him. "I guess I should let you go." She stood. He stood with her.

"I'll bring the cards and the cribbage board over when Mike gets home." He stepped closer. Without asking, not wanting her to say no, he kissed her. Her lips felt so soft, so welcoming. The breath they shared meant everything to him. More than sexual, her touch soothed him, filling that void he hadn't been aware stood empty. He caged her in his arms, feeling protective, unsure about their future yet wanting it with his last breath.

He let her go when she stepped back. Their eyes met. Hers light brown, questioning. He could only imagine what she saw in his. Likely a nightmare.

She took a deep breath and let it out. "I'll see you soon." She walked to the door, looked at him again and waved, then left.

Half an hour later, he and Colin waited for Mike on the couch. They watched some lame show while debating Colin's aptitude for the theater. Three more times the kid had cried on command, put on an angry face, or looked pitiful. Mike really had his hands full with this one.

They'd finished the popcorn and some juice. Colin didn't need to go to bed until nine, so Flynn wasn't breaking any rules by letting him stay up. Mike entered the house at eight-thirty looking majorly pissed.

He gave Colin a hug and a kiss on top of his head. "Colin, buddy, go put your PJs on. I need to talk to Uncle Flynn."

Colin glanced from his dad to Flynn and made a face.

Flynn snorted. "Go on, you monster. Let your dad yell at me without an audience." He knew damn well the kid would linger in the hallway eavesdropping.

The minute Colin left, Mike hauled him to his feet by the collar of his shirt. "Hey."

"What the fuck did you say to Mom?"

"Ah, what?"

"Don't pull this shit with me," Mike lowered his voice. "Mom just spent the last hour grilling me about *Abby*. What the hell? She told me you had second thoughts about the last time you'd talked to her. *The last time?* That you had fucking concerns about my relationship with women and that with Abby here, I might be confusing the past with the present."

The truth—Flynn *was* concerned. Okay, it hadn't exactly been fair to sic their mother on Mike, but if she'd gotten him to open up, the tiny lie had been worth the effort. Not to mention Flynn had gotten some quality time with Maddie, as well as an invitation to her place. A win-win.

He dodged Mike's fist and shoved his brother back. The ox. "Look, I thought I was sharing some personal feelings with Mom. I had no idea she'd narc on me and pull you into this." Well, at least the part about her telling on Flynn.

"For the last time, I loved Lea," Mike rasped. "She's dead, and no one's bringing her back. Abby is nice, she's our neighbor, and that's *all* she is. I know it. Colin knows it. Abby knows it. Now leave it alone."

It felt good to hear Mike admit it. He never said Lea's name unless pressed. But Flynn had the smallest niggle of doubt that maybe Abby's resemblance hurt Mike more than he'd let on. But no, his older brother just looked mad as hell, not hurt.

"Good to hear, buddy." He ducked another punch. "Hey. I was concerned. And you never talk about her. Colin asks stuff, you know?"

Mike paused. "He does?"

"Yeah. Like what Lea was like, how the two of you used to act, how you met. I tell him the truth. About how annoying and gross it was when you were kissing. Or how much he reminds me of her sometimes." Flynn knew none of this was easy on his brother. "He needs to hear it from you too, Mike. The picture on his bed stand is great, but the kid misses his mom."

"He never knew her." Mike coughed and looked away, and Flynn felt like an ass for forcing this. But hell, someone needed to talk to Mike about his avoidance. He didn't know why his mother never pushed it.

"Yeah, but *you* knew her. Show him it's okay to laugh about her. You say you're over her passing, but it's been almost six years and you still aren't. Maybe talking about her will help." He couldn't imagine what Mike had gone through when Lea had died, and he'd been there. What if it had been Maddie? Flynn had this huge ball of tangled feeling for her, and they were still in the infancy of their relationship. Not married yet, not with a child on the way.

The thought struck him between the eyes.

Not married. *Yet*.

"Dude? I'm not going to hit you again," Mike said gruffly. "You look ill. Relax. I'm not that mad. Anymore. I'll talk to Colin," his voice rose, "who should be getting ready for bed."

They both heard scrambling and a door slam.

"Bed, right. Hey, I need to borrow the cribbage board. I'll see you later. Sorry about Mom."

Mike sighed. "Yeah, right. But don't think I don't know you're scamming on the redhead. I'll take it out of you later."

Not willing to risk his good fortune, Flynn grabbed the board and the cards and bolted.

—∿—

Maddie typed in the office she presently shared with Abby, comfortably ensconced at the small desk now organized and outfitted with her own all-in-one printer/fax/copier, laptop, and electronic filing system. She had a stack of books in the bookcase behind her, as well as a rolling file cabinet holding receipts, schedule books, and other odds and ends.

Empowered, organized, and overworked. Pleasantly tired from the many jobs she'd been working on the last three weeks, she couldn't have been happier with her new life. Hampton's Designs had become a distant memory, especially since she'd given her version of her treatment at the place to a lawyer needing testimony on behalf of *another* woman Fred had apparently harassed.

She no longer feared losing money with her staging business. She had her own crew, a rhythm of sorts, new contacts through Linda, and a few other real estate firms looking to take advantage of her services. Apparently, Grace, her Howe Street client, had a big mouth, and she'd told all her friends how well Maddie had worked on her house.

Keeping busy wasn't a problem. Managing Flynn was. They spent all their time together.

Sometimes in the evenings they took walks through different parks, always holding hands. They'd gone miniature golfing. Watched a few movies. She'd laughingly enjoyed bowling with him and his idiot brothers. And one Saturday, she'd given up a spa day with her friends to go to a ball game with him. Even more shocking, she'd had fun listening to his witty remarks and watching the game.

He was constantly surprising her by bringing her coffee or lunch when he had the chance, making her whole day brighter with just a glimpse of his smile. She'd never been with a man who seemed to like her so much, who made her like *herself* so much. With Flynn, Maddie saw herself as a strong woman worthy of admiration—for more than her looks.

And their relationship showed no sign of slowing down. He didn't react if she had to cancel on him, other than to show regret. He'd been busy himself, getting more work because of the jobs he'd done up north. She didn't like him spending so much time away from her, and that worried her.

Oddly enough, the times spent at her house, they didn't have sex. Whether he thought she might be embarrassed around her friends or he was, she didn't know. She only knew it bothered her that they had boundaries between them.

Boundaries you put up first.

"Hey, anybody home?"

Her heart raced. Flynn had arrived. She had butterflies thinking about taking that next step with him. For now, best to keep to what she and Flynn did best. Have fun and have sex.

"In here."

He opened the screen door she'd kept unlocked for him and eventually found her in the office. "Hey, beautiful." He smiled at Abby, then turned a feigned surprised look her way. "Oh, and you too, Maddie."

She poked him in the stomach.

Abby snickered. She twirled in her chair to face them. "I told you he had taste. Now shoo, you two. I'm working and I need the quiet. Go pal around outside or upstairs. Whatever."

Flynn dragged Maddie from her desk. As if he had to try that hard.

"Where's Vanessa?" He wore that wary look on his face he usually had regarding her cousin.

It didn't help that Vanessa had nearly bashed his head in with a baseball bat the first night Flynn had slept over. But in the dark, she'd had a right to be afraid.

"She's hanging with Cam, I think," Abby called from behind them.

"Cam?" Flynn frowned. "I thought he was out of town."

"I guess not." Maddie didn't pull her hand from his, warm at the feel of his calloused fingers cupping hers with a gentleness he seemed to hold just for her.

"I don't know if I like the thought of your cousin corrupting my brother."

She laughed. "You're kidding, right? Vanessa's tough, but I doubt anything can scare a McCauley."

The intense look he gave her scalded her to her toes. "You'd be surprised."

She increased the wattage of her smile, pleased when he blinked. "Speaking of surprises, I have a few for you tonight. Want to go for a walk first?"

He narrowed his eyes in suspicion. "Together?"

"Yes, together, you moron."

He squeezed her hand. "Do I have to let you go?"

"Do you want to?" she teased, feeling very unlike herself.

He pulled her in close and kissed her with one of his trademark bone-melting embraces. She shivered when he pulled away, as always, aware of the powerful muscles that surrounded her. Part of the thrill with Flynn was that he could so easily dominate her. Physically. Yet he left the control in her hands, unless they made love.

Not made love, had sex, Madison. Get it right.

"You okay?" he asked.

She shook off the pathetic emotional whiner within and nodded. "Yep. Let me get my shoes and we'll enjoy the sun before it goes down."

They walked down West McGraw Street to Queen Anne Avenue and mingled with the other evening walkers. The foot traffic had thinned, and they spent their time laughing and enjoying one another's company. He bought her an ice cream cone that he ended up eating as well.

"I love chocolate." He kissed her, then stole another lick of her cone. "But it tastes better on you." His gaze wandered over her lips to her breasts, and she could almost hear him thinking.

"Uh-oh. Too cold, no matter how you try to lick it off."

He grimaced. "Don't say things like that out in public. It's embarrassing to walk around with wood."

"With what?" She frowned then blushed when under-standing dawned. "Flynn. You're so crude."

"Well, yeah. I'm a guy." He yanked her with him, and they passed a few people Flynn and she knew.

"Did you see that?" he asked, sounding way too satisfied.

"What?" All she'd seen, and tried to ignore, was the way the women had been ogling Flynn. Hell, they were holding hands. Just as friends, but those women didn't know that—or did they?

"They were looking at us. At you and me, together."

"Really? Looked to me like you had some fan-girls checking out *your* ass. Or maybe it was your wood, hmm?"

Flynn had just taken another bite of her ice cream and sputtered. "Jesus, Maddie. Keep it down." His cheeks turned red, which she normally loved. Except she noted yet another woman's gaze lingering over him. Used to ignoring the way women watched him, she suddenly found herself irked.

"Take your own advice, studly. Well?"

"Well what?"

"Is there a reason women around here seem to think you're available? All those late night plumbing jobs? Are you doing more than fixing sinks, Mr. McCauley?"

"What?"

She lowered her voice, suddenly annoyed. "I'm talk-ing about sex, dumbass. You have women checking you out all the time, but those last two were practically foam-ing at the mouth. Is there something I should know?"

He stared at her wide-eyed. "Oh my God. You're jealous."

"I am not." Good Lord. Could she have been more obvious?

His grin made her feel two inches tall. "Madison Gardner. You. Are. Jealous. Green with it."

"Shut up, Flynn." She pulled her hand from his and stalked away with *her* ice cream. She tossed the melting mess into the trash and found a new route home.

"Hold up, babe."

Then he had to make her feel worse. *Babe.* She felt so sexy whenever he called her those intimate names. *Baby, babe. Sweetheart.* But he usually used those words during sex, and they sounded sincere because he made no effort to use them outside the bedroom.

Not that she should allow it. She tried to get mad. "*Babe?*"

"Baby? Is that better?" Flynn kissed her hard on the mouth before she could say anything. "I think we should get back."

"Why? So you can duck out to go play with Bambi and Bubbles?" Why couldn't she keep her mouth shut? Every time she spoke she sounded more and more— *damn it*—jealous.

"Because my *wood* is getting hard to hide, even in these jeans. I told you how much it turns me on when you get mad. And you do have a temper, Maddie. Oh yeah."

Stunned and aroused that he could possibly want her after her immature display of jealousy, to which she had no right because they *weren't* dating, she followed his advice. They made it back to the house in record time and rushed upstairs to her bedroom.

She locked the door behind him and leaned back against it. "I actually have plans for tonight," she said in between breaths.

He paused at the button to his jeans, not even winded. "You do?"

"Yeah, with you. So take off your clothes and lay back on my bed. No talking." She turned on her iPod and set the speakers high enough to mask the deep moans she hoped he'd soon be making.

"Yes, ma'am." He flashed her a wicked grin and stripped.

"Talk about impressive." His cock stood stiffly at attention, thick and hard. Flynn had nothing to ever be embarrassed about his body. Sculpted muscle, a clean, masculine power that made him smell like sex and hunger all rolled into one. And Lord love him, but he knew what to do with what he'd been given.

"It's always hard around you. Not my fault you're so hot."

She flushed with pleasure. "Yeah, right. Now lie down. Good." She found a small bag by the bed and unzipped it. Then she removed four scarves and a blindfold.

He sat up. "Is that for me or you?"

"You."

He didn't move. But then he lay back with a big grin. "I didn't know you were into games. You just keep getting better and better."

"Than what?" she muttered, wondering to what, or to whom, he compared her.

"My fantasies of you. I have this one, but in it I'm tying you down."

"Well, then, you'll have to dream on while I have fun, my way."

"Whatever you want. Should I call you Mistress?"

"Shut up, Flynn." She chuckled and tied his wrists and ankles to the bed.

"Now, Maddie, the blindfold isn't necessary."

"Then maybe I'll use it as a gag if you don't zip your lips."

"Witch." He muffled a smile as she tied the material behind his head and adjusted it over his eyes. "Oh yeah. I feel more without my sight. Okay. Get busy. I'm all yours."

She looked at him, really looked at him, and wondered how she'd gotten so lucky. As usual, a rush of panic followed that thought. Gardners weren't good at relationships. Her mother had spent over two decades with no life and had just now started dating. Maddie didn't want to follow in her footsteps.

"Hello? Still waiting."

Feeling like an idiot for wasting this man in this position, she hushed him. "I have a ball gag, and I'm not afraid to use it."

"Just remember, I'm all about payback. And I'm stronger than you." He pulled at his wrists and his muscles bunched.

"Gee, Flynn. I'm so impressed." She laughed softly when he swore. "I'm taking off my clothes, give me a minute."

He stilled like a stone. His cock bobbed in anticipation.

Once naked, she crossed to him and planted a soft kiss on his ankle.

"A little higher."

She smiled. Her kisses trailed up his calf to his knee, thigh, and higher. Past his hips. She lingered over his nipple, gratified by his hiss of pleasure. Then she sucked on his neck and ran her tongue over his ear. "Hmm. You taste good."

"You're good at this." His thick voice excited her. "How about my mouth, Maddie? You haven't kissed me there yet."

"No. Or your cock. I haven't kissed you there, either." She knew he liked it when she used frank language.

He groaned and met her mouth when she kissed his lips. She let him push his tongue into her mouth and tease her with dominance, but then she took back control. She scooted down his body again and tortured his other nipple, refraining from using the clamps that also sat in the bag. Abby and her bag-o-treats. The woman claimed she needed them for reference material. Personally, Maddie thought her roommate had a kink streak she needed to explore.

But Maddie couldn't complain she wasn't enjoying it. Flynn looked delicious bound and hard under her. She stroked his body, absorbed in his figure as more than fine art. As part of the man she had a large fear she'd fallen in love with.

Chapter 18

Just the thought of the L word freaked Maddie the hell out, so she took her mind off it with some naughty talk.

In a low whisper, she told Flynn what she planned to do with him. Each announcement met with strained muscles and his whispered pleading to go free and take charge, which she had no intention of allowing. She drew circles on his skin over his belly, his ribs, his hips. She traced the muscles in his thighs, drawing closer but not touching his shaft.

"Maddie. You're killing me," he rasped, arching his hips. "God, I'm so fucking hard. I want you, baby. So bad."

She smiled and kissed his thigh, her cheek right alongside his cock.

He swore.

"Shh. I don't want to have to gag you."

"Then stop playing. Put your mouth over my dick and I'll—*shit*." He groaned and his entire body tensed as she sucked his cockhead, licking her way down and kissing the rigid length of him.

She sucked him and took his cock as far back down her throat as she could until she wanted to gag. Then she let up on him and pulled her mouth off. She lifted his shaft and sucked his balls, pumping his cock while she nuzzled him.

"Fuck. Oh fuck, Maddie. Shit, that's so good."

She'd reduced him to a bundle of swear words. Nice work.

But she'd revved herself as well. She joined him on the bed and brushed her body over his as she sought his lips. Before she kissed him again, she whispered into his ear, "I'm so wet for you. You're gorgeous, just lying there so hard and thick. But my pussy is empty, baby."

His chest rose and fell in rapid breaths, and he turned his head to steal a kiss. With unerring precision, he found her lips and kissed her until she couldn't think. She pressed herself against him, grinding her pelvis against his erection as the kiss intensified.

She pulled away, gasping, and realized he'd taken charge.

"Oh yeah. Grab one of the condoms from my pants and roll it over me. Then slide down, baby. Let me come inside that pussy."

She'd planned tonight to finally relent and trust him. She wasn't worried about disease—they'd already confirmed with each other that they were clean. She considered her birth control one level of defense against unplanned pregnancy. But to let him go without a condom… A condom would practically nullify the possibility.

She always made her partners wear one. Without fail. But Flynn was different.

She scooted down his body again and sucked his cock, trying to show him how deeply she felt. How much affection she had for such a strong man with a caring manner he tried to hide under gruff jokes and in those odd moments he thought she didn't see.

The looks he shot her, full of confusion and tenderness. The way he had of making her life easier. He never judged, didn't order her around—unless in bed—and supported her without being condescending.

"Maddie, I'm gonna come, baby. Oh fuck. You have to slow down. Or suck harder," he groaned.

She let him go and rubbed her breasts over him on her way back up his body. "I want you to come." She nipped his earlobe. "Deep inside me."

"Yes."

"Just you and me. No rubber."

He tensed. "What?"

"I'm on birth control. I-I want you inside me. To feel you come in me."

"You sure?" he asked through gritted teeth when she rubbed her body against his again.

"Yeah." She rose and put her nipple by his lips.

He latched on and sucked, playing with her until she wanted to scream. She moaned. "Let go."

"Other one," he mumbled around her flesh.

"Okay." She leaned back and he released her. Then she settled her other breast near his mouth and watched him work her. So sensual. All that pleasure, that focus he centered on her.

She tweaked his nipples and ground over him, smoothing her arousal into his skin.

"Oh yeah. Fuck me, Maddie. Ride me hard. But take this blindfold off. I want to watch you. I *need* to watch you."

She pushed it off his head and sat up, taken with the glittery emeralds of his eyes. "Oh Flynn. You are so sexy."

He stared at her breasts, her belly, and her pussy. "Put yourself over me, but go slow. Let me watch you take me inside."

"I thought I was in charge." She held him as she slowly settled over his girth.

"You are, Maddie. Oh fuck. You are in charge."

She took him inch by inch and sat all the way down on him, impaled and loving it.

"So sexy. Move over me. I can't believe how warm you are. I can feel it, every bit of that soft pussy, baby."

She rose up and sank down.

"Yeah. That's it. Fuck yourself on me. Come over my cock, beautiful." He sounded hoarse, and he had yet to look away from where they joined.

She rode him, up and down, faster then slower. The fullness was indescribable, and knowing nothing lay between them as they made love shoved her headlong under his spell.

Slamming over him, she took him harder and deeper inside her. So huge, he felt as if he touched the heart of her womb, and she couldn't wait to watch him come, to see him cry out as he shot deep inside her.

"Touch yourself. I want you to come with me," he ordered.

Domineering, even tied to the bed and under her. Her Flynn.

She fingered herself as she rode him, and his body locked up tight.

"Oh yeah. Maddie, baby, I'm coming. I'm coming *hard*."

He moaned as he released, and the agonized pleasure on his face threw her into her own bliss. She pinched her clit and clamped down on him, awash in the prolonged ecstasy of Flynn spilling inside her as her inner walls seized with contraction after contraction.

Shaking, she fell on top of him, wanting to feel his arms around her.

It took her a minute or two to realize he *was* holding her.

"What—"

"I could have gotten out of them earlier, but you seemed to like being in charge." Flynn kissed her cheeks, her nose, her mouth. "I think you need a little lesson in who's really in charge, don't you?" He twitched inside her, and the smile that grew on his face reflected in his eyes.

He let her protest and squirm over him while he chuckled.

"Flynn, it was fun though, wasn't it?" She pushed her hair out of her eyes and studied him, trying to see if he might be a touch mad about it. He had agreed, after all, but she'd had fun torturing him.

"Baby, that was fun we're going to have again. Tonight." He looked deeply into her eyes and pulled her face down to kiss her.

The touch of his lips shook her. There was nothing carnal or dominant about it, but a sharing of mouths and minds and hearts. The softness and care, followed by a hug that held them close and didn't lessen, eased her worries that he hadn't liked it… and furthered *more* worries because it grew harder to deny the truth of how she felt about him.

He pulled away and smacked her hip. "Now I think it's time for a little payback. Don't you?"

Flynn smiled at the picture she made. All cleaned up and fresh. And tied down with the ball gag, so he didn't have to hear her curse at him. "Now, is that any way for such a pretty girl to talk?"

She scowled at him behind the gag.

"What's that? I can't hear you, honey." He leaned back, admiring his handiwork. He'd tied her wrists to her headboard but left her legs free. That way she could wrap them around his waist when he took her this time. "Spread your legs, you naughty girl."

She didn't move, showing a sexy stubbornness that only aroused him more.

"It would be a good idea to obey me, Maddie. You're all tied up and gagged. How well do you really know me? I mean, I could fuck that ass right now, and you couldn't say no."

She shot him a death glare and her eyes glinted with a fire he intended to put out. Was there anything more beautiful than an annoyed redhead glowing with anger?

"Oh man, I want to bang you so hard. Look at me." He held his erection in one hand, not surprised to see himself just as big as he'd been previously. "You sucked a lot of come out of me, but I'm ready to go again. How about you, baby? You ready for me?"

He'd been teasing her on and off for a good half hour. Enough time for them both to have cleaned up and recovered for round two.

He moved back between her thighs and lowered his mouth to taste. "Not wet enough, I'm afraid."

Kneeling between her legs, he toyed with her folds,

sliding his fingers along the soft flesh before pushing through. Her heat constantly amazed him. Why, he didn't know. But every time he shoved his dick or his finger inside her, it felt like coming home into a hot, welcoming place.

Watching his finger disappear inside her made his balls hard. He pulled out his finger and slid it down toward that taboo area that seemed to excite her well enough. Her nipples, those hard little berries, begged for a nip. And as he rimmed her anus, he sucked her tits until she whimpered around the gag.

He pushed the tip of his finger inside her, and she froze.

A bite to her nipple shocked her, and he shoved a bit more of his finger inside her.

"It feels thick, like it's too huge. But it's not. Just a little tease to keep your attention, hmm?"

She shook her head, and her wine-red strands teased the upper slopes of her breasts.

"You're so pretty, Maddie." He removed his finger from her ass and leaned down to suck her clit again. "So sweet."

He sucked and licked until the constant moaning behind the gag got to him as well. "Okay, I'm going to take away the gag. You have to promise not to yell at me."

She frowned.

"Promise."

She rolled her eyes and nodded.

He unstrapped the gag but didn't give her time to reply. Quickly straddling her neck, he lowered his balls to her mouth. "Suck them, baby. See how hard I am for you."

She licked and sucked his sac, and he had to force

himself not to grind against her face. She had to feel more than just lust for him if she tolerated all this. Sucking him, licking him, letting him gag her…

He pulled away and blanketed her body, positioning himself between her legs. He rested his cock against the entrance to her pussy.

"Why me, Maddie? Why let me make love to you without a condom?"

"Does it matter?"

He wanted to say no, but it did. Sensing she wouldn't answer, he slowly pushed inside her. When she would have closed her eyes, he stopped. "No, watch me. I want to see you while I love you."

She bit her lip but didn't break eye contact as he continued to push inside her. So deep, so hot. He glided across her curves while his cock filled her, made her his. Once seated all the way inside, he stopped and rested his upper body on his elbows.

"Kiss me, baby. Show me what you feel," he whispered and lowered his mouth to hers.

She closed her eyes at the last second, and he did as well. The feel of her transcended everything. He tried to hold still but as she teased with her tongue and lips, he lost himself to his instinctive need to tie himself to her. Thrusting with a slow, steady pace, he enjoyed the teasing, gentle seduction of her mouth.

She'd been rough before, and playful when she wanted to be. But tonight, she appeased. She accepted. She urged him to give her all of himself. Despite his attempt to go slow, he couldn't help speeding his rhythm.

Her legs wrapped around him, deepening his angle of penetration. He continued to graze her clit with each push, and she moaned as she linked her ankles behind his back.

He trailed his mouth to her cheek, her neck, and fucked her harder and deeper.

"Yeah, that's it. Take it, Maddie. Take me deep inside you. All of me." *Love me, honey.*

She twisted her hips and groaned his name, climaxing so beautifully. Her ripples stimulated his own rush to the edge, and he shuddered as he came inside her. Her breasts teased his chest, her legs rubbed his sides, and he continued to pump until he had nothing left to give her. Nothing but a sappy heart and a proposal sure to send her screaming out of the city.

He kissed her, wishing he could just blurt his feelings. But the woman had only just allowed him to hold her hand in public. It wasn't the time to push the commitment button, no matter how much he wanted to. He released her bonds and rubbed her wrists, captivated by her soft skin.

Maddie hugged him tight and placed a soft kiss at the base of his neck.

He sighed and held her close. Not planning to let go anytime soon. Or at all if he had his way.

The next morning, Abby watched Flynn and Maddie during breakfast, trying not to be obvious about it. Flynn looked like the cat who'd eaten the canary. She'd done her best to steer clear from the upstairs last night, but she'd heard a few love moans anyway.

And boy, that hadn't helped her get any sleep. So she'd switched gears and worked on her manuscript. She supposed she should thank the lovey-dovey pair. The love moans had filled some gaps in her story. She'd had to use her imagination, but she hoped Maddie might fill in a few details later today about the bondage gear Abby had loaned her.

Maddie, the lucky witch, had a post-coital glow that had yet to fade. Tall, pretty, and now getting regular sex. Three outstanding reasons to hate her best friend.

"Who burned the bacon?" Vanessa groused as she entered the kitchen wearing a sleep shirt that barely hit her mid-thigh.

Flynn, oblivious, barely waved at her before he stared back at Maddie with a dopey, dreamy smile.

He had it bad. Abby was happily heterosexual, but even she couldn't look away from Vanessa's hopelessly long legs. The woman had an attitude but a killer body.

"He didn't stare. Barely blinked at you," she murmured to Vanessa, who sighed.

"I know. I guess we're going to have to get used to all that male groaning after all." She cleared her throat and in a louder voice said, "Thanks for the attempt at breakfast." Her eyes widened on the counter. "And that, with the bow? Where did that come from?"

Flynn shrugged. "I figured since I've been spending a few nights over, I might as well say thank you for putting up with me."

"It's the high-end model. It grinds the beans. Oh, and an attachment for frothed milk. Yummy." Vanessa acted like a kid at Christmas, and Abby had to laugh. While Vanessa read the directions on the espresso-coffeemaker, Abby took a whiff of something delicious coming from the... oven?

"What's in there?" She'd come to breakfast a few minutes before Vanessa.

"Homemade sticky buns, courtesy of my mother. Sorry. I can grill and cook the basics, but I'm not into baking."

"Neither is Abby, though she tries," Vanessa said while fiddling with the coffeemaker. "Okay, Flynn. You can stay. But if you're serious about hanging out, next time let Maddie gag you. I had a hell of a time falling asleep last night."

Maddie turned red, and Flynn choked on his coffee but nodded.

"Wow. This is outstanding. Now I don't have to settle for that stupid Mr. Coffee in the morning."

"Hey, there is nothing wrong with Mr. C." Abby treasured her ancient coffee pot. A caffeine addict, she had a hard time functioning without her daily java infusion. "I'll move it into the office. Save myself a few trips every morning."

"Yeah, like your ass needs the break from even that much daily exercise." Vanessa snorted.

"Leave her alone, Vanessa." Maddie smiled. "I think you should use that open corner in the office for your coffee table. A mini coffee area, like the one I used to go to each morning when I worked for my old employer."

Since Maddie seemed fine mentioning her old boss, Abby decided to reveal something she'd recently learned. "Speak of the devil, did you know Fred Hampton stepped down as CEO of Hampton's Designs yesterday?" Everyone gaped at her. She shrugged. "Robin and I had a conversation. I would have shared it, but I'd forgotten about it and figured you would have heard about it already."

Maddie smiled at Flynn again, her heart in her eyes. *Oh my God, the girl has fallen in love.* Abby shared a stunned look with Vanessa, who pretended to strangle herself.

"Right. So." Abby cleared her throat. "We're going to go shower. Me and Vanessa." Knowing how that sounded, she amended, "Not together or anything." Flynn didn't even look up at that. She dragged Vanessa with her from the room. The big-footed blond still had a death grip on her instruction manual.

"Okay, okay. Ease up." Vanessa grimaced. "Wouldn't want to flash Flynn my ass and cause the poor man to dump Maddie flat." She snickered.

"Whatever." Abby shoved Vanessa up the stairs ahead of her.

At the top of the stairs, Vanessa paused and cracked a wide yawn. "I'm still tired. I wasn't kidding about all that moaning last night. Man, it was enough to have me fanning myself. He must be hot as hell in bed. I can't believe Maddie did him here. She's pretty shy about that kind of thing." Vanessa shook her head. "I hate to say it, but you're right. The girl is in love. I don't suppose you want to bet on how long it takes her to screw it up?"

Abby sighed. "I give it a month."

"Please. A week at most. Twenty says I'm right."

They shook hands and parted. Abby wished she could have bet against Maddie messing things up. But she knew the girl too well.

Chapter 19

NEARLY A WEEK HAD PASSED, AND MADDIE FELT LIKE she was walking on clouds as she sat in the office near Abby, trying to focus on work. She couldn't think of her new clients without mentally thanking Flynn's aunt, which led to thoughts of Flynn. The way he smiled, how his lips crooked and his eyes twinkled right before he'd kiss her. All week long she'd lived with her phone glued to her hand in case he sent her a text. They'd spent alternating nights at his place or hers. Last night they'd accepted Mike's invitation to dinner. She'd let Flynn hold her hand, not at all worried about what anyone might say. It had "girlfriend move" written all over it. And she didn't care.

To her surprise, Flynn's brothers had been perfect gentlemen. They'd been fun to be around and demolished her chocolate chip cookies. Colin ate three. When she'd asked him about Ubie, he'd looked confused, until Flynn reminded him about the bear. Then he'd raced from the room to get his most favorite stuffed animal.

Brody remained the only fly in the ointment. He continued to watch her with what she swore was distrust. It bothered her. Brody and Flynn might as well have been brothers.

Why didn't he like her? Had she done something to come between the two of them? Was Flynn not working as hard, distracted like her, because of their as-yet-unnamed relationship?

She frowned, knowing the feeling. Despite her giddy happiness with the way her relationship with Flynn had blossomed, she still feared calling them an actual "couple." Which made little sense. But she worried her new *boyfriend* would change the moment she labeled them.

He hasn't changed since letting me tie him up. Maybe it's me who's changed.

Her stupid subconscious wouldn't shut up today.

Someone knocked at the outer door then rang the bell.

Maddie hadn't expected Flynn until later. She wanted to jump up and race to the door to see him. So she didn't. This leaping at texts and running to greet him like a damn dog had to stop. No reason for her to lose her mind and heart any time he neared. If only he didn't look at her with such proprietary interest. If only he'd act less like he cared for her, she might have been able to calm her rising discomfort. Plain and simple, she cared too much about him. She... *loved*... Flynn McCauley.

Oh shit. Shit. I really do. I love the guy. Me. In love. She stared blankly at her monitor.

"Gee, don't get up. I'll get the door." Abby jumped up from her seat at her computer and stomped through the hallway. For such a short person, she made a lot of noise.

Maddie distracted herself by opening her email. One message in particular stood out. A request for design help. Excited, she read the request over again before jotting down the phone number listed as a contact, along with the woman's name. Bonnie Weir.

Before she could make the call, Abby returned to the office with an odd look on her face.

"Abby?"

"You have a visitor."

"What's wrong?"

Footsteps sounded and she looked up, expecting Flynn, only to see Ben Foster instead. The old flame, Doctor Superior.

"Hi, Maddie. I wondered if we could talk."

Stunned, she glanced from him to Abby, who made a face but erased it when Ben looked at her.

"Don't mind me. I just write for a living. Let me clear out and let you two kids have some space." Abby left in a huff.

Moments later, Maddie heard the back door slam, probably Abby headed into the yard to pull weeds.

Maddie stood and motioned Ben to take a spot on the love seat by the far wall. She wheeled her chair from behind her desk to sit across from him, needing the distance.

She had to admit, the man looked good. Tall, dark-haired, and blue-eyed, he had a lean grace and easy confidence that had attracted her from the first. His low voice wasn't as gravelly as Flynn's, but reflected the cultured tones of a man raised to know his dessert spoon from his soup spoon. She'd been suitably impressed with him, in hindsight because his background had been so different from hers.

"You're looking good, Maddie. Really good." Ben smiled.

"You too. I'm surprised to see you here."

He nodded. "I figured. I would have called, but I wanted to see you in person." His face softened. "I miss you."

She didn't know what to say. She'd never expected this. "Ben, you told me to leave. So I left. I moved on with my life. It's been over three months."

"True." He sighed. "It's just… You're a lot to handle, Maddie Gardner. Beautiful, passionate, intelligent."

He was hitting all the right buzz words, but none of what he said really mattered.

"Ben, why are you here?"

He continued as if she hadn't spoken. Some things never changed. "I had a hard time keeping my ego with you. I used to try so hard to impress you. But you never seemed to need me around. When you pretty much told me to, and I quote, 'man-up or man-out,' I was stunned. I'd thought things were okay between us. Not perfect, but well enough. Do you have any idea what it's like to hear that the woman you love doesn't want to spend time with you?"

She paled. "Love?"

"Yes. It took me a while, but our time apart made me realize how much I missed you."

"You chose to cut me out of your life."

He laughed, but it wasn't a sound of mirth. "You're kidding, right? During our time together, any time I tried to get close to you, you froze me out. We didn't even make love at the end. We spent weeks apart. I got tired of it all."

"Oh?" True, at the end, she'd been the one to deny him. But months spent lying under him, waiting for him to please her, only after he'd pleased himself, had grated.

"The minute we'd finish screwing, you'd kick me out of bed or leave to go back to your place. I had a hard time handling that. And you didn't seem to care."

She definitely had a different recollection of events than he did. "Really? Because I don't remember the sex as much of a problem, at least not for you. But I do remember your tantrums whenever I couldn't make one of your doctor luncheons or work around your schedule. Any time I tried to devote extra effort to *my* career, you'd make me feel guilty for it."

"Extra effort?" His voice rose, and he made an obvious effort to tone himself down. "Maddie, you spent *all* your time working." He paused. "I once called your office looking for you. When I jokingly complained about all your overtime, the girl there told me you didn't get paid a dime for it. That you willingly volunteered all your hours, making the rest of them look bad."

She blushed. She'd told him a small lie about getting paid for her extra work in an effort to avoid hurting his feelings. Ben understood money. But putting design before him had always been an issue. Unfortunately for him, spending time with Ben had never been huge on her agenda.

Ben shook his head. "I sometimes worked harder at my job than on our relationship, I admit. But my practice demanded it. I knew yours didn't."

"Yes, but I wanted to make my career work. I busted my tail for that place."

Odd how she'd hadn't thought much of it the past few weeks.

"The thing is, Ben, you never seemed to understand how important my work was to me. You're a successful doctor from an affluent family. You come from money. I never begrudged you that," she said to forestall his objection. "You are what you are. I've worked my entire life to make my way. I grew up relying on myself. I never needed you for your money."

His eyes narrowed. "And maybe that was part of the problem."

"I'm not a gold digger. How is that a problem?"

He blew out a breath. "It wasn't that you didn't need my money, but that you didn't need me. I was convenient. We made a nice couple, handy when it came to professional functions where we needed a date. Everyone said how perfect we looked together."

He was right. Their looks had complemented each other, as had their designer clothes and white-collar jobs.

"It was more than that," she protested.

"Was it? Can you tell me you've thought about me since we broke up? Don't you miss me at all?"

She missed his friendship, but not being a couple. Not sure how she would have answered, she didn't get the chance.

A low, annoyed voice interrupted, "What the fuck is this?"

She pulled back from Ben and stood, feeling out of sorts. Some stupid girly part of her wanted to cheer at Flynn's jealousy, while another part of her wanted to remind him that no one owned her. "Flynn, this is Ben. Ben, Flynn."

"Ben?" Flynn turned his accusatory glare on her. "The same Ben who dumped you right before you left your job?"

"Who the hell is this?" Ben sounded irritated, but in command of himself. He also sounded a little haughty. "McSons," he read Flynn's shirt and blinked. "Wait a minute. You're one of the guys David's been talking about?"

"David?" Flynn looked torn between fury and confusion.

"David Weir. He's a friend of a friend," Ben added in that snooty way only he could. "He and Bonnie are building Mountain Pass. You know, that development in Anacortes?"

"Bonnie Weir?" Maddie had a bad feeling about the coincidence of so many names. "Hold on. Ben, why exactly are you here?"

"I miss you. I love you. I want you back." He threw out the words, more like a challenge than a declaration of love.

Flynn looked ready to burst a blood vessel. "Are you kidding me? You tossed her out, now you want her back?" To her he said, "This is your foot doctor?"

Ben fumed. "Foot doctor? Not that again. Maddie, really."

She still wanted to know what Bonnie Weir had to do with Flynn. "Hold on. Why did I just get an email from Bonnie Weir asking me about design help?"

Flynn's expression lightened. "She contacted you already? Good."

"Did you tell her to email me?" The surge of rage took her by surprise. How dare Flynn act like he owned her? Between Ben's posturing and Flynn's growls, she felt like a bone in a tug of war between two mangy dogs.

His slow smile stopped. "Yeah. She was talking to David about getting a professional to do some work for them on the development. A few predesigned houses in addition to the club house. I thought of you."

"I take care of myself, Flynn. I don't need your help. I'm doing fine on my own."

"Yeah, I can see that." Flynn shook his head. "This isn't about me giving my girlfriend help, is it?"

"Girlfriend?" Ben scowled.

"I'm not your girlfriend."

In a soft voice, Flynn asked the question she'd been asking herself for weeks, "Then what are you, Maddie? What are *we*?"

"I, we—"

"Are we a carbon copy of you and Ben? A pair who fuck, hang out for a while, have some fun, then go our separate ways when *you* decide we're done? What say do I have in this?"

Ben answered him. "If you're like me, you won't have one. I'm sorry, Maddie. I can see it was a mistake to come here." He turned to leave but stopped at the doorway. "You never needed me, Maddie. That was the problem with us. It was your call, all of it. I only told you the answer you wanted to hear when I left." He glanced at Flynn and shook his head. "Good luck, buddy. You're going to need it."

Ben left, but she and Flynn stood there staring at each other.

To her shock, she felt tears spill down her cheeks.

Flynn didn't seem to care. His face was stony, his eyes dark. "I'm sorry I interrupted your little lovefest."

Her temper rushed to the fore. "Screw you, Flynn. He was a surprise. But this, with you… it's been a long time coming, I guess."

"Yeah, I can see that. Is this where I get the man-up or man-out speech? Where you cut me off by the balls and tell me to stop clinging to you? I hate to break it to you, Maddie, but I'm not a pussy to be shoved around. Hell, you want the truth? I love you. I have *feelings* for you. Real feelings. And yeah, I mentioned your name to Bonnie and David. Because in my business, that's what we do. I also mentioned Gary and Rick, friends who are electricians. It's a way to hook up friends with potential clients. But if you're not any good, you won't get the job."

"I don't need your help. I'm not some charity case." She clung to the idea he pitied her. No way he meant that part about loving her.

"Christ, you're an idiot."

"What?"

"It's not charity to accept a reference. Do you really think it's pitiful that my aunt mentions my company to anyone needing a good plumber?" He shook his head, looking at her as if he couldn't stand the sight of her.

She sniffed and wiped her eyes, dismayed she couldn't stop the tears. "It's not the same."

"Bullshit it's not the same. How is it—"

"It's not," she shouted, shocking him to silence. "You're great at what you do. You're talented, smart, funny, handsome. You have an incredible family. Everyone you know loves you."

"Except you."

She talked over him. "I have to earn my way with every step. Every failure and every success. I don't want to have to rely on a 'boyfriend,'" she ended defensively with a sneer.

"Oh no. You're not putting this shit on me. You want the truth? You don't *want* to hear how I feel. You don't want to know. You just want to bury your head and run away. Not needing anyone. God forbid you actually rely on me for anything. That you ask to come over to dinner or hang with my family without an official invitation.

You like my dick, and you like my company until I'm an inconvenience. Then you just want me to go away."

"That's not true."

"It is true. And you know what? I'm sick of it. Get your head out of your ass and think about what you want from me, and what you're willing to give me. I'm not your foot doctor. I'm not going to come crawling back to you begging you to take me back. Figure out what's important, Maddie." He looked like he wanted to say more but didn't. He stormed away from the room and slammed his way out of the house.

She hadn't noticed Abby standing at the office entrance, her eyes wide. And right next to her stood Vanessa. Maddie felt sick. As if she'd died but her body hadn't yet caught up to the idea. Flynn had the audacity to act as if she was just using him for sex or casual company? Their first big fight and he wanted to throw in the towel?

"Boyfriend my ass." She ended on a hiccup, burst into tears, and slumped back onto the love seat.

To her surprise, Vanessa didn't comment. Her cousin left and returned minutes later with a hot cup of tea. Abby didn't say anything either. She just sat with Maddie on the love seat, offering her support just by being there.

The three of them sat in silence for several moments, the occasional hitch in Maddie's breath the only interruption until Vanessa drawled, "Well, you really stepped in it this time."

Abby groaned. Maddie couldn't hold back more tears.

"Flynn was right. He could have been a little nicer, sure, but Maddie, you need to listen. You're smart and successful. I have no doubt you'll one day have more money than both me and Abby combined."

Abby frowned.

"But I'm worried about you. You never used to be like this. So afraid to take a chance. You seemed so happy with Flynn, so different with him. He never tried to control you, either. Not like Ben. He's a genuinely nice guy. Abby and I have seen some of the losers you've dated."

"Th-thanks a lot." She sniffed.

"I hate to agree with Vanessa on this, but she's right." Abby patted her knee. "I'm sorry, Maddie. But you're a little nutty when it comes to relationships. Flynn never pushed you for more than you wanted to give him, but he didn't let you brush him away either. He's the first guy I've ever known you with that you actually let close."

"And now look. He broke my heart. The jerk." She tried to stop the next crying jag before it started but couldn't.

"For once, I think you have the right to cry." Vanessa surprised her out of her tears. "You're throwing away something great, Maddie." She uttered the soft words with such sincerity Maddie couldn't tune her out. "I've seen the way he looks at you. The way he treats you. Like you're valuable but not breakable. He wants to help you, not hurt you. Why is it so hard for you to let him in? To let anyone in?" She reached for Maddie's hand and held it tight. "You wouldn't let me or Abby help you without paying us every last cent, and we're family. Closer than sisters. What's going on with you?"

Maddie didn't know. "I just… It's so hard for me to ask for help. It was Mom and me for so long. Vanessa, you don't know what it was like. We didn't have any money. Not *any*. I spent my days going to school and my nights helping my mom wait tables or clean houses. For a year we even lived in a shelter. Nothing was ever easy or free. It was all about surviving."

Vanessa looked shocked. "Why didn't you guys stay with us? We had plenty of room."

"Why? So Grandma could tell Mom what a loser and slut she was? So I could hear how I was a mistake and we'd never amount to anything? And Vanessa, get real. Aunt Loretta and Uncle Scott barely tolerated our visits when we did come."

Vanessa sighed. "You have a point. They barely tolerate mine."

"It sounds to me like your problem is pride," Abby offered. "We met in college. I'm not a part of your family's past. I didn't grow up with you, but you've told me how it was. Did you really like your mom making you work so hard? What would it have hurt if she'd asked for help for you? Not for her, for *you*? Maybe she'd have been called a few names or dealt with your pompous aunt and uncle." She bit her lip. "No offense, Vanessa."

"None taken."

"I know what you're both saying." Maddie sniffed. "It's just, Mom taught me to stand on my own feet. It's not safe to rely on anyone but yourself, she always said. Then I lose my job, and it all comes crashing down." She coughed, her heart sick, and admitted the root of the problem. "I don't need Flynn feeling sorry for me."

"Um, Maddie. I don't think you heard him right." Vanessa shook her head. "That man feels a lot of things for you. Sorry ain't one of them."

Abby agreed. "He did for you what he'd do for any of his friends. If you worked a job and someone needed a good plumber who wouldn't rip them off, wouldn't you recommend him?"

Vanessa smacked her in the back of the head.

"Ow!"

"Jesus, Maddie. Don't be dense. You're all but living in each other's pockets and have been for weeks."

"Not true."

"Abby? Tell her."

Abby sighed. "Yeah, well. Think about it, Maddie. You don't like labels, we get that. But you and he are exclusive."

"We're friends with benefits. It's just safe sex with someone I can trust."

"It's sex, *period*," Abby emphasized. "You either spend your nights at his apartment or here. You spent time with his family the other night. And he's had plenty of breakfasts in our kitchen."

"Not that we mind," Vanessa added. "Since he cleans up better than you do."

Maddie surprised herself by laughing.

Abby continued. "He's always doing stuff for you and trying so hard not to freak you out about it. I didn't want to tell you about this, but who do you think got your printer and your software for you at such a great price? Because it wasn't me."

"But you said you did."

Abby didn't flinch. "I lied. Flynn gave me the stuff and told me not to say anything, because of your many issues. The guy knows you. And despite that, he loves you. Hell, he admitted it in there. Laid himself on the line."

"Yep." Vanessa nodded.

Abby sighed. "The guy has it so bad for you, Maddie.

He's spent weeks letting you keep him at arm's length. Then you denied him—not his girlfriend?—in front of Ben and us."

"But he left me."

"Do you care?" Vanessa prodded.

"Of course I care."

"Then, as Flynn said, get your head out of your ass, realize you want *him*, and talk to him about it."

"The only man who might ever have truly loved me—for me—just walked out the door." Hearing herself say it, Maddie wanted to pull her hair out and shriek. She was scared out of her mind she'd just ruined the best thing that had ever happened to her. She felt so confused. She didn't know what to do.

"I think you love him, you're just too dense and terrified of admitting it." Trust Vanessa to call it like she saw it. "Don't you see? You've never shared yourself with anyone else the way you have with Flynn."

Was Maddie in love? Could a Gardner feel that elusive emotion for a man? An emotion she'd always wanted but had been cautioned all her life to beware? It had ruined her mother, made her—

"Hey, Aunt Michelle? Yeah, it's me, Vanessa. Hmm? I'm great. How are you?"

Why was Vanessa talking to her mom on Maddie's phone?

"Well, that's good. I'm sorry to be bugging you, but your daughter's head is stuck so far up her butt she can't see. She's in love and she just kicked the man of her dreams out the door. Can you talk some sense into her? Please?"

Vanessa nodded, beamed, and tossed Maddie the phone. "Just remember, you owe me for this. Name the first girl Vanessa. Unless she's ugly. Then name her Abigail."

Abby frowned. "Damn it, Vanessa."

Maddie brought the phone to her ear, still in shock over all that had transpired. "Um. H-hi. Mom?"

"Oh, baby. What can I do?"

Baby. What Flynn used to call her. She broke down in tears again.

Chapter 20

FLYNN GOT RIP-ROARING DRUNK IN THE PRIVACY OF HIS own apartment. He didn't want witnesses watching him in the aftermath of the biggest fuck-up in Flynn McCauley history.

He passed out some time around four in the morning. Maybe. He rose to puke a few times in the toilet, then crawled—literally—back to his bed and passed out again.

"Damn it, wake up."

The noise hurt his head and he swore.

"There you go." More background chatter. "Get him up. Over here."

"Hell. He stinks." Was that Cam?

"Th-thought you were out of town." His youngest brother, the baby of the family. The thought made him grin. Then he started laughing.

"Shit. He's still drunk."

"You think?" Brody's sarcasm didn't faze him.

The guys said a few more choice comments. Something hard poked him in the chest. Flynn blinked up at the light fixture on his bedroom ceiling and groaned.

"Hey there, sleeping beauty. What do you know? You slept the day away. It's after six *PM*. Get up already."

He avoided Brody's grabby hands and rolled out of bed. He stumbled into the bathroom and thought he pissed in the toilet. Or at least near it. He washed his hands, dried them on his rumpled shirt, then made a beeline for his kitchen and reached into his refrigerator for another beer. *For the woman that ails you.*

His bender had worn off. Now he felt pain, both physical and emotional. His head throbbed. His stomach refused to accept its emptiness and churned with the need to regurgitate more. But it was his heart that bothered him most. Taking a can from the refrigerator, he turned to his brother. "See, Cam? Not pussy beer. This is for real men."

Cam glanced from the beer to his face, his derision clear. "It's Bud Light, manly man. You on a diet?"

"They didn't have anything else at the store." He'd grabbed the first thing he'd seen on the way home. A case to drown his worries, of which he'd imbibed too much, added to shots of tequila. And maybe a glass or four of whiskey to make himself really forget.

He drowned his misery with another can. Or at least, he tried to. Cam yanked it out of his hands.

"Flynn, sober up. You're an ugly drunk."

"Fuck you."

"Snappy comeback." Brody huffed at him. "Now how about you tell us what the hell this is all about. You missed our three o'clock today, but luckily the client forgot as well, so we have a do-over next week. I kept the schedule light so you and Red could spend the day together. Didn't you have plans?"

"She dumped me."

Brody snapped his fingers. "I knew it. I knew that redhead would be nothing but trouble."

Cam eased Flynn into a chair. "See if you can tell us what happened while I make you some coffee. You look—and smell—like shit."

"Thanks." He flipped his brother the finger, but Cam's back was turned and he missed it. "I showed up last night to her place. We were gonna do the festival downtown."

"Which one?" Brody asked.

"Who the fuck cares? I showed up to see her chatting it up with her loser ex-boyfriend. The doctor."

"Ouch."

He didn't want Cam's sympathy. "She dumped him. I think." His memory of their conversation was fuzzy, mostly because he'd been too busy battling rage when he'd seen the guy reaching for her to pay attention to their words.

"So what happened? Was she seeing him on the side or something?" Brody looked annoyed—on his behalf no doubt.

"No. He was begging her to come back while she argued with him. Instead of just telling him she had *me*, she sat there asking him stupid questions."

"Ah." Cam nodded.

"What the hell does that mean?"

"You sure it's not a pride thing with you, Flynn?"

Brody intervened before Flynn could leap out of his chair and body-blow Cam to the floor. "Nice, Cam."

Cam shrugged. "Flynn's always been a little full of himself. It's kind of weird to see him drinking away his sorrows because he's a little jealous. I'm surprised he didn't fight for her if he wanted her."

"She didn't go with him, Cam," Flynn growled. "The dickhead left when she and I started arguing. She told me she's not my girlfriend. Then what the fuck is she?"

"A fuck-buddy?" Cam offered.

"That's what *she* said! I love the woman, and she

can barely tolerate me. What the hell is wrong with this picture?" he asked on a moan.

Brody patted his shoulder. "Oh man. So she rejected you? The big *love* hanging out there between you now, huh?"

"Yeah." *Stupid, stupid*. "We fought, I told her to get her head out of her ass. Then I left."

Cam and Brody just stood there and stared at him.

"What?"

Cam frowned. "Okay, tell us again what happened between you two?"

He'd just finished explaining when Mike pushed through his front door. "What the hell did you do?" He rushed to Flynn.

Worried Mike might kill him, Flynn jumped from his chair and shoved Brody in his path.

"Thanks a lot, Flynn." Brody held Mike back, barely.

Mike swore and stalked away. "You see? This is why I told you to leave them alone, Flynn. At eight o'clock this morning, Vanessa was at my house demanding I talk to you."

Flynn could only focus on Maddie. "Why? Is Maddie okay?" As much as she'd pissed him off, and she had, he didn't want to think about her being hurt.

"According to Vanessa, the girl is miserable right now."

He groaned and avoided Mike's glare, feeling overwhelmed by so many people in his small apartment.

Mike sighed. "Since I'm pretty much the only one with real relationship experience, let me give you some advice."

Cam took exception. "I've had girlfriends."

"Yeah, I've had my share of dates." Brody glared when the others just looked at him. "Sex counts."

Mike continued. "Flynn, you need to get yourself together. If you care about Maddie at all, just give yourselves some time. It's good to argue. It's healthy."

"Fuck. We argue all the time. Woman is too damn bossy as it is."

Brody shrugged. "So dump her. Move on."

"I can't. I love her." The confession came out in a croak.

"Shit," Mike groaned. "He's done. Dad has it for Mom. I had it for Lea. It's a McCauley thing."

"That you-only-love-once bullshit is old, Mike." Brody shook his head. "But in Flynn's case, it might be true. I saw it from the first."

"You did not," Flynn snapped, annoyed with Brody's arrogance. "That woman is the most illogical, aggravating, emotional woman I've ever met. She puts two and two together and gets five. Not my girlfriend?" Furious all over again, he stood and would have thrown something if he'd had anything in his hands. "We shared ice cream. We talk all the time. Trade nights at each other's places. I let her tie me up, for God's sake."

Brody blinked. "Yeah, how did that go?"

"Never mind. The point is, I can't stop thinking about her. She's *it*. And she barely lets me hold her hand." Not exactly true, but he still felt like just getting to hug her in public was a huge accomplishment. Flynn McCauley, a man who had a list of women he could call at any given moment, wanted a woman who could barely call herself his girlfriend.

Flynn clutched his head, wishing he could go back and redo yesterday. "I wish I didn't love her. She's an idiot."

"With her head up her ass, don't forget that," Cam added to be helpful. He chuckled, and Flynn raised his head to glare at him. "You sure do have a way with words. Look, Flynn, either she loves you or she doesn't. There's not much you can do about it at this point. You left the ball in her court, now wait for her move. Hopefully, she'll go on the offense, straight for the hoop."

"Not basketball references." He felt nauseous. "I think I'm gonna be sick."

Mike looked embarrassed and crossed his arms over his chest. "Over Bud Light? You are such a girl."

He heard the others laughing as he rushed to make friends with the toilet again. *Note to self: Bud Light and getting dumped don't mix.* As his stomach lurched, he wondered what Maddie was doing, and if she missed him at all.

—◦◦◦—

Maddie spent the first week after their argument pouting, and she knew it. Her roommates had been supportive yet annoyed with her for not putting things right with Flynn. They didn't seem to understand she needed time. Her mother had been less than sympathetic, which had shocked Maddie.

From a woman who had steered clear of male entanglements all her life, a *kudos* wouldn't have been out of place. But Michelle Gardner was suddenly seeing the error in her ways. Now dating some guy she couldn't get enough of, she wanted the same for Maddie. She talked about accepting help from family, letting people in, that men weren't the enemy... All of it gave Maddie one whopper of a headache.

That, and she cried herself to sleep every night, missing the hell out of Flynn. The little frog's eyes seemed to follow her around her bedroom, so she'd buried him in her sock drawer. Then she'd felt guilty and put him right smack in the middle of her bed.

She used the following week to fully work herself into exhaustion each night. She'd engaged in multiple jobs at a time, and she'd made some decent money by doing a lot of the moving work herself. It took her mind off her personal life and helped her professional reputation. But she knew avoidance wouldn't solve her problems forever.

Something she'd refrained from doing kept slapping her in the face, and as she lay in her bed, beyond tired, she let down the last barrier shielding her fragile heart. She finally let herself think of what Flynn might be going through. Putting herself in his shoes, she had to acknowledge he had a right to be annoyed with her. More than annoyed. Furious. Enraged. She just hoped he wasn't angry enough to never want to see her again.

"I am so stupid." She groaned and thought back to their argument.

If that weren't bad enough, he'd spotted her with an old boyfriend. What if she'd interrupted him with an ex? The thought of any woman with Flynn but her enraged her, but did she have a right to feel jealous? She'd been adamant to keep their relationship casual. Meanwhile, she'd given him encouraging signals indicating they meant more to one another. Sex, the blow job. No more condoms. Holding hands. Spending all their time together.

Of course he'd thought they meant more to each other. And why shouldn't he? He loved her.

She couldn't stop replaying his words in her mind.

Agitated and more than a little worried, she took a few deep breaths and called Flynn.

The phone rang four times before he answered. "Hello?"

"Flynn?" she sounded terrible, and she hoped he couldn't hear that she'd been crying.

"This is Flynn."

Terrific. He wouldn't make this easy. Then again, he didn't need to apologize. She did. "I, ah, I hope I'm not bothering you." At ten o'clock on a Thursday night, she was just happy to catch him.

"Trying to get to sleep after a long day at work." He paused. "So what do you want?"

"I wanted to say I'm sorry." Is that what he wanted to hear?

Apparently not, because he growled, "That's it?"

She didn't know what else to say. She had so much to make up for; she didn't know where to start.

But he must have taken her silence for disinterest, because he snorted in disgust. "Look, I have a long day tomorrow. I don't have the time or energy to deal with this right now. I'll have to talk to you later."

He disconnected, and Maddie lay there feeling worse than before. Hearing his voice had made everything all right, until he'd ditched her. He sounded as tired as she did. Guilt ate at her, knowing she'd taken a good thing and trashed it.

One thing she knew. As soon as she caught up on rest and thought about what she needed to say, she planned to see Flynn and straighten this mess out. She'd worked her entire life for what she wanted. The time had come to figure out how much she wanted Flynn in her life, and what she'd do to get him there.

The day after Maddie's phone call, Flynn sat next to their accountant in a restaurant, not sure what this evening was supposed to accomplish. He couldn't fake interest in the woman, no matter how attractive he found her. She had long brown hair, big breasts, and a tiny waist. And Tara liked both men *and* women. What Brody had called the mother lode.

Unfortunately, a stubborn redhead refused to leave his thoughts. He'd expected more after she'd called to apologize. Such a terrific sign that things might get back to the way they should have been. And then… nothing.

"Come on, Flynn. Have a crab cake. Brody swears by them." Tara pushed the appetizer plate at him.

He glumly lifted a piece to his mouth, not tasting anything but ash as he chewed.

"Dude, liven up." Brody frowned next to him. "Face it. It's over. If a woman treated me the way Maddie treated you, I'd make her crawl to me, begging to make up. Then I'd dump her ass again."

Brody was his best friend for a reason. "Yeah, that would be something to see. But I don't see her crawling anytime soon." So why couldn't he let her go and move on with his life? He'd had several old girlfriends call him looking to hook up. No doubt Brody had clued them in to his single status, if he was in fact single.

Maddie seemed to think so, but he couldn't convince himself to agree.

"He really is sweet. So heartbroken." Tara shook her head. "You know, if things don't work out with Maddie, I'd be more than willing to heal that broken heart."

Brody clinked his glass with hers. "What a woman. Tara, I swear, if we weren't in business together, I'd give you the night of your life."

"You're so unselfish, Brody." Flynn forced a grin, trying to be pleasant and mingle with the living again. He'd only gone out this evening at Brody's insistence. But this birthday celebration for Tara felt anything but festive. He hated dragging her down and tried to be more fun.

A glance around the restaurant once more made him wonder why in the hell Brody had insisted on frou-frou for Tara instead of a real meal. Since Tara preferred beer and pizza to things he could barely pronounce, it couldn't have been to impress her. Unless Brody was putting a move on their accountant, which no way in hell would Flynn approve.

At that moment, a hint of movement by a table at the end of the restaurant drew his notice. Maddie Gardner looked around the place, searching for someone. When she spied him, she lit up. God, she looked incredible.

"Here she comes," Brody said under his breath. "Look alive." In a louder voice, when Maddie reached the table, Brody welcomed her with a pleasant voice. "Hey, Maddie. Nice to see you again. What are you doing here?"

Maddie came to rest right behind Flynn's chair, so he couldn't see her expression. "I'm supposed to meet my roommates for dinner."

"You could join us if you want and round out our table." Brody nodded to a space next to him. "I don't think Flynn and his date will mind."

Not sure what the hell Brody was talking about, Flynn shot him a sharp look but said nothing when Tara's hand covered his on the table.

Tara smiled. "Hi, Maddie. I don't think we've met. I'm Tara."

He would have given his left arm to see Maddie's face, especially when Brody smirked.

"Nice to meet you, Tara." The ice frosting her words gave him real hope for the first time since that phone call. "Flynn, I was actually hoping to talk to you again. Maybe when you're done with your meal?"

Flynn took a deep breath and resolved to play his part. Maddie didn't like him dating Tara, did she? She wanted to talk to him? How badly did she want the conversation?

Brody kicked him under the table.

"Maddie." He turned and gave her a tight smile. "What did you want to talk about?"

There was a long pause.

"It can wait."

"Well, I hope you have a nice evening." He deliberately smiled at Tara. "I'm enjoying mine."

He glanced back at Maddie but didn't see anything more than her bland nod. The hand around her purse clenched tight though, and he fought the urge to grin. *Good. Get nice and jealous, Maddie. Feel it, baby. You care, I know you do.*

"I'll go look for Abby and Vanessa. Sorry for interrupting. Maybe we can talk tomorrow?"

"Call me. I have work with Brody first thing in the morning. Barring any major problems, I should be finished up by four."

"You have to work first thing in the morning?" Tara

pouted, sounding breathy and sexy all at once. "I was hoping we could go out after dinner."

"Sure, Tara. But I can't stay out too late." He winked at her, and she winked back.

Maddie didn't spare a glance at Tara. She glared at *him*, her whiskey gaze hot enough to burst into flames. "Fine. I'll call you and set up an appointment." She bit out the T, turned on her heel, and stalked away.

The table remained silent until she left the vicinity.

"Wow." Tara blew out a breath. "You sure you two are over?"

"I don't know." She still wanted him, she *had* to.

"Flynn, you okay, man?" Brody frowned. "If I'd known you'd get even mopier, I wouldn't have tricked her into coming. I kind of mentioned to Abby that we'd be eating here tonight. We all want to see you two talking again."

And that answered how Maddie had happened to dine at the same restaurant this evening. She'd either left or she sat in another area, because he didn't see her. He should have been upset with Brody's meddling, but he was too tired of the whole mess to drum up much annoyance.

He spent the next hour trying to relax and laugh with Brody and Tara, who proved to be a good sport. Apparently Brody had filled her in on his pathetic partner and she'd been gung ho to help in any way she could.

Flynn wished he'd fallen for someone like Tara. A pretty, laid-back woman without half the hang-ups a certain redhead had in spades. The night drew to a close, and he left the pair with a promise to be in to work early and not looking like hell. The short drive back to his apartment seemed too long, and as much as he wanted to head straight to Maddie's and get the confrontation over with, he forced himself to leave it in her hands. She'd done him wrong, not the other way around.

He could almost hear Brody nagging him. *Be a man. Suck it up, dipshit, and let the woman make her play. Then show her who's boss.* Of course, this advice from a man who had yet to have a serious girlfriend in thirty one years of life.

As Flynn slipped off his clothes and tucked into bed, he tried to see the positive in Maddie looking so angry. She'd looked like a woman on the verge of slugging Tara right in the mouth.

That had to be good, right?

Chapter 21

FLYNN HAD A FITFUL NIGHT'S SLEEP. THE NEXT DAY, he and Brody wrestled with a busted pipe that had to be dug up and replaced, as well as tracing a leak in an upstairs shower. Tired and annoyed with the owner, who thought anyone could have done the job, Flynn asked the obnoxious husband why he'd bothered calling them since he apparently knew every goddamn thing. Then Brody stepped in and sent Flynn home.

He didn't bother swinging by Mike's, not wanting to possibly see Maddie before he had his head screwed on straight. Instead he headed home and slammed into his apartment, wanting nothing more than a cold shower to wash away memories of Maddie. Just a few minutes of peace wasn't too much to ask. He'd stripped all the way down to his boxer briefs and was halfway through the living room before he realized he wasn't alone.

He swung around and tackled the person behind him, landing hard on him—her.

"Maddie?"

She squeezed her eyes shut and moaned. "I'm sorry. You don't have to beat it out of me."

Astounded, he leaned up, concerned he might have hurt her. "What the hell are you doing in here?"

She shoved ineffectually at his shoulders. "Brody gave me his key."

The feel of her hands on his bare skin had the same

effect they always did. His cock hardened. He stared down at her, seeing the strain on her face, the shadows under her eyes. Her dark red hair spilled over the floor, the soft strands making him itch to bury his hands in the stuff.

"I needed to talk to you," she whispered, her hands no longer pushing, but stroking his shoulders. "I was hoping to catch you alone. Not with that perky cheerleader you were sitting with last night."

"Who?" He couldn't think past the need to be inside her.

"We'll talk right after, I promise."

He frowned. "Right after what—?"

She pulled him down to her with surprising strength and kissed him. Pent-up passion, need, and frustration spilled into him with the strength of a tornado, and he returned the kiss with equal force.

He tugged her shirt off and made short work of her bra, baring her chest in seconds. Her hands somehow moved between them and buried beneath his underwear. She gripped him hard, teasing his cock with frenzied strokes. His slit was so wet, she slid over his shaft as if he'd lubed.

"Keep it up and I'll come all over you before I'm in you," he panted and sucked hard at her neck. The subtle scent of perfume and lust rolled off her in waves. Lightheaded, he could only give her whatever she wanted. Forgiveness, his head on a platter, his cock… He didn't care.

He physically hurt, his cock stiff and throbbing with the need for release. He'd been celibate since she'd left, unable to touch himself without thinking of her.

He latched on to her nipples, sucking with sheer pleasure.

"Yes, Flynn. Oh yeah. I missed you so much."

Words he'd been dying to hear for too long. But a part of him didn't like her coming to him like this. Sexually starved for her, he'd take what she offered. But he wouldn't let her get something for nothing. He couldn't. To watch her deny their connection again would hurt too much. The woman had to know she needed him.

He shoved his hand beneath her pants and panties and speared her pussy with his finger. Christ, she was wet. Her heat surrounded his finger as he rubbed her clit, pushing her to the edge. He took comfort in the knowledge she still wanted him.

"You need my cock, honey? That why you're here?"

It hurt to say, but he wanted the truth before he laid his heart at her feet *again*.

The woman took him by surprise. She let go of his cock and shoved at his chest. "I came for you, jackass. Not just your wonder cock." Obviously angry, she yanked on his hair, and he expected her to push him away. God knew he didn't have the strength to leave her.

Instead she tugged his mouth to hers and bit his lower lip. Not hard, but enough to shock him. The minute he opened his mouth, she shoved her tongue inside.

He rubbed against her, body to body, arching against the willing, warm woman who mattered most. He wanted to but couldn't deny her satisfaction.

He leaned up and stripped off the rest of her clothes and his briefs, then put her right back under him. "Spread your legs." It would be fast and furious, but they both needed this.

She did and clutched him to her, kissing him like a starving woman.

He nudged her thighs wider and found her wet entrance. He plunged inside. The ecstasy of her flesh around him was intense. He lost himself to the feel of her, her scent and touch. So familiar, yet she stoked his primal desires and stirred his buried anger.

He pounded inside her, for once not concerned about her climax as much as he was about reminding her where she belonged. And each thrust brought pleas for more from the stubborn redhead.

"You're mine, Maddie. My *girlfriend*." He fucked her deeply, stroking against her body with each pass, determined to make her beg. "My lover. I'm fucking *my* woman." He added a twist to his pelvis and felt her entire body clench. Then he forced himself to stop.

"Flynn. *No*. Don't stop. Oh God. *Flynn*."

"Say it. Tell me you belong with me." He sucked on her breast, biting her nipple while using his weight to still her movements. He ached to come, but he refused to let her take the easy way out.

"Yes, yes. I'm yours. Please, Flynn. Make love to me."

Make love, not fuck. Semantics, but he knew the difference. And so did she.

Flynn pulled out before shoving deeper inside her. He made love to her with long, drawn-out thrusts. She cried out, scratching his shoulders as she squirmed around his cock.

"Mine. I'm going to fill you. And then you're going to lick me off, suck all your sweet cream off me, and make me hard again. You'll watch me fuck your mouth, and you'll beg me for it, won't you?" he ended on a

moan when she clamped down on him and keened his
name as she came.

"Maddie, yes, yes. *Oh fuck*." He poured into her, lost
in the connection while his scorching orgasm left him
weak and shaky. He lay there, in her, so close he could
feel her heartbeat. God, he loved her so damn much.

He tried to pull it together as he caught his breath.
Then Maddie took charge.

She rolled them over onto his back so she could move
off him. Despair struck, that she would leave now that
she'd gotten what she'd come for. She stunned him by
kneeling by his side, her hair like a fire around her face,
framing innocence and carnal knowledge in those big
brown eyes. She watched him with a soft, wondrous
smile. The look of a woman in… love?

She caressed his legs, his hips, his cock. "Do you
want me to beg you now? Or should I wait until you're
coming down my throat?"

He groaned and flopped an arm over his eyes, trying
to remember exactly what he'd said in the heat of the
moment. The temptress leaned close and took his semi-
erect cock between her lips.

"Maddie." He wished to hell he could get his
hard-on right back. She licked him, and knowing she
tasted herself turned him on. But fuck, she'd drained
him. It would take him some time to get his strength
back. "So is all this because you saw me with Tara
last night?"

As he'd meant her to, she pulled away and glared at
him. "Yeah, let's talk about your new *girlfriend*."

Oh hell no. He deserved an apology, not more of her
anger. "What do you care? You made it plain you didn't

want me. I was nothing but someone to make you come, right, Maddie?"

She blinked back her hurt, but he saw the tears. He felt like a horse's ass, yet he wanted her to be honest with him.

"Tell me the truth. Am I just a stand-in for Ben? What's the difference between me and him? Or me and all the other assholes you've dated?"

"Shut up for a minute and I'll tell you." She raked back her hair, the flyaway strands giving her a wild appearance. He'd never seen her look sexier. Her tits were heaving, her nipples hard. Her slender belly quivered, and he wanted to trail bites across the creamy flesh then…

Maddie's eyes narrowed when she saw where his attention had wandered, but he only raised a brow.

"What? This is what you came here for, right? An orgasm. Shouldn't you be on your way?" He was being a real asshole, but he couldn't stop pushing. He wanted his redhead to come apart, to fly at him, shout at him, scream. Anything but glare and seethe in silence.

"I came to apologize," she said through gritted teeth. "I shouldn't have said what I did, and not in front of Ben."

Not what he'd wanted to hear. He sat up, not liking her looming over him. He felt vulnerable enough. "Sorry. I guess you should have waited until your foot prince left."

He'd intended the words to be snarky, but instead of annoying her, he made her laugh.

"Foot prince? Yeah, he was that." She chuckled, her laughter misplaced, at least to him. "Okay, Flynn. I love you. Now would you please shut the hell up and let me apologize?"

He sat, stunned, and waited for her to finish. Could she mean it? Should he believe her? Because he wanted to, so fucking much.

Maddie sighed. "After my lame apology over the phone, I was going to find you and beg you to take me back. But I had a few emergencies at work, and I chickened out. I had no idea how to tell you how wrong I was. You didn't deserve any of that argument, and I'm so incredibly sorry if I put you through half the hell I've been through. So when I saw you at that awful restaurant, I figured I had the perfect opportunity to apologize." She glanced down at herself and huffed. "As usual, you screwed everything up."

"Me?"

The glare she gave him shut him up.

"That tart you were with last night made me lose my head. I was so jealous. It killed me seeing you with her. I had plans to… Oh hell. Flynn, I was a bitch to you from day one. Not my fault, really, because I was having a really bad day, and there you were, the enemy, looking incredibly handsome, sexy, and in control while I ranted and raved like a crazy woman. The next day, you were so *nice*." She drew out the word like a curse. "And so hot in your underwear. You really shouldn't walk around in those if you don't want to get jumped." She glanced at a similar pair lying on the floor next to them.

He couldn't help grinning.

"I'm a sucker for good abs." She bit her lip. "And a nice package. You're that and more. Flynn, you make me laugh. You made me cry too, and I'm not pretty when that happens."

"I know."

She scowled, and his heart threatened to burst from his chest. She held up a hand. "Let me finish."

He nodded.

"I said a lot of things I regret. I'm sorry I flipped out on you." She took a deep breath and let it out in a rush, but she didn't break eye contact. "I appreciate you mentioning me to the Weirs. I did call them, and the job sounds perfect." She blushed, which amused him, considering she'd just been thoroughly fucked and still sat naked in front of him. "I guess she also heard of me through a few friends I still have at Hampton's. So it wasn't just your recommendation that got me the job, but my work for them as well."

"Like I told you. They wouldn't hire you if you weren't good."

"Okay, okay. You told me so. I know. I was wrong. Capital W wrong. It's just, you don't know. I haven't talked a lot about my past because I don't like thinking about it. I never went into how hard it was growing up, but I think that's where a lot of my issues stem from. Don't get me wrong. I always knew my mom loved me, but she worked so hard. I used to feel like she'd have had an easier life if I'd never been born."

He frowned.

"I know, stupid to feel that way. She loves me to death. But we grew up pretty poor."

"Maddie, money isn't important to me—"

"Not to me either, which is weird, right? I should be hunting a rich man."

He shifted. Truth to tell, between his work and Cam's investment strategy, he didn't worry overly about money. Mostly he worked hard because that was what he knew.

"But for me, it's not about wealth, though I wouldn't say no to it. It's about not having to struggle like my mom did. I just wanted to prove I could make something of myself. I put myself through school and interned my ass off for a great job—or what I thought was a great job. You met me on a downswing." She gave him an apologetic grimace. "Instead of super-confident Maddie, you got the world-is-going-to-end Maddie. I was afraid I'd be back cleaning houses and waiting tables."

She brushed back a tear. He wanted to comfort her, but he didn't want her to stop talking.

"You're so successful at what you do," she continued. "It made me feel like I wasn't. This job is new to me, and I'm making mistakes."

"Maddie, we all do. Brody and I have been in business together for years and we still make them."

She nodded. "I know. I'm stupid. It's just, you're not like the other guys I've dated. Flynn, you matter to me," she confessed in a whisper. "I started falling for you, and I was afraid."

Though she tried to resist, he pulled her into his arms but kept a small distance between them so he could see her face. "Oh baby. Why? I'd never hurt you."

"But you would if you left. In case you can't tell, I like you a lot." She sniffed, and her eyes filled. "I didn't want to give you the man-up or man-out speech. All of my exes always manned out."

He hugged her tight and kissed her tears away. "I'm

not *them*, Maddie. I'm not going to settle for your ultimatums. It's not clingy to want to spend time with you."

She smiled through her tears. "Not when it's you. You're so strong. You make me feel safe. I just," her voice caught on a sob. "I was so scared you'd leave, so I pushed you away first." She wiped her nose with the back of her hand. "I'm so gross right now."

He chuckled. "Funny, I was thinking I've never seen you more beautiful. Those watery eyes, that pouty mouth. Maddie, you're intelligent, you don't take any crap from anyone, and you're sexy as hell. But I've met plenty of women who fit that description. It's you, what's inside you, that's what I miss when we're apart. Look, I'm not the most sensitive guy. I make mistakes. I love your body, so yeah, sometimes when you're talking, I'm imagining my dick between your lips, or my mouth on those beautiful breasts of yours." He loved seeing her flush. "But when I'm inside you, it's different. It's like I'm giving you something more."

The silence between them made him feel stupid. Could he be any more of a pussy? Maybe he should start his own Hallmark line—

"Oh Flynn." She hugged him to her, holding him so close he could feel her every curve and breath. "I've never loved anyone before, not a man, I mean. My dad didn't exist, and my mom made sure to warn me about the dangers of falling in love with the wrong person." She pulled back. "But you're not the wrong person. I panicked that I'd finally found the right one and you wouldn't want me."

"Maddie," he chided and kissed her. "Why wouldn't I want you?"

"I have a temper. I'm too emotional. I need to lose ten pounds, and I'm a mess at work right now. I'm under-billing your aunt, and I can't—"

He chuckled. "No, wait. One, your temper gets me hard." He pulled her back and forth over his growing erection. "You're a natural redhead. And you're so my type it's not even funny. I like that you're emotional. It's when you hide how you feel that I'm not that happy with you. You're perfect the way you are. I'm not seeing the extra ten pounds anywhere, but if you decide to lose them, take them from anywhere but your ass, tits, or stomach. I love passing that belly when I'm about to go down on you."

Her eyes darkened.

"About my aunt… talk to Cam. He's a wonder when it comes to billing people. Seriously. Or talk to Brody."

"He doesn't like me." She sounded pitiful.

"Yes he does. He's just worried for me. He saw how hard I fell for you. Like Abby and Vanessa with you, he and my brothers always have my back." He held her in his arms, content to stay this way for the rest of his life. "We're lucky people, Maddie. I love you. I want to *marry* you, and I'm willing to wait as long as it takes to prove to you I'm not going anywhere. You're it for me. Mike tells me it's a McCauley thing."

She nodded. "Okay."

It couldn't be that easy. "That's it? Just okay?"

She squirmed and rubbed against his cock again, fill-ing the damn thing out. "The first time was hard for me to say, but now I can't stop myself. I love you. I love everything about you, Flynn. Except maybe your taste in dinner partners."

Should he tell her the truth about Tara now or later? "Um…"

"I'll be honest. The thought of the future scares me. But I know I don't want to be with anyone else but you." She swallowed loudly. "I've been so scared of making my mom's mistakes, of getting pregnant before I was ready. That's why I've been on the Pill and why I made my partners wear condoms." Her eyes shimmered. "You're the only one who's ever come inside me. I love you so much, Flynn. When we were at Mike's, and I was holding Colin and sitting with you, I imagined what it would be like… to hold *our* baby."

She bit her lip, watching him for a reaction. Did she expect panic? Worry?

Elation filled him. "Oh honey, me too. But hell, you'd barely let me hold your hand, let alone refer to you as anything closer than a casual friend." He rubbed her belly. "Someday, when you're ready, when *we're* ready, we'll make that happen."

"Really? Even though I broke your poor heart?" She didn't sound very sorry about that. He thought her conceit could use a knock or two. But the pleasure, the love in her eyes captivated him.

"Broke it into tiny pieces." He had to clear his throat not to cry like a goddamn girl. If he shed a tear and the guys found out, he'd never hear the end of it. Then she smiled, and he couldn't contain his joy. One spilled over. "Shit."

She laughed and cried with him. "I won't tell. I promise."

He rubbed the offensive tear away with the heel of his hand. "I'll give you all the time you need, Maddie. I promise I'll be right here waiting. But breaking my heart the way you did, that's going to take one hell of an apology to forget. Maybe some groveling, on your knees, your mouth open, waiting for me. That might help speed my forgiveness."

She crawled out of his lap and knelt before him. She licked her lips. "I should make it up to you, shouldn't I?" A glance at his cock had her smiling. "What was that you said before? Something about sucking you deep and begging."

"Why don't you show me how sorry you are, you little witch?" His abs contracted as she ran her fingernails up his legs to his belly. "You owe me."

"I do. I love you, Flynn. Please, let me show you how much."

He stood and spread his legs, braced for her touch. Yet the hot friction of her lips around his cock still made him tremble. "Maddie, baby. I love you so much."

She moaned and sucked. Cupping his balls, she scraped those fuck-me nails over his scrotum and down his thighs, not hard enough to break the skin but just enough to drive him insane.

He panted, whispered her name, and prayed to last. But she gave him no respite. She breathed through her nose as she worked him, owning him with little more than the sweep of her lashes, the glance of her bright eyes.

"You're mine," he stated, unable to look away. "And I'm yours. Always, baby."

She sucked hard, licking and stroking with her tongue. Her breasts heaved as she blew him, and then she sucked him deeper and took him to the back of her throat in a move that shocked the hell out of him.

The added stimulation against his cockhead became unbearably good. He rocked into her mouth, though he'd done his best not to do anything to make her more uncomfortable than she had to be.

Yet she looked so eager, so into pleasuring him he couldn't think, only react.

Her hand again cupped his sac. His balls were rock hard, and he couldn't stop himself from thrusting deeper. Agony and ecstasy gathered at the base of his spine and pushed throughout his body as he released.

"Baby, yes. I'm coming… so hard…"

He groaned her name as he jetted down her throat, unaware of when he'd gripped her shoulders as he pushed deeper still.

When he could again function, he withdrew and heard her suck in a huge breath.

"Oh shit. I'm sorry." He sounded drunk and had trouble keeping his balance.

She shook her head and evened her breathing. "No, I'm sorry. I was wrong before. But I'm here now. And I'm not leaving." Was she convincing herself or him? Either way, he didn't intend to let her go again.

"Good. Because one good turn deserves another." In control of himself once more, he pulled her to her feet and lifted her over his shoulder. As he started for his bedroom, he slapped her on the ass. "Be a good girl and spread those legs for me once we're on the bed. Time for an early dessert, lover."

Epilogue

A MONTH LATER, STANDING OUTSIDE THE BACK DOOR to Mike's kitchen, Maddie glared at her hottie by the grill. Flynn had been driving her nuts lately and seemed to revel in pissing her off. He claimed seeing her angry aroused him, but she thought he was just getting her back because she'd given him such a hard time at the start of their relationship.

Almost five months together and they still had hot sex all the time. They laughed and played. She looked forward to the end of her work day to spend time with him and their interlocking families. His clan had fully embraced her and her roommates. They spent time together, all of them, and the warmth of acceptance had yet to fade.

"Hey, Red, stop dreaming and grab the plate for the burgers." Brody treated her like an extension of Flynn, but without all the cursing and roughhousing, thank God. They truly acted like brothers in every sense of the word.

She grabbed the plate off a nearby table and shivered at the wind that whipped through the open door, wishing she'd brought more than her fleece jacket. As they neared Halloween, the weather had become downright nippy.

"I'll give it to Flynn." Vanessa took the plate and sneered at Maddie's jacket. "Do you need me to dress you, too? I got you a great rental rate on the house you now barely live in, I still take care of your books, and I landed you a hot boyfriend."

Flynn must have overheard, because he turned around and saluted Vanessa by lifting a bottle in her direction. Brody muttered under his breath as he took the plate and darted back to Flynn's side.

Once he'd gone, Maddie said, "You didn't land me anything. If I remember right, you thought he was a user."

"Not so. I just think good-looking men can be a little too sure of themselves sometimes. Helps to take them down a peg or two." She lowered her voice. "I don't know if you've noticed, but something's going on between Abby and Brody. She won't talk to me about it yet, but I'm wearing her down."

Maddie was ashamed she hadn't noticed. Ever since she and Flynn had opened up to each other, her entire world seemed right. She didn't flinch when he talked about love or marriage anymore, and she fantasized about kids and a life with him all the time—except when working. There she'd become more than good at compartmentalizing.

Cam took that moment to nudge Vanessa and Maddie into the house, like herding sheep.

"Watch it, you jerk," Vanessa snapped then flushed when Cam pointedly looked at the small boy by his side.

Colin gaped. "Oh man. She called you a jerk."

"Now, Colin." Cam shot Vanessa a smug look. "You know we're not supposed to say bad words in the house."

Vanessa wasn't having it. "I was standing outside, spongebrain."

"Spongebrain!" Colin laughed and raced past his grandmother in the kitchen, no doubt to share this newest insult with the family.

No longer amused, Cam turned his back on Vanessa, who deliberately left the door open when she exited the house. "She's letting all the heat out," Cam complained and shut the door again before turning to frown at Maddie too. Through the window, she saw Vanessa stick her tongue out at the back of his head.

She grinned at Cam. "You sure the heat's out? Because you look pretty hot under the collar."

"You're not that funny." He nodded at his mother, working in the kitchen, then left Maddie when his father called to him from the living room.

Next to Beth, Abby stood eating a carrot and tapping her foot to some rock music playing softly in the background.

Maddie shook her head. "Aren't you supposed to be helping?"

Abby grinned and swallowed a mouthful of food. "I'm the taste tester. Try Beth's killer dip. I told her it's fine, but she keeps wanting to add more dill."

Beth chuckled. "I need more than your opinion. You like everything I cook."

"But isn't it flattering? I think I've gained an extra ten pounds from your dinners alone."

Beth preened. "Well, it is nice to know I'm appreciated. Some people," she raised her voice and glared in the direction of the living room, "don't know how good they have it."

Maddie exchanged a glance with Abby but took her friend's headshake to heart and let it pass.

Beth smiled, and Maddie saw Flynn in the expression. Though the woman had to be in her mid- to late fifties, she had the energy and looks of a woman a decade younger. The McCauleys had good genes.

Flynn would make such pretty babies.

She frowned, wishing she could stop thinking about procreating for more than two seconds at a time.

"Everything okay, Maddie?" Beth frowned.

She smiled. "Fine. I was just wondering how to—"

"Grandma!" Colin's shrill voice sounded from outside the kitchen. "I need you." Somehow he stretched the word *need* into four syllables.

Beth wiped her hands on a towel and rolled her eyes. "Boy is just like his father. Needy and not shy about telling you."

They snickered at the description of big tough Mike, who walked through the kitchen looking annoyed.

"Colin's that way," Maddie pointed. When they were alone, she turned to Abby, "So Abby, what's this about you and Brody?"

Abby's eyes widened. "What?"

The squeak gave her away. Before Maddie could press for details, the back door opened and Brody came in. Abby froze. Brody stopped in his tracks. The look Brody gave her best friend made Maddie blush for her.

Then a freight train bore down on both of them.

Abby bumped into her to avoid a monstrous canine barking up a storm. Flynn raced by them, swearing as he tried to catch the thing. Brody joined him after a moment, but he tripped over Abby's shoe and knocked her into Maddie. The three of them went sprawling to the floor in an ugly, painful heap.

"Ow. How is it I'm on the bottom of this?" Maddie winced and tried to scoot out from under Abby and Brody, who felt like he weighed more than her car.

"How do you think I feel?" Abby's muffled words mixed with Brody's laughter. "I'm the lean turkey in this sandwich."

"Lean turkey?" He laughed harder and moved off them. Then he picked Abby up as if she weighed nothing.

Maddie scooted back to brace herself against the cabinets. She heard barking and several male shouts as the others struggled to grab the dog.

"Okay, thanks. You can let go of me now." Abby stopped speaking when she looked into Brody's face.

Maddie wouldn't have believed it if she hadn't seen it. The suave, joking Brody Singer looked dumbstruck as he stared at Abby. His gaze traced her friend's features with something more than mere attraction.

Then he dropped her like a hot coal and joined the others trying to capture the dog.

"Wow." Maddie would have teased her when Cujo returned, sliding over the tile with muddied paws.

The dog looked like he ate people for breakfast, lunch, and dinner. As large as a wolfhound but with a mishmash of other breed traits, at best he could be called a mutt. At worst, a nightmare. And he headed straight for her.

She screamed. He stopped. The crowd behind him froze.

"Maddie, don't move," Flynn said quietly.

"Oh hell. This is my fault." Brody ran a hand through his hair. "It's okay, he's friendly. I swear."

The dog took a few steps closer and proved it by licking her face with a long, wet tongue.

"Ew. Get him off me." Maddie tried to push him back, but the dog took her touching him as a sign of affection and tried to crawl into her lap.

Nice, except he stunk to high heaven and wasn't a lap dog.

A few laughs and then everyone was talking and pointing and moving around at the same time.

Brody tugged the dog off her, bringing attention to the fact the thing had a collar.

"Is he yours, Uncle Brody? You have a dog? Really?" Colin jumped up and down. "Can I pet him? Can I ride him? Do you feed him squirrels?"

Where did the kid get his information?

Flynn helped her to her feet. He leaned close to kiss her then backed away. "You smell like dog."

"Thank Brody." She glared at the man doing his best to make nice with everyone while keeping the dog from slobbering on him.

Flynn steered her toward the door. "Come on, honey, let's go clean you up." Flynn said to his mother, "We'll be back. Maddie's going to grab some clean clothes."

Vanessa appeared at the back door, standing safely outside. She opened the door wide for them. "Oh, and she needs you to help her?"

"Hey, where were you when I was being attacked?" Maddie asked her.

"You weren't attacked," Brody corrected in a loud voice. "Mutt's friendly."

"Mutt?" Abby eyed him and the dog like a disease. "That's your dog's name?"

"Come on, let's get out of here." Flynn pulled her

with him out the back door and past Vanessa, who watched them go with amusement.

Back at her house, Maddie hurried upstairs to change. She stripped out of her shirt and dirtied pants, then hustled to the bathroom to wipe off her face and neck, where a mess of dog spit had dried. So gross.

"I'll be right down, Flynn," she called as she walked down the hall to the bedroom. Only to stop and stare as he waited for her with a huge smile.

"Shut the door and turn around."

Conditioned to that look in his eye, she melted. Her body readied for him in an instant.

"Bend over the dresser, baby. Watch me fuck you."

That he wore all his clothes while she had on only her panties and bra made it naughty—hotter—and then he slipped his hand down her ass and nudged her thong aside.

He unzipped his pants and she felt him there, behind her. The rough denim scraped against her ass as his cock found her wet entrance.

"That's it." He slid inside her, thick and tight. "Fuck. I love this. You're so good, baby." He rocked into her, gripping her hips as he increased his pace. "I was hearing you laugh. Watching you with my family. And I wanted you. Wanted to be inside you right then."

He drove harder inside her while she took it. In this position, he had such deep penetration.

"Flynn. You feel so good."

"Touch yourself. Get off before I do, which won't be long."

She put her hand down her panties and stroked her clit, knowing Flynn loved when she touched herself while he fucked her.

"You're wet, aren't you? That clit hard, baby?"

His raspy voice made her moan. "Yeah. Hard for you."

"That's it. Oh fuck. Come on, Maddie. Come. I can't last much longer."

She plucked her nub and imagined them at the club again, where one of his friends might catch them in the act. The shock and arousal would be too much for the voyeur to bear, and he'd be helpless as he watched while they finished.

"Yes, oh yes." She gritted her teeth and came around him, right before he swore and emptied into her.

He rotated and pushed, filling her until he shivered. Then he withdrew and buttoned himself up.

"You were thinking about the club, right?" He grinned, into her fantasy. He'd been the first to suggest it, that she liked the thought of being caught. Not actually having people see them have sex, but the possibility of it really aroused her.

"Maybe." She took the towel he handed her, amused he'd prepared for their little tryst. "We need to get back before they know what we did."

After she cleaned herself, he took the towel from her and tossed it to the ground, then hugged her back against him and kissed her neck. "I don't care about them knowing."

"It's embarrassing."

"It's hot as hell. You're so sexy, and you're mine. I like knowing they might want you, but they can't have you."

She blinked. "They wouldn't want me."

"Why not? You're a beautiful woman. But my brothers would never make a move. Like I said, when we fall, we fall hard. You're it for me. And only me," he growled.

"I can barely handle you as it is," she teased and stepped out of his arms to dress. Once more garbed in jeans and a sweater, she faced him. "Have I told you lately that I love you?"

The soft love in his eyes brought her to tears. How had she ever thought to throw this away?

"You can never tell me too many times."

She wanted to confess what else she'd been thinking about. To see what he thought. "Flynn, I know we haven't been together all that long. And we talked about marriage and maybe babies in the future." She swallowed, nervous yet spurred by the hope on his face. "I don't have any more refills for my pills. Just one more month and I need to go back in for a checkup."

"Yeah?" The gritty tone made her smile. She could almost feel him willing her to say what came next.

"So I was wondering. Do you want me to stop taking them? I know it's soon, but I can't stop thinking about babies for some reason."

He pulled her to him and kissed her. "I'm in. Forever. And I can't wait to have kids with you. But you have to be sure. That you'd even ask me now… Maddie, we're going to take this slow. How about we get married first? Six months, a year. Then we'll try. We're still young. We don't have to rush this."

Part relieved and a little frustrated he'd rejected her offer, she wanted to argue. But the relief was too powerful to deny. "You're right," she heard herself say.

"I know. I'm always right. See, that's what you need to learn before you'll be perfect. You're close, but not quite there. You just need to learn and believe that last bit. Say it with me. Flynn is always right."

She punched him in the gut, pleased when he whooshed out a breath. "Jerk."

"But you love me." He grinned.

She grinned back. "But I love you."

"Maddie, when we have kids, there won't be any doubt in your mind. Don't do it for me, but for us."

"I know. I just have so much love right now. I'm too emotional."

"You're just right." He straightened and grabbed her hand. "Now I have a present for you. How would you like to pull a fast one on the family?"

Abby didn't like the way Brody kept looking at her. He must have somehow found out she wrote for a living and had read one of her books. She just knew it.

Flynn and Maddie returned holding hands. The sparkle in her friend's eyes told Abby in no uncertain terms what she and Flynn had been doing.

Lucky girl.

She wondered wistfully what it must be like to have someone accept you, flaws and all. With Flynn, Maddie could be herself. Slightly neurotic, obsessively organized, beautiful and confident enough—at least in her looks—to know it. Abby could do neurotic, and she had her office as neat as a pin, but confident in any way? Hell no.

Every other day she expected a rejection from one publisher or another. Her agent had so far stuck with her and seemed keen on making them both money. But

Abby knew she was only as good as her last book. The minute her sales dropped, she could find herself ass-out of an agent, an editor, and the royalties she needed if she wanted to eat.

Though come to think of it, missing a meal or two couldn't hurt.

So pleased for her best friend, she also couldn't help feeling a tiny bit envious. Abby lived out her fantasies through her books and characters, but reminders of her solitude ate at her every time she stepped away from her computer.

"Hey, you okay?"

The others sat in the living room yelling at the television. She'd thought herself safely apart in the hallway, looking for Colin. How had Brody found her unless he'd been looking for her?

She cleared her throat. "Fine. Just looking for Colin."

He arched a brow. "Really? 'Cause he's sitting on Pop's lap."

Pop and Bitsy—what he called James and Beth McCauley, the people who'd raised him. She still wanted the full scoop on Brody Singer, but she couldn't ask outright because then Maddie would think she was interested in him. And she wasn't. Not really.

A woman would have to be a lesbian not to desire Brody. Yet even Robin had commented on how handsome and sexy he might be to a poor straight girl. Like Abby.

That dark blond hair—which she'd never liked, but on him looked right—those light brown eyes that reminded her of honey when he grew angry. And that body. She sighed. For someone who had issues with sweets and how they fell directly to her thighs, she shouldn't have set her sights so high. But Abby had always been a sucker for trim, lean men. Brody had surpassed lean thirty pounds of muscle ago.

"Abby?"

She blinked and saw her stare centered on Brody's chest. She sure hoped he hadn't noticed… She blushed when she met his gaze, annoyed at the smirk he wore. "What?"

"Like what you see, honey?"

She snorted. "Honey? Please. I'm about as sweet as vinegar, and you know it."

He leaned close, and she made the mistake of breathing him in. Her nipples stiffened, and she praised the weather for being cold enough to make a sweater necessary, hiding her reaction.

"I bet you're sweet all over." His eyes flashed with heat. "I'd be more than happy to indulge my sweet tooth. Any time you say the word."

She burst into laughter. "Sweet tooth? Does that line ever work on anyone?"

He seemed annoyed but grinned too quickly to think he'd meant anything serious by the comment. "You'd be surprised."

She snorted. "Probably not. Your type seems to go for the empty-headed bimbo."

"Really? So I have a shot then?" The hopeful look on his face made her laugh.

"Good one. I'll give you that."

She could have sworn he said, "I'm hoping you'll give me a lot more," before Flynn dragged her away.

"Yeah?"

"Quit picking on Brody. You placed my money, right?"

She patted his arm. "I did. This means our sprinkler system is a done deal when the weather heats up in the spring, right? That is, after the wedding."

He winked. All that McCauley charm bottled up for her best friend. Damn.

Flynn stepped away from Abby and motioned for Maddie to join him. Abby took a subtle step back and started when large hands pulled her into a hard frame.

Brody stood behind her and wouldn't let her go. He whispered into her ear, "What did Flynn say to you just now?"

She barely controlled a shiver while her body flushed with heat. Annoyed by her reaction to him, she stepped on his foot. When he grunted and let her go, she took refuge next to Colin, who'd moved to be near his Uncle Brody.

"Good move, Abby." Colin let her rest a hand on his shoulder. A big deal considering the kid never stood still.

"If I could have everyone's attention." Flynn said it again, louder, and the room quieted.

Abby noted the nods between Flynn's brothers. A glance at Brody showed a smug smile.

Beth and James sat next to each other on the couch. Beth looked so happy, Abby almost felt bad for what was about to happen. Except she knew Flynn's mom had bet on today as well.

Flynn took Maddie's hand in his and held it up for everyone to see. "Maddie is the love of my life. She knows it, and it's time everyone knew it."

A bunch of "hear hears" and "It's about times" scattered through the room. Vanessa joined in, looking satisfied. Probably taking credit for putting the pair together.

"I wanted to do this with friends and family to witness. It's been almost five months, the best five of my life." Flynn put on a burst of emotion that seemed fake to Abby, but everyone else seemed to buy it.

"Not enough tears," Colin whispered.

"I know," she whispered back. "Shush." Figured the little con man would see through him.

Out of the corner of her eye, she saw Brody's gaze narrow on her.

"And so, with all of you here to witness this special occasion, I'm just going to ask her." Flynn bent down on one knee, his hand still holding Maddie's. Despite knowing what was coming, Abby couldn't help thinking how romantic the scene looked.

For some reason, her gaze met Brody's. She couldn't read his expression and quickly turned back to Flynn and Maddie.

"Madison Gardner," Flynn boomed. "Will you do me the great honor"—he took something from his pocket—"the incredibly important role, of becoming my…"

Everyone stopped breathing.

"Girlfriend?" He opened his palm and on it sat two dazzling emerald earrings. "Will you, my sweet, wear these earbobs as a token of my extreme affection?"

The earbobs line had been Abby's touch. She'd been reading a historical romance the other week and was stuck on how much she liked the word.

Beth looked heartbroken. The others mumbled unflattering comments while she, Flynn, and Maddie laughed.

"Pay up, suckers." Abby collected money from

everyone who'd bet Flynn would pop the question today. They'd been placing wagers for a month. Abby had mentioned it to Maddie, who'd told Flynn. In an effort to win some money, Flynn had planted some hints he might ask her at the family barbecue.

"Hey, does this seem rigged to anyone else?" Brody frowned as he dug in his wallet.

"Rigged is such an ugly word." Maddie put on her earrings and smiled. "They're beautiful, Flynn. I love them."

"And I love you." He kissed her.

Beth finally stopped frowning and smiled. "You'll have such pretty babies."

Colin gagged and pretended to have a seizure on the floor.

"Maybe a girl this time," Beth said with a frown at him.

Mike nodded. "Yeah, a girl or two… to kiss cousin Colin!" He jumped on his son and tickled him until Colin cried *uncle*, to which three men answered, "Yes?"

Abby laughed and gave Maddie a hug, stunned when Vanessa willingly did the same.

"What?" the blond asked. "I can't show some love?"

Abby waited.

Vanessa lowered her voice and admitted, "Well, Maddie cut me in on the take. I made twenty bucks off Cameron and James, enough for a few lattes next week. Nicely done, ladies."

Abby grinned. "And this is where I'd type *The End*."

———※———

Brody watched Abby with her friends. The sexy little liar. He shook his head.

Flynn went out back and returned scowling. "Hey, Brody. Go get that thing you call a dog before he breaks the leash and attacks the grill. And just so you know, it's not the dog I'm afraid for. It's the steak."

"Dick," he mumbled under his breath. "Yeah, yeah. I'm coming, Mr. Romance. Earbobs? Extreme affection? What the hell, man?"

He met Abby's gaze as he passed, and his pulse jumped the way it always did around her. *Nope, Not The End, Abby Dunn. This is just the beginning.*

Here's a sneak peek at book 2 in
the McCauley Brothers series,

How to Handle a Heartbreaker

THEY STARED AT EACH OTHER, LIKE DUELING GUN-slingers waiting to see who would draw first. She'd be damned if she'd blink before he did. Despite his sheer size, drool-worthy body, and oh-my-God sex appeal, Abigail Dunn refused to budge on this issue. Her roommates might think she was one big pushover, but she knew better. It was time *he* did too.

After several tense moments in silence, Brody Singer rolled his eyes, then pinched the bridge of his nose and sighed in defeat. "Okay. Jesus. You're such a hard-ass. It's not his fault, you know."

"No. It's *yours*." She crossed her arms over her chest, doing her best not to turn pink when his gaze immediately followed the movement. And stayed there. After a moment, she cleared her throat. "My eyes are up here, Brody." She pointed to her face.

He slowly lifted his gaze to her face but didn't stop leering. Instead, the charming idiot wiggled his brows. "Beautiful. So…big. And so…brown."

She wore a brown sweater today, so she couldn't be sure if he referred to her breasts or her eyes. By the expression on his face, she was betting on the former. Anyone else talking to her like that would have received a kick in the teeth. But from Brody, she felt simultaneously irked and turned on. *So* not good.

"You know, you're really very good looking."

He looked puzzled that she'd compliment him, but as he started to smile, she added, "Too bad you ruin it the moment you open your mouth."

He had the gall to laugh. "And the guys think you're shy."

Now she flushed. Dear Lord, did Mike and the others talk about her? Her neighbor, Mike McCauley, was the oldest of the four McCauley brothers, of which Brody had been unofficially adopted at a young age. She'd been dying to get the scoop on the whys and hows of his life, but asking would make it seem as if she wanted to know. And heaven help her if her roommates started on the sparks flaring between her and Brody again. Her head hurt just thinking about it.

Realizing he continued to stare in a way that made her all too aware of her now tingly girlie parts, she blurted, "I *am* shy."

"Not with me you're not." And that pleased him for some stupid reason, because his grin grew wider.

Abby planted her hands on her hips and counted to ten in her head. In a calmer voice, she explained, "I don't have time for this. I have to make my deadline by Halloween—in *five more days*. Get that mongrel out of our yard or else."

"You won't call the pound." He didn't seem to be taking her threat seriously.

Abby turned and stared out the back door of her kitchen, not surprised to see dog slobber and a furry face against the door pane. The smashed nose and tongue occasionally gave way to a gaping mouth of sharp teeth as Cujo tried to get more oxygen into his freakishly large body. "Pound? I was thinking National Guard. That thing is nearly as tall as I am."

"But you're short."

"Petite."

"Not with that rack," he muttered.

"*What?*"

"Nothing." He swallowed hard but to his credit kept his gaze above her neckline this time. "Look, I'm sorry. He *likes* you, Abby. Mutt just wanted to give you a token of his affection."

"You mean the bone he buried in our backyard last week? *That* token?" She fumed, remembering the broken flower pots and her mauled garden beds. "I don't know why I bother. This isn't even my house. You want to piss off Beth and James, feel free. But when we move out, I'm getting my rent deposit back. If not from them, from you."

He frowned. "You're leaving? You guys just moved in eight months ago."

She hadn't realized he knew that. But considering their many connections, it shouldn't have surprised her. "You're spending too much time with Flynn and Maddie." Maddie, her roommate and best friend, had found a real treasure in Flynn McCauley. Great for Maddie, not so great for Abby.

Flynn and Brody were best friends and business partners. Mike was her neighbor. And Abby, Maddie, and Vanessa—her other roommate—had been pseudo-adopted by the entire McCauley clan. Which meant seeing Brody on a regular basis. She could handle his aggravating attempts at charm, but her libido was making it really hard to remember all the reasons why she should give this man a wide berth.

Like now, when he wouldn't stop staring at her.

"Cut it out."

"What?"

Did he just step closer? She backed up and found herself against the door. Behind her, that mammoth of a dog whined.

"See? We like you, Abby." Brody smiled, his amber eyes bright, like his golden hair, shining through the gloom of yet another bleak Seattle day.

She held up a hand and met his chest, doing her utmost to ignore the firm muscle under her palm. "Stay." To her bemusement, he did. She did her best not to laugh hysterically at the comparison of man to dog. "I think I made myself clear. Your dog needs to stay at *your* place. He keeps getting out of Mike's yard, and he's already torn up my garden."

"Garden?" Brody looked over her head through the door window. "You mean that dirt in a box? Anything out there was already dead, honey."

"It was dormant and would have been perfect for springtime next year, *honey*, but Fenris out there already dug up my bulbs."

"Hmm. Fenris."

"Yeah, Fenris. Loki's son? A demon dog who ends the world?"

He seemed to consider the name. "Catchy, but no. Doesn't fit him. Guess we'll stick with Mutt for now."

She gritted her teeth. "I don't care what you name your dog. Just get him *out*. Of. My. Yard!"

She stormed past him in a whirl of anger, frustrated

lust, and hopelessness that she'd be able to concentrate on writing her story now that Mr. Wrong had shown his pretty face to distract her again. Bad enough she saw him in her dreams or when he tagged along with Flynn. But now he invaded her working hours.

"Oh. You stupid muse." The damn thing needed to get laid. Then maybe it would stop painting her hero with Brody's face and smile. *Riiight. It's your muse that's been celibate for a year. Not you, oh she of the wide ass, freakish desires, and air of desperation…* Kevin's words were never far from her mind, and at that moment, she hated him and Brody equally. Kevin had been a jerk, but Brody made her wish for things she'd never have. She paused in the hallway at the doorway to her office.

The front door opened, and Maddie entered with Flynn on her heels. "Hey, Abby, what—"

Abby pointed at Flynn. "This is your fault. Take care of *that*…" she thumbed at the noise behind her ". or I will." She seethed as she closed herself in her study—what she used to think of as her sanctuary—and did her best to ignore Brody's low voice and the happy barking no doubt forecasting a mess in the kitchen.

At the thought that Vanessa would soon be returning, Abby smiled with evil glee. The blond dictator would take care of it. She'd take care of *everything*. "Now if only she could type…"

Acknowledgments

Thanks to Leah for giving me a shot. Sorry to see you go. And to my editor, Cat C., for consistently helping me make this a better story. You rock!

About the Author

Caffeine addict, boy referee, and romance aficionado, *USA Today* bestselling author Marie Harte is a confessed bibliophile and devotee of action movies. Whether hiking in Central Oregon, biking around town, or hanging at the local tea shop, she's constantly plotting to give everyone a happily ever after. With more than ninety books under her belt, she's well on her way to making that happen. Visit http://marieharte.com and fall in love.

How to Handle a Heartbreaker

The McCauley Brothers

by Marie Harte

USA Today Bestselling Author

———

He can't get her out of his head

It's lust at first sight when Brody Singer first lays eyes on Abby Dunn. The dark-haired beauty looks a lot like a woman he once knew, who died years ago. At first Brody fears his attraction is a holdover from that secret crush, but Abby's definitely different. She's a lot shyer, a lot sexier, and, despite her attempts to dissuade his interest, absolutely mesmerizing.

She can't get him out of her books

Abby isn't having it. She's still trying to put her last disastrous relationship behind her and overcome the flaws her ex wouldn't let her forget. But somehow Brody isn't getting the hint. It doesn't help that when writing her steamy novels, she keeps casting Brody as the hero.

Brody is more than happy to serve as her muse and eager to help make sure her "research" is authentic. But when their research turns into something real…will she choose her own happily ever after?

———

Praise for Marie Harte:

"Harte has a gift for writing hot sex scenes that are emotional and specific to her characters." —*RT Book Reviews*

For more Marie Harte, visit:

www.sourcebooks.com

Ruining Mr. Perfect

The McCauley Brothers

by Marie Harte

USA Today Bestselling Author

———

It's tough always being right

Vanessa Campbell is a CPA by day and a perfectionist by night. She's fit, smart, healthy…and decidedly lonely. She can't stop thinking about the youngest McCauley brother, Cameron. He's just like her: smart, beautiful, and usually right—except when dealing with her.

…But someone's got to do it

Cameron McCauley likes the look of Vanessa a little too well. She's a blond goddess and she knows it. She hates to be wrong, just like him. They tend to rub each other the wrong way, which is unfortunate considering how well they could fit. He's dying to shake Vanessa up—get her to let loose. But if he succeeds, can his heart handle it?

———

Praise for Marie Harte:

"Off the charts scorching hot. Ms. Harte wows with sex scenes that will make your heart pump." —*Long and Short Reviews*

For more Marie Harte, visit:

www.sourcebooks.com

What to Do with a Bad Boy

The McCauley Brothers

by Marie Harte

USA Today Bestselling Author

She can fix anything...

It's great that all his brothers are finding love, but Mike has been there, done that. He had his soul mate for a precious time before she died giving birth to their son. She left him with the best boy a guy could want, so why is everyone playing matchmaker? He's sick of it... until he meets Delilah Webster. For some reason, the foul-mouthed, tattooed mechanic sets his motor running.

But can she fix his heart?

When Del first met Colin, Mike's young son, she fell in love with the little scam artist. But his father's like an overprotective pit bull. Too bad they rub each other the wrong way, because Mike is seriously sexy. But when a simple kiss turns hot and heavy, she can't get him out of her head.

Mike can't forget that kiss either. He sees the loving woman buried under the rough exterior. But the closer they get, the more the pain of past wounds throws a monkey wrench into a future he's not sure he can handle...

Praise for Marie Harte:

"Charismatic characters and sexual tension that is hot enough to scorch your fingers." —*Romance Junkies*

For more Marie Harte, visit:

www.sourcebooks.com

The Day He Kissed Her

by Juliana Stone

—◦◦◦—

Coming home is the only way to heal his heart.

Mackenzie Draper thought he had everything he ever wanted when hired by a hotshot Manhattan architectural firm. But he still needed one last visit back home to Crystal Lake to face the demons of his past. For Lily St. Clare, the charming small town she just moved to was a haven. Big cities only wanted to eat you up and spit you out.

Neither was expecting to stay very long...until the day they found each other, and one amazingly red-hot night followed. But old wounds almost always leave a mark, and Mac's scars run deeper than most. With her flirty charm, Lily could be exactly what he needs—if he's willing to give love one more chance.

—◦◦◦—

Praise for Juliana Stone:

"Stone wastes no time establishing her ability to tell an enthralling story." —*RT Book Reviews*

For more Juliana Stone, visit:

www.sourcebooks.com

Find My Way Home

Harmony Homecomings
by Michele Summers

—◦◦◦—

She's just the kind of drama

Interior designer Bertie Anderson has big dreams for her career, and they don't include being stuck in her hometown of Harmony, North Carolina. After one last client, Bertie is packing up her high heels and heading for her dream job in Atlanta. But her plans are derailed by the gorgeous new owner of that big old Victorian she's always wanted to renovate…

He's vowed to avoid

For retired tennis pro Keith Morgan, Harmony is a far cry from fast-paced Miami—which is exactly the point. Keith is starting a new life for himself and his daughter Maddie, and he's left the bright lights and hot women far behind. Bertie's exactly the kind of curvaceous temptation he doesn't need, and Keith refuses to let their sizzling attraction distract him from his goals. Keith and Bertie both have to learn that there's more than one kind of escape, and it takes more than wallpaper to turn a house into a home.

—◦◦◦—

For more Michele Summers, visit:

www.sourcebooks.com

The Longest Night

by Kara Braden

—⁓—

Two fiery personalities living together in a remote cabin

When a car accident leaves gorgeous but prickly genius Ian Fairchild with a debilitating injury and an addiction to painkillers, this city boy has to find a safe place to recover. He escapes to the remote Canadian wilderness, as far from the lights of Manhattan as he can get—and in the company of a woman he has no reason to trust.

Will they make it through the winter?

Former Marine Captain Cecily Knight prides herself on being self-sufficient. Her nearest neighbor is miles away, she has to fly to town for basic necessities, and she can go weeks without seeing another soul…and that's the way she likes it. But when she's called on to repay a debt, she agrees to allow Ian to stay with her in her isolated cabin, on one condition: just because he's invading her privacy doesn't mean she's willing to open herself up to him, even if he is as tempting as sin.

But as they spend day after day in in the wilderness together, Cecily and Ian's wary friendship turns into a love these two lost souls needed more than they ever knew.

For more Kara Braden, visit:

www.sourcebooks.com